CW01513258

THE
FACTORY GIRL

ania Crosse

www.ariafiction.com

About *The Candle Factory Girl*

1930s London

Work at Price's Candle Factory in Battersea is tedious for intelligent, seventeen-year-old Hillie Hardwick, but she knows she is lucky to have a job at all. Her home life is no better, as she constantly battles with her exacting and bullying father in order to protect her mother and five younger siblings from his abuse. Her only solace is her loving relationship with the chaotic Parker family and her best friend, Gert Parker.

When matters violently escalate for Hillie, smitten Jack-the-Lad Jimmy Baxter seems her only salvation. But could this be the biggest mistake of her life, and should she be looking for protection nearer home?

A story that crackles with unease where courage and friendship are the only hope.

For my darling husband
For always being at my side, and for being you

Chapter One

A Friday Morning in June 1932

'Blooming heck, Hillie! Can't you wait for us?'

As she neared the corner of the street, Hilda Hardwick heard the hurrying footfall of her lifelong friend scurrying up behind her, and she slowed her own step. She turned round, and though she itched with exasperation, she couldn't help but smile. Gert was rushing towards her, pulling on her old, fraying cardigan over her work dress as she went. Hillie could see that one of her hastily tied shoelaces had already come undone and was threatening to trip her up. To complete the chaotic image, Gert's naturally frizzy auburn hair stood around her head in a blazing halo, flying about her shoulders in a fiery cloud. She always reminded Hillie of one of the Titian paintings they had admired together on a rare trip to the National Gallery in Trafalgar Square. It was 1932 and members of the fairer sex had been cutting their hair short for nearly two decades. However, these two factory girls from the backstreets of London's Battersea had yet to catch up with the fashion.

'I *have* been waiting for you,' Hillie chided, pulling her lips back into a displeased line and resuming her brisk pace now that Gert had caught her up. 'If I'd waited any longer, it would've made me late for work and I wouldn't want to risk the consequences of *that*. And some of us can't afford to catch the tram. And my dad's already… well…' She pulled herself up short, knowing she'd said too much. So instead she finished the sentence with, 'Gone on ahead.'

Gert's jaw dropped as she guessed what Hillie had nearly let slip. 'Oh, Hillie, you don't mean…? 'Cos I kept you waiting?'

Hillie instinctively turned to her with a brief, wistful grimace as they half ran along Battersea Park Road.

Gert caught her breath as she glimpsed the telltale pink hand mark on Hillie's cheek, and she flushed with remorse. 'Oh, Hillie, I'm so sorry.'

'It's not your fault my dad's like he is,' Hillie mumbled under her breath.

But Gert obviously still felt guilty. 'You shouldn't have waited for us, not when you know what he's like.'

'Someone's got to stand up to him.'

Hillie said it quietly, but Gert knew there'd be no arguing. They'd had the same discussion on umpteen occasions before. Harold Hardwick was a bully and there'd never be any changing him.

Gert knew the story by heart.

'Me and Hillie's mum'd been friends for years,' her mother had told her, so many times that Gert could repeat it virtually word for word. 'She was the timid little thing from the grocers' round the corner, and I was the big girl trusted to do the shopping for me mum. Used to make Nell laugh, I did. Always said it should've been the other way around. *She* should've had the posh name of Evangeline, not me! Anyway, the years went by, and when things got tough for her and she married that Harold, I got them the house on the street. 1914 it was, just as the war broke out. Nell found she was preggers the same time as I did, and you two popped out within days of each other, May the next year, 1915. Both of you girls, too, except that Hillie was Nell's first and I already had Kit.

'So you two was friends from the cradle. Just learning to walk, the both of you, when they brought in conscription. Your dad and Harold found themselves together in the same Pals' Regiment as they called them. Only Harold'd always been a bully, keeping poor Nell under his thumb. But he was just what they was looking for in the army, someone to keep order. So he quickly rose through the ranks to sergeant. Inflicted his rigid discipline on every poor

3

bugger what came under his command, so your dad says. Never got a scratch on him. Mind you, you know your dad only got a bit of shrapnel in his leg in all the two years they was in the trenches. Kept his head down did your dad, and I was grateful for that. And when he came home, he was his old, lovely self. But Harold, huh! Remained a sergeant ever since, even if he was back on civvy street. If he was strict with poor Nell before the war – and with Hillie, too – he's been a blooming tyrant ever since.'

Gert released a bitter, desperate sigh. A tyrant and a bully were good ways to describe her best friend's dad! But as Hillie had grown up, instead of giving in to him like her mum did – anything for a quiet life – she'd started challenging him. The consequences of Harold's resulting temper were often dire. Gert so often wished, as she did now, that Hillie would hold back, but no end of persuasion could change her mind.

'And where's *your* dad?' Gert realised her dear friend was asking now.

'Well, he really *is* running late, so he's *got* to catch the tram,' Gert sighed knowingly.

'I know where you get it from, then!'

To Gert's relief, Hillie was grinning at her, a teasing light dancing in her eyes. They scuttled along, passing under the railway bridge just as a train rumbled overhead, its wheels clunking slowly and rhythmically along the track. The sound was so familiar that the two girls scarcely noticed it. All they were concerned about was arriving at Price's Soap and Candle Factory on time to clock in.

It hardly mattered to them that it was a glorious June morning. Shopkeepers were starting to open up their premises, setting up displays of their goods outside on the pavement, while pedestrians were striding along on their way to work, dodging the tramlines as they crossed the busy street. It was a working day, but hearts were generally lighter because of the pleasant weather. But neither Hillie nor Gert would see much of the sunshine that day as they would soon be swallowed up into the candle-packing shed at the factory.

They'd reached the point where Battersea Park Road became York Road, and still Gert hadn't succeeded in taming her rebellious mop of hair into a bun at the nape of her neck.

'Hang on a tick,' she panted, stopping to pin up a rogue hank that kept escaping. 'Don't I wish my hair was more like yours and not so much like a bleeding bush.'

Hillie was tempted to remind Gert that her own hair was a riot of curls that needed pinning down with Kirby grips when she tied it back for work and that Gert simply needed to allow herself more time to do the same! But Hillie was happy to stop and wait for her to ram her old cloche hat on top of her finally conquered locks. No matter that it was hardly worth it.

They were almost there and though she didn't possess a watch, Hillie knew that they'd arrived on time as they joined the mass of a thousand or so workers at the factory who were converging on the extensive eleven-acre site alongside the River Thames.

It was as Hillie gazed about at the stream of humanity heading for the factory that she noticed the young man loitering by one of the gates. He was craning his neck this way and that as if trying to pick out someone from the crowd. Hillie knew who he was: Jimmy Baxter. He worked in deliveries, and because of that he knew every inch of the factory, and everyone in the factory knew him.

Raw materials of all sorts, delivered by boat and barge at the factory's wharves, were stored in the relevant warehouses all over the site. There was even a light railway system for transporting them, the area was so vast. Jimmy Baxter was part of the team who delivered the materials from the warehouses to the different processing sheds as they were required. A bit of a Jack the Lad was Jimmy Baxter, and everyone knew it. Even the girls who went out with him knew it was only likely to last a few months at most. But despite his reputation, he was a solid and dependable worker and good at his job.

As Hillie passed him, she sensed him push himself away from the wall and fall into step beside her. She quickened her pace, but he kept level with her shoulder, and when she stopped abruptly, so did he.

'What d'you want, Jimmy Baxter?' she demanded, spinning to face him.

If she'd expected to throw him off track, she was mistaken. He shrugged casually, but his cheeky, chocolate brown eyes never left hers. 'Just wanted to walk into work with the two prettiest girls in the factory,' he answered nonchalantly. Before they could escape him, he'd stepped between them and wrapped an arm about each of their waists, pulling them tightly against his sides.

Gert wasn't at all sure how to react and eyed her friend warily. Jimmy might be a bit cocky but he was generally quite liked among the factory staff, even if he was known to play the field as far as girls were concerned. So Gert was really quite relieved when Hillie extricated herself from Jimmy's hold with an irritated jerk of her arm.

'Well, I don't want to walk into work with *you*, so you can keep your dirty hands off me. And you can let go of Gert and all,' she ordered, dragging a bemused Gert free as well. 'We don't want anything to do with you. We know what you're like. Anything in a skirt and you're after it.'

Jimmy's expression twisted into one of mock hurt. 'Oh, come on, Hilda Hardwick. I'm not that bad. I just can't resist a pretty face, and yours is one of the best.'

'And I'm sure you've said that to every girl whose poor heart you've broken over the years. So bugger off and leave us alone.'

She grabbed Gert's hand and stalked off, leaving Jimmy Baxter standing there, utterly amazed and enduring a chorus of derisive laughter.

'Met your match there, eh, Jimmy!'

'Have to work your charms a bit harder on her, lad!'

And all the male workers went off to the different parts of the factory, chuckling with amusement and shaking their heads. Jimmy Baxter had been put down by that slip of a girl. That was a turn up for the books, if ever there was one.

'Tough little nut, that one,' someone commented.

'Have to be if you're Harold Hardwick's daughter,' someone else chipped in.

'What, that bloke in the moulding house? Blimey. Poor little sod. Wouldn't want to be in her shoes.'

'Looks like it's taught her to stand up for herself, mind.'

'Huh, rather her than me. Avoid him if I can.'

But though he was aware of their comments, they were like whispers on the wind to Jimmy. He stood for a second or two, quite mesmerised by his encounter with Hillie Hardwick. My, she had spirit, and that was something he deeply admired in a woman. It was also what had deterred him from approaching her before, if the truth be told. For though he hated to admit it to himself, he liked to be dominant in any relationship. He treated all his girlfriends well and had never forced any of them to do anything that was seriously against their will. If a bit of a fumble was as far as they wanted to go, he'd never cajole them into something they'd later regret. He'd simply move onto the next one and see what was on offer there.

No, he wasn't an ogre. He prided himself on that as much as his good looks. He allowed himself a moment to watch Hillie and her friend disappear round the corner of one of the factory's enormous brick buildings before setting off for the warehouses and his own day's work. But the image of her still hovered in his head. She was beautiful, even if he'd only ever seen her in unflattering, workday clothes, hair dragged back in a thick, swirling bun. She must be exquisite with her tresses hanging softly about her face, and the thought took his breath away.

The thing was, Jimmy Baxter knew himself to be in awe of Hilda Hardwick. He'd been trying to summon up the courage to make an overture to her for months. It had cost him a huge effort to jump her and her friend at the gate. Not that he'd ever want anyone to know that. But could he ever persuade her that there was more to him than people thought?

She was right that he'd had a string of girlfriends in the past, but none of them had been serious. Not on his part, at least. So he supposed he only had himself to blame for his reputation, and his mouth screwed up with regret. For now he felt even more drawn to her than ever. Their brief contretemps – now that was a word that might impress her – had done something to his heart he couldn't rightly explain. He felt sorry for her, too. The mark on her face hadn't gone unnoticed and from what he knew of her father, it wouldn't surprise him if his was the hand that had made it. Because of his job, Jimmy knew everyone in the factory to some extent, and Harold Hardwick was disliked by most. The thought of him hitting his daughter made Jimmy's blood boil.

Of course, it was by no means the first time Jimmy had spoken to the poor girl, although only in passing. He had to make deliveries to the packing shed pretty well every day, and when he first went in, he always called out a cheery, 'Morning, ladies!' or 'Afternoon, ladies!' followed by, 'How are we today?' or words to that effect. Most of his girlfriends came from that enormous workshop. Girls liked to go out with him, even if it was understood that he wasn't the settling down type. He took them to the cinema or dancing, or treated them to fish and chips or tea and cake. And if he was short of cash, he could always entertain them with his jokes and make them laugh – until he started getting bored and called it a day.

Hillie Hardwick, though, was a different kettle of fish. He'd hardly noticed her when, as many did, she'd first come to Price's after she'd left school at fourteen. She'd been a tall, skinny kid back then. But in the – what would it be – three years since, she'd blossomed, still tiny of waist but filling out in all the right places, which more recently had begun to draw Jimmy's attention. She also had the most striking, silvery blue eyes and a prettily bowed mouth that he ached to kiss.

But it wasn't just that. She intrigued him. She wasn't the silly, giggling type. Maybe that father of hers had beaten the gaiety out of her, the sodding bastard, but Jimmy felt sure he could cheer her up. Almost saw it as his duty. He usually made the girls laugh, and he'd always got a polite smile, though nothing more from Hillie if he made a comment to her as he passed.

'Looking lovely today,' he might wink cheekily.

'You say that to all the girls,' she might reply with a half-smile so that he was never quite sure of her.

That was it, he supposed. He was attracted to her – her friend, Gert was pretty, but Hillie far surpassed any other girl in the factory for looks – but she was also a mystery. And he was determined that the heated words they'd exchanged that morning wouldn't be his last conversation with her. And if he played his cards right, it'd be the first of many. She'd be a challenge, what with her spirit and that father of hers, but he certainly felt far more smitten than he had with any other girl before.

He thrust his hands into his pockets and pursed his lips ready to produce his usual, carefree whistle. But somehow no jaunty tune would come into his head and he walked on instead in thoughtful silence.

*

Hillie stretched her tall, lithe body in a graceful arc and then grinned at Gert across the workbench. 'Lunchtime. At last!' she exhaled in relief.

'Don't know about you, but I'm starving,' Gert declared. 'Dad was bringing me sandwiches in, so I'll have to go and find him.'

'OK. Looks like the sun's still out, so fancy going down and sitting by the river? Then we can grab a cuppa before we go back.'

'Righty-ho. I'll find you down there.'

They pulled off the voluminous overalls they were obliged to wear, and stepped outside together. Though the numerous buildings shadowed each other with the result that sunlight couldn't reach the few narrow passages in between, the strip of sky Hillie could see overhead was a bright, duck-egg blue. The two girls parted company, weaving their way inside the maze of different departments of the factory, since much of the site was completely covered with no space at all between the buildings. But both girls knew it like the back of their hands, and Hillie finally emerged into the warm sunshine along the south bank of the Thames.

She wasn't the only one wanting to escape the drudgery of the workplace for half an hour and enjoy the welcome June weather. The wharfs were heaving with factory workers who had flocked outside and were already munching their packed lunches. People were sitting on the ground because every conceivable seat – every box, barrel or mooring bollard – had already been occupied. Barges were moored three abreast in places, cranes had been abandoned in mid-air, and merchandise littered the quayside.

Hillie went to stand by the river and gazed across the wide expanse of shimmering grey water. Wharfs spread along the bank in both directions as far as the bends in the river allowed her to see, serving the numerous other factories beyond the candle manufactory. It all had a certain industrial beauty to it, though, she mused, with cranes and hoists silhouetted against the clear blue of the sky. The chatter of the hundreds of workers squeezed into the narrow space was a happy buzz in her ears, filling her with contentment.

Or was it?

It was true that Price's had provided employment for her father and so many others throughout the previous years when millions over the country had been out of work, and Hillie supposed she should be grateful for that. Despite the fact that the market for general domestic candles had been slashed first by gas lighting and now by the rapidly expanding National Electricity Grid, trade was still brisk. Night-lights were still hugely popular, and Price's had long ago diversified into decorative products for every conceivable occasion, from the beeswax candles burned in churches down to tiny cake candles. They even still held the Royal Warrant and the contract to provide candles for every state occasion dating back to the wedding of Queen Victoria and Prince Albert, something the workers still felt very proud of. In addition, for years, Price's had also manufactured lubricant oils for motorcars and other machinery, as well as glycerine and fine soaps. Amazingly, the company still produced edible candles made from a mixture of refined tallow and coconut oil called stearine, as opposed to the usual high percentage paraffin ones. These were supplied for expeditions to remote places all over the world, such as botanical trips to the Andes and attempts on Everest, so that in dire circumstances, the candles could be eaten as food. Famously, Price's had supplied Captain Scott's final expedition to the South Pole in 1910 with over two thousand pounds of stearine candles, as well as Shackleton's trips to the Antarctic in later years.

Hillie knew all this because every candle product passed through her hands for packing. But she also found it fascinating that although Price's had in fact been taken over by Lever Brothers shortly after the war, it was allegedly still the largest manufacturer of candles in the world. It had factories in every far-flung corner of the globe, particularly in less developed countries where electricity had yet to make its mark and so demand was still sky-high.

The majority of candles were paraffin-wax based but blended with palm oil to give the perfect non-smelling, non-smoking, brightly burning flame. But was it that very knowledge that made Hillie restless? She could imagine dazzling places where it was warm and the sun shone all year round, acres of palm plantations that provided the oil for the candles. Wouldn't it be wonderful to visit some of these exotic places rather than just dream about them? She could probably have a job as a packer for the rest of her life. But was that what she really wanted? Did she want to stand at the same bench, day in, day out, packing one box after another, and another and another, with one week's holiday a year, for the rest of her working life?

At school, she'd always been top of the class, relishing every lesson, every map she pored over, every essay she wrote. She was clever enough to go on to grammar school, her teachers had said. But no, her father had insisted that she went out to work at the earliest opportunity, and had secured her a job at Price's the very week she'd turned fourteen. And now she was trapped. Working full-time, she had no opportunity to go in search of better employment. Besides, with the state the country was in, new jobs were few and far between, and Hillie knew she was lucky to have the one she did. No, for the moment, she'd have to put up with life as it was, and live for the weekends. In her case, the best time was after she finished work at Saturday lunchtime. Every week on her way home, she made a detour to the library on Lavender Hill to change her library books. She knew that it wasn't the way most girls spent their spare time, but for her, reading stories or books about far-away places helped her escape the humdrum life she was destined for.

Her mouth firmed to a disgruntled line as she silently pondered the slow-moving, majestic waters of the River Thames. Would she ever find a way out? But could she ever leave her mother and younger brother and sisters to defend themselves against her father's temper?

'Hillie?'

She almost jumped at the voice in her ear and turned her head to find Doris Sedgeworth at her elbow. The older girl's dark eyes were like sorrowful pebbles in her pale face.

'Sorry, Doris, I was miles away.'

'Not dreaming of Jimmy Baxter, I 'ope,' Doris said tentatively.

Hillie's eyebrows arched in surprise. 'No, not at all. Should I be?'

'Definitely not. Only I 'eard what 'appened this morning. He's a rat, is Jimmy. We was going out the last few months, but he dropped us just like that last week. Just when I was starting to fink fings was getting serious for us. And he done the same to so many before me.'

'Well, there you are, then,' Hillie tried to be gentle, 'it's what you should've expected.'

'Hello, you two,' Gert butted in cheerfully, brandishing her brown paper bag of sandwiches so Hillie knew she must have found Stan at his post in the factory's sawmill. 'Long faces you both got.'

'Just warning Hillie about Jimmy Baxter. Build up your 'opes an' then break your 'eart, he would.'

17

Gert threw up her head with a loud guffaw. 'Don't think you need to worry about that. Sent him away with a right flea in his ear, she did. Should've heard her!'

'Have to admit my language was none too savoury.' Hillie felt colour creep into her cheeks. 'But I reckoned it was the only sort of thing someone like Jimmy would take any notice of.'

Language none too savoury, Gert repeated in her head. You wouldn't hear many workers at Price's using those sorts of words! A cut above was Hillie. Must be all those books she read. Didn't quite get it herself, did Gert. Much rather go down the flicks of a Saturday night. Sometimes Hillie came with her, of course. But she'd often prefer to stay at home with her nose in a book. Mind you, Gert knew that Hillie's dad made her hand over virtually all of her meagre pay so she couldn't afford to go out every weekend anyway.

'Well, you did the right fing,' Doris nodded. 'Wanted to do you know what wiv us, he did, but when I says no, he was off like a shot. Didn't press us or anyfing. Just went. Anyway, I need the bog, so I'd best be off. You know 'ow old Miss Bossy Drawers don't like us going during the shift.'

'Yes. And thanks for the warning about Jimmy,' Hillie added.

'No skin off my nose,' Doris shrugged as she turned away, but Hillie could tell by the set of her shoulders that in reality Jimmy Baxter had upset her very much indeed.

'Poor soul,' Gert murmured. 'Reckon he broke her heart really.'

'Yes, that's the impression I got.'

'Got to hand it to Jimmy, mind. Didn't press her,' Doris said. 'Might've left a string of broken hearts, but no one's ever accused him of forcing himself on them, and he's not left a string of, well, you know, girls in trouble, to put it politely.'

'So now he's a saint, is he?' Hillie asked, her jaw set.

Gert frowned in confusion. 'I wasn't saying that exactly.'

'Oh, Gertie, you should see your face!' Hillie chortled in a burst of laughter. 'I was pulling your leg! I've no intention whatsoever of entertaining Mr Jimmy Baxter.'

Gert blew out her cheeks in relief. 'Good. I didn't think you'd be so daft. But anyone else you fancy here?'

'Not really,' Hillie shrugged. 'Not really interested in men, me.'

'Oh, must be someone, surely? Come on, spill the beans, girl!'

But Hillie shook her head. 'No, honestly. Anyway, I'm not sure I want every aspect of my life to revolve around Price's.'

'What, you expecting some knight in shining armour to ride out of the sunset like in one of them books you read?' Gert teased, her eyes dancing.

'No.' Hillie gave a wistful laugh. 'I don't kid myself. Life's not like that. But what about you, if you're so keen to match me up with someone?'

'Me?' Gert tried to look bashful, but a peachy hue flushed up beneath her freckles. 'Well, keep it to yourself, but I quite fancy that Tom Ferrers in the print shop.'

Hillie lifted her eyebrows. 'Oh, I know. Quite good-looking, I suppose. And quite pleasant. But isn't he—'

'Engaged. Yeah. Just my blooming luck.'

'Oh, well, never mind. Have to wait for someone else to come along, won't you?' Hillie sighed sympathetically, opening her own packed lunch. 'Come on. Let's have our sandwiches before we die of starvation.'

'Yeah,' Gert agreed, laughing too, now. 'Me stomach thinks me throat's been cut. Look, someone's just got down off that bit of wall over there. We can sit on that. Me feet's killing us.'

'What are they doing then? Wrapping themselves round your neck and squeezing tight?'

'Oh, you,' Gert chuckled, heaving herself atop the wall. 'You know what I mean.'

'Course I do,' Hillie agreed, settling herself beside her friend. 'It's my back that gets me more. May and Ethel and their cronies have worked here all their lives. All through the war, standing at the same flipping bench for years on end. Can you imagine that?'

'Expect that'll be me,' Gert sighed glumly as she chewed enthusiastically on her sandwich. 'But you, Hillie. Now I reckon you're destined for better things.'

'If only,' Hillie scoffed sadly.

'Oh, that reminds us. Dad said there's an advert been put up this morning on the noticeboard. There's a vacancy come up in the offices. Reckons you should apply.'

'Really?' Hillie's thoughts started racing. It'd be easy to apply for the position, wouldn't it? And if she got it, it would doubtless mean more money. She could rent a room of her own. Get away from her dad. Independence. But above all, a job in the office would be far more interesting than the stultifying, repetitive one she had now! 'What about you, though, Gert? You should apply, too.'

'What? Oh, no, not me,' Gert shrugged. 'If you apply, you'd get it over me. And I'm not sure it's really what I'd want anyway. But if you get it, you can treat us to an ice cream once in a while.'

'Oh, Gert, I'd do more than that! You know I would! Best pals we are. Always have been and always will be.'

She hugged her friend tightly, being careful that neither of them slipped off the wall as a result. But over Gert's shoulder, she spied a pall of black smoke rising from one of the factory's chimneys, spreading its evil fingers across the blue sky and getting thicker by the moment. Within seconds, the sun would be obliterated by a filthy, menacing cloud.

'That's it. Fun over,' she announced grimly. 'Won't be able to breathe in a minute.'

'Oh, damn. But I could do with a cuppa to wash this down anyway.'

In unison they carefully folded their paper bags ready to reuse the following day, then slid down from the wall. Arm in arm, they made their way towards the canteen, Hillie keeping a sharp eye out for the ominous figure of her father. She wanted to avoid him at all costs, for no way did she want him to spoil the happy dream that she was hugging to her breast.

An office clerk. It wasn't quite the stuff of dreams, but it would be a start, anyway.

*

Jimmy Baxter had kept himself apart that lunchtime. Some of his mates had been knocking a football around in a little yard that opened up between two of the factory sheds, but he'd declined the invitation to join them. They'd be shot if they were caught. And there'd be hell to pay on top of a new pane of glass if a window got broken! Besides, Jimmy had other things on his mind.

He couldn't drive the image of Hillie Hardwick from his brain. Not only was she beautiful, but she had guts, too, and the word was that she had brains and all! Bloody hell, she'd be a challenge, and Jimmy was all for that. But there was something else he couldn't quite define. For the past few months, even before he'd started walking out with Doris, Hillie had always set his heart pattering in a most curious manner whenever he saw her. Poor kid, having such a pig for a father, and that made Jimmy feel protective. But somehow he felt something for her he'd never experienced with any of the countless other girls he'd held in his arms before. And it made him feel utterly confused.

He slid through the passageways and various factory sheds down towards the river. His keen eyes scanned the wharf. It took some minutes, but at last he spotted her, talking to that silly little Doris Sedgeworth. God knew why he'd ever asked *her* out. Jimmy pulled back round the corner of the building that housed the toilet soap and pharmaceutical departments, carefully peering out until Doris had gone. Hillie was left chatting with her friend, Gertrude Parker. Everyone knew they were bosom pals and both girls were pretty. But Jimmy only had eyes for Hillie, and suddenly she filled every fibre of his being, swelling his heart with a passion that both astounded and delighted him.

Chapter Two

'Suppose you're off to the library, eh, Hillie?' Gert asked.

'Certainly am. You coming? I can recommend you some good stories to read.'

Mentally, though, Hillie was crossing her fingers. They'd just clocked off from their Saturday morning shift and now they'd reached the junction with Falcon Road on their walk home. Hillie hadn't had a chance the previous afternoon, but that morning, she'd been into the vast offices at Price's and had a chat with a Mrs Harrington there about the advertised vacancy. Now an application form burned between her fingers – or more accurately between the pages of the book she had to return to the library. She wanted to sit quietly at the table in the public building to fill in the form. Her entire future could depend on that sheet of paper. She wondered if it knew that it might hold the key to a new life for her. Fanciful, perhaps, but for her, paper and the words written thereon had an existence all of their own. And this sheet of paper in particular. Much as she loved dear old Gert, she needed to be alone to complete it to perfection.

To her immense relief, Gert pulled a face. 'Last one you told us to read was *Black Beauty*. Blooming sad it was. And so many flaming words.'

'You generally find a few of those in books,' Hillie teased, and Gert giggled back.

'See you later, then. What you doing tonight?'

'I'm not—'

'Bleeding hell, Hillie.' Gert dropped her voice to a sharp whisper, as she shrank away from her friend. 'Here comes your dad.'

Oh, God, she could do without him just now. Hillie instinctively clutched the book more tightly against her chest. She went to walk on, pretending she hadn't seen Harold, but a lead weight dropped down inside her stomach as she felt an iron hand on her shoulder.

'Don't think you can sneak off somewhere that easily, young madam,' his familiar, odious voice snarled in her ear.

'Hello, Dad.' Hillie turned to him with a smile whose sarcasm she scarcely attempted to conceal. 'Didn't see you there.'

'Don't give me that, you little smart-arse. And remember I heard what happened with you and that Jimmy Baxter yesterday morning. Like I said last night, don't let me ever catch you—'

'Well, you'll also have heard that I sent him packing with a flea in his ear. So you've no need to worry, have you?'

'Huh,' Harold grunted. And then as if searching for some other way to reprimand her, he went on, 'Suppose you think you're going to the bloody library again. Well, I can tell you, you're not.'

'Oh, yes I am.' Hillie's silver blue eyes flashed like rapiers. 'My book's due back and you wouldn't want me to have to pay a fine, would you?'

'Humph,' was the grudging response. 'Don't you be long. Your mother needs help in the house.'

'Help her yourself, then.'

Hillie was just about to add that if he hadn't saddled her poor mother with five more children after her, there wouldn't be so much work to do, when Harold grasped her wrist in a vice of steel.

'You little brat!' he spat, so that spittle spraying from his lips showered her face. 'Don't you dare backchat me!'

'Well, you know I do loads to help Mum. Now,' she hissed, catching the horror on Gert's face, 'you're hurting me, so let go before I call for a policeman. And you're causing a scene. People are looking.'

She made a deliberate show of swivelling her gaze about them. She knew her father had some strange notion that he deserved respect no matter what. Her mum always said he'd come back from the war obsessed with demanding obedience from everyone around him, but Hillie didn't think he'd like to be shown up as a bully on the street! Sure enough, he sucked in his cheeks, his mean mouth almost disappearing, and he dropped Hillie's wrist with such a jerk, she winced in pain before relief set in. He stalked off, and it wasn't until Gert was sure he wasn't going to turn back that she stepped up to Hillie again, shaking her head.

'Blimey, Hillie! Don't know how you stand it. I know I couldn't if my dad was like that.'

'Not much choice. Not at the moment.' Her eyes dropped to the secret held between the pages of the book, and her heart took an excited bound. 'Now promise me you won't tell a soul,' she said, lowering her voice to a whisper, 'but I've got an application form to fill in for that job you told me about.'

Gert's eyes lit up. 'Really?' she breathed. 'Oh, I am pleased. And no. Course I won't tell no one. But I'll keep me flipping fingers crossed for you. D'you think you'll get it?'

'No idea. I've never applied for an office job before. Depends who else applies, I suppose.'

'Well, I think you should get it. You know all about the factory, but you're wasted on the shop floor.'

'Thanks, Gert,' Hillie replied ruefully. 'We'll just have to see. But I'd best get on now. If I'm too long at the library, there'll be hell to pay,' she concluded, jabbing her head along Battersea Park Road in the direction her father had taken.

'And that wasn't? Hell, I mean.'

'Oooh, no.'

Hillie gave a short, ironic laugh and waved to Gert before setting off with a brisk step along Falcon Road. The sooner she arrived at the library, the sooner she could put her mind to completing the application form. The long walk alone, though, under the rank of railway bridges crossing the road as the multiple tracks left Clapham Junction Station, and then up Lavender Hill as far as the tall, brick building of the public library, gave her time to think. She'd given the form a cursory glance and had a rough idea of what it contained. It was only short, so she needed to make a glowing impression in a few words.

The library was silent but for the hushed sounds of people scanning the shelves to choose new books. It was a busy period, Hillie knew. As most people were at work the rest of the week, there weren't many in this industrial part of south-west London who could visit the library at any other time.

Hillie found herself an empty table and sat down. She carefully unfolded the sheet of paper and smoothed it out with reverent hands. She'd brought her fountain pen with her, a prized present from her mother, wrapped up in a sheet of blotting paper in case it leaked. Now she tore off a narrow strip of the absorbent paper and wound it round behind the nib of the pen. She wasn't going to risk any ink splotches marring her chances of getting an interview!

Personal details, that was straightforward enough. Concentrating on writing them down in an impeccably neat hand seemed to calm her nerves. This could be the gateway to releasing the real Hilda Hardwick, whose heart burst with a passion for life beyond the backstreet where she lived and the factory where she worked. It would be but a small step, but it would be a job where she could use her brain a little more, and the extra money would allow her a little more freedom of whatever type she chose. Presuming her dad didn't get his dirty hands on it, of course!

Qualifications, now that was trickier. She had no shorthand and typing skills, but Mrs Harrington had explained those weren't necessary as this was a strictly clerical post. The only academic qualification Hillie had was her school leaving certificate, but with 'excellent' in every subject, that must surely prove her intelligence. In case she ever needed it, she'd proudly stored the certificate in her drawer in the bedroom she shared with Joan, Trixie and Daisy, three of her five younger siblings.

Experience. Well, she'd worked at Price's for three years, only as a packer, perhaps, but she knew every kind of candle the factory produced, every shape and size, the type of wax for different uses, the differing wicks and how they were prepared from cotton or flax, and the various companies they manufactured candles for that required their own labels to be affixed rather than Price's own. She'd also done a stint in the soap-packing house when there'd been a huge, urgent order to fulfil. She'd really enjoyed that, with all the fragrances and pretty colours in the silky smooth bars. And although she had nothing to do with the lubricating oil production at the factory, she had a reasonable idea of the processes involved. So overall she had a pretty good notion of the entire factory and how it worked, which surely must stand her in good stead for a position in the office. She also added that she was a conscientious worker, young and enthusiastic, and quick to learn any new skill that was required of her. They would also see from her records that she was never late and had only been off sick once in her three years of service.

Hillie paused to chew the end of her pen. She mustn't be too long or her dad would come down on her like a ton of hot bricks. She didn't want him to know about her application. He'd see it as her getting too big for her boots, and he'd want to keep her in her place. And if she didn't get the job, it'd only provide fuel for his cruel mockery of her, and she didn't want that! She could just imagine him ridiculing her for trying to prove herself better than she really was.

Well, she'd do her level best to prove that she *was* worth more than standing at a bench packing candles all day! She went back to finishing off the form. It had taken her half an hour to complete, and when she'd finished, she sat back to observe it with a critical eye. It certainly *looked* good, almost like a work of art, her handwriting small, slightly and evenly slanted, artistic and yet utterly legible, and not a crossing out or an ink blot. It was as perfect as she could make it; even if she wasn't successful, at least she wouldn't have disgraced herself. With a proud sigh tempered with apprehension, she slid it back into the envelope Mrs Harrington had provided and then went to choose a new book to read during the week. She deliberately chose one large enough to conceal the envelope and then set off home, nervous excitement simmering in her young breast.

*

'There. That's everything done, isn't it, Mum?'

Hillie and Nell Hardwick surveyed together the back room of their terraced house in the Latchmere area of Battersea. It served as both kitchen and dining room, with a rustic kitchen table placed in the centre. A curtain across the recess at one side of the narrow chimney breast hid the pull-down bed where Luke, the eldest of Hillie's younger siblings, slept at night. Off the room was a scullery which housed the enamel gas oven on its tall legs on which Nell cooked for her family of eight, and the chipped butler sink with its corroded cold tap perched on the end of a lead pipe protruding from the wall. All was as neat and tidy as it could be, everything washed up and stowed away in its rightful place after Sunday lunch.

'Yes, I think so, Hillie dear. Thanks for your help. And I'm glad you applied for that job,' Nell said, dropping her voice. 'I won't tell a soul. I understand why you don't want your dad to know.'

'Thanks, Mum. It was a nice dinner, by the way.'

Hillie beamed at her mother, who returned her affection with a timid curve of her mouth as if she was almost afraid to show her pleasure. She appeared so small, so vulnerable, that Hillie was overwhelmed with an irresistible surge of protectiveness and enveloped Nell in her arms. Her mum just about came up to her chin, and Hillie wondered for the umpteenth time where she got her own height from, since her father wasn't particularly tall either.

'Oh, get away with you,' Nell pulled away, blushing shyly. 'And it wasn't a nice dinner at all.'

'It wasn't at all bad, and it was the best you could do to feed so many of us on the pittance Dad gives you for housekeeping.'

'And what *you* give us,' Nell corrected, cheeks pinked with embarrassment. 'If I had my way, we wouldn't be taking so much of your wages from you. You deserve to keep more money for yourself.'

'But you couldn't manage on any less. And what would I do with it, anyway?'

'But your father always has enough for his cigarettes and more than a few pints every week.'

Hillie clamped her jaw. She'd thought the same herself on numerous occasions. She was convinced her dad earned more than he let on. But she had enough to argue with him over without challenging him on that score as well. Besides, their rows upset her mum so much that she often gave in for Nell's sake.

She was saved having to find a suitable reply, though, as her father came in through the back door from the yard, pulling up his braces. Hillie knew he'd been using the outside lav. It was his ritual after Sunday lunch, and everyone else had to wait. Now his broad, stocky figure filled the doorway between the scullery and the kitchen, casting an ominous shadow over the two women. Hillie sensed her mother shrink against her.

'You done everything properly?'

Hillie's chin shot up. 'Of course. Can't you see? So I assume you'd have no objection if we all go to the park for the afternoon? It's such a lovely day.'

'Humph,' Harold snorted, knowing he was bested since the room and the scullery were immaculate. 'Make sure you're back to help your mother with the tea.'

'Of course. Come on then, Mum. The others are all waiting outside.'

'Just get my hat, dear.'

Hillie bit down her frustration. She couldn't wait to get away from the suffocating atmosphere her father created in the house. But her mother was of the generation who couldn't put her head outside the door without sticking some sort of covering on it.

'Where d'you think you're going?' Harold's voice sliced through the stiff air as he leaned forward to grasp his wife's arm before she even got as far as the dark, depressing hallway. 'I didn't say *you* could go, did I?'

Hillie waited for the indignation to scorch down through her body and land heavily in her boots. Why shouldn't her poor, downtrodden mother have a few hours' pleasure wandering through Battersea Park and playing with her children? She had little enjoyment in her life as it was.

Hillie's mind raced. How could she diffuse the situation without aggravating her father even more? 'Why don't we all go, Dad?' The words tumbled gaily out of her mouth before she could stop them. And then, cringing at her own actions, she linked her arm through her father's. 'You'd enjoy it. I've probably got enough in my piggy bank for us all to go on the boating lake.'

'What would I want to go boating for? Take the little uns if you want,' her dad barked back, snatching away his arm. 'Keep them out of my hair for a few hours. Give your mother and me a bit of time together.'

He drew the tip of his tongue over his suddenly drooling bottom lip, and Hillie felt sick. She knew what her father had in mind. Oh, her poor mum. If her dad was as domineering in the bedroom as he was in everything else, her mother must be desperate. And Hillie was desperate to save her mum from the ordeal, this once at least.

She opened her mouth to make some sort of protest. They might not get such a lovely day again for weeks, perhaps? But her mother caught her eye with an almost imperceptible shake of her head.

'You go along and enjoy yourself, Hillie dear,' Nell said, a false smile trembling on her lips. From the pleading expression on her face, she didn't want Hillie to interfere. And perhaps it'd be worse for her mum if she did, Hillie considered, though her rancour towards her father stuck in her throat.

'OK, then. See you later.' She tried to force some brightness into her voice as she skipped out of the front door into the blinding brilliance of the afternoon sun. But in truth all she felt inside was bitterness and anger towards her father.

Having lent a hand with the washing up earlier, Luke and Joan, the eldest of her younger siblings, had been allowed by their father to go off and find their own friends. Odd how he allowed them to get away with a lot more than *she* ever did when she was that age, Hillie always thought. But the youngest two, little Daisy and Frances, were playing on the doorstep under Trixie's watchful eye. Hillie sometimes wondered if Trixie was more like their father than any of them. She never allowed her charges much fun, but though only eight years old, she could be relied upon to keep her younger sisters safe.

'Hey, you lot,' Hillie addressed them fondly, trying to keep her mind off what she knew was about to take place indoors. 'We're going to the park. We can... Oh, never mind.' Damn. She was so riled up about her dad that she'd forgotten to run upstairs and raid her piggy bank, but she certainly wasn't going back indoors now! 'You wait here. I'm going to call for Gert and see if any of them want to come, too.'

'Goody! Will you ask Jake to bring his football?' Daisy piped up.

Hillie laughed, grateful for the diversion from her unhappy thoughts. She went a few steps down the street and knocked at the front door to the Parkers' house. It was opened only seconds later by a little tot barely tall enough to reach the latch. The child stared up at Hillie, eyes huge in a pinched face that still bore evidence of the meal the family had recently eaten.

'Hello, Trudy!' Hillie beamed. 'Is Gert in?'

Ermintrude Parker's enquiring expression moved into a grin. 'Hillie!'

Holding up her arms, the little urchin leapt into the air, obliging Hillie to catch her. In time-honoured fashion, Hillie hoisted her onto her hip – and immediately wished she hadn't. She could feel that the toddler had wet her knickers and nobody had noticed – and Hillie was wearing her best summer dress, taken, freshly washed and ironed, from its hanger that morning. To her utter relief, though, Trudy started to wriggle herself free the instant she spied Daisy and Frances through the open door. Hillie set her down on her feet again and the child rushed outside. Hillie knew she'd be perfectly safe playing hopscotch on the pavement under Trixie's strict command.

Hillie stepped inside the house and walked down the narrow hallway with its chipped brown paintwork and walls of similar hue. The door to the front room stood wide open, revealing the single bedstead where Gert's grandmother, Old Sal, slept. Half hidden behind the door was another bed that Hillie knew little Trudy shared with her brother,

Jake. Even though the windows had been opened, the room smelt of stale urine. But when Hillie's nose screwed up, it was from bitterness rather than distaste. Why wouldn't her dad allow *their* front room to be used as a bedroom, instead of insisting it was kept as a pristine but spartan parlour only he was allowed to set foot in? It would certainly ease the crowded conditions in the bedroom four of them squeezed into; and even though he was probably the brightest in the class, poor Luke had been caned more than once for falling asleep at school. But it was no wonder when his bed was in the kitchen and he couldn't go to sleep until his parents had retired for the night. And what would happen as the youngest, Frances, who still fitted in the cot in her parents' room, got bigger? But their father's word was law, no matter how often Hillie tried to reason with him over their sleeping arrangements – and received a cuff round the ear for her troubles.

Her frustration, though, was quickly forgotten as lively chatter filtered through from the back room of Number Eight. As Hillie pushed the door wider, the happy atmosphere wrapped its welcoming arms about her. In shape and size, the room mirrored that in her own house, but that was as far as the resemblance went. Yes, there was a table in the middle, but it was still littered with the detritus of Sunday lunch – and probably the past week's meals as well. Hillie grimaced to herself as she reflected that her dad would have a fit if he came home to a table like this. Unadorned with the starched white tablecloth that he insisted was replaced every day, the Parkers' table was always bare, deep scratches and burns from scalding pans placed directly on the wood unashamedly on show. Bread and cake crumbs, so stale they'd dried into minute solid lumps, were scattered across its surface among ring marks and dirty crockery. Hillie noticed greasy gravy dripping from the spout of a cracked jug and congealing on the table, even though the pudding, the remnants of which looked as if it might have passed as jam crumble, had already been served and eaten.

But what did all that matter? The clash of merry conversation – each voice raised higher and higher to make itself heard – didn't cease as a sea of faces turned to Hillie, drawing her into its chaotic bosom. The very goodness of it all made her heart ache with envy.

'Wanna cuppa, ducks?' Evangeline Parker called out from the scullery. 'Just putting the old kettle on.'

'No thanks, Mrs P,' Hillie called back. 'I'm just taking my lot up the park and wondered if any of you wanted to come.'

'Course,' Gert gulped through her last mouthful of whatever it was. 'I'll just get me hat. I'll take the kids and all, Mum, so you and Dad can get some peace.'

'No. You go, too, Eva girl,' Stan insisted, emerging from behind his newspaper. 'I'll stay 'ere and keep an eye on Old Sal. And clear away the battlefield,' he added, winking at Hillie as he disappeared behind the sports page again so that she wondered if so much as a teaspoon would have moved by the time they got back. Dear Mr Parker, so different from her own father, Hillie sighed to herself.

'D'you mind if I have a cuppa first?' Eva asked from the doorway now.

'No, go ahead,' Hillie answered. 'We're not in any hurry.'

'Better tidy these two up, anyway,' Gert grimaced, getting to her feet and waving her hand towards her younger brother and sister, Mildred and Jake. 'I'll change Baby Primrose's nappy, too. Just had a feed, hasn't she, so she'll sleep in the pram for a few hours if we're lucky.'

'I think Trudy needs some attention, too,' Hillie whispered as Gert passed. 'She's gone outside with mine, but she's wet her knickers.'

'Righty-ho,' Gert chanted amiably, disappearing off to her tasks like a proper little mother, and Hillie wondered what on earth she'd do without Gert and her happy-go-lucky family.

It was only as the crowded room cleared that Hillie realised Gert's elder brother was perched on the far chair, patiently feeding Old Sal her pudding. As the old lady had no teeth left, eating was always slow. The poor thing was riddled with arthritis and spent most of her time in an armchair by the fire. The seat sagged and stuffing was hanging out of the upholstery here and there, but it was more comfortable than the wooden kitchen chairs everyone else had to make do with.

'Hello, Kit. Come round for Sunday dinner, then?'

Kit smiled briefly over his shoulder as he used the spoon to catch the custard that dribbled from the corner of Old Sal's wrinkled mouth. 'Best roast in Battersea.' He shot Hillie another glance, one eyebrow arched ironically. 'Apart from your mum's, of course.'

Hillie returned his grimace. Nell *was* a good cook, but as her dad never allowed any visitors into the house, Kit Parker and anyone else had to take Hillie's word regarding her mother's culinary skills.

'Not working today?' she asked, neatly changing the subject.

'Night shift,' Kit told her without turning his head. 'Passenger trains might stop, but freights go all night.'

Hillie nodded. Bright was Kit. Now when *he* had been offered a place at the grammar school, Stan and Eva had scraped every penny to afford the uniform and all the extras that hadn't come free with the scholarship. But Kit had a passion for trains and when he was sixteen, his uncle – Stan's brother – who'd worked at Clapham Junction himself from a boy, had managed to get his nephew taken on in the office. Being one of the brightest recruits, Kit had been selected to be trained on the telegraph. It was a lowly but good start. Kit had been there for six years now, and was gradually working his way up the ladder.

'You still planning on being stationmaster one day, then?' Hillie enquired, half teasing.

Kit's strong mouth spread into a grin. 'Of course!'

'Bit ambitious, aren't you? Clapham Junction's one of the busiest stations in the world. And the biggest in Britain, isn't it?'

'That's what they say,' Kit confirmed. 'And I intend to be in charge of the whole operation by the time I'm forty.' His grin broadened, eyes shining like stars. Hillie wasn't sure if he was being serious or not, but somehow felt she could detect solemnity behind his jocular smile. Perhaps it wasn't a joke but a deadly serious ambition. And why not?

'Your digs still OK?' Hillie asked next.

'Yes, thanks, Hill. Works out well and I couldn't go on living in this bedlam. Right, all finished, Gran.' He turned his attention back to Old Sal, wiping her mouth with a stained cloth which didn't look as if it'd seen the inside of a washtub for weeks. 'All right?'

Old Sal smacked her lips over her toothless mouth as she nodded, and her dull, drooping eyes brightened as she noticed their visitor. 'Hello, Hillie dear,' her chin appeared to articulate without her lips making any contact with each other.

'Hello, Sal,' Hillie beamed back at her. 'Enjoy your dinner?'

'Yeah. This nice young man give it to me.'

'I'm sure that's a compliment, Gran, but I'm your grandson, Kit. Christopher.'

The old lady peered at him through a bemused frown. 'No, you're not. He's only this high.'

'I've grown, Gran. I'm twenty-two now.'

'How old?' Old Sal still looked puzzled. 'How old am I, then?'

'You're eighty-six, Gran.'

The frown deepened. 'And who's this, then? Do I know her?'

'Yes. It's Hillie. From a few doors down. You've known her since she was a baby. You said hello to her just now.'

'No, I didn't. Who is she?'

'Oh, dear. Not a good day.' Eva plonked herself down in the next chair, spilling tea from her chipped mug all over the table. The cloth she pulled from the pocket of her dirty apron was not, however, for mopping up spills. It turned out to be a scarf, remarkably clean for her, which she proceeded to tie over the curlers in her hair. 'There,' she announced proudly. 'Just swallow me tea and use the lav and I'll be ready.'

'You coming with us, Kit?' Hillie asked, feeling so much happier than when she'd left her own house.

'If you'll have me. Shift doesn't start till six. That's if you can manage on your own, Dad?'

'Yeah, yeah.' Stan flapped his hand at his eldest offspring. 'You go and enjoy yourself with the others.'

There were relaxed, genuine smiles all round, and yet again, Hillie felt so envious. If only her family were allowed to be like this! She gritted her teeth, driving away the odious shadow of her father. It was a beautiful afternoon, hot for the time of year, and she was about to spend a few hours with her best friend and her family among the grassy spaces and neatly tended flowerbeds of Battersea Park.

But the image of what Harold was doing to her poor mother kept coming back to haunt her.

Chapter Three

Harold Hardwick swung his legs over the side of the bed and sat on the edge of the mattress to pull his drawers back on. He looked down between his legs and a smirk twisted his face. He'd performed well, but twice was enough for him. Nell was too much of a cold fish in the bedroom department for his liking. Always had been. He knew why, of course. It still galled him how he'd been tricked all those years before. So he always enjoyed taking his revenge, and it made him feel good that he could still make the hussy suffer in such an intimate way.

He glanced over his shoulder at his wife's naked form on the sheets beside him, curled up on her side with her back to him. From behind, she still looked like a young woman, slender-limbed, firm buttocks, graceful neck. Even from the front, she was still attractive, face only faintly lined and her hair in the neat perm he insisted on. It was only the loose skin on her otherwise flat stomach that gave away her multiple pregnancies, and her breasts didn't sag so much that he didn't enjoy kneading them, seeing the pain and fear in her eyes. He swallowed the saliva that had collected in his mouth. Perhaps he should turn her on her back again. Take his pleasure for a third time. But he was hot, his armpits running with sweat. He didn't want to humiliate himself by not being able to finish what he'd started.

He pulled his shirt on over his vest, his mind wandering, unsatisfied. Perhaps he should seek out some younger comfort. He never had before. It somehow seemed beneath him, and besides, he'd seen young lads who'd got the clap out in France during the war and the agonising treatment they'd had to endure. So perhaps he'd better stick with humiliating Nell as often as he could.

He picked up his trousers from the floor and put them on again. Now what? The entire house was like a new pin. He saw to it that Nell was too terrified to let it be otherwise. Part of her punishment. But none of it was enough for him. He was always looking for ways to make her pay for what she'd done.

He went to go downstairs, but as he stepped on the tiny square of landing, he noticed that the door to the back bedroom was ajar. Perhaps he could find something amiss there that would be cause to reprimand young Hillie. He could punish her, and that would be even greater torture to her mother. But to his annoyance, the room couldn't be tidier and you could eat off any of the surfaces, or the floor for that matter.

Harold lowered himself onto the narrow bed the girl occupied. It was underneath the window, on the opposite side from the bunks Joan and Trixie slept in, with Daisy's little cot-bed slotted behind the door. The wardrobe the four girls shared stood on one side of the chimney breast, and the chest of drawers on the other. It was cramped, but with the military tidiness Harold expected, it wasn't uncomfortable.

He lay back on the bed, hands behind his head. To think this was where the little madam rested each night. The pillow was hard, though. Why was that? He slipped his hand beneath. Ah, a book, of course. She had nowhere else to keep it, after all. So, what was she reading that kept her so engrossed?

As he pulled the book from its resting place, something slid from between its pages. An envelope. So what was the sly monkey hiding? A love letter? Well, he'd soon put a stop to any secret relationship she might be having. No one was going to try and trick him and get away with it ever again!

He turned the envelope over in his hands, anger simmering deep inside. It wasn't addressed to anyone. What did that mean? It was sealed, but not all the way, as if it had been done in haste. So could he possibly steam it open?

He slunk down the stairs to the scullery and turned on the gas under the kettle. Nell wouldn't be down, but he'd listen out just in case. But he wasn't disturbed. As the steam loosened the glue, he slid the blade of a knife underneath and, hey presto, the envelope revealed its secret.

For a few seconds, Harold was confused. Why would Hillie not tell them she was applying for another job? It didn't make sense. And then it hit him like a fist in the belly. If she got the job, it'd be more money, possibly enough for her to leave home. She'd have it all arranged before she told them, wouldn't she? The crafty little so-and-so. And then he couldn't go on using her to get back at her mother. Couldn't go on punishing her. Not only that, but the brat could taunt him by claiming she had a better job than him, was climbing the ladder when he'd only be a candle moulder for the rest of his life. With her tongue, he wouldn't put it past her.

Well, he'd damned well make sure she wouldn't get the job! So what could he do? She believed the envelope was sealed, so she wouldn't be looking at the form again, would she? It was almost a work of art, it was so neat. But what if the ink was badly smudged? A sly leer twisted Harold's lips as he wetted his hands under the tap and allowed the water to drip from his fingers onto the paper. The ink leeched out of the words in pretty blue stars. Not too many or it would look deliberate, but just enough to ruin Hillie's chances. A few moments to let it dry, then return it to the envelope, seal it up and replace it in the book. Hillie would never realise what had happened and would think she didn't get the job because she wasn't bloody good enough! That'd teach her to go behind his back and think she was cleverer than him.

Oh, what joy! Harold's heart danced as he crept back up the stairs.

*

They made a motley procession walking down to Battersea Park that sunny June afternoon. Leading the way was Eva Parker, pushing the battered old pram with nine-month-old Primrose, pretty as a picture, asleep on her back. Proud as Punch was Eva of all her offspring and it was a delight to her to have them all together on an outing, especially her eldest, Kit, who didn't live with them anymore. He was piggybacking little Trudy – now in dry knickers – while Gertie herded Mildred and Jake across Battersea Bridge Road, minding the rattling trams, and Hillie did the same with her three youngest sisters. Kit was smartly attired in his railway uniform as he was going straight to work afterwards, but apart from that, the difference between the two families was that while the Parkers provided a scruffy sight, the Hardwicks were clean and neatly turned out, even if their clothes were all hand-me-downs. Nell wouldn't dare let her children be otherwise unless she wanted to answer to Harold!

'You'd think me mum was the flipping queen, wouldn't you?' Gert chuckled in a low voice, jabbing her head at Eva who was several paces ahead as they trooped down Cambridge Road. 'If she had a crown on her head instead of curlers and a scarf, you could be mistaken, she looks so proud and royal like.'

'And if she'd taken her apron off,' Kit observed, trying to keep a straight face. 'Remembered to change out of her slippers, mind.'

'That's a wonder,' Gert grinned. 'Right, hold me hand, you two,' she commanded as they reached the vast junction of Albert Bridge Road and Prince of Wales Drive.

They all crossed over in dribs and drabs according to the traffic, Eva waiting by the lodge house just inside the ornate, wrought-iron gates and arched stone pillars of the park's Sun Gate. Her warm, maternal smile graced her homely face as they all caught her up.

'Right, where shall we go, then?' she asked brightly.

'I wanna play wiv me football,' Jake whined. 'That's why I bringed it all this way,' he moaned, twirling said object in its string bag.

'I want to go to the aviaries,' Trixie pouted.

'We can do everything,' Hillie told them. 'Got plenty of time.'

'And I've got some crusts to feed the ducks and the swans,' Eva put in. 'Do that first, shall we?' Not that she gave anyone the chance to disagree as she set off in the direction of the lakes, everyone trailing along around her in a little cluster. 'Your mum not wanted to come, then?' she asked, glancing sideways at Hillie.

Hillie hoped the rush of heat she felt in her cheeks didn't show. 'Thought she and Dad would have a bit of peace together,' she replied, cringing at the half-truth.

'Pity. Poor Nell works so hard, I hardly ever see her, and her living only a few doors down and us being friends since we was kids. Well, you tell her I'm coming to see her in the week, no matter how busy she says she is,' Eva announced, heaving up her bosom so that Hillie wondered quite what she was thinking.

Hillie would never have guessed, of course. Eva's thoughts had wandered back to the time when she'd befriended the little girl at the grocers' when she was running errands for her own mother, Old Sal. Nellie Fenton, as she'd been then, was a pretty, shy soul, a bit vulnerable and not streetwise like Evangeline. But the two had become bosom pals. Then the war had come along and Nell's parents had eventually lost all their money. With all the food shortages, they'd refused to deal in under-the-counter goings-on, and as a result of their scruples, business had collapsed. They'd both died in poverty in the 1919 influenza pandemic.

By then, of course, Nell had been married to Harold for five years, Hillie was a little tot of four and Nell had been pregnant with Luke. Unlike the Hardwicks, when Stan had returned from the war, he and Eva had waited to see what life would bring before they extended their family. They'd used those rubber things to stop anything happening; how they'd fallen about laughing the first time Stan had tried to put one on! But when he'd got the job at the sawmill at Price's factory and his future looked secure, the babies hadn't come straightaway – unlike Nell who seemed to produce them on a regular basis, the four-year gap between Trixie and Daisy being the longest interval. But now Eva had six children of her own, perhaps it was time she shut up shop. She wasn't getting any younger, after all.

'Got the bread then, Mum?' Mildred asked, tugging at her sleeve and snapping her from her reverie.

'Yeah, here you go. There's not much. Can't afford to feed the blooming ducks that much. So make sure you share it equal like.'

Eva lowered her plump frame onto a bench by the hooped railings and released a sigh of contentment. Ah, how lucky they were to have this whacking great park on their doorstep with its lovely lakes, wide open spaces and all the other amenities. The huge formal flower beds were carpeted in colour, and some flowering shrubs whose names Eva didn't know were still covered in frothy blossom. Nell would've loved it. Perhaps if there was another fine day in the week, Eva could persuade her to come for a stroll in the park. Eva's brow furrowed in pensive bitterness. Poor Nell. But Eva's lips were sealed. What good would it do, anyway?

'Bread's all gone now,' Gert announced cheerily.

'Blimey, you didn't half make short work of that!' Eva laughed, her comely bosom wobbling. 'So, bird cages next, is it, young Trixie?' she asked, since she couldn't quite remember the posh word Trixie had used for them.

The little army set off again, this time with Eva and the pram bringing up the rear. The younger ones skipped and danced on ahead while Hillie, Gert and her brother were in the middle. Kit obviously said something funny and teasing, and Hillie playfully pushed his arm in response. Eva's heart gave a little bound. It'd be nice if those two got together. Her Kit needed someone intelligent, and she was a pretty kid, too. No, not just pretty. She was beautiful. And Kit wouldn't be a bad catch either, even if Eva said so herself.

'Right, who's for an ice cream?' Kit asked when they'd had their fill of poking their fingers through the wire of the enclosures and being told off by a brown-uniformed keeper.

Kit was met by a chorus of delight, and ushered the troop away with a blushing apology to the keeper. Taking his hands, Mildred and Jake almost dragged their big brother along to the pavilion near the river embankment. They queued patiently enough, though, even if they were jumping up and down with excitement.

'Now calm down and hold it carefully. Look, like Trixie,' Kit ordered as he handed each of his younger two siblings their treats. 'If you drop them, you won't get another one. Hill?' he asked, turning to Hillie who was overseeing little Daisy and Frances as they carefully licked their cones.

Hillie was sure she flushed. 'Can you afford it?' she replied in a low whisper. 'There's an awful lot of us.'

'Course I can,' Kit assured her, dismayed that she'd felt she had to ask. But he knew from Gert how tight Harold Hardwick was with money and how he snatched most of Hillie's wages, so she certainly wasn't used to having a treat very often! 'I'm on reasonable money,' he explained, to make her feel better about it. 'My digs are quite cheap so I manage to save a bit each week, so I'm sure I can afford to buy the girl of my dreams an ice cream.'

His eyes had gleamed rakishly as he said it and Hillie laughed aloud as he ordered another cone. 'Give over,' she grinned, and would have dug him in the ribs if there hadn't been the risk of his dropping her ice cream as he'd warned the younger ones not to do.

They were lucky to find an empty bench nearby and sat the little ones down in a row to enjoy their cones without mishap. When they'd finished, they skirted the bandstand where military marches were enthralling the audience, pausing for ten minutes to listen to the music before ambling off through the extensive cricket grounds where a match was in full swing on one of the immaculate pitches. They at last reached the vast grassy area devoted to football. With the season over, it was less well-tended, and people were dotted about the edges, sitting on picnic rugs. They managed to find yet another bench for Eva to rest on so that she could jiggle the pram back and forth on the flat path since Primrose was threatening to wake up. The others all went off to a patch of grass to knock Jake's football around where they wouldn't disturb others, until the two youngest, Frances and Trudy, were getting tired, and Gert and Hillie brought them back to stretch out on the grass beside them and have forty winks.

'Good with the little ones, isn't he, your Kit?' Hillie said lazily as she watched a bee investigating the first daisies to appear that year.

Gert wrinkled up her nose in a shrug. 'Get used to it, I suppose, if you're the eldest of a big family. But you should know that, Hillie. Hey, you don't fancy our Kit, do you?' she giggled after a moment's pause.

'What?' Hillie was taken aback by Gert's teasing question and her eyebrows shot up towards her hairline. 'Kit?' she questioned. 'Well, no. I mean, I suppose he's good-looking enough. But Kit's... well, he's just Kit,' she shrugged. 'Your brother, and... Well, he's like a brother to me, too.'

'I suppose you'd rather Jimmy Baxter?' Gert suggested, attempting to keep a straight face. But she couldn't do so for more than a few seconds before she burst out laughing.

'Oh, you!' Hillie chuckled back, reaching out to give her friend a playful shove. 'You're incorrigible, Gertrude Parker!'

'That's why you like me so much. And trust me with your secrets.' Gert's face suddenly moved into serious lines and she hesitated a moment, glancing round as she dropped her voice. 'You filled in that form yet?'

'Yes, I have,' Hillie whispered back. 'I'll be handing it in tomorrow. I told Mum, but you won't say a word to anyone else, will you?'

'Cross me heart,' Gert assured her with a dramatic gesture. 'If you get it, mind, I'll miss having you next to us at the bench. Won't get all highfalutin with me, though, will you?'

'Course not. I've got to get it first, anyway.'

'They'd be daft not to choose you.' Gert stated her opinion so forcefully that it brought a rueful smile to Hillie's lips.

'Oh, I don't know,' she sighed.

Gert tipped her head enquiringly to one side. 'I can read you like a book, Hill. What's up?'

Hillie met her friend's steady, demanding gaze and knew she had to give an answer. 'Oh, sometimes I just wish,' she began hesitantly, 'that we could get away from all this, you and me. You know Price's factory at Bromborough? Opposite side of the Mersey from Liverpool?'

'Yeah? Well, I mean, I've never been there as you know, but I've heard talk of it. They built it 'cos everything from West Africa comes in there, including all the palm oil for the candles?' Gert looked puzzled for a moment, and then her eyes stretched wide as realisation dawned. 'You doesn't think with all this electric thing and the new power station they're building just over there' – nodding her head towards the massive construction site at the far side of the park – 'that Price's will have to close York Road down, do you? And that some of us might have to go up to Bromborough? Or else lose our jobs?'

Hillie shrugged her eyebrows. 'The thought had crossed my mind. But it mightn't be a bad thing if I was offered a job there and my dad wasn't. When they built the factory at Bromborough, they built a whole new village for the workers as well. It might've been back in Victorian days, but it was so good that Levers copied it for their Port Sunlight.'

'And then Cadbury's built Bourneville for their workers along the same lines, didn't they?'

'That's right. Well, I've often thought, wouldn't it be great if you and me could move up there, and live in one of those little houses together? But I know you wouldn't want to leave your family.'

'No, sorry, kid, I wouldn't.' Gert lowered her eyes. 'And you wouldn't really want to leave yours either, would you? I mean, it'd mean you could be free of your dad, but you wouldn't want to leave your mum at his mercy, would you? Or the little ones?'

'No. Not really. Silly of me.' But Hillie shook her head in desperation. 'Oh, Gert, sometimes I feel I'm being pulled apart, and I don't know which way to turn.'

She was almost drowning in Gert's sympathetic green eyes, and didn't see the figure approaching them until she felt a shadow blocking out the sunlight. She looked up at a black silhouette outlined against the brilliant sky, but she recognised who it was at once.

'Sorry to interrupt, ladies,' a familiar voice said.

Hillie squinted grudgingly up at Jimmy Baxter. 'What you doing here?'

'Same as you, I imagine,' Jimmy shrugged. 'Enjoying me day off. Only in my case, it's not been a whole day. I do a Sunday lunchtime shift at a pub. The Falcon. Down St John's Hill. Know it?'

Hillie had never seen the inside of a public house, not even the Duke of Cambridge on the corner of their street. But she knew where Jimmy meant. 'Well, yes, I do. Of course,' she answered warily.

She watched as Jimmy linked his thumbs under the braces just visible beneath his open jacket, and ran them up and down, leaning back with his thin chest puffed up as he surveyed the scattered crowds in the park. 'Lovely day, ain't it? And all the better for meeting you two beautiful ladies. And who are these little cherubs?' he asked, jabbing his head at the two toddlers dozing on the grass beside them.

Amazingly, Jimmy seemed genuinely interested, and anyway, Hillie could think of no reason to lie to him. 'This one's my youngest sister, Frances.'

'Pretty little kid. How many of you are there, then?'

'Six. I'm the eldest.'

'And this one? Looks more like you, Gertrude, if I'm not mistaken.'

Gert blinked at him, almost ready to laugh. She was never called by her full name, and to hear it from the lips of this cocky devil seemed ludicrous. 'She's me sister, yeah. But not the youngest. She's in the pram over there. With me mum. Why don't you come over and meet her?' she suggested, since Frances and Trudy had been disturbed by the intruder and were coming to. Meet her mum. Now *that* should send Jimmy Baxter packing!

To her amazement and annoyance, Jimmy declared that he would love to. He followed the girls – who exchanged horrified glances – over to where Eva had almost nodded off herself, and when they introduced him, he held out his hand politely.

'Very pleased to meet you, Mrs Parker,' he said in the most cultured tone he could muster.

'Likewise, I'm sure, young man.' Eva straightened her curlers. Mmm. Nice-looking enough. Not as handsome as her Kit, but more than passable. And seemingly quite charming. Might her Gertie be interested?

'So you not out with Doris today?' Gert asked pointedly, knowing full well that Jimmy had dumped

Doris Sedgeworth and catching the expression on her mother's face.

Jimmy's frown was only fleeting. 'Oh, we're not walking out anymore,' he announced quite openly. 'She wasn't mature enough for us.'

'Hello, who've we got here, then?'

Hillie noticed that, curiously, Jimmy seemed to jump as he swivelled round to face Kit as he came up behind them with the rest of the tribe. Jimmy's expression tightened, his eyes travelling over Kit's railway uniform. His shirt was open at the neck, though, and he was bare-headed, having left both his tie and cap at his parents' house in readiness for work afterwards. Jimmy's face seemed to relax, then, and he held out his hand once again.

'Jimmy Baxter,' he introduced himself. 'I work at Price's with Hilda and Gertrude. And you are?'

'Kit Parker. Gert's elder brother. And this lot are divided between us,' Kit explained, waving his hand at the flock behind him, his own siblings decidedly grubby while the other Hardwick children had done their best to keep clean.

Jimmy's face spread into a grin. 'You all look hot and bothered. Would you all like an ice cream?'

'Yeah!' a general cheer replied.

'No,' Hillie said sharply. 'You've already had one, and if you have another one, you'll be sick and Dad'll be cross. Now, you lot, thank Mr Baxter for his offer. It was really kind of you, Jimmy.'

'Not at all. Another time, perhaps.' Jimmy tugged his forelock as the line of urchins mumbled their thanks, shooting grudging pouts at Hillie. But it was soon forgotten when Jake found a large stone to kick along the path and the others tried to turn it into another game of football. 'See you at work tomorrow, then, girls. Goodbye, Mrs Parker. Nice to have met you.'

Jimmy sauntered off, whistling, hands thrust deep in pockets. Kit met his sister's gaze and they both shrugged. Jimmy Baxter meant nothing much to either of them.

As they eventually set off home, it was Hillie who noticed the smart trio entering the park through Sun Gate as their happy, scruffy band was about to leave through it. The middle-aged man cut a fine figure in a well-cut, lightweight suit. Below a beige homburg hat, however, his sour face was adorned with a handlebar moustache whose twizzled ends curved menacingly across his cheeks. On his arm strutted a plump, similarly aged woman, impeccably dressed in the latest fashion, nose in the air as if the summer scent from all the flowers was coming from a rubbish tip. They were as familiar to those who were walking towards them as the backs of their own hands. As was the pretty young woman who was walking beside her parents, equally as well dressed but with her face glowing and alert as she took in the displays of flowers and shrubs around her. It was the Braithwaite family who lived in one of the grander houses on the opposite side of the street. As soon as she recognised the straggling band coming towards her, the daughter, Jessica, hurried forward to greet the two girls.

'Hello, Hillie, Gert!' she grinned. 'Fancy meeting you here!' she joked.

'Hello, Jessica! Good to see you,' Hillie beamed back. And as Jessica's parents caught up, she said politely, 'Hello, Mr and Mrs Braithwaite. Beautiful afternoon, isn't it?'

Jessica Braithwaite's lovely face had exploded in a friendly smile, but before she had a chance to say anything else, her father grasped her with his free hand and directed her straight past.

'You know I don't like you speaking to that riff-raff,' he barked. 'Bad enough that we live on the same street.'

'Come along, Jessica, your father's right,' the girl's mother sneered, looking disdainfully down her nose.

Hillie stopped dead, slack-jawed, turning her head to watch the Braithwaites continuing along the path. Jessica was being almost dragged away, but kept glancing back over her shoulder with both apology and regret written across her face.

'Stuck-up cow, that Hester Braithwaite,' Eva muttered under her breath. 'And he's just as bad. I'd like to see him—'

But Hillie didn't hear what Eva wanted to see. Probably something she didn't care to hear anyway. Her attention was diverted by Kit's hurrying back and planting himself in the Braithwaites' path.

'I would suggest you take that back, Mr Braithwaite, sir,' Hillie heard Kit's clear, steady voice. 'My family might not have had the benefit of your supposedly superior upbringing, but they're just as good people as you, and I'd thank you to remember it.'

Hillie could only see the back of Mr Braithwaite's head but she could imagine the sneer on his face as she heard him scoff, 'And who do you think you are, you jumped-up scum? Remind me what you do for a living? Oh, yes, you just work on the railway, don't you?'

Hillie saw Kit's features harden and he drew himself up to his full height, which she was grimly gratified to note exceeded Mr Braithwaite's by an inch or so. 'We'll see, Mr Braithwaite. We'll see what the future holds. In the meantime, my family might be poor, but at least they're happy. Whereas you'd better watch out you don't drown in your own misery.'

Kit gave a sharp bow of his head and then hurried to catch up with the others. Hillie could feel her stomach churning as she glanced at Kit's set face. Behind him, she saw the Braithwaite family pause, and then move on as if nothing had happened. Jessica, though, glanced back again, and for a brief instant, her gaze met with Hillie's, something desperate and pleading in her eyes.

'That told him, son.' Eva bobbed her head up and down in proud approval. 'He's only a shopkeeper himself. I reckon you got the best of him then. And if he doesn't like our street, he can blooming well move away. It's the girl I feel sorry for, poor kid.'

Yes, Hillie thought as they came to the main road and she gathered up her sisters to shepherd them across the traffic. Charles Braithwaite, she knew, was actually the manager of an entire floor at the prestigious Arding and Hobbs department store near the main entrance to Clapham Junction Station. But he was just as strict and heartless towards his daughter as Harold Hardwick was towards Hillie. As the troop reached the far side of the busy junction, it struck her that she and Jessica Braithwaite were two of a kind. The difference was that Hillie doubted Jessica stood up to her father in the same way she did to hers. And her heart plummeted as her thoughts returned to what her mother would've had to endure while *she* was enjoying a pleasant afternoon in the park.

Chapter Four

It had been by pure chance that Jimmy Baxter had come across Hillie and Gert and their families in the park, but Jimmy couldn't help believing that fate had played a hand. Just when he'd been wondering how on earth he could make another approach to Hillie, the opportunity had presented itself quite out of the blue. The chance meeting had given him confidence and set hope flickering inside him once more.

Hillie in a pretty summer dress – short sleeves revealing her slender, graceful arms, and her crown of tawny silvery curls rioting about her shoulders – had been a vision that had truly made him gasp. He'd always thought she'd be beautiful out of her working overalls, and he was right. But she always struck him as intelligent, too. Far too bright to be packing candles all day. Jimmy prided himself on having a quick brain, too. You had to be sharp to do his job, delivering all over the factory. So they should be well-matched. If only he could get her to see beyond his reputation.

And he needed to act quickly. He didn't know Gert had an older brother, and a handsome devil he was, too. And presumably he wasn't blind, either! Surely Kit Parker couldn't help but have eyes for

Hillie? And he'd given Jimmy a fright when he'd first seen him. That uniform – well, thank goodness it was only to do with the railway!

Jimmy's mind had been whirling as he sauntered away. Hillie was... he couldn't quite describe what. All he knew was that he'd never felt like this about anyone before, and he'd never experienced such rumblings of jealousy, either. He hadn't really been aware of where he was going. Just regretting that he was putting more and more space between them when what he really wanted was to run back and take her in his arms.

And then the idea had come to him in a flash. He could use the opportunity to find out where she lived, if nothing else. He continued walking in the same direction, making for the trees on the far side of the open grass area. But when he reached them, he looped back beneath the cover of the avenue. He was just in time to see Hillie and the others making for Sun Gate, and Jimmy followed. There was some sort of altercation with a toffee-nosed-looking older couple and a girl Jimmy guessed must be their daughter. Now *she* looked a bit of all right as well, but way out of his league! He then continued to shadow Hillie across the junction and down Cambridge Road where he'd had to be careful not to be seen. On the far side of Battersea Bridge Road, the group of adults and children turned into Banbury

Street. And Jimmy gasped as he spied them all splitting up and disappearing into two different houses.

Ooo. Jimmy drew the knowledge close to his breast. It wasn't that he wanted to stalk Hillie, but it felt good to know where she lived, although quite what advantage it gave him, he wasn't entirely sure. He went back to the room he rented in Candahar Road, with its gas ring and little gas fire in front of which he could toast a slice of bread stuck on the end of a fork if he had the patience. When he'd moved in many years ago now, he'd felt like a king. Suddenly though now, the damp patches on the ceiling, the paper hanging off the walls and peeling paint on the windows jumped out and took him by the throat. He'd have to do a lot better than this if Hillie was going to take him seriously. But first of all, he needed to work up to asking her out on a date – and think of how he could deal with that father of hers!

He went to bed, the cogs of his brain whirring as they never had before.

*

Jimmy woke to the pattering of rain on the window and the first thing that leapt into his head was a picture of Hillie walking along the road under an umbrella. The idea galled him, especially after the idyllic vision of her in the park the previous afternoon. If only he could stop her from getting wet.

But he could, couldn't he? He wasn't that hard up. He'd got used to the squalid room, but the rent was cheap and his was by no means the worst paid job at the factory. With only himself to take care of – and with his weekly stint at the pub and the odd 'extra' that came his way – he had cash to spare. He even had a Post Office savings account!

He took extra care shaving that morning and brushed his hair to a smooth shine before he left. And he left early, because he wasn't going directly to work, was he? He was planning a little detour, and he wanted to make sure he was in time.

He'd worked out where Hillie must come out onto Battersea Park Road, and he would – by chance, of course – appear on the street just at the same time, albeit a few turnings down and on the opposite side of the road. He'd pretend to have just seen her and cross the road to join her. She would doubtless be with Gert, but he'd have to put up with that. And there'd be safety in numbers, giving him more confidence.

When Hillie appeared, though, she was alone, and Jimmy's heartbeat accelerated. He swallowed hard, taking a hold on himself, and turned the corner onto the opposite side of the road, praying it didn't look too obvious.

'Hillie!' he called as he threaded his way through the traffic and went to meet her. He was thrilled to see that the surprise on her face when she caught sight of him displayed no displeasure as it might have done a few days previously. 'What a change in the weather, eh?'

'Yes,' she answered, stepping along briskly but peering at him from under her umbrella. 'You must live near.'

'Yeah, I do. Candahar Road. Tell you what, I was going to catch the tram, it's raining so hard. Look, there's one coming,' he announced as he glanced behind them to see a Number 31 trundling towards them on the opposite side of the road. 'D'you want to join me? My treat instead of getting you an ice cream yesterday.'

Hillie flashed a glance at him, and then at the approaching tram. She'd have to make a snap decision. She couldn't afford the fare and would have to let Jimmy pay anyway, and she didn't particularly want to be in his debt. But the rain was coming down hard and it was pretty miserable. But most of all, she didn't want the envelope hidden in the paper bag with her sandwiches to get wet. She'd slipped upstairs to fetch it just before she left, wishing she had an inside breast pocket in her coat like men did in their jackets. Sliding it between the greaseproof wrapping round her lunch and the brown paper bag was the best she could do. She had no excuse to take in a book today as it wasn't Saturday and everyone knew she'd spend her lunchtime chatting with Gert rather than reading.

'All right, thanks, Jimmy,' she found herself saying.

'Come on, then. Quickly!'

He put his hand on the wet arm of her coat, his fingers tingling with delight, as he directed her through the traffic to the other side of the road. The queue of people waiting at the tram stop had already climbed aboard, and Jimmy and Hillie had to jump onto the platform as the tram began to move off.

'Standing room only,' he grinned at her, and his heart soared as the tram lurched and he put a steadying arm about her as she was using both hands to close down her umbrella and couldn't grab hold of the rail.

'Thanks,' she smiled at him, and he thought he'd gone to heaven.

'Where's Gert this morning, then?' Jimmy asked after he paid their fare.

'Oh, she'll be in at the usual time. She knew I wanted to be early. Need to call into the office for a minute. They got my wages wrong last week,' she lied. She didn't want Jimmy knowing the truth, of course, in case it got back to her father, and she wasn't going to explain to Jimmy the reason why she wanted to keep her application a secret. As it was, her dad hadn't batted an eyelid when she'd left early, and she wanted him to remain unsuspecting!

'Underpaid you, no doubt.' Jimmy gave an ironic laugh. 'Not the other way round.'

'How did you guess?' Hillie smiled back. Wasn't so bad, after all, was Jimmy. 'It's a job, though, isn't it? We should be grateful when there's so many out of work.'

'Yeah, I guess so. People will always need candles despite gas and electric. And you can burn a night-light for hours for a fraction of the cost. Started off in the night-light wicking room, I did.'

'Really? That's even more boring than packing. At least we have lots of different shapes and sizes to deal with, and boxes to match. And then putting on the labels. My favourite's doing the fancy candles, though. You know, like the ink-printed ones we do at Christmas, and putting them in pretty boxes rather than plain cardboard ones.'

She stopped abruptly, wondering quite why she was engaging in polite conversation with Jimmy Baxter, of all people. But she was saved any further awkwardness as the tram came to yet another rattling halt.

'Here we are, then,' Jimmy announced. 'Don't take long on the tram, do it?'

Having had to stand on the platform, they were the first to get off. Jimmy jumped down in front of Hillie, then astounded her by turning round to take her hand and help her step down. No one had ever treated her like that before. Like a lady. Or was it all part of Jimmy's using his false charms on her?

'Thanks, Jimmy,' she said with cool politeness when they reached the opposite pavement next to the vast buildings of the factory that fronted the road. 'I'm very grateful.'

'My pleasure,' Jimmy smiled, since it genuinely was. 'Good luck in the office. And I hope you get some pretty candles to pack today.'

He doffed his cap, and they went their different ways, Hillie shaking her head in confusion. But she had better things to ponder just now, and went off to find Mrs Harrington and hand in her application form.

*

Hillie didn't have fancy candles to pack that day. Instead she was wrapping up plain white utility ones, a dozen in each packet. But rolling them up in the thick paper, pleating the ends neatly and sticking labels on top to hold them in place made a change from stuffing boxes. The process required skill and concentration as fingers worked with deft swiftness, and it was lunchtime before she knew it. Rain was still streaming down outside, so Hillie and Gert went to the canteen to eat their sandwiches and get themselves a cup of tea to wash them down.

'Don't let him fool you,' Gert warned with a wise nod of her head when Hillie told her how Jimmy had rescued her from the rain. 'I mean, it was nice of him. I got blooming soaked, so I wish I'd been with you and got a free ride meself. But we all know what he's like.'

'Don't worry,' Hillie reassured her. 'Forewarned is forearmed. But I think there's a kind side to Jimmy nobody's ever given him credit for. Oh, talk of the devil,' she said quickly as she happened to glance across the busy canteen. 'Don't turn round, but he's coming over.'

'Oh, blimey,' Gert groaned, rolling her eyes. 'Last few days, you can't turn a flipping corner without him being there.'

'Hello, ladies. You both look a bit glum. Bad morning?'

Hillie swivelled her eyes up to Jimmy's smiling face, and for some strange reason, her heart felt lighter. 'No, not especially,' she answered amiably. 'Just the weather. Makes you feel miserable, and it's supposed to be summer.'

'Well, look at it this way. It can rain all it likes during the week, so long as the sun comes out at one o'clock on Saturdays and stays out till Sunday night.'

'Put in your order, have you?' Hillie teased.

'Of course! One o'clock on the dot.'

Jimmy had kept a serious face and now he astounded the girls by standing back from the table, turning his feet out and, with a theatrical flourish, opened up an imaginary umbrella. He then walked up and down a couple of times in a perfect impersonation of Charlie Chaplin, straight-faced and with little jerky movements of his head. He stopped before the two girls, put his free hand to his ear as if listening to a clock chiming, consulted his watch, gazed skywards whilst holding his palm out beyond the reach of the umbrella which he proceeded to close down, and then he swaggered on, using the umbrella as a walking stick.

It had all been executed so perfectly that applause broke out from those who'd been near enough to see the brief amusing mime. Jimmy turned round and gave a couple of exaggerated Chaplinesque bows before coming to sit with Hillie and Gert.

'That was very good,' Hillie giggled. 'Never knew you could do that.'

'Ah, well, there's a lot you don't know about us,' Jimmy said mysteriously, and then he laughed. 'Comes of a misspent youth going to the pictures all the time. When I first got me freedom and discovered films, you couldn't keep us away. You and me could go, if you want.'

He said it with his eyes flickering between both girls, but they came to rest on Hillie's face, and she felt her heart give a little jerk of pleasure. When Gert said, 'Nah, not me,' her voice came to Hillie as if from afar as she returned Jimmy's smile.

'Maybe,' she replied enigmatically since she wasn't sure herself if she meant it or not.

'I think they're gonna be showing *Brother Alfred* again,' Jimmy answered, looking more than pleased with himself. 'That comedy with Gene Gerard and Molly Lamont. I missed it when it came out in the spring. I'll find out what time it starts if you fancy it. And now I'll leave you to finish your lunch in peace.'

He folded his arm across his chest and gave a short bow before walking, deliberately pigeon-toed, to the end of the row of tables, swinging his imaginary umbrella in circles as he went.

Hillie chuckled at his back, shaking her head. 'Didn't realise he could be so funny.'

Gert's response brought her back down to earth. 'Don't you get taken in by him,' she said fiercely. 'And how could you say you'd go to the flicks with him?'

'I didn't. Well, not exactly.' Hillie felt herself turn on the defensive, even though doubt had set into her mind.

'Well, I'd say he's expecting you to go now! Must've taken leave of your senses. He'll only hurt you. And you know what goes on in the back row. This is the first time you've ever been asked out, and I don't want you getting carried away.'

'Don't worry. I'm not some stupid, giggly little girl. Nothing will go on in the back row with me! If I go to the pictures with Jimmy Baxter, it'll be to watch the film and have a good night out. I've no intentions of becoming romantically involved with him.'

Hillie saw the look of horror on Gert's face but misinterpreted it, and it wasn't until a hand landed on her shoulder, fingers digging in painfully as he pulled her round, that she realised Gert had been trying to warn her that her father had come up behind her.

'I saw all that,' Harold hissed into her face. 'And I tell you, no daughter of mine's going out with that cocky young sod. Get you up the spout before you know it and then expect me to provide for it. Though God knows why he'd wanna look at you in the first place! But I'll beat you black and blue if I see you anywhere near him.'

The sinews in Harold's neck were standing out like knotted ropes he was so cross. Just the sight of him made Hillie heave with rebellion, and chips of ice formed in her eyes.

'Don't you trust me?' she snapped back. 'And when has any girl ever accused Jimmy of getting her in the family way, eh? Tell me that!'

She saw her dad's head retract on his neck, and knew she'd beaten him. But he wasn't going to back down so easily. His fingers clamped even more tightly around her thin shoulder making her fight to stop the pain reflecting in her face.

'You just keep away from him, or else, d'you understand me?'

His eyes bore into hers like red-hot coals before he released his hold with such force that her chair nearly overbalanced. Hillie watched him stride down the gap between the rows of tables, several shocked faces turning to follow him. For a few awkward moments, Hillie wasn't the only one holding her breath. But muted conversations were starting up again, and Hillie turned back to Gert with a mixture of embarrassment and lingering defiance.

Gert's eyes were still stretched wide. 'Bleeding hell, your dad don't muck about, do he? I'd be bloody terrified of him.'

'He's a bully and no mistake,' Hillie answered between clenched teeth. 'But I'm not going to let him run my life. If it wasn't Jimmy, it'd be anyone else I wanted to go out with. Thinks he's still in the army and expects us to obey his every command.'

She flexed her shoulder, wincing at the discomfort Harold's vice-like fingers had caused. Gert tipped her head sympathetically.

'I know your dad's a pig,' she dared to say, 'but I have to agree with him about Jimmy.'

Hillie gave a light laugh, feeling the tension ease, and squeezed Gert's hand. 'If I can handle my dad, I'm sure I can look after myself as far as Jimmy's concerned! But you can't blame me for wanting a bit of fun in my life.'

'No, I suppose not. But you be careful, Hillie.'

'Of course I will,' she promised. 'And anyway, Jimmy might not actually ask me out. But if this rain keeps up and he wants to pay my fare home on the tram as well, I'm not going to say no, am I? And if you stay next to me and play your cards right, you might get a free ride and all!'

'Well, I wouldn't say no to that!' Gert grinned back.

*

'That was a lovely evening, Jimmy. Thanks ever so much.'

As they walked up the main road the following Saturday night, the diffused light from the street lamps allowed Hillie to see Jimmy pull a face. 'Not the best film I've ever seen, but it was funny in places.'

'Oh, you were laughing your head off whenever I looked at you,' she teased merrily.

'Maybe that's 'cos I was in a good mood, having such a pretty girl next to us.'

Hillie felt herself flush. She didn't want any compliments from Jimmy, and Gert's warning flashed across her mind. 'Well, it was very kind of you to take me out,' she said politely.

'You make it sound like the evening's over. It's not half past ten yet.'

'But I need to be in by eleven, or my dad'll have my guts for garters.'

'He's a right bastard from what I've heard.' Jimmy's voice rang with bitterness now. 'Everyone at the factory says so.'

'Do they, now?' Hillie grimaced.

'Well, not *everyone*, of course. But those what know him. Or know *of* him. And don't forget, in *my* job, delivering stuff all over the site, I see and hear all sorts. Keep most of it to meself, mind.' He paused to tap the side of his nose with knowing pride. 'Never know when some bit of knowledge might come in handy. Like when someone's got something what's fallen off the back of a lorry, for instance. For a bob or two, I can pass it on to someone to sell down the market.'

Hillie gasped and her eyes opened wide. 'But, Jimmy, that's against the law, handling stolen goods.'

'Yeah, I know,' he shrugged, though Hillie noticed that he had the grace to look a touch abashed. 'It's only petty stuff, mind, and not so often. People shouldn't be so careless. A big factory owner's not going to miss the odd box of silk stockings, is he?'

'You don't... take the odd box of candles, do you?' Hillie was aghast.

'Course not.' Jimmy sounded affronted. 'What, and risk me job? I'm not that bloody stupid. Oh, I'm sorry, Hillie. I shouldn't have told you. I can trust you, though, can't I?'

'What? To keep quiet? Yes, of course you can,' Hillie answered, though she was quite astounded at herself for saying so.

'Good. I thought as much. Anyway, what fun'd life be without a bit of excitement, eh? Look at *you*, sneaking out with me and telling your dad you was going out with Gert!'

Hillie's heart suddenly leapt into her throat. 'You won't tell him, will you? Or anyone else? He'd kill me if he ever found out. From now on, you keep completely away from me at work. No conversation, nothing. I can't risk anything getting back to my dad.'

'Yeah, course. I understand. I'm not an idiot. Besides, it makes us even, don't it? Having a secret of each other's to keep.'

'Yes,' Hillie agreed reluctantly. 'But I wish you wouldn't… do what you do. What if you got caught?'

'Would you care if I did?'

Hillie stopped in her tracks, her pulse racing as she turned to face him. She felt her emotions turning somersaults, but one thing was certain: she had enjoyed Jimmy's company that evening.

'It'd be your own fault, but yes, I would,' she told him honestly.

'Then I promise not to do it ever again. If you promise to come out with us again next week.'

The teasing lilt had returned to his voice, and Hillie wasn't sure if he was being serious or not. 'D'you mean that?' she quizzed him. 'That you'd stick to the straight and narrow just for me?'

'Cross me heart and hope to die.' He made the accompanying gesture with such solemnity that Hillie was inclined to believe him. But then his teeth flashed in the darkness as he grinned at her. 'And I might just die if I don't get something to eat. Fancy sharing a bag of chips? Have to be quick. They'll be closing any minute.'

'As long as I'm back by eleven.'

With that, Jimmy dived inside the fish and chip shop they were passing. Hillie waited outside, her mind spinning in circles. But soon they were making their way through the backstreets in the direction of home, and Hillie thought she'd never tasted anything so good as they walked along in the still night air.

'We'd better say goodbye here,' Hillie said reluctantly as they reached the corner two streets from where she lived.

'You sure?' Jimmy sounded genuine enough. 'Don't like the idea of you walking home alone in the dark.'

'Safer than if my dad finds out I've been out with you.'

She heard Jimmy release a sigh. 'All right, then. But be careful.'

'I will,' she assured him.

'See you Monday, then.'

'Yes, but we ignore each other, remember? In case—'

'Yeah, I know. Your dad. See you, then.'

He turned and walked away. Hillie wasn't sure if she was relieved or disappointed that he hadn't so much as given her a peck on the cheek. Oh, well. She walked on in a state of confusion until the vision of going indoors and the lies she'd have to tell her father stole menacingly into her mind.

What she didn't know was that once she'd rounded the corner, Jimmy turned back to follow her at a distance all the way home to make sure she got there safely. He didn't like the idea of her having to bluff her way through her dad's inquisition, but there was nothing he could do about that. At least he'd seen her go indoors safely, and turned on his heel to make his way back to his own rented room.

He shouldn't have told Hillie about his little dealings on the side, he considered as he turned the key in the lock to the front door of the house. He'd just felt so relaxed and happy with her by his side that he'd let down his guard. Could he keep his promise to her? Just now, he felt he was on top of the world. If it meant he could have Hillie as his girl, maybe even more in time, he felt he could do anything!

*

Hillie was making her way across to the toilet block. Although it was mid-morning and they weren't really supposed to leave the workbench, it was her time of the month and she could feel she was leaking through her sanitary pad. She had stomach cramps and both her back and head were aching, and the thought of standing up at her work for the rest of the day filled her with misery. But she had no choice. She was lucky to have a job and couldn't risk losing it by going home. Three and a half million people were out of work, although the problem was more in the north of the country, and she could imagine her dad's wrath if she were to join the ranks of the unemployed just because she had a bit of stomach ache! She'd taken some aspirin and once that started working, she'd hopefully feel better. At least the worst would be over by Saturday evening when Jimmy wanted to take her out again. He said he planned on treating her to something a bit more special than the pictures, and she wanted to feel her normal self by then.

'Oh, excuse me.'

A female voice cut through Hillie's thoughts. She looked round at a young woman, she guessed just a few years older than herself and dressed smartly in a navy skirt reaching to her mid-calf, matching tailored jacket and a small hat placed at an angle on short, permed hair. Beside her, swathed in her factory apron over a drab working dress, Hillie felt small and inferior, even if she was some inches taller than the stranger.

'Can I help you?' she answered somewhat tartly.

The girl looked relieved. 'Yes, please. I've come for an interview for a job in the office, only I seem to have got a bit lost. Could you tell me where I can find a Mrs Harrington?'

Hillie's heart began to pump furiously. Interview? For a job in the office? Was it the same one she'd applied for? So why did not have an interview? She felt so angry, she could have left the girl standing where she was.

'This way,' she said curtly, and marched off in the direction of the offices, grimly satisfied as she glanced over her shoulder and saw the stranger's nervous expression.

Inside the offices, Mrs Harrington seemed to be waiting at her desk. 'Take a seat over there,' she smiled when the young woman had said who she was. 'Next to the other candidates. I'm afraid the interviews are running a little late.'

The girl nodded, and went to sit next to two others waiting anxiously for their turn. They were all dressed similarly, and Hillie's eyes smarted with tears of humiliation. Was that why *she* hadn't even got an interview, because she didn't *look* the part? Because she didn't have those sorts of clothes? Even though she knew the factory inside out?

'Thank you, er… Hilda, isn't it?' Mrs Harrington gave a brief dismissive smile and turned her attention back to some papers on her desk.

A spasm of pain twitched at Hillie's face and it took all her strength to summon up her courage. 'Er, Mrs Harrington, may I ask, is this for the job that *I* applied for?' she enquired in a small voice that she scarcely recognised.

Mrs Harrington looked up again, her eyebrows squeezed in irritation. 'Yes, it is,' she answered with no more compassion than if she had been swatting a fly.

'And I didn't get an interview? Can you tell me… why not? Even when I've been working here for three years and know all there is to know about the place, and they know nothing?'

She wanted the ground to swallow her up as Mrs Harrington gave a deep sigh and slapped her hands on the desk in exasperation.

'If you really want to know, firstly they all have a much better education than you and didn't leave school at fourteen like you did. And secondly, well, to be frank, your application form was a mess.'

'A mess?' Hillie's voice was more like a squeak. 'It was immaculate.'

'What you wrote was very good, I admit. But we couldn't have someone working in the office who hands in something looking like that.'

Hillie shook her head in bewilderment. 'I… I don't understand,' she stammered.

'Oh, for heaven's sake, see for yourself.' Mrs Harrington shuffled through a file on her desk and extracted a sheet of paper. 'Surely you didn't expect to get anywhere with *this*?' she demanded, holding it out.

Hillie took it in a hand that had begun to tremble. She lowered her eyes and gasped at the spoilt document, a desolate fist tightening inside her. 'But… it wasn't like this when I handed it in.'

'I'm afraid it was. I opened it myself. Now I believe you have your own job to get back to, unless you want to lose that as well.'

Mrs Harrington's face had closed into a hard mask and Hillie wilted under her gaze. She turned and left the office, her feet dragging as she made her way back towards the toilet block. She couldn't understand what had happened. She'd kept the paper dry, she *knew* she had. And yet it was splattered with blobs of something that had made the ink bleed and smudge.

She went into the ladies' and locked herself in one of the cubicles. She lowered herself onto the toilet seat, head in her hands. It would only have been a small step, but now her dreams lay shattered at her feet and she burst into tears.

*

'What's up, love?' Nell asked in a sympathetic voice that evening after the younger children had gone to bed and they were sitting together on the front doorstep enjoying the last vestiges of the day. 'You've been really quiet since you got in from work.'

Hillie didn't answer for a moment as Jessica and her parents appeared at their front door and came down the steps, obviously off out somewhere for the evening. Hillie vaguely wondered where. Mr and Mrs Braithwaite had their noses in the air as normal, but Jessica managed to sneak her a little wave. Hillie couldn't bring herself to speak until they were out of sight and she felt no one could hear her. Luke and Joan had gone to see some friends who lived round the corner, and Hillie glanced back inside the house to make sure her dad wasn't in earshot. Suddenly the events of the day crowded in on her, making moisture well up in her eyes.

'I found out this morning I didn't even get an interview for the job,' she blurted out miserably.

Nell's face creased with compassion. 'Oh, Hillie, I am sorry.' She put her arm around her daughter's shoulder and rubbed her arm.

Hillie looked sideways at her mother, chin quivering as she bit back her tears. For two pins, she could have told Nell why, but what good would it have done? She was still feeling so raw and confused over what had happened.

'I don't know, Mum,' she groaned, twisting her head. 'I thought it would be just one little step. Something for me. Maybe it could've been the start of something better. I don't want to be a factory girl forever.'

'You won't be.' Nell pulled Hillie towards her, tucking her head under her chin as if she were a child again. 'You're destined for better things than this,' she murmured into her hair. 'Something will turn up, I'm sure,' she said wistfully. But as her eyes wandered up and down the street, she couldn't really believe in what she'd said. It hadn't happened for her, had it? She just prayed that her beloved eldest daughter would have more luck.

Chapter Five

'Hello! It is you, isn't it? You helped me find my way to the office the day I came for the interview.'

Hillie looked up from trudging across the main yard, the largest open space on the whole site. It was July, and ever since that day a few weeks back now, she'd felt utterly disgruntled, and nothing – not even her Saturday nights out with Jimmy who did his level best to cheer her up – could lift her from the black pit she'd fallen into. And she could well do without another reminder of it.

She flicked her head round, ready to give the speaker short shrift. But the older girl was smiling broadly, holding out a gloved hand.

'I just wanted to say thank you,' she said in such a pleasant and friendly tone that Hillie felt ashamed of her own churlish attitude.

'You got the job, then?' Hillie answered, taking the girl's hand despite herself, and marvelling at the feel of the fine cotton glove.

'Yes, I did. But if you hadn't helped me, I'm sure I'd have got even more lost and been too late for the interview. Belinda, by the way.'

'Hilda. But everyone calls me Hillie.'

'Hillie? Oh, that's nice. I'm called Belle at home, but I hate it. Makes me sound like something out of a Walt Disney film.'

Hillie couldn't help but chuckle. She seemed all right, did this Belinda. And then Hillie noticed the other girl's brow furrow into an apprehensive frown.

'I couldn't help overhearing on the day of the interview that you'd applied for the job, too. So I hope there'll be no hard feelings and we can be friends.'

Friends? Hillie dropped her hand as if it were a red-hot poker. Friends, indeed! But Belinda's face was creased with anxiety and Hillie's reason got the better of her. It wasn't Belinda's fault, after all.

Hillie released a big, fat sigh. 'Tell you what. D'you want to meet Gert and me in the canteen at lunchtime? Gert's my best friend. If it's nice, we usually go outside, but it looks like rain to me.'

'Thanks, yes, I'd like that.'

'We can tell you things about working on the shop floor you won't hear in the office. As long as you can keep it to yourself.'

Belinda grinned in reply, and they went their separate ways. But the meeting set Hillie's mind going over events, and as a result, the rest of the morning flashed by. She was also looking forward to the prospect of making a new friend. Perhaps, though, Belinda was simply being polite. Certainly when lunchtime came round, there was no sign of her in the canteen.

'I bumped into that girl this morning,' she told Gert as they munched their sandwiches. 'The one who got the job in the office.'

'Oh, yeah? Right cow, I expect.'

'Actually she seemed very nice. Said she wants to be friends. I asked her to sit with us, but I don't see her.'

'Yeah, well, there you go.' Gert sniffed disparagingly. 'Say one thing but mean another.'

Hillie gave a shrug. 'Maybe. But it got me thinking. You know, my application form was in perfect condition when I put it in the envelope. I sealed it and then I hid it in the book I was reading. And then *that* was under my pillow where I always keep my library books. And then I took it out just as I left for work on the Monday morning.'

'Raining that day, though, wasn't it?' Gert mumbled through a mouthful of food. 'You sure it didn't get wet?'

'Definitely not. I was very careful, and that was the day Jimmy paid for me to go on the tram with him. It wasn't even damp when I handed it in.'

'How come it got spoilt, then?'

'That's exactly it. I've been asking myself that ever since. But...' She paused, drumming her fingers on the table and gazing straight at Gert as her train of thought rushed on. 'We all went to the park on the Sunday afternoon. D'you remember? It was only my mum and dad who stayed behind. So, what if someone happened to find it and managed to steam it open while we were out? I mean, it never even occurred to me to check that it hadn't been tampered with.'

'You… don't think…? Your dad?' Gert swallowed the food in her mouth so hard she almost choked. 'Never! Surely even he—'

'Just think about it.' Hillie dropped her voice to an urgent whisper and leant across the table towards Gert. 'It's the only explanation. It's been at the back of my mind for some time but I just didn't want to believe it.'

'You mean, you think he didn't want you to get the job? But… why?'

Hillie shook her head in bewilderment. 'I'm not sure. I mean, he likes to think he's top dog, so maybe he didn't like the idea of me working in the office. It would've meant I was one up on him.'

'Yeah, but you'd've been bringing home more money. You'd think he'd be pleased. No, it don't make sense. Unless,' Gert paused thoughtfully, as if an idea was dawning, 'he thought you might earn enough to be able to leave home altogether and take your wages with you.'

Hillie nodded, sucking in her cheeks. 'That's exactly what crossed my mind. But I don't know, Gert. He's always taking it out on Mum and me. I mean, he's strict with all of us, but I've always had the feeling he hates Mum and me. As if he wants to make us suffer. On the odd occasion I've tried to broach the subject with Mum, she just says it's 'cos of what he went through in the war. Being in the trenches and all that. But I think there's something else as well. Something she won't tell me.'

'Oh, hello! I found you, at last! Don't mind if I join you, do you?'

Hillie pulled back and looked up into Belinda's smiling face. 'Course not. Take a pew.'

She managed to move her own mouth into a smile, praying that Belinda hadn't caught any of their conversation but glad of the opportunity to lock her thoughts away. But as she moved along so that Belinda could sit down, she happened to glance across the canteen. Men and women were flocking in, in twos and threes or small groups, chatting and laughing as they anticipated passing the lunch break in good company. Only one solitary figure stood out and Hillie's heart thumped in her chest. Her father. People were shying away from him or, at best, ignoring him. At that moment, Hillie felt her own hatred fly across at him like an arrow.

It was with the greatest relief that she turned her attention back to the stranger who had just sat down beside her. Belinda was a pretty girl with short permed hair framing a petite face. But despite her smart clothes and the fact that she'd landed the job over all the other applicants, she wasn't the least over-confident.

'Belinda, this is my best friend, Gert,' Hillie introduced them. 'We work together in the packing shed.'

'Pleased to meet you, Gert.' Belinda politely held out her hand, her gesture accompanied by a broad smile, and Hillie could tell Gert was a little taken by surprise. It wasn't the usual sort of introduction people of their class were used to.

'Hello,' Gert answered guardedly, shaking Belinda's hand.

'How was your first morning?' Hillie asked, determined to break the ice.

'Oh, well, you know, a bit daunting,' Belinda admitted. 'Obviously there's a lot to learn. Different places have different systems, of course. It's a case of getting used to them.'

'You worked in an office before, then?'

'Oh, yes. I worked in customer accounts for the gas board, but I got a bit bored dealing with just figures all the time, so I thought I'd look for something more varied.'

'How old are you, then?' Gert quizzed her.

'Nineteen. And you?'

'We're both seventeen. Born the same week.'

'Well, I never! Known each other long, then?' Belinda asked brightly.

'All our lives,' Gert informed her, seeming to warm to the stranger at last. 'Our mums were friends long before we came on the scene. And you? Got lots of friends? Where d'you live, then?'

'A few old school friends, yes. And I live in Parsons Green with my mum and dad and one of my brothers.'

'Brother, eh? How old's he?'

Hillie had to smile to herself as Gert's eyes brightened. Since she'd been going out with Jimmy, Gert seemed to have been paying more attention to the opposite sex as well!

Belinda replied with her sweet smile. 'Rob's twenty-one. Maybe you'll meet him one day.'

'Maybe we will,' Gert grinned now. 'Can I get you a cuppa? I feel it in me bones we're all gonna be good friends!' she declared, getting to her feet.

Hillie exchanged a smile with the newcomer. She, too, had the feeling that this was the beginning of a new and lasting friendship.

'Now tell me more about yourself,' she invited her.

'Come on, gorgeous, what's up? Hardly said a word, you have. Ain't upset you, have I?'

Hillie blinked hard and her mouth curved into a wistful smile. 'Oh, Jimmy, I'm sorry. I was miles away. And of course you haven't upset me. I was just thinking, that's all.'

'Penny for them, then.'

Hillie drew in a breath. She couldn't tell Jimmy the truth somehow. And sure as she was of her father's deceit, she didn't have definite proof. What good would it do, anyway? If Jimmy confronted her dad, it could well end in fisticuffs, and she didn't want that. Harold would put an even tighter rein on her, and she wouldn't want that either! Every Saturday when she'd gone out with Jimmy, she'd let her father believe she was with Gert, and she didn't want to upset the applecart. Sometimes Gert did come with them, but recently she'd been more inclined to go somewhere with Belinda rather than play gooseberry. Hillie was pleased that the two were becoming such good friends as she'd been feeling somewhat guilty at abandoning her lifelong pal now that she had a boyfriend.

She gave a casual shrug, hoping it would throw Jimmy off the scent. 'Oh, I don't know,' she sighed, trying to think of some way to explain her strange mood. 'I guess I'm just enjoying the summer too much. Here we are in the middle of July with a couple of months of fine weather still to come—'

'If we're lucky.'

'Well, it might not be fine *all* the time, I grant you. But here we are, able to walk in the park on such a beautiful evening. Well, until it closes, at least. And it doesn't matter that we don't have any money. We can just enjoy being together and it doesn't cost us anything. But it'll go all too fast, and before we know it, it'll be cold and dark again—'

'And we'll just have to go to the flicks or something more often. There's more cinemas round here than you can shake a stick at.'

His words made Hillie chuckle. 'What an old-fashioned expression!'

'I'm an old-fashioned chap,' Jimmy grinned back, one eyebrow raised sceptically. But then his lips fined to a solemn line. 'It's true, despite what people say about me. I just hadn't found the right girl until you came along.'

He danced around in front of her, stooping slightly so that he was twisting his head to gaze up at her cajolingly. She couldn't help but smile at his antics, and he laughed back.

'There we go. At least I didn't have to resort to doing Charlie Chaplin again. Not here in the park, anyway.'

'Oh, Jimmy, you are good for me.' She shook her head, but really she couldn't throw off her morose thoughts. 'I just wish, well, that I could rescue my mum and Luke and the girls from the life we lead. From being cold in the winter because we can't afford enough coal to heat the house properly. And from things like having hand-me-down shoes that've been mended so often, they're more patch than shoe.'

'And from your dad,' Jimmy put in sagely.

Hillie met his gaze steadily. 'That, too,' she answered, caution slowing her words. 'Though he's not so strict with the others. It's mainly Mum and me he goes for all the time.'

Jimmy pursed his lips but a second later his face brightened. 'You need cheering up, my girl. Why don't we go up the West End? See if there are any tickets left for one of the big shows?'

'You can't afford that, and I certainly can't.'

'Oh, yes, I can.' Jimmy puffed up his chest. 'Well, I haven't got the money on me. But I could draw out some of me savings and we could go next week.'

'That's so sweet of you, Jimmy. But save your money for the future.'

'*Our* future, you mean?' Jimmy looked pleasantly surprised.

'Maybe. As long as you can buy me a grand house with lots of servants and a roaring fire in winter—'

Jimmy interrupted her with a proud smirk and offered her his elbow in a gentlemanly fashion. 'I can do better than that, milady. Come with me,' he instructed.

Hillie obediently threaded her arm through his so that when he broke into a run, she was obliged to match his pace. They sped along, chortling with mirth as they pulled each other this way and that. Jimmy was directing her towards Albert Gate and she tagged along, swathed in mystery as he led her out through the park gates and then turned right to cross over Albert Bridge.

'Just look at that sunset!' he crowed, dragging her across the road between the traffic.

They stopped, side by side, gazing over the side of the bridge. The sun was a sphere of molten gold casting coral veils across the dying brightness of the sky and reflecting like sparkling jewels on the myriad ripples of the Thames. Battersea Bridge just upriver wasn't as pretty as Albert Bridge, which always made Hillie think of a wedding cake, but the view was overall quite stunning. Just beyond Battersea Bridge, the towers of the Lots Road Power Station were silhouetted against the peach and apricot streaks in the translucent sky, lending an industrial beauty to the scene. A barge with a red sail was drifting upriver on the incoming tide, and a couple of leisure craft were enjoying the Saturday evening sunset.

Hillie felt herself relax and the truculent mood emptied out of her. 'Oh, Jimmy, of course. It really is beautiful. I was just being silly.'

The next thing she knew, Jimmy had turned her round to face him, hands gently on her shoulders and his mahogany eyes for once serious. 'My girl silly? Not a bit of it. I understand how you feel. And I promise that one day I'll take you away from all this.'

She was about to say that he didn't understand how she felt because she didn't want to be taken away, at least not without taking her family with her – minus her father, of course. And anyway, she couldn't see that Jimmy could ever afford to keep such a generous promise. But she didn't get a chance to voice her misgivings. Jimmy bent his head tentatively and the next moment, his handsome mouth came down slowly and brushed against hers.

His kiss was like a gentle balm soothing her sorely tried spirit and her heart danced an unexpected waltz in her chest. It wasn't as if a deep passion had exploded somewhere inside her, or that her pulse had suddenly started racing with excitement. It was more like a tender dream, merely the next sweet thread of a growing understanding between them.

Jimmy pulled back, his smiling eyes searching her face. She blinked at him, trying to untangle her emotions. She'd never been kissed before, and she didn't feel quite as she'd imagined she would. But this wasn't some fictitious romance she was watching at the cinema or reading about in a book. This was for real, and though she didn't feel swept up in a whirlwind of delight, she had to admit that she liked it!

'Come on.' Before she had time to catch her breath, Jimmy had laced his arm about her waist and was walking her to the far end of the bridge. 'There ain't many evenings like this, so we should make the most of it. Come along, milady. I want to show you your new abode.'

His eyes were teasing now and Hillie was grateful he hadn't pushed her any further. 'And where might that be, my good man?' she answered with mock haughtiness. 'And who d'you think you are to choose a new home for me?'

'Well, I'm Lord Rumpelstiltskin and I'm going to lock you in my ivory tower, Lady Rapunzel, and keep you all to myself!'

Jimmy let go of her, bending double and drawing up his arms with hands retracted into claws. Hillie laughed aloud, putting the unexpected kiss with its confusing effects behind her. Once again, Jimmy was lifting her out of the chasm of despair she'd fallen into because of her suspicions over her father.

'Now then, madam.' Jimmy's brow puckered into a frown as, with a sweeping gesture, he indicated the long row of opulent mansions along the Chelsea Embankment. 'Which one takes your fancy?'

'Hmm.' Hillie paused to consider, her eyes roving over the majestic buildings on the opposite side of the road. 'They're all rather nice. And they've got the lovely view across the river with the park on the other side.'

'Naturally. That's why I chose it for you. I know how you love the park. But does any particular one of them stand out for you?'

'Well, it's difficult to say without seeing inside. And do they have proper gardens? I simply must have a proper garden,' Hillie proclaimed imperiously, falling into the game, 'rather than the yard we have at present. It's scarcely big enough to hang out all the washing, and then it gets covered in smoke and smuts from everybody's coal fire and all the factory chimneys.'

'Oh, yes, madam, they all have gardens,' Jimmy assured her. 'But the laundry rooms are so big that you dry the washing inside. Sadly we can't guarantee there won't be any smuts around, especially with all the chimneys going in the winter.'

'Well then, I shall purchase the house with the biggest garden. Of course, it all depends on which ones are up for sale.'

'No need to worry about that. Just choose the one you want and I'll put a spell on them to make them move out. Or make them an offer they can't refuse.'

'In that case, I think it'd better be the spell.'

Try as he might to keep a straight face, Jimmy couldn't help grinning from ear to ear. Hillie, too, tried to contain her mirth, but when she started giggling and Jimmy responded with a theatrical bow more suited to a pantomime than the embankment, she burst out in a guffaw of laughter. No matter that they drew bemused glances from passers-by, they fell about in uncontrolled gaiety, holding onto each other with sides ready to split.

'Oh, come on, Jimmy,' Hillie spluttered at last, wiping the tears from her eyes. 'We can't keep this up all evening. People will think we're crackers.'

'Let 'em think what they like. I really don't care so long as me girl's happy.'

'Yes, I am.' Hillie finally brought her laughter under control. 'Thanks, Jimmy. You've really cheered me up.'

'Good. And it don't hurt to dream once in a while. And on a beautiful evening like this, who can blame us, eh?'

He offered Hillie his arm once again and she took it, resting her head on his shoulder as they proceeded to stroll along under the trees of the wide embankment. They eventually sat down on one of the raised benches so that they could gaze back upriver, watching until the daylight had faded and the ornate Victorian lamps were casting a diffused glow into the night.

'I bet it's no nicer than this out in Los Angeles,' Hillie said dreamily, breaking the easy silence.

'What made you think of that? Oh, I suppose it's them Olympics.'

'Yes, that's right,' Hillie mused. 'Start on the thirtieth, don't they? Stan, you know, Gert's dad, he's really keen on sport. He says we've got a really good chance of some medals in the rowing. He'll be glued to the radio for the first two weeks in August!' she chuckled.

'And what about this thing they're calling television or something? They say it'll be like the flicks only you'll get them in your own home like a radio. Don't understand it meself.' Jimmy shook his head with a frown. 'They say they're gonna start experimenting with it soon. But I can't see it taking off meself. And who's gonna be able to afford something like that? But I guess they'll make some *Pathe News* films of the Olympics, so Gert's dad can go to the cinema to watch 'em. Don't interest me much. I'd rather be sitting here with me lovely girl. Ten o'clock and still warm enough to sit outside,' Jimmy sighed contentedly, glancing at his watch.

Hillie's back stiffened. 'Is that the time? Oh, Jimmy, we'd better start walking back. I must be in before my dad gets on the warpath. And we'd best part company in case he's out and about. All hell'd break loose if he saw us together.'

'Blooming bastard,' Jimmy muttered as they got to their feet and began walking back the way they'd come. 'If only I was the sort of person he'd approve of rather than a foundling what was brought up in a children's home and had to fend for meself from when I was fourteen.'

'Well, I think you've done very well for yourself. At least as good as my dad ever did. And his parents were still alive when he was that age to give him support. And he was an only child, so it wasn't as if they had to divide their attention between a horde of kids. But I don't think it'd make any difference if you were a rich businessman or a teacher or whatever. My dad just seems to have it in for me, no matter what.'

It was on the tip of her tongue to tell Jimmy what she suspected her father had done, but she bit her lip just in time. Better to keep it to herself. She knew Gert would never let on – heaven knew they'd had to share enough secrets about Harold over the years. But Jimmy, well… Much as she'd grown very fond of him in the month or so they'd been walking out, Hillie could imagine that his impulsive nature might make matters worse as far as her father was concerned.

They crossed back over the bridge, the river now swirling dark and menacing below them. Hillie tried not to let fear of bumping into her dad spoil the last minutes of the precious hours she'd spent with Jimmy, but as they passed down the side of Battersea Park, which was in total darkness now, she couldn't stop the churning that gripped her stomach. It was as they reached halfway along Cambridge Road that Hillie slowed her step and turned to Jimmy.

'We'd better split up now,' she told him nervously. 'We're already too close for comfort. He could be drinking in the Duke of Cambridge. I should've arranged to meet up with Gert and walk back with her.'

They'd stopped between the pools of light from two street lamps, but even so, Hillie saw Jimmy's eyes flash towards the pub on the opposite side of Battersea Bridge Road which crossed the far end of the street.

'Don't like all this skulduggery, I don't,' he grumbled. 'Wish you'd let us have it out with the old devil.'

Horrified at the very idea, Hillie grasped Jimmy's arm tightly. 'No! Trust me, that's *not* a good plan. Besides, we don't know each other that well yet. Let's wait and see... well, how things go. And if we get really serious, that'll be the time to approach him.'

She heard Jimmy draw a deep, reluctant breath through his teeth. 'All right. If you insist. But it makes me feel like a coward.'

'A sensible coward, mind,' Hillie grinned back, relieved. 'Anyway, it'd probably be me or Mum he'd take it out on, not you so much. There are times when discretion really is the better part of valour, you know. So I'd better go, and you give it five minutes before you follow on, and don't come down my street. Or better still, go back to the park and make a detour round that way.'

Without giving him a chance to protest, she gave him a quick peck on the cheek and then hurried away. It was a good excuse not to have another proper kiss. It wasn't that she hadn't liked the first one, but it was a new experience for her and she wanted time to ponder on her own feelings. She liked Jimmy very, much, but she wasn't sure she was in love with him. But then, did she really know what love was?

She was so engrossed in her thoughts – as well as keeping her eyes peeled for the threatening figure of her father – that she didn't see the body sprawled on the pavement of Banbury Street until she all but tripped over it. She nearly landed on the ground herself, and nervously spun back round, not knowing what to expect.

'Here, you, look where you're going,' a slurred voice reproved as its owner staggered to its feet.

Hillie took a step backwards, hand over her mouth as the stench of gin and vomit stung into her nostrils. 'Oh, not drunk again, are we?' she admonished, recognising Dolly Maguire from a couple of houses down. It was common knowledge that Dolly had lodgers in her upstairs rooms to help pay her own rent, but the slovenly woman's house was in such a state that they never stayed long. The rats attracted by the rubbish piled up in her backyard stayed longer!

'What's it to you?' the woman spat, swigging on a near-empty bottle. 'Stuck-up little bitch.'

'At least I'm sober and don't smell like a distillery,' Hillie retorted in disgust.

'Like a what?' Dolly lurched forward so that Hillie was obliged to leap out of her way. 'Bah, get yourself back to that sparkling clean palace of yours and your upright bloody family. But don't – think – your – mother's – as – white – as – she – makes – out!'

She prodded Hillie hard in the chest with each sneering word. Hillie was too stunned by the drunkard's vicious insinuations to back away, and it was several seconds before she was able to retaliate.

'You nasty, dirty liar!' she hissed back. 'And we all know where you get your gin money from. If it's not lodgers in your bedrooms, it's visitors to your *bed*!'

Hillie backed away, appalled by her own attack. The times Dolly had been seen stumbling, blind drunk, into her house with an equally as inebriated man in tow were too numerous to count. There was no proof, of course, of what went on once they were inside, but it left little to the imagination. All Hillie wanted was to escape the woman's filthy tongue. Finding her feet at last, she ran along to her own home, fumbled through the letter box for the string with the key tied on the end, and let herself inside, in her outrage forgetting all about her father.

Dolly's wavering gaze struggled to follow her. She was about to yell out that she knew what the strumpet had been up to as well! Before Dolly had collapsed in a drunken stupor, she'd spied the girl wandering down Cambridge Road from the park, arm in arm with a man. The park gates were locked, but it wasn't so difficult to climb over. Dolly had done so herself enough times in her younger days to earn a few extra shillings among the shrubbery. That self-righteous prig was little better. But it might be more worth Dolly's while to keep her mouth shut about what she'd seen.

For now, at least.

Chapter Six

'Have a nice weekend, you two.'

Belinda turned to Hillie and Gert as they left Price's at one o'clock one Saturday afternoon in September. Although the sun was shining, there was a definite autumnal tang in the air, and the girls were determined to make the most of the good weather while it lasted.

'You, too, Belinda. Pity we won't be seeing you.'

'Oh, I'm sure you'll manage without me,' Belinda grinned. 'But didn't you say you're not going out with Jimmy tonight, Hillie?'

'Sh! Keep your voice down!' Hillie's eyes flashed Belinda a warning. 'You know if it gets back to my dad—'

'Oops, sorry.' Belinda bit her lip in remorse, dropping her voice to a whisper. 'It's not the sort of thing I'm used to.'

'I know, but she's coming out on her own with me instead!' Gert crowed as quietly as she could. 'Be like old times, it will. I won't have to play bleeding gooseberry all night!'

'You know we never mind you tagging along,' Hillie told her. 'But anyway, Jimmy was asked to run an errand this afternoon for some chap who comes into the pub a lot, and he's going to pay him loads for it. And then he was asked to do an extra shift in the bar tonight as well. He didn't want to turn it down. If there's ever going to be a future for us, we'll need every penny we can get hold of.'

'You really think there will be? A future for you and Jimmy, I mean?' Gert quizzed her.

Hillie ignored the niggle of uncertainty at the back of her mind. 'Possibly,' she answered vaguely. 'We all rather misjudged Jimmy, you know.'

'Well, much as I'd love to, I can't stand around here discussing Jimmy Baxter's attributes or otherwise,' Belinda told them, 'especially when I hardly know the fellow. I must be off, I'm afraid.'

'Oh, I'm sorry, Belinda. Wish your dad a happy birthday from us.'

'Yeah! Hope he has a lovely party.'

'It'll be great, I'm sure. See you Monday, then!'

'Will do!' the other two girls chorused as Belinda turned with a wave and then was lost in the crowd of those factory workers who were making their way in the same direction as her. Hillie and Gert exchanged a smile before setting off up York Road in the company of the hundreds of Price's employees going the opposite way.

'Belinda's fitted in with us so well, hasn't she? But I do envy her,' Hillie sighed on a wistful breath, grateful to steer the conversation away from Jimmy.

She knew the risk she was taking and didn't like talking about Jimmy anywhere near the factory. 'Sounds as if she has such a happy home life.'

Gert cocked an eyebrow. 'I'm sure she does. But I think the words grass and greener spring to mind.'

'It's all right for you. Your family are so easy-going. And it sounds like Belinda's dad and both her brothers have reasonable jobs, too. The older married one as well as the younger one, Rob. Still haven't met them, have we? But it must be nice having a bit more money and not having to watch every penny.'

'Money's not everything, gal.'

Hillie nodded ruefully. 'I know. But I wish our family had a bit more. It'd be a lot less strain on my mum if Dad wasn't breathing down her neck over the housekeeping all the time. And if I'd got Belinda's job, I could've given Mum a bit more money each week. Treat her to a little something sometimes.'

'Your dad has a lot to answer for, don't he? And you still think it was him what ruined that application of yours?'

Hillie's jaw clamped down in anger. 'The more I think about it, the more convinced I am. It's as if he wants to punish me all the time.'

'I just hope for your sake he don't find out about you and Jimmy.'

'He might have to one day.'

Gert shot her a sideways glance. 'If you get serious, you mean? And *are* you getting serious? You didn't seem too sure when I asked just now.'

Hillie hesitated a moment, trying to put some sense into her own tangled emotions. 'I do like Jimmy very much,' she confessed. 'I seem to live for the weekends and the time I spend with him. Mind you, it means I don't get so much time for reading. I miss having my nose in a book all the time. But Jimmy makes me laugh, and he's kind and thoughtful, too. We both like films and walking in the park, and gazing at the stars and dreaming of a better life. But does that mean I truly love him?'

Hillie was hoping her dear friend would have some words of wisdom to offer, and was disappointed when Gert merely shrugged.

'Search me. Seeing as I've never had a boyfriend, how should I know? But tonight, Miss Hardwick,' she announced, her face illuminating with cheer as she linked her arm through Hillie's, 'it's gonna be just me and me old mate. So what we gonna do, then? Flicks? Or dancing, maybe?'

'Oh, I don't really mind. Whatever you want. If it stays fine, I'm happy just walking in the park till it closes. I like being there at the end of the day when it's quieter, but with the evenings drawing in, we won't get much more chance to do that. But it's up to you.'

'Tell you what, then.' Gert's happy smile broadened. 'Got to help your mum this afternoon, ain't you? But call for me about five and we'll go for a stroll in the park, and then maybe catch a train up the West End. We can't afford a show or anything, but it's fun just being there and seeing all the lights, ain't it? We can celebrate.'

'Celebrate? Celebrate what?'

'Why, *us*, of course. Us being best mates forever and ever.' Her face was stiff with solemnity, making Hillie's eyebrows dip in bemusement. Then Gert burst out laughing, eyes twinkling with teasing. 'Know your trouble, Hill? You take life too blooming seriously. No wonder you need the likes of Jimmy Baxter to cheer you up. But tonight, girl, it's just you and me against the world!'

Hillie forced a smile to her lips. She was looking forward so much to spending the evening with Gert, so did that mean she didn't love being with Jimmy as much as she thought? Walking out with him felt like the end of an era: the end of the childhood she and Gert had shared. But when Jimmy took her in his arms and his mouth sought hers more passionately now, she felt the excitement frothing up inside her. It felt *right* in her heart. But when she stood back as she was now, she wasn't really sure what she felt.

*

'Hello, Kit!' Hillie greeted Gert's brother as he opened the door to her later that afternoon. 'Nice surprise! Gert didn't say you'd be here.'

'That's 'cos she didn't know,' Kit grinned back, his generous mouth curving pleasantly. 'I'm just leaving actually. Only popped in for a few minutes. I must say, though, you look very fetching,' he observed with an approving nod of his head. 'Gert's not quite ready. As usual.'

'Oi, you! I heard that!' a disembodied voice squawked down the stairs. 'Just putting on me lipstick.'

'War paint,' Kit corrected, muttering under his breath. 'Anyway, have a good time whatever you end up doing. Gert says this Jimmy fellow of yours is doing something else tonight. Not two-timing you, I hope.'

Hillie's eyes flashed at him. Kit was smiling in that enigmatic way he had, and Hillie wasn't sure if he was pulling her leg or whether there was some serious inference in his words. But, no. She refused to doubt Jimmy. After all, she could easily go to the pub to check up on him, and surely he wouldn't take that risk if he was aiming to lie to her.

'He's been asked to do an extra shift in the bar at the Falcon tonight,' she answered, her tone crisper

119

than she meant it to be. 'And Gert would've been on her own, so it's worked out well. Tell you what, mind,' she went on, not wanting to seem churlish, 'why don't you come with us?'

The idea was actually quite appealing. Kit was always good company, and to be honest, she'd feel more comfortable with a man beside her in the heaving heart of London. So she found herself feeling somewhat let down by Kit's reply.

'Kind of you to ask,' he said with a shrug of his shoulders, 'but I'm going out for a pint with some of the lads from the station later on. Never mind, another time. When your Jimmy's not around,' he concluded. But as he stepped past her onto the pavement, he suddenly turned back. 'You know, Hill,' he said, his forehead wrinkling into an anxious frown, 'I wish you weren't going out with him. It's too dangerous for one thing. I know your dad disapproves, and if he found out—'

'Well, he's not going to, is he?' Hillie's eyes snapped back at him. 'Only you and Gert and your mum and dad know, and none of you are going to give me away. I haven't even told my own mum 'cos it's better she doesn't know. And at work, Jimmy keeps right away from me. Only Belinda there knows, and she can be trusted to keep her mouth shut. So you've no need to worry.'

'But I do, Hill. I'd feel awful if anything happened to you.'

The expression on his face was so earnest that Hillie relaxed into a smile. 'It's nice of you to be so protective. Like you always have been. Like a big brother,' she grinned now. 'But it's not necessary.'

But she couldn't coax a smile from him. 'Well, I still don't think he's right for you,' Kit insisted. 'I have to agree with your dad on that. You're bright and intelligent. And what's Jimmy? Don't you ever wonder what it is he does on these so-called errands he runs every now and then? And why doesn't he seem to have any friends? Do people not trust him?'

Hillie felt herself bristle again. 'People don't know him,' she protested.

'And you do?'

'Yes. And he makes me laugh and forget that I'm stuck in a boring job and a boring life with a father who's always at my throat and my mum's.'

Kit drew in a deep breath as he stared at her, and then shook his head as he let it out in a disapproving stream. 'Well, don't say I didn't warn you.' And then laying his hand on her arm, he looked intently into her eyes as he told her, 'You know I'll always be there for you, Hill. No matter what.'

Leaning down, he took her by surprise by brushing a kiss on her cheek. But before she had time to react, he called out a last goodbye to his family and strode off down the street.

Hillie stood there for a second or two, frowning in bewilderment. Kit was wrong about Jimmy, but he was right that she was taking a huge risk. She'd just have to make sure her dad never found out, unless things got really serious between her and Jimmy and he had to be told. It was good of Kit to be so concerned, of course, and when she searched inside herself, Hillie was disappointed that he wasn't coming with her and Gert up to the West End.

But she wasn't going to let their conversation spoil her evening out. Gert still hadn't materialised, so Hillie went down the hallway to the back room, knowing the Parker family would be gathered round the table. Sure enough, the familiar tableau greeted her as she opened the door: Old Sal in her armchair by the empty fireplace, toothless mouth wide open as she snored for England, Stan lost in the sports page of that morning's newspaper, and the four younger Parker offspring sitting at the table, stuffing their tea of bread and dripping into their hungry little mouths. Eva was lovingly supervising baby Primrose who was wriggling around in the scratched and battered wooden highchair, the tray of which looked little more sanitary than the kitchen table.

'Hello, Hillie love,' Stan welcomed her, half-smoked cigarette dangling precariously from the corner of his mouth. 'Did you know Fulham's doing quite nicely in the new season? In Division Two, but stand a good chance of getting promoted if they play well enough. I'd've liked to have gone to today's match, only it was away to Notts County.'

'Oh, Stan,' Eva reprimanded him. 'Hillie don't want to hear about that, do you, ducks? I hear you and our Gert are gonna paint the town red tonight.'

'I'm not too sure about that,' Hillie chuckled, grateful to forget her discussion with Kit, 'but I'm sure we'll have a good time.'

'Sure you will. But just you be careful, two pretty young girls alone in the big city. And watch out for pickpockets.'

Hillie had been on the receiving end of the very same lecture from her own father, except that his had been delivered in such strident terms that she'd been worried he was going to forbid her to go at all. But now she smiled back reassuringly at Stan. 'I haven't got anything worth stealing. And don't worry. We'll stick—'

'Ready!' The door flew open, bouncing back on its hinges, and Gert burst into the room in her favourite, well-darned summer dress. Her bright hair had been scooped up into an untidy chignon, and her lips glowed a cardinal red. But then, Gert would always be Gert, and Hillie didn't think there'd ever be any changing her. Besides, she'd never want her friend to be any other way.

'Right. Off we go, then. Bye, Mr and Mrs P.'

'Enjoy yourselves!'

'Thanks, we will!'

'You've certainly dolled yourself up,' Hillie giggled as they stepped out into the street. 'You wearing mascara?'

'I am that.' Gert lifted her chin proudly. 'What d'you think? It's quite hard to put on. You have this little block of black stuff and a stiff little brush you have to wet to put it on with.'

'Well, I reckon you've put a bit too much on, but for a first effort, it looks pretty good.'

'You're being diplo-what's-it, ain't you?' Gert's face fell. 'Oh, Lordy love, you don't think I look tarty, do you? I want to find meself a man, but he's got to be the right sort.'

'Don't worry, I'll protect you!' Hillie laughed, and they linked arms, snuggling close as they'd done all their lives.

It was as they turned the corner of the street that they all but collided with a figure backed up against the wall of the pub as if it would like to disappear into thin air. The girl was gnawing on her tightly clenched knuckles, whimpering like a terrified animal. Hillie couldn't believe her eyes. It was Jessica Braithwaite! They both stopped dead in their tracks.

What on earth had happened to upset their young neighbour so much? She was in a right old state!

'Whatever's the matter?' Hillie was the first to speak. 'Have you hurt yourself?'

'Oh.' Jessica's eyebrows were almost joined in her angst, her white lips trembling. 'I-I've got…'

The poor girl seemed unable to speak and instead dipped her head sharply down towards the side of her skirt. Just above the hem, a thick smear of something dark and nasty was encrusted on the pretty floral print. As Hillie frowned down at it, her nostrils latched on to the familiar evil odour, and realisation dawned.

'Oh, heck, is that what I think it is?' she sympathised. 'How did you manage that?'

At her question, Jessica recoiled like a frightened rabbit, her pretty china-blue eyes wide like saucers. Everyone found dog mess vile and distasteful, but Hillie sensed that her posh neighbour must have an exceptional horror of it, and her heart went out to her.

'You'd best get home and wash it off before it stains,' she advised gently. 'What bad luck. Tripped over in the street, did you?'

'N-no,' Jessica stuttered. 'Y-you don't understand. I-I can't go h-home like this.'

Her voice tightened to a squeak and Hillie exchanged bewildered glances with Gert. Her instinct was to invite Jessica into her own home to wash the offensive stuff from Jessica's skirt for her. But her dad was indoors and Hillie couldn't imagine how he'd treat the daughter of the hoity-toity prigs across the road, as he referred to the Braithwaites. The last thing poor Jessica needed was to be on the receiving end of his tongue! So Hillie was relieved when Gert came to the rescue.

'Blimey, you don't half look scared. We was just going out, but you'd best come indoors and we'll clean you up a bit.'

Jessica didn't appear any the less petrified at Gert's generosity, and as the two friends ushered her along the street, her eyes were swivelling in every direction, shoulders hunched as if she were trying to melt into the ether. Once inside, she seemed equally as nonplussed by the strange surroundings, although Hillie noticed Gert's affronted expression when Jessica couldn't help but wrinkle her nose at the unpleasant smell as they passed the open door to the front room.

'Mum!' Gert called as she pushed open the further door, and six pairs of eyes, including baby Primrose's, turned to stare at the three young women unexpectedly entering the room. Only Old Sal slept on regardless.

'You forget something?' Eva asked in surprise, and then spying Jessica, her face stiffened and she hitched up her ample bosom. 'Oh, look who've we got here, then.'

'Jessica fell over and got some dog muck on her skirt and she's scared to go home 'cos of what her parents might say,' Gert explained in a matter-of-fact way.

Eva's expression at once softened and her natural maternal instincts got the better of her. 'Mean to say they'd tell you off just for that? You poor lamb.'

'Let's have a butchers at the damage.' Stan relinquished his newspaper and came round to the other side of the table. 'Oh, is that all? Well, if Gert can lend you something to slip on for a few minutes, I'll wash it off for you out in the yard.'

'And you look like you could do with a nice cuppa,' Eva nodded, the trusty cup of tea being her answer to all ills. 'But first, you go next door to change,' she instructed as Gert went out of the door and they all heard her clumping up the stairs.

Jessica, though, appeared rooted to the spot, so Hillie herded her into the front room. She wasn't sure what Jessica would think of this parlour converted into a bedroom for an incontinent old lady and two small children, one of whom still wet the bed on occasion. But if Jessica had any feelings of distaste, she hid them well enough, not even wrinkling her nose this time. A few minutes later, they were all back in the kitchen, Jessica wearing

Gert's spare skirt, and Stan took the soiled garment out into the yard.

'I don't know, strange folk what'd give you a ticking-off for that,' Eva muttered under her breath as she bustled around the kitchen, suddenly inspired to wipe the crumb-strewn table with a suspicious-looking grey cloth. 'Tripping up in the street with these blessed uneven pavements. Could happen to any of us.'

'Oh, no.' Jessica suddenly seemed to come to life, warmed perhaps by the steaming tea Eva had thrust into her hand. If she had noticed that the mug was chipped, she didn't make any comment. 'That isn't what happened,' she said openly, and then instantly clapped her free hand over her mouth, eyes stricken fearfully again. 'Oh, you won't say anything, will you?'

Eva had picked Primrose out of the highchair and was now cuddling the child on her lap. 'To your parents, you mean? And when did either of them engage in conversation with the likes of me, may I ask?'

Jessica cast down her eyes and a peachy hue flushed into her pale cheeks. 'They do both think a lot of themselves, I know. In Daddy's case, I think it's from being in charge of so many people at work, and having to keep them in check all the time.'

Eva glanced up from reaching across with her free hand to help Trudy as the little ones clambered down from the table and then charged out into the yard. 'Ought to have this lot to take care of,' she pouted. 'Then he'd know what keeping bodies in check *really* means.'

Hillie had to smile to herself. Eva was a wonderful mother, but the good lady could hardly claim to have too much control over her family. If asked to describe the Parker household, the word chaotic would have instantly sprung to mind!

'Your father's a floor manager at Arding and Hobbs, isn't he?' Hillie asked, trying to divert the conversation.

'Yes. He has the jewellery and expensive glass and china departments under him. So he has to be very careful. Thank you for the tea, by the way, and for being so kind.'

'Not at all,' Eva beamed proudly. 'You was in a proper state. But I still don't see what all the blooming fuss was about.'

'Forgive me, but you don't know my parents.' Hillie noticed Jessica's eyes move darkly from one to the other, and she chewed on her bottom lip before continuing. 'You see, they hate dogs. Well, animals of any sort. Call them dirty, nasty things. But the thing is…' She broke off, hesitating once again, but then apparently made up her mind. 'Well, I love them.

And twice a week, I go for a piano lesson. Wednesday mornings and Saturday afternoons. Only on the way home, I call into Battersea Dogs' Home and help out for half an hour. That's how I got the mess on my skirt. But it wasn't until I was almost home that I realised.'

'So that's why you were so scared,' Hillie said, piecing it all together.

'Yes. My parents would kill me if they knew what I'm doing behind their backs. Daddy'd probably confine me to my room and the atmosphere would be awful for days.'

'But couldn't you just say that you fell over in the street like we thought you had?' Hillie asked, thinking that being sent to her room would be better than the slap or worse her own dad usually meted out as punishment for anything he considered a misdemeanour.

'Yes, but my father would want to know chapter and verse. Exactly where I fell over so that he could complain to the council if it was because of an uneven paving slab or something. And then he'd be on about dog-fouling and trying to find out whose dog it was. I just couldn't face all that.'

'Well, it's a crying shame when a girl's frightened of her own parents,' Eva declared fiercely. 'Give them the length of my tongue, I will, next time I—'

'No, please, I'd rather you didn't,' Jessica pleaded. 'If they had any suspicions about what I've been up to, they'd stop me going out on my own at *all*.'

'I know how that feels,' Hillie snorted wryly.

'Really?' The surprise on Jessica's face was genuine. 'But I always thought—'

'There we are then.' Stan shouldered his way through the back door, proud as punch with himself. 'Not a trace. Bit wet, mind.'

'Let me see.' Eva bustled forward, taking the garment from her husband and holding it up to inspect it. 'Hmm, well, it *looks* clean,' she conceded, 'but it still pongs a bit.'

'I've got some perfume upstairs,' Gert offered brightly. 'Well, it's 4711 eau de cologne, but that should be just right. Not too obvious. I'll pop up and get it.'

'Oh.' Jessica's glance followed Gert as she hurried out of the room and they all heard her charging up the stairs again. 'You've all been so kind, I can't thank you enough. I just wish there was something I could do for you in return.'

'No thanks needed, dearie.'

'Well, if ever I can do anything, you'll be more than welcome,' Jessica replied with more confidence now as Gert re-entered the room clutching the little bottle of cologne. 'With the help you've given me, Mummy won't suspect a thing, and Daddy shouldn't be in for another half-hour,' she stated, consulting her watch that Hillie noticed was encrusted with tiny sparkling gems. They weren't diamonds, were they? 'I can just put my skirt in the laundry basket for Mrs Dawson to wash on Monday morning, and no one will be any the wiser.'

'Your woman what does, I assume?' Eva sniffed with more than a little inverted snobbery.

Jessica actually laughed back. 'Well, you wouldn't find Mummy lifting a finger to do anything. And I'm not allowed to. Ever since I left school, I just have to sit around twiddling my thumbs. Sometimes I sneak in a bit of baking and pass it off as Mrs Dawson's. So thank goodness I have my piano and my visits to the dogs' home. Otherwise I wouldn't know what to do with myself all day.'

'Couldn't you get a job?' Gert suggested naively as she squirted some of the 4711 onto the drying patch on Jessica's skirt.

Jessica released a weighty sigh. 'Daddy won't let me, and Mummy agrees with him.'

'So what you gonna do with your life?'

'Wait until my parents come up with a suitable husband for me, I suppose. And go to coffee mornings and the Townswomen's Guild, just like my mum.'

'Oh, you poor thing. You must feel like a prisoner.' Compassion was etched on Hillie's face.

'My dad rules me with a rod of iron, at least he would if I let him. But he's happy enough for me to go out to work as long as I hand over almost all of my wages at the end of the week. And he lets me go out at weekends provided I've done all my chores and he thinks I'm with Gert. Even if I'm not,' she concluded under her breath.

'We're much the same, then. I never realised.'

Hillie smiled back with a rueful nod of her head. From what Jessica had said, Mr Braithwaite didn't react in quite the same way her own father did. She'd seen for herself the icy coldness in the man's eyes, and could well imagine him freezing his daughter to the bone with one glance. She doubted his wife was much better. But at least his answer wasn't to raise his fist.

Jessica put her own skirt back on in the privacy of the other room and, repeating her thanks, went to the front door with Hillie and Gert. They checked that Mrs Braithwaite wasn't watching out of the window of the house opposite, and then Jessica scuttled across the street, giving them a brief wave as she slipped inside.

'Well, that was a turn-up, wasn't it?' Gert declared as they set off for the second time. 'All that rumpus, and Gran slept all the way through it!' she mused fondly.

'Wish we could get to know Jessica a bit better, though, don't you? She seems really nice.'

'Maybe we could if she stood up to her dad a bit more like you do with yours. Only she seems a bit too soft for that.'

Hillie replied with a wry twist of her mouth. It didn't always do her much good, did it, when her dad's response to any disobedience was to give her a clout around the head that made her ears ring? God knew what he'd do to her if he discovered she'd been secretly walking out with Jimmy all summer.

So perhaps Jessica was the sensible one, after all.

Chapter Seven

A violent shiver rattled through Hillie's bones as they turned the corner into the street, and it wasn't just from the cold and wet. Rain had lashed down all afternoon from the leaden November sky, and Hillie had been keeping a wary eye on it through the windows of the candle-packing house, praying it would stop before home time. But it showed no sign of letting up, and when the three girls stepped out into the dark evening, the rain at once drove into their faces like pins of ice.

'See you tomorrow!' Belinda called, disappearing in the opposite direction, and the two other girls waved back.

'Cor, can't wait for the crowd to thin out so I can get me umbrella up,' Gert declared, turning up the collar of her threadbare coat as they were jostled among the throng of workers leaving the factory.

Hillie replied with a mere grunt. Autumn could be a beautiful season, and she'd walked in the park with Jimmy, admiring the hues of gold and copper, cinnamon and amber, as the trees had taken on their glorious mantle. She and Jimmy had played in the ocean of crisp, dead leaves strewn across the ground, kicking them in the air as they strolled along, or picking up handfuls to shower over each other. Now the memory danced fleetingly across Hillie's mind of a particular moment when she'd squealed with laughter as Jimmy had chased her around with some dried, brittle leaves cupped in his palm. He'd finally caught her by the arm, tossing them over her in a glowing arc. They were so close then, Hillie's mouth open in a roar of glee and Jimmy grinning boyishly. They stood for a moment, catching their breath, and Jimmy started to pick the leaves carefully from her hair. His smile faded, and the brightness in his eyes altered to a deep intensity.

'I love you, Hillie,' he'd croaked, his breath ragged. And Hillie had felt herself fly to the moon.

But a period of wind and rain had set in soon afterwards. Now the trees were bare, their naked branches dark and damp and their fallen leaves forming a soggy, miserable carpet on the grass and roads in the park. Winter was on its way, making Hillie feel really down in the dumps. It wouldn't have been so bad if they could have snuggled together in front of a blazing fire, watching their dreams in the merry flames. But they had nowhere to go. Jimmy's landlady, lax though she was, had threatened him with eviction on the one occasion he'd taken Hillie up to his room.

'We're only talking,' Jimmy had argued.

'And we all know what talking can lead to,' the woman had insisted. 'Now out with her, or pack your bags.'

'Sorry about that,' Jimmy had murmured as they went back downstairs. 'But I don't want to move out. It's cheap and you know I'm trying to save every penny for us.'

'I know,' Hillie had whispered back. But it had hurt that the landlady had considered they were up to no good. She was as bad as Hillie's father.

No, Hillie corrected her thoughts as she and Gert hurried along in the rain. She didn't think anyone, not even the cold and humiliating Charles Braithwaite, could be as bad as Harold Hardwick.

'I think you've made a mistake, Dad,' she'd said the previous Saturday afternoon when she had, as usual, handed over her wage packet to her father. He'd opened it, picked out a silver coin to give back to her, and then pocketed the rest. 'That's a shilling piece,' she corrected him, staring at the shiny disc in her palm. 'It should be half-a-crown. You've always let me keep half-a-crown a week. Ever since I started at Price's.'

'Well, it's going to be a shilling from now on,' he hissed back, baring his teeth. 'Winter's coming and coal's not getting any cheaper. And your brother's feet have grown so much, he needs some new boots. Want him to go around barefoot, do you?'

'No, of course not, but—'

'But nothing!' To emphasise the point, Harold raised his hand threateningly. 'And if you backchat me again, I'll make it sixpence.'

Humiliation burned inside her at the recent memory as Hillie tied her scarf over her head. 'At least you *have* an umbrella,' she muttered as Gert was at last able to open hers.

Gert shot her a frowning glance. 'Where's yours, then?'

'Another couple of spokes snapped the last time I used it. Had to throw it away and I can't afford a new one.'

Gert eyed her suspiciously, but made no comment. 'Suppose you can't afford the tram fare, neither?'

Hillie sucked in her lips, shaking her head in reply, and she saw Gert lift her shoulders in a casual shrug. 'Nor can I. But I'll let you share my umbrella. Unless Jimmy's around and wants to fork out for both of us to go on the tram,' she added as a hopeful afterthought.

'Couldn't risk Dad seeing us together even if he were. Actually, we didn't see Jimmy today, did we? Wasn't any reason for him to come to the packing house.'

'Come on, then. Keep close.'

They huddled together as best they could, trying to dodge the puddles that had formed on the pavement. Sharing the umbrella wasn't easy especially with Hillie being so much taller than Gert. Before too long, they both had rain running down the back of their necks and Hillie could feel water seeping into her oft-mended shoes.

'Blimey, the rotten sod!' Gert suddenly stopped dead and jerked her head towards where Harold was just climbing on to a tram. 'Thought you said he'd docked what you normally keep 'cos he needs the money for coal and whatnot?'

'He did,' Hillie seethed through clenched teeth. 'But he can afford the tram for himself while I get soaked to the skin.'

'Bastard,' Gert said for her. But then she pulled her friend forward. 'Well, we'll just have to get soaked together,' she grinned, 'and the quicker we get home the better.'

Hillie returned her smile and a warm tide flushed through her despite the pouring rain. What would she do without Gert? Jimmy made her brim over with excitement, and when he kissed her, a delicious euphoria tingled down her spine. But it was still Gert who was the rock of her life, and guilt snapped at Hillie's heart. She felt somewhat as if she'd abandoned her dearest friend. Gert had never said in so many words, but Hillie knew she didn't entirely approve of her relationship with Jimmy. And yet she'd been prepared to keep up the pretence that she always went out with Hillie in their spare time – not a particularly safe thing to do when she was effectively lying to a man like Harold Hardwick. No. Gert was one in a million, and Hillie felt she was treating her unfairly. If only Gert could find herself a boyfriend, they could go out as a foursome, and Hillie would feel much better about the situation. She was sure it would enable Gert to see the good in Jimmy, too.

'Penny for the guy, miss?' a little voice cut through the clatter of rain.

Both girls stopped and looked down on a scruffy urchin huddled in a shop doorway.

'Where is it, then, your guy?' Gert demanded.

'Couldn't bring it out in this, could I? It'd get soaked and then it wouldn't burn.'

'Well, if I had a penny which I don't, I'd give it to me own brothers and sisters.'

'I'll give you a farthing. It's all I can spare, I'm afraid,' Hillie said, searching for her purse.

'Cor, thanks, miss.'

'Soft, you are,' Gert declared, dragging her onwards. 'His family's probably better off than ours are.'

'Well, our dad won't let us have fireworks, so at least I can think of that kid enjoying some. And I felt sorry for him. Made me think of all those people on the hunger march. They can't afford to eat, let alone have fireworks.'

'Yeah, awful business, wasn't it? A million signatures on the petition, Dad said he read in the papers, and they never even got it to Parliament. And to think they was greeted by a hundred thousand supporters in Hyde Park.'

'That was the problem, though, really, wasn't it? They sent thousands of police in, mounted as well, and it all ended in violence.'

'Well, sorry as I might be for them, I'm not putting the world to rights hanging about in the bleeding rain. Let's hurry up and get home.'

They hurried on as quickly as they could, squeezed together under the umbrella. By the time they reached the corner of Banbury Street, they were both drenched through and shaking with cold. Hillie's feet were squelching in her shoes and she could feel the rain had seeped through her coat on the shoulder that had been outside the umbrella's protection. The skin down her back was cold and wet, her sodden skirt clinging about her legs, and she was chilled to the marrow. She felt utterly miserable and couldn't wait to get inside, strip off her dripping clothes, step into some dry ones and warm herself by the fire. She knew Gert must feel exactly the same.

'See you tomorrow, then,' Gert said as cheerfully as she could as they reached Hillie's front door.

'Just hope my shoes will've dried out overnight,' Hillie grumbled, but then feeling that was a bit churlish, she added, 'Thanks for sharing your umbrella.'

'That's what friends are for, kiddo,' Gert grinned back, and set off the few paces to her own home.

Hillie let herself inside and shut the front door on the wind and rain as quickly as she could. God, it was good to get indoors. She clicked the latch home and stood for a moment, watching the water drip from her coat and ooze out of her shoes onto the mat. She pulled off her headscarf and her coat. Now where would be the best place to hang them to dry without making a puddle on the floor?

She suddenly realised that the house was unbelievably quiet. That was odd. The younger children's shoes were in their normal military line, each pair sitting exactly beneath the relevant coat on the row of hooks on the wall above, smallest to largest in precise order. Only Harold's and Nell's outdoor clothes were permitted to grace the hallstand that Nell polished each day until it gleamed. So, everyone was home, just as Hillie would have expected. So why was the house so silent?

She'd scarcely had time to kick off her shoes when she had the answer.

'Harold, please, stop!'

Her mother's thin squeal gasped desperately through the front-room door which Hillie noticed now was slightly ajar. The next instant, she heard her father's roar of rage, the resounding thwack as something slammed against its target, and then a woman's agonised scream of pain.

Hillie was imprisoned in shock for no more than a second or two. She dropped her coat and scarf on the floor and catapulted forward, flinging open the door. The sight that met her eyes cut her to the quick. Her father's arm was raised above his shoulder, wielding the heavy belt that normally kept his corduroy work trousers in place around his sturdy waist. Cowering at his feet, Nell was attempting to protect herself, yet at the same time was gazing up as if to beg him for mercy. One cheek was already swollen from a hefty slap, if the fingermarks were anything to go by, and on the floor next to her, lay the small book Harold kept for his accounts, its tiny lock smashed open.

'How dare you!' Harold was bellowing like an enraged bull, so enflamed with anger that he was oblivious to the fact that Hillie was standing in the doorway behind him. 'I've told you before to look in my book!'

'I didn't!' Nell tried to protest. 'It fell on the floor and broke. I haven't looked inside, I promise.'

'Expect me to believe that? I saw you looking. No, you forced it open, you liar!'

With that, Harold swung his arm back to gain momentum. But he got no further. Hillie was so incensed that she felt no fear. She sprang forward, launching herself onto his raised arm. Her weight wrenched on his shoulder, dragging him round with such force that she fell back against the wall. In the split second it took her to regain her balance, she stared into the cruelty in his eyes, and her hatred for him froze solid somewhere deep and irrevocable inside her.

'And I suppose it was you put her up to it!' Harold snarled, and he whipped the belt through the air again, this time in Hillie's direction.

But she was too quick for him, dodging away with lightning speed. The leather strap crashed against the wall, making an indentation on the raised pattern of the paper. Hillie dropped on her knees, covering her mother with her own body and glaring up at her father, her eyes sparking dangerously.

'That's it! Be a man and hit a defenceless woman!' she challenged him.

'It's her own fault. She shouldn't have disobeyed me!'

'She didn't! You know jolly well she'd be too damned scared of you to break open your precious account book. And anyway, *I'm* the one who should want to see inside it since all my wages go into it!'

'Only paying for your own board and lodging.'

'And a lot more besides! Just because *you* can't provide for your own family.'

At her words, her father's face suffused to an alarming puce and his eyes bulged as if they were in danger of popping out of their sockets. Next to her, Hillie was aware of her mother's stricken expression and she heard her tiny whisper begging her to stop. But all the years of bitter frustration suddenly spiralled to the surface.

'No, Mum, I won't stop! It's about time we aired some home truths. That's why you steamed open my application for that job, wasn't it, and deliberately ruined it?' she demanded, turning back to Harold. 'Because if I'd got the job and was earning more money, you were afraid I'd get a place of my own. Leave home and take my wages with me. And you didn't want that, oh, no. Didn't think I'd worked it out, did you? Well, I did, and it just proves what a conniving, despicable bully you are. But if you lay a finger on Mum again, I'll go straight to the police.'

Her eyes scorched into her father's, watching his mouth open and shut like a goldfish. She could almost see the cogs of his evil mind turning, and wasn't surprised to watch the taut, furious lines on his face rearrange themselves into a sarcastic leer.

'You little fool!' he guffawed, lips curled with malice. 'The police can't interfere between a man and his wife.'

Hillie pulled herself up short. Damn. She'd heard that before somewhere. But she wasn't going to be thwarted. 'Maybe not,' she answered as an icy calm overtook her, her hatred so palpable she could taste it on her lips. 'But there are others who would. Good men at the factory who know what you're like and wouldn't think twice about giving you a taste of your own medicine.'

'Huh, that's what *you* think!' Harold sneered. 'They'd be too worried about losing their jobs, or getting into trouble with the police themselves. So I suggest you think again before making any more idle threats. Just shows what a stupid little bitch you are!'

He threw up his head with a tormenting laugh, calmly replacing the belt around his waist. Then he swiped the book with its broken lock from the floor and bowed mockingly out of the room. Hillie heard him in the hallway, and a few moments later, the front door opened and then clicked shut behind him.

Hillie remained motionless, listening to her pulse cracking inside her skull. She'd never felt such savage anger before. It had astounded her, but the satisfaction of telling her father exactly what she thought of him was all-encompassing. Her mind had been on fire, and she'd felt a strange sort of freedom.

She'd experienced some euphoric strength, and now that she had, she wasn't going to let it elude her ever again.

'What've you done, Hillie?'

The barely audible voice that scraped from Nell's throat brought her back to reality with a resounding thump.

'Oh, Mum, you can't let him go on treating you like this,' Hillie said desperately, her heart snapping as she noticed her mother wince as she helped her to her feet. 'I know this isn't the first time he's hit you. Or me for that matter. But using a belt... And what next?'

Nell straightened up, her face strained. She seemed about to speak, but just then the door slowly opened and the younger children sidled into the room that was normally forbidden to them. Hillie wondered how long her father had been beating her mum before she'd arrived home. She realised now that was why the house had been so deathly quiet. Her brother and sisters had been terrified into silence by what they could hear going on in the next room. Now the girls clustered about their mother, trying to comfort her and at the same time to take comfort for their own terror. Only Luke stood back, his young brow creased agonisingly.

'I should've stopped him,' he croaked miserably, his low voice meant for Hillie's ears alone. 'But I thought I should keep the little ones out of his way.'

Hillie felt her heart rip at her brother's anguish. 'You did the right thing. But you shouldn't have had to. You're only thirteen, for heaven's sake.'

'Come along.' Behind them, Nell's brave tone as she gathered herself together nonetheless held an underlying quiver that only the two elder siblings recognised. 'Let's finish tea, shall we?'

She flashed a watery smile at Hillie and Luke as she herded the four younger girls back into the kitchen. Elder sister and brother exchanged glances, and Hillie went over to retrieve the duster and tin of polish she spied on the small table where the sacrosanct account book usually sat. The crisis was over for now. Or was it?

'What can we do, Hill?' Luke's whispered question stabbed into her thoughts. 'He's getting worse.'

'I know,' she murmured back. 'I'll try and think of something. But I might just have made things worse.'

'I thought you were great. Heard every word you said. Wish I'd had the courage to stand up to him like that.' Luke shot her an awe-inspired look. 'Did you really try to get another job?'

Hillie nodded, sucking in her lips. 'Much good it did me. I didn't want Dad to know I knew what he'd done. I thought I might've been able to use it against him at some time, but I was so angry, it just came out.'

'Well, I think you played a trump card there. It let him know he can't always get away with things.'

'D'you think so?'

'Let's hope so, anyway, eh?'

Hillie lifted her eyebrows as she followed her brother back out into the hall. It was only when she saw her coat and scarf on the floor that she was reminded of the damp clothes on her shoulders and the saturated skirt that still clung to her trembling knees. She wearily retrieved her outer garments and hung them over the newel post, then with a shudder of strung-out emotions, shot up the stairs to peel off her wet clothes and exchange them for her spare set. She snuggled her feet into her worn slippers, which were at least warm and dry, and then shook her wet hair from its bun so that it would dry more quickly.

She came back down, carrying her wet clothes to hang on the wooden clothes horse by the fire and fighting to hold down the bitterness that still churned in her stomach. But she must take a hold of herself for the sake of her four sisters who were sitting back at the table, tucking happily into their baked beans on toast now that everything seemed back to normal. Only Joan was still watching anxiously as her mother poured out mugs of tea made with the same leaves she'd been using all day.

Hillie's own scant meal stuck in her throat, and she had to force it down. But as the minutes ticked by and they fell into the nightly routine of getting the younger ones off to bed, Daisy and Frances first, followed by Trixie and then Joan an hour later, Hillie's heartbeat gradually returned to normal and the horrible feeling of something trundling through her breast gradually subsided.

'Your father's still not back,' Nell croaked when it was just the three of them left downstairs.

Hillie had been immersed in her own resentful reverie, but at her mum's nervous words, her mind filled up with determination. 'Good. Give him more time to wrestle with his own conscience. If he has one.'

'Well, in a way, it was my own fault,' Nell said limply. 'I'd left the duster and polish on the table and went to get them because I knew he'd be cross about that. Then I heard him come in and it gave me such a fright that I accidentally knocked the book off the table and the little lock on it broke as it hit the floor. I picked it up and it was still in my hand when he came in the room.'

'And he put two and two together and made five, and thought he'd take his belt to you for it.' Hillie could feel the hatred bubbling up inside her again. 'What sort of a man does that to his wife?'

She paused, waiting for her mother to give her an answer, but Nell simply lowered her eyes and Hillie had to swallow down her exasperation. She glanced across at Luke whose young face was tense with a blend of consternation and expectancy. He was looking to her to do something, wasn't he? She wasn't sure what, but with a deep breath, she took her courage in both hands.

'Look, Mum,' she said, trying to disguise the tremor in her voice. 'We can't let things go on like this. It's by no means the first time he's hit you. Or me. How long before he starts on the others?'

Her mother's eyes suddenly flashed at her, and Hillie frowned, meeting Luke's perplexed gaze. Her brother was such a gentle soul, but he was also very sensitive to others' needs. Now he got quietly to his feet and backed towards the scullery.

'Just going out to the lav,' he muttered. 'I'll be a while, if you know what I mean.'

Hillie nodded. She knew he wasn't referring to bodily functions. He wanted to give Hillie time to talk to their mum alone. Once the back door was shut, she turned back to Nell but had no need to prompt her.

'He won't. Start on the others,' her mother told her.

Hillie's frown deepened. 'How can you be so sure?'

She noticed a faint flush rise into Nell's cheeks, but her mother looked at her steadily.

'You... you don't understand. There are reasons. But he won't, I assure you.'

Hillie tipped her head in confusion. 'All I understand is that he's violent and can lose his temper over the slightest thing. He's constantly humiliating you, and yet you take it lying down. Just look at you. Your cheek's all swollen, and look here.'

She pointed to her mother's neck where there'd been nothing to protect it from Harold's belt. A red weal cut angrily into her pale skin, and Nell, head hanging, allowed her eldest daughter to draw her blouse and cardigan from her shoulder to reveal a lattice of raised scarlet lines, some of which were smeared with traces of blood.

Hillie sucked her shock through her teeth. 'Why don't you divorce him, Mum?' she couldn't stop herself from saying.

'Divorce?' Nell blinked in surprise. 'On what grounds? I'd have to prove he's been unfaithful, and he hasn't. And as he rightly pointed out, the law can't come between a man and his wife for violence. And you need money to get divorced.'

'Well, we need to get away from him somehow,' Hillie said fiercely. 'Somewhere he'll never find us. At the other end of the country if need be.'

'But, Hillie—'

'I'll borrow some money. And… I know someone who'll help us.' Her thoughts had sprung immediately to Jimmy. He'd been saving hard for their future, but that would have to wait. She was sure he'd lend her the money and he people. People who he'd had dodgy dealings with in the past, it had to be admitted, but who could maybe be persuaded to help them now. Spirit them away. And once they were settled somewhere far, far away, she would get a job. Anything, it wouldn't matter, as long as it paid. Luke could pretend he was a year older than he really was and get a job, too. Eventually Jimmy would join them and they could live as one happy, *safe* family.

It would be hard, but she was sure they could do it. The only thing was they'd have to break all contact with Gert and the Parkers. It wouldn't be fair on them if Harold thought they might know where his family had started a new life. She wouldn't be able to tell Gert. Or even say goodbye. It would break her heart, but…

'No.' Her mother's sudden fearless confidence shook her rigid. 'I won't leave him.'

The blood seemed to drain from Hillie's head and her insides screwed into a bewildered, tangled knot. 'What on earth d'you mean?'

A serene smile lifted Nell's face. 'You're a good girl, Hillie. The best. But forget your wild plans. Believe you me, he'd find us, and that'd make things even worse. And whatever you might think, he's been good and loyal to me. There are reasons why he's like he is. The war, you know. Some men came home as nervous wrecks. Some had nightmares and tried to strangle their wives in their sleep. They reacted in all sorts of strange ways. Your father... well, he came home with this obsession about obedience. And with this anger inside him. Sometimes it just takes over. He's not the same man I married, but neither am I the same woman. And I owe it to him to stick by him.'

Hillie stared at her, drowning in disbelief. 'B-but...' she stammered as words failed her.

Her bewilderment deepened as Nell smiled calmly at her and reached out to take her hands in hers. 'But I'd understand if you wanted to go. In fact, the more I think about it, the more I think you should. And is that what happened? With your application for that job? Did he really deliberately ruin it?'

'Yes.' Hillie pursed her lips in bitterness. 'I always suspected it, but you saw his reaction just now. He confirmed it himself.'

'Oh, Hillie,' her mum sighed. 'I do love you, more than you can imagine. But maybe he's done you a favour, stopping you getting that job. You should move right away. Get a job in another part of the country. I'd miss you terribly, my darling. We all would. But at least I'd know you were safe. It's not fair the way he takes it out on you. And maybe if you weren't here—'

But Hillie never got to hear the rest of her mother's words as just then Luke came back indoors, throwing her a questioning, worried look, and Nell covered herself up again. Luke's return brought the conversation to a close, and Hillie was left reeling. Much as she yearned to escape from her father, how could she possibly leave her mum to face his vicious temper alone? She understood how the horrors of war had damaged so many men, scarring them mentally as well as physically. She'd grown up seeing men with missing arms and legs, and there was a chap she often saw in Battersea High Street whose face was horribly disfigured but who wore several medals on his jacket. And there was something called shell shock that still affected some men and made them unable to work. But even if something like that was the cause of her father's violence, it was no reason for her mum to put up with it. There must be something else, something that meant her father had some other sort of hold over her mum. Why else did she seem to accept the situation, to make excuses for him?

Hillie's lips firmed into a determined line. How could she find out what it was? She simply *had* to find a way…

Chapter Eight

'Haven't you finished that yet?' Harold snarled.

Hillie sat back on her heels and glowered up at her father. It was the Sunday exactly a week before Christmas. Lunch had consisted of two meagre slices of roast belly of pork eked out between them all, but there'd been plenty of roast potatoes and boiled cabbage to go with it. Even before the meal was over, Harold had insisted the scullery needed a good clean. As soon as the washing-up was done, Nell had begun scrubbing the oven with soda crystals dissolved in hot water, using a Brillo pad on the more stubborn grease stains. By the time she'd finished, the whole thing gleamed inside and out, but her fingers were raw and aching. Meanwhile, Hillie washed the quarry-tiled floor and then finished it off with a coat of Red Cardinal polish. She was buffing the tiles to a smooth sheen when her dad appeared at the back door after the weekly ritual of his ablutions in the outside toilet.

'I couldn't do that last bit until Mum had finished the oven, could I?' Hillie retorted caustically. 'And I hope your shoes are clean, or you'll make marks.'

Harold made a deliberate show of checking the soles of his shoes before looking down again at her with a mocking sneer. 'As a whistle,' he proclaimed before storming through so that Nell was obliged to leap out of his way. 'You two make sure you've finished properly before you go out,' he barked. 'Though why you want to go to a bloody carol concert, I don't know. All Christmas does is cost me money.'

'Well, at least the concert's free!' Hillie called after him.

She clenched her jaw, going over where his feet had nonetheless made distinctive prints where the polish wasn't quite dry. She almost wished that her father held the strict belief, as some did, that you shouldn't do any work on a Sunday beyond preparing food and drink. That way, her poor mum would at least be spared from her domestic drudgery on one day of the week. But her dad didn't have a religious bone in his body.

However, at least he hadn't struck either Nell or Hillie since the appalling incident some weeks ago now. Or if he had hit his wife, she'd concealed the fact with complete success. But Hillie remained convinced there was something her mother wasn't telling her. And what had she meant when she'd said she wasn't the woman her father had married? Hillie had thought of asking Eva, but that would be like sneaking behind her mum's back, and it could put Eva in a difficult position, so she'd decided not to.

Hillie kept turning that dreadful evening over in her mind. How could her mum refuse to leave her dad when there was that constant tension between them, as if Harold was taking every opportunity to belittle and humiliate her? Hillie just couldn't understand how her mother could kowtow to Harold all the time. Yes, the war might've made him into more of a bully than ever, but he must surely have some other secret hold over her, but what? Every so often, Dolly Maguire's half-cut words slipped unbidden into Hillie's mind. Vicious though she was, had there been some truth in the drunken woman's insinuations?

'There, that's the oven done so you can finish off now, Hillie, love,' Nell told her. 'I'll just get the others ready to go out. Concert's at three, isn't it?'

'Yes. We'll just make it,' Hillie answered over her shoulder as she took up the scrubbing brush again, thrusting her thoughts aside. 'Won't matter if we're a few minutes late for the start, though.'

She nevertheless worked as swiftly as she could to finish off the floor. The old tiles did, though, look refreshed and friendly, even if the dank odour rising up through the solid concrete floor could never be eliminated. The tap over the chipped butler sink in the scullery leaked slightly, too, giving off the sharp, metallic tang of wet lead. Harold had given up trying to cure it. After all, if their landlord didn't seem to care about it, why should he? His attitude made Hillie grit her teeth. He was so finickity about her and her mum doing their chores properly, yet he was happy enough to let this go!

It was the last thing on Hillie's mind, however, as she went to collect her hat and coat. The children were lined up in the hall, scarves wound about their necks in readiness, their young faces shining with anticipation. They wouldn't be having a Christmas tree. Their dad had proclaimed the greengrocer had put the prices up far too much this year and he wasn't prepared to spend that sort of money even if he had it. Hillie would've loved to treat her family to a tree, but since Harold had reduced her allowance, she truly couldn't afford it. Not if she was going to give everyone a little gift. Instead she and Luke had put up the previous year's coloured paper chains and the few pieces of dusty tinsel that were still in the box, but that was about it for decorations.

It was no wonder the children were looking forward so much to the concert. The Salvation Army were to play in the bandstand in the park, and there was to be a tall, decorated tree. Hillie smiled ruefully to herself as the family trooped out into the cold, wintry afternoon, chattering with excitement. The sky was a solid grey, but it looked as if the rain would hold off. A chilly wind teased the hems of their coats and blew up inside the girls' skirts, but nothing could dampen their high spirits.

'Hello, you lot!'

The door to Gert's house opened just as they reached it and out spilled the entire Parker family, pandemonium breaking out in the quiet backstreet. There seemed to be children everywhere, voices shrill with excitement, girls holding hands and skipping along the pavement, while young Jake copied Luke as he balanced precariously on the kerb.

'Glad you've been let out to play for once,' Eva nodded at Nell with a hint of bitter irony. 'I see the old bugger ain't coming, thank goodness. Wouldn't want him spoiling the afternoon.'

Hillie had to chuckle. Didn't mince her words, did Eva. Hillie noticed she was giving her best coat an airing in honour of the occasion. She'd bought it for next to nothing, Hillie recalled her saying, in a pawnshop years earlier. It would have to do her until she died, she'd proclaimed proudly. And it would probably have to!

'Hello, Mr and Mrs P, Gert, kiddies,' Hillie beamed, her dragging heart lifting at the prospect of spending some time with this jolly family she loved so much. And then she noticed that Stan was assisting Kit to manoeuvre Old Sal's wheelchair over the threshold and onto the pavement. The old lady was so swathed in blankets and scarves that Hillie could scarcely see her wizened little face, but Old Sal's eyes were like bright, shiny beads. It was so difficult to take her out that it was a rare occurrence. Hillie doubted she understood what was going on, and admired the family for making such an effort.

'Hello, Kit,' she greeted Gert's brother as he heaved over the back wheels. 'Not working, then?'

'Early shift, so I've finished for the day,' he replied pleasantly. 'It's early to bed and early to rise for me at the moment. I'll be heading back to my digs and my bed straight after the concert.'

Hillie fell into step beside him as he trundled his grandmother along the street. 'You all right, Old Sal?' she asked, leaning forward and raising her voice, and the old dear answered with a gummy grin. 'I wonder if she appreciates it,' Hillie commented as she straightened up. 'D'you think she knows it's Christmas?'

'Not sure, but it was the only way we could all come out together. You know we can't leave her. God knows what she'd do.'

'Set the house on fire probably,' Gert joined in the conversation. 'Or have a fall. But I'm sure she'll enjoy coming out, and we've got her well wrapped up.'

'Yes, so I see,' Hillie chuckled, smiling first at Gert and then at Kit as she walked along between them. Kit was the only one of the six children who took after his father in looks, Hillie reflected. Stan must have been good-looking in his youth if Kit was anything to go by. Funny that, she mused. But she supposed you didn't normally consider such things when you'd grown up with someone. But the thought slipped away as her attention was drawn by her mother nattering away with Eva, and she breathed a sigh of contentment. It was wonderful to see her mother having a good time when most of her life was lived under a weighty cloud.

As they reached the corner of the street, the unusual sight of a motor vehicle turning in from Battersea Bridge Road drew Hillie's curiosity. She looked back to see a black taxi pulling up outside Number Three on the opposite side. Out climbed Mr and Mrs Braithwaite, heads held high in their habitually superior manner. While Charles Braithwaite paid the driver, Hillie saw Jessica slip out of the cab behind her mother, looking downtrodden and cowed despite her fashionably tailored coat and cloche hat with its turned-back brim. But it seemed Jessica couldn't help glance across at the large, rowdy group gathering on the corner of the street. When her eyes met Hillie's, her long face moved into a broad smile.

Hillie didn't allow herself the luxury of hesitation. It was only when she'd crossed the street behind the departing taxi that she found herself making a deliberate attempt to steel her nerves.

'Good afternoon, Mr and Mrs Braithwaite. Hello, Jessica,' she called with apparent confidence. 'Been somewhere nice?'

With her back to her parents, Jessica rolled her eyes. 'Lunch with another manager at Arding and Hobbs. It was *so* boring.'

'Ah,' Hillie nodded knowingly, then raised her voice again. 'Not coming to the carol concert in the park?'

Jessica's face lit like a beacon. 'Oh, I'd love to!'

'Well, *I'm* not sitting round in the cold with the hoi polloi,' Mrs Braithwaite proclaimed curtly, stabbing a disparaging look in Hillie's direction.

Hillie ignored the woman's remark. 'Jessica's welcome to come with us if she wants.'

'Now look here, young lady.' Already halfway up the stone steps to the front door, Charles Braithwaite turned to sneer down his nose at Hillie. 'My daughter doesn't want to mix with the likes of you.'

Hillie felt the hairs on the back of her neck bristle with resentment. 'What you mean is *you* don't want her mixing with us. But this is just a carol concert by the Sally Army. I don't see how you can object to that. It'll be over in an hour or so. Hardly time for us to corrupt her. And she wants to come, don't you, Jessica?'

Hillie held her breath as Jessica appeared to waver in her resolve, but then to Hillie's relief, she gave a decisive nod. Hillie saw the slight hesitation on Charles's face and seizing the opportunity, grasped Jessica's hand.

'Come along, then,' she said, drawing Jessica away. She chose to ignore Charles's open mouth as he went to protest, but he didn't come after them as they hurried across the street to catch up with the others making their way towards the park.

'Oh, my goodness, well done.' Jessica had hunched her shoulders as if she expected her father's wrath to descend upon her. 'I'd never have had the nerve.'

'Look upon it as a first step,' Hillie grinned. 'Maybe we can work on it.'

'I don't know about that.'

Jessica arched a wry eyebrow as they hurried along to join the two families walking past the opulent mansions in Cambridge Road. Gert had watched what had happened, her jaw dropped in awed astonishment at Hillie's bravado.

'You joining us, then?' she called.

'It would seem so, yes!' Jessica replied, still bewildered at her freedom. 'Thanks to Hillie here.'

'Oh, you can rely on our Hill to stir things up. Come on. This is me brother, Kit,' she announced as they finally caught up.

'Oh, hello. Yes. I've often seen you coming and going.'

'Of course. And I, you.' Kit briefly took one hand from the wheelchair handles to shake Jessica's. 'Hope you've got some gloves. Your hands are cold already.'

'Yes, I have. In my pocket.'

'Hello, Jessica, ducks,' Stan welcomed her over his shoulder, and Eva nodded a greeting, too.

Nell turned back to add her own warm smile. 'Nice to meet you properly, dear. Sorry I can't shake your hand. Got to hold onto these two tykes until we get into the park,' she explained, jabbing her head down at Daisy and Frances who were skipping boisterously along on either side of her.

'Gosh, there's so many of you. Let me help,' Jessica offered, starting to look so relaxed and happy that Hillie was pleased she'd made the decision to stand up for her.

And so it was that quite a little army crossed over Albert Bridge Road together and entered the park through Sun Gate. Once inside, they joined the throngs of people making their way towards the bandstand, and soon the group got broken up by the surging crowd. The little ones were some way ahead with Nell, Stan and Eva who was pushing a vociferous Primrose in her pram, since now that she was walking, the toddler wanted to join her siblings on her own two feet. Jessica came next, chatting with Kit as he propelled Old Sal along in her wheelchair, and Hillie and Gert were just a little behind them.

'Hello, miss. Not with your young man today?'

Hillie's wide-stretched eyes alighted on one of the park's brown-uniformed keepers, and a slick of sweat oozed down her back. The man was smiling genially, litter-spike resting in his hand like a javelin. He was a jovial, friendly fellow who'd chatted to her and Jimmy on many occasions. But his innocent comment was the last thing she wanted to hear just now. It was sod's law she should bump into him just there when he patrolled the whole flipping park!

'Not today,' she muttered feebly.

'Enjoy the concert, then!' the park-keeper called, and went on his way.

Hillie released a sigh of relief. She and Jimmy had been so careful to keep their relationship hidden. They'd even agreed not to give each other a Christmas present. If Harold discovered she'd stowed away a gift suitable for an adult male, there'd be hell to pay. Likewise if Jimmy gave her something, where could she say it had come from? No. Far better not to take any chances and just wish each other a Merry Christmas instead.

As it was, they often just walked in the park on their dates, but if the keeper had recognised her from that, perhaps they'd better not go there anymore. Everyone else who knew about her and Jimmy was sworn to secrecy, but she'd kept her own family in the dark as she couldn't risk it getting back to her father. But as luck would have it, her mother was well ahead of her with Eva and Stan, with all the children cavorting around out of earshot. Jessica, who as yet didn't know about Hillie and Jimmy, was still engrossed in conversation with Kit, so neither she nor Nell had been aware of the keeper's words. So the dangerous moment had passed unnoticed and Hillie relaxed as they reached the bandstand area in plenty of time.

'Oh, look, there's Belinda!' Gert cried, waving frantically. 'She said she'd try and meet us here. And who's that handsome fella with her? Here, you don't say she's been hiding something from us, do you?'

'Hello, Belinda!' Hillie greeted their friend as she weaved her way through the crowds. 'Glad you made it!'

'Oh, I'm looking forward to it!' Belinda grinned. 'And this is my brother, Rob.'

'Pleased to meet you. I'm Gert.'

Hillie had to smile as her best friend blinked up at Belinda's good-looking brother. In her head, she could hear Gert saying, 'Cor, he's a bit of all right, ain't he?' Rob was unattached, they knew. Wouldn't it be good if he and Gert hit it off? With a sister as nice as Belinda, he must be a good sort.

Hillie quickly introduced Jessica to Belinda and her brother, and then all conversation was lost in the scramble to get everyone seated. Kit parked Old Sal's wheelchair to one side and stayed standing beside her, while Eva managed to sit on the end of a row so that she could have the pram beside her, and the others vied to find seats among the thousand places available. To make room for others, each child was seated on an adult's knees, and Jessica ended up with Trudy on her lap. Hillie noticed that Jessica seemed to delight in having such close contact with the little girl and didn't mind a jot that the tiny, none-too-clean fingers were constantly playing with the earrings that twinkled on her earlobes.

'Here we go, then. "The Holly and the Ivy",' Gert announced as if she'd arranged the concert herself, beaming at Rob who she'd managed to sit next to, even though she had Mildred wriggling about on her lap. 'The women don't half look funny, don't they, in them old-fashioned bonnets?'

'It's their traditional uniform,' Hillie whispered sharply on her other side. 'They do such wonderful work. *Of all the trees that are in the wood,*' she sang gustily, and with a cheeky grin, Gert joined the entire audience in belting out the familiar words.

'Quite magical, isn't it?' Jessica breathed in the break before the next carol. 'There must be over a thousand people here. Every seat's taken and there's loads of people standing.'

'Something about music in the open air,' Hillie agreed. 'And the cold somehow adds to the atmosphere.'

'Yeah, everyone's breathing out clouds!' Gert put it. 'Oh, "Once in Royal" is next.'

Music rippled out across the park again, and voices were raised in happy exultation. As the day began to fade, hurricane lamps were lit around the bandstand, and the tinsel and baubles on the Christmas tree glittered prettily in the flickering lights. Hillie watched the wonder on the faces of the little ones and a lump came to her throat. She wished so fervently that she could do something more for Luke and her sisters, but how could she? Then she saw her mum smile at her over their heads, and that nagging feeling began tugging at Hillie's heart again. What was it that made her mum bend to her father's cruel will all the time? But they were all together, safe and happy for now, and she should put all else aside to enjoy this delightful moment. If only she could have shared it with Jimmy, it would have been perfect. But they'd decided it was too dangerous to risk any contact, however fleeting, at the concert. Hillie kept looking round, though, hoping he might have come anyway, but keeping his distance. She was both relieved and disappointed when she didn't spot him.

As it was, the concert was over all too soon. As the final rousing chorus of 'Oh, Come all ye Faithful' died away on the early evening chill and people queued to leave their row of seats, sadness stole into Hillie's heart. The majority of those in the audience would have little to spend on Yuletide celebrations, yet she could imagine them spending a happy Christmas with their friends and families. And so would Hillie – if it weren't for her father's menacing presence and the fact that she couldn't risk trying to see Jimmy.

'Hello, there. It's Miss Braithwaite, isn't it?'

They were all wending their way down the avenue away from the bandstand when a man's voice interrupted the lively conversation between the three young women. Hillie realised that the fellow must have picked Jessica out of the milling crowds, and her curiosity was drawn for more reason than one. He was tall and dressed in a good quality coat, but even in the gathering dusk, one glance showed Hillie that his skin was as dark as coal! Hillie hadn't seen many people of his race in her life, and he looked a bit frightening at first, but he was well-spoken with a lovely lilting accent and seemed friendly enough. Hillie judged him to be about thirty, and once the initial shock had worn off, she thought he actually looked quite attractive in an unfamiliar and exotic way. Waiting patiently beside him was a beautiful dog, ghostly pale in the gloom and gazing up alertly at its master. Who could this chap be, and more to the point, how on earth did Jessica know him?

'Do you remember me?' the man asked.

Hillie glanced across at Jessica and was intrigued to see recognition dawn on her friend's face.

'Yes, I do,' Jessica said slowly. 'I did the paperwork when you collected Honey from the dogs' home. But I'm afraid I don't recall your name.'

'Ah, well, that is no surprise,' the stranger chuckled amiably. 'My name is Akpobio. But please do call me Patrick. But I am afraid I changed Honey's name to Africa to remind me of my homeland every day.'

'Well, I think that's lovely. And it's really nice to see her again and looking so healthy.' Jessica bent to ruffle Africa's fur behind both ears, setting the animal's tail swishing vigorously. 'She's such a gorgeous dog. I don't know how anyone could've abandoned her.'

'Perhaps she was lost,' Patrick suggested.

Jessica shook her head. 'I doubt it. If a stray doesn't have a collar, we contact the police and it didn't seem as if anyone was looking for her.'

'Their loss and my gain.'

Jessica straightened up and Hillie was surprised to see the pair smiling at each other hesitantly, not quite knowing what to say next, but as if hoping the conversation wasn't over. Could Hillie detect some sort of instant attraction between them? But, oh Lord, they were from two very different cultures, oceans apart. If they wanted to be friends, Hillie could only see problems ahead, especially given the Braithwaite's superiority complex. But even in the fading light, she caught the delicate hue blossom on Jessica's face.

'Do you mind if I walk with you?' Patrick found his tongue at last. 'I go out through Sun Gate.'

'So do we.' Jessica's voice quivered with pleasure, though Hillie was sure there was some nervousness there as well. 'These are my friends, Hillie and Gert. They live in the same street.'

'How do you do, ladies? And do you work at the dogs' home, too?'

'Nah, we work at Price's.'

Hillie exchanged meaningful glances with Gert. Belinda and Rob had already set off in a different direction, but not before inviting Hillie and Gert to a New Year's party at their parents' house in two weeks' time. They asked Jessica as well, but Jessica had said she was expected at a party with her own parents. But now Hillie knew exactly why Gert had put on her most working-class accent in reply to Patrick's question. She, too, could see that no good could come of any relationship between Jessica and this stranger. She was doubtless trying to put the clearly cultured chap off by letting him think Jessica's best mates were uneducated factory girls. But it didn't work!

'Indeed? I must say I admire their beautiful decorative candles. I have a box of Christmas ones all ready to light, but alas, no one to share them with. I have no family in this country, and no one wants to spend Christmas with their dentist.'

'Dentist!' all three girls chorused.

Patrick looked somewhat abashed. 'For my sins. Every mouth is fascinating, you know. It tells a story. But I am sure you do not want to hear about that.'

'On the contrary, I should love to,' Jessica answered breathlessly.

'Then… perhaps I could make so bold as to ask you out? Would you like tea at Claridge's, perhaps? Oh, my goodness, all this and I have yet to ask your given name.'

Hillie held her breath. *Claridge's!* Blimey. But surely it could only end in tears? So she slumped with relief when she heard Jessica's reply.

'It's Jessica. But I'm afraid that wouldn't be possible. My parents wouldn't allow it.'

'Because of the colour of my skin?' Resignation trembled in Patrick's voice.

'My parents can be very prejudiced,' Jessica apologised. But then she flicked up her head. 'But

I'm not. Give me your telephone number and I'll ring you when the coast is clear.'

'Why, yes, of course,' Patrick almost stuttered, fumbling inside his coat. 'Here is my card. And here we are at Sun Gate. I go this way, and you?'

'Over there,' Jessica told him.

'Well, it has been a delight to meet you all, ladies.' Patrick gave a half bow. 'I hope it will not be the last time. And may I wish you all a very Merry Christmas!' He turned away, Africa trotting along obediently by his side. Hillie saw him give a little skip and then swivel back to face them. 'You could always feign toothache!' he called, and with a cheery wave, he disappeared into the now total darkness.

'Well, I never.' Hillie broke the silence as they crossed the road and hurried back along Cambridge Road.

'Need to tread blooming carefully, if you ask me.' Gert wrinkled her nose. 'Dentist, indeed. How d'you know he's telling the truth?'

'The dogs' home do check on people before they let them take a dog home,' Jessica assured her.

'And there's a dentists' register, isn't there?' Hillie suggested as they caught the others up. If Jessica was keen to pursue the matter, she ought to support her. After all, if it hadn't been for her, Jessica wouldn't have been in the park in the first place. 'You've got a phone. The operator should be able to connect you.'

'Who on earth was that, then?' Kit asked, grunting as he manoeuvred Old Sal's wheelchair down the kerb to cross back over Battersea Bridge Road.

'Some bloke Jessica met at the dogs' home. *Says* he's a dentist.'

'Ah, yes, I think I've heard of him. Can't be many black dentists around here. Someone at the station went to see him and said he was excellent.'

'There you go, then. So, you going to contact him again?' Hillie asked.

Jessica puffed out her cheeks. 'If I get the chance. I wouldn't even have thought of it if it hadn't been for the way you stood up to my father just now, Hillie. Perhaps it's rubbing off on me! Anyway, what are you all doing at Christmas?'

'You know, the usual sort of thing,' Gert told her. 'Just nice to have the family together. And you?'

They'd reached Banbury Street now, and Jessica's answer floated over Hillie's head as her thoughts turned to her own home. The magic of the carol concert, the children's faces entranced by the lights dancing in the gloom, would dissolve into fleeting memories the instant they all got inside. Harold would be waiting, ready to scorn and hurt with his spiteful tongue – or worse. Schooling her face into a smile, Hillie said goodbye to the Parkers, and then watched Jessica let herself in to Number Three. Then, following her own family to their front door, she prepared to face the music.

Having said goodbye to everyone, Kit was left standing alone on the pavement. He could hear the muffled, happy voices of his own family from the other side of the closed front door, but the street itself was quiet and still in the darkness. A bus rumbled across the end of the road, then all was silent again.

Kit paused for a moment, letting the chill wind entwine itself about him. He drew deeply on the evening air, and then watched his breath billow out in a little cloud. The afternoon had been wondrous. Even more so because *she* had been there. From his position standing next to his gran, he'd watched her unobserved across the crowd, her lovely face lifted in contentment. Yet he knew she had problems of her own with that bastard of a father. He longed to take her in his arms, wrap his own strength around her. But his stupid pride had made him want to make something of himself first. To have a decent home, security, to offer her before he declared himself. But he'd left it too late, and now she had that chap from the factory. She must be smitten to risk her father's wrath by seeing this Jimmy fellow when she knew how strongly he disapproved. Dear God, Kit prayed he'd be around to protect her when the devil found out.

His gaze was drawn to the Hardwicks' front door, and he stood, rooted to the spot, his heart aching.

'No good lusting after 'er. Got some other geezer, ain't she?'

Kit smelt rather than heard Dolly Maguire come up behind him. He threw the drunken old witch a withering glance before spinning on his heel and striding off down the street.

Dolly Maguire chortled aloud. Hit a raw nerve there, hadn't she? So she was right. That stuck-up little puss *was* seeing someone – and Dolly would bet her last farthing that Old Man Hardwick didn't know. But how could she make the best use of that little nugget? She'd have to think about that one…

Chapter Nine

'Here you are, Mummy. Happy Christmas!'

Little Daisy stepped forward and gave Nell a small package. Nell pulled her daughter onto her knee as she unwrapped the brown paper with deliberate slowness.

'Oh, what have we here?' she said excitedly, making her fingers work as clumsily as they could. 'Oh, a bath cube! And this one's lavender,' she beamed, 'so now I have rose, lily of the valley, orchid, hyacinth and lavender,' she declared, adding it to the line of tiny gifts on the kitchen table. 'I'll use just a half each time I have a bath, and then won't I smell lovely!'

'Will you use mine first, Mummy?' Trixie piped up.

'No, mine,' Joan pouted.

Nell glanced up wistfully at Hillie, and their eyes met. Nell knew full well that with Harold refusing to give his children pocket money, Hillie had given her brother and sisters the few pennies to buy the bath cubes at Woolworths in Lavender Hill. It was all she could afford, since her father had cut what she could keep from her wages each week.

Earlier that morning, after opening their stockings that were nothing more than one of their own socks, in each one of which Nell had placed an orange and one of the new Mars chocolate bars, they had all gone to church. Everyone except Harold. The whole idea had been to get away from him for an hour and a half, rather than from any religious convictions, although singing carols had been uplifting. But back home, the atmosphere was hardly jolly with Harold's mere presence putting the dampers on everything.

'Well, I think I'll muddle them all up and choose with my eyes shut,' Nell pacified all her children. 'That way it'll be fair.'

'OK, Mum,' Luke shrugged. 'I just wish I could've got you something better.' His eyes flashed meaningfully to the door. Their father had sneered at the ceremony of exchanging gifts, and had taken himself for a cigarette in his parlour. The older children all knew of his meanness. He could afford cigarettes and beer, but scarcely a penny for them.

'And I've got you this, Mum,' Hillie said quietly, handing Nell another small packet. Like the others, it was wrapped in brown paper, but at least it was tied with a length of coloured string, the only thing she'd ever purloined from her work in the packing shed. But it was only a small piece, just about long enough to tie round the minuscule present that would have been no use at Price's and therefore thrown away.

'Oh, a lipstick.' Nell's eyes shone for her eldest daughter. 'Thank you, love.'

'And thank you for the mittens and the beret, Mum. They're lovely. You're so good at knitting.'

'Yes, thanks, Mum,' the others chorused, since they'd all received something made by Nell's hand: a scarf or a pair of gloves, and a jumper for Luke who'd grown so much and was in desperate need of something to fit.

'Well, let's lay the table now, ready for dinner. It's only scrag end of lamb, I'm afraid, but I've got a surprise for pudding,' Nell winked.

'Can we put out the crackers we made?' Frances wanted to know.

'Of course!' Hillie grinned, remembering the laughter she'd heard coming from the kitchen when she returned from work the previous evenings and found her mum and the others up to their eyes in newspaper and glue. 'And Price's gave us each a decorated pillar candle this year,' she went on. 'I'll put mine on the table, too, to make it look pretty, but we won't light it until it gets dark.'

'Best leave your dad's one on the mantelpiece,' Nell commented to Hillie under her breath. 'He might go mad if it's moved. And when we've done that, we'll play some games until it's time to put the vegetables on,' she went on, lifting her voice again. 'But better not make too much noise so we don't disturb your father.'

When all was prepared, Nell produced an old snakes and ladders board that had been hers as a child, which kept everyone happy until it was time to eat.

'Isn't it ready yet?' Harold demanded, barging into the kitchen.

'Almost, dear. You just sit down and relax.'

'Huh,' came the grunted reply. 'And I suppose I've got to open my own beer.'

'Well, if you're not too busy,' Hillie retorted, and just dodged her father's flying hand. But ignoring the gesture, she said brightly to the others, 'Open the crackers carefully now, and see what's inside.'

The crackers were merely twists of newspaper, and inside each was a halfpenny bar of chocolate and a newspaper hat. Daisy's Robin Hood-style contraption was too big and fell down over her eyes, making everyone laugh, except her dad who considered it all a load of bunkum. While Luke swapped his Nelson hat, which was too small, with Daisy, Harold tore his in half.

Hillie struggled to hold her anger in check, but as soon as Christmas dinner was over, the surprise being a plum pudding Nell had made especially,

Hillie announced that she was going to call in to see Gert.

'Huh, if you must desert your own family on Christmas Day!' Harold growled. 'Well, don't you be long, or I'll be coming to get you.'

'No, I won't, Dad,' she answered, seething, and hurrying down the hallway, let herself out of the front door, gulping in her freedom. No, she wouldn't be long. But if she didn't get away from her dad for an hour, she thought she would scream. Some Christmas Day! She couldn't get to the Parkers' quick enough!

*

'And where d'you think you're going, missie? You spent half the afternoon at the library, and now you're wanting to go out again.'

Harold poked his angry face so close to Hillie that she could see the individual hairs up his nose. It was Saturday afternoon, and New Year's Eve. When Price's had closed at lunchtime, Hillie had indeed gone to the library to change her book. But Gert had gone with her, and afterwards they'd spent some time window shopping since Hillie wanted to put off for as long as possible going home and putting up with her dad's obnoxious presence.

'I'm going out, of course,' Hillie answered him crisply now. 'It *is* New Year's Eve. And it's Sunday tomorrow, so I haven't got to get up early for work in the morning.'

'And what if I say you're staying here?' Harold snarled, grasping her arm so tightly that his fingers pinched her even through her coat sleeve.

Hillie lowered her eyes slowly to her arm, and then raised them again to meet his gaze with steady determination. 'Then I'd go anyway. People are expecting me, and they'd wonder why I didn't turn up.'

'And what people would that be, then?'

'Belinda's family are having a party and she's invited Gert and me. You know, Belinda in the office? Who got the job I might've done if you hadn't ruined my application. I haven't forgotten that, even if you have.'

Hillie saw the mere shadow of guilt flicker across her father's face. 'So where does this Belinda live, then?' he sneered.

'Parsons Green,' she snapped back.

'Parsons Green!'

'Yes, you know, on the other side of the river.'

'I know where it is, you cheeky monkey! Well, I won't have you wandering back all the way from there in the middle of the night, even if you are with that Gert hussy.'

His words were like a red rag to a bull. 'Don't you dare speak about Gert like that! And we won't be walking back. One of Belinda's brothers is going to bring us home in his car.'

'So you've got it all worked out, then?'

'Of course. I'm not the fool you take me for, you know. So you can let go of my arm and get yourself off down the pub to enjoy yourself, knowing I'll be perfectly safe and you won't have to worry about me,' she concluded with burning sarcasm.

Harold's eyes narrowed, but then he released his fingers, raising his hand in a mocking gesture. 'I might stay in actually, and enjoy the evening with your mother.'

Hillie didn't like the way he said it, but then she wasn't meant to, was she? She knew he wanted her to think he meant to take her mother upstairs for *an early night* once Luke had got into his pull-down bed in the kitchen. The devil was trying to goad her into changing her mind, wasn't he? And a vile, sick feeling landed in the pit of her belly. But if it wasn't then, it would be some other time. And if her mother refused to do something about it, why should Hillie feel responsible? She'd made several more attempts to persuade Nell to try and escape Harold's clutches, but each time her mum insisted that she wouldn't leave.

But the fact was, Hillie did feel responsible. At that moment, though, it seemed pretty pointless, whereas defying her dad was paramount. So, although she was seething, she gave what she hoped would appear as a casual shrug and rammed on her head the gaily patterned knitted beret her mother had made her for Christmas. 'I'll see you next year, then,' she said flatly, wishing it meant in a year's time rather than the following day!

She stepped outside onto the pavement, making a conscious effort to tamp down her resentment. She'd have liked to slam the door, but that would only give her father the satisfaction of knowing that he'd angered her. He really made her blood boil. If only she could be free of him, but she couldn't see any way she could ever have him out of her life while he had this unidentified hold over her mum. And she certainly wasn't going to leave her mum to face him alone! There were times when she wanted to scream, but what was the point?

She covered the few yards to Gert's house, shivering not just from the cold. The smell of damp was sharp in her nostrils, mixed with the heavy tang of coal smoke spiralling from every chimney. There wasn't a breath of breeze to blow it away and it caught at the back of her throat. But she was used to it, and wasn't going to let it spoil her evening out.

Most people she knew were too broke after Christmas to celebrate New Year, and it was the first time she'd ever been invited to a New Year's party. She could scarcely contain her excitement. Mind you, she hadn't told her dad that before they walked across Wandsworth Bridge towards Belinda's home, she and Gert would be calling into the Falcon. Jimmy didn't normally work there on a Saturday night, but with it being New Year's Eve, the landlord wanted extra staff and Jimmy didn't want to turn down the chance of extra pay. He'd be busy behind the bar until midnight as the pub had extended its licence for the evening. So Hillie and Gert were going to spend an hour or so there before they went on to the party. It was only the second time either girl had been in a pub, and being under eighteen, they'd only be allowed to have a soft drink. But as neither of them had ever tasted alcohol, they hardly minded.

'You look nice, ducks,' Eva said as Hillie went into the kitchen at Gert's house. 'Oo, you got them proper stockings on? That Belinda girl gave our Gertie a pair for Christmas and all.'

Hillie bit her lip. If she'd got the job, it would have been *her* giving everyone nice presents. Not that she felt any resentment towards Belinda herself. She'd turned into a good friend, and it was kind of her to be so generous.

'Wish I had some decent shoes to go with them, mind,' she answered. 'These are falling apart. Tell you what, though. Some nice warm boots wouldn't come amiss. It's turned cold tonight after all the mild weather we've had.'

'Better wrap up warm, then,' Gert pronounced, breezing into the room. 'Mum's lent me her best coat, see?'

'Well, can't go out, can we, with me mum and the little uns?' Eva said almost apologetically. 'Me and Stan've got in a few bottles of stout and we're going to cuddle up in front of the fire, ain't we, Stan?'

Hillie had to smile to herself at the crimson that suddenly coloured Stan's face. It was all so different from what would be going on between her mum and dad, and her heart lurched.

'Oh, sounds like someone at the door.' Stan snatched at the opportunity to change the subject.

'We'll see to whoever it is on our way out,' Gert told him. 'Bye-ee! Have a nice evening!'

Hillie added her goodbyes, and then followed Gert out into the hallway. 'Hope to God it's not my dad decided to try and stop me going out after all,' she groaned as Gert opened the door. She mentally crossed her fingers, but to her utter surprise, it was Jessica standing on the doorstep.

'Oh, hello!' Gert said, equally taken aback. 'We was just going out, but come in for a minute. Anything up?'

'Oh, well, no,' Jessica stammered as she stepped inside and Gert pushed the door to. 'I mustn't make you late.'

'Nah, a minute or two don't matter for a friend,' Gert insisted. 'You must've wanted something, or you wouldn't be here.'

'Well,' Jessica faltered, 'you know I said I was going to a party with my parents? That's why I couldn't go to Belinda's. It's an annual event thrown by Daddy's boss. I hate going so I pretended I had a headache. And, well... I phoned Patrick and asked him round. But he won't come unless you two come as chaperones. I know you're going to Belinda's party, but I thought that wouldn't be until later.'

'It isn't,' Hillie faltered, and her glance snagged on Gert's as she bit her lip. 'Well, the thing is, if you can keep a secret, I've got a boyfriend. Only my dad doesn't approve, so we're just going to see Jimmy briefly at the pub where he's working tonight before going to the party. You won't say anything, will you?'

'Hardly. Not with you knowing about me and Patrick,' Jessica assured her. 'But if you're going out now—' she went on, sounding a little crestfallen.

'No, that's OK. We could go a bit later. But are you sure about this, Jessica? What if your parents come back early?'

'No, they won't,' Jessica told them. 'Daddy likes to suck up to his boss, and won't leave till the very end. And I like to see Patrick, if only for an hour. I checked up and he who he says he is.'

'Tell you what, then,' Hillie said decisively. 'Ring him back and tell him to come round in about three quarters of an hour. That'll just give us time to pop down to see Jimmy and tell him we can't stay. Never much fancied being in a rowdy old pub, anyway. We'll come back here, but just for an hour, and go on to the party afterwards.'

'Won't get there till late, though, will we?' Gert questioned, somewhat irritated since she couldn't wait to meet Belinda's brother, Rob, again.

'That wouldn't matter, would it?' Hillie said, glaring at Gert. 'Belinda said it won't finish till gone midnight.'

'S'ppose so,' Gert shrugged back. 'All right, then, Jessica. We'll come.'

At Gert's words, a thousand stars danced in Jessica's eyes. 'Oh, that's so good of you! But only if you let me give you some money for a taxi to your party.'

'Oh, no, we couldn't—' Hillie began.

'Cor, blimey, we'd really arrive in style, then!' Gert crowed. 'You're on, girl!'

'I'll see you a bit later, then. And thanks ever so much.'

They watched Jessica cross back over the street with a spring in her step before setting off themselves.

'Never been in a taxi before, but you sure this is a good idea?' Gert asked as they turned the corner.

'Not entirely. But I know how she feels, so I suppose that's why I want to help her.'

'Well, on your head be it,' Gert warned. 'If it goes wrong, and her dad finds out and then he tells your dad, you'll be right for it.'

'Don't I know it,' Hillie murmured under her breath. But she said out loud, 'But Old Man Braithwaite's not going to find out, is he?'

She just wished she felt as confident as she sounded!

*

Dolly Maguire was slumped in the snug at the Falcon, staring at her empty gin glass. It was still early, but she'd already tossed a couple of doubles down her throat. The shakes had stopped, so now she could start savouring every sip that passed her lips. The only problem was that she was short of the readies. She'd had to cough up the bloody rent that afternoon, and she'd had to dip into the money she'd put aside for her evening out. Damn and blast. She'd already squeezed an extra bob or two from her lodgers, so what could she do? It was bleeding New Year's Eve, and she was going to have a good time, no matter what.

There was only one thing for it. Sit there quietly and watch through the gap in the finely etched-glass partition for some likely punter in the main bar. Dolly never usually came to the Falcon, so she didn't know its customers. But there was bound to be someone. Some fellow on his own, looking a bit down in the mouth. A bit scruffy and not too young. A toff, or anyone under about forty-five, wouldn't look twice at her. She wasn't daft about that. Didn't flatter herself. But it didn't matter who he was as long as he was willing and had a bit of money in his pocket. Enough to buy her a few drinks in exchange for a bit of company and a laugh.

Maybe she'd strike even luckier. Sit with her victim in this secluded snug. Lend a sympathetic ear if it was needed. That was always a good one. If he seemed the right sort, she'd slip her hand under the table, rest it on his knee. Watch his face. Slowly walk her fingers up his thigh until she found what she was looking for. Tease him. Excite him to fever pitch. Offer to take him home. Or they could do it under the railway arches. She knew where you wouldn't be seen. As long as he paid up, she didn't care. On second thoughts, the railway arches would be best, 'cos then she might get more business after that. And that hoity-toity young bitch a few doors down couldn't accuse her of turning her house into a knocking shop! If only she could goad the little tart with the truth about her own mother. From the way she'd reacted, the kid obviously didn't know, and she'd never believe it anyway, so there wasn't much point.

Dolly leant forward so that her bloodshot eyes could get a better view into the main bar. The accumulating fug of cigarette smoke dulled the glint of the gleaming brass fittings as more and more customers, mainly men, of course, were coming in from the frosty streets. Dolly squinted at them with a calculating eye as they waited, two deep, to be served, their voices loud and raucous as they called over the heads in front. The clamour increased, and someone began bashing out familiar songs on the honky-tonk piano, tuneless voices joining in. What a bleeding racket! No one would notice Dolly if she stayed where she was. But what if she went over to the piano? She knew all the words. She wouldn't kid herself about her looks, but she still had a good, strong voice. At least someone would stand her a drink or two.

She rose unsteadily to her feet, squeezing round the table. It was then that she spied the two girls sidling uncertainly through the corner door. Flaming heck. Talk of the devil, it was that prissy madam she'd been thinking of just now and her blooming friend. What the bloody hell were they doing here?

Dolly drew back just enough so that she could watch without being spotted herself. The girls seemed to hesitate, and then suddenly stepped forward when they caught the eye of one of the young lads rushed off his feet behind the bar.

Dolly all but lost her balance when the penny dropped. She hadn't recognised him before, but now she was sure the boy behind the bar was the very same she'd seen Hillie Hardwick with on that evening back in the summer. And as if to confirm her suspicions, he lifted the hinged section of the wooden bar and came round to the two little floozies. They spoke for no more than a minute, the Hardwick girl doing most of the talking. The lad nodded, they were all smiling at each other like bloody Cheshire cats. And then Dolly's heart sprang up inside her as the boy took the little trollop fleetingly in his arms and gave her a plonking great kiss.

Dolly rolled gleefully back to her seat. Ho, ho, ho! Luck was on her side that night, after all.

*

'What part of Africa do you come from?' Jessica asked, handing Patrick a cup of tea.

'I come from Nigeria,' he answered, and once again, Hillie could understand why Jessica was attracted to him. His voice was so gentle and lilting, his accent so intriguing.

'It must seem an awfully long way away,' she put in, watching Jessica sit down and place her stockinged legs discreetly to one side. 'You must miss it.'

'Yes, of course. It is a long sea journey. I have only been back twice since I came here, and I miss my family very much.'

'Why did you come here, then?' Gert asked bluntly. 'Wouldn't leave my family behind all that way.'

Patrick gave a wistful smile, his large teeth flashing between his full lips. 'I came here to study. I had received the best education my country had to offer, but to become a dentist was a different matter. I wanted to obtain the best training I could. Nigeria is a British Protectorate and English is our main language, so London was the obvious choice.'

'It must've taken a lot of courage,' Jessica said, and Hillie could see the admiration glowing on her face.

'Yes. At first, I found it very difficult. Many people distrust the colour of my skin. They think of black people as savages, but once they get to know me, they realise that is not so. It was particularly difficult when I first set up my practice, but it is growing steadily. It is my dearest wish one day to be able to set up my own school of dentistry back in Nigeria, and to pay back my family's generosity.'

'I suppose it must've cost a lot for you to come here,' Jessica observed.

'Yes. But my family is not poor. Nigeria is made up of many chiefdoms that the British authorities have always maintained. Back home, my father is a chief and I, for my sins, am what you might call a prince.'

'Blimey!' Gert nearly choked on her tea.

Patrick's mouth stretched into that winsome smile again. 'It was simply a matter of birth,' he said almost apologetically. 'I could have been born the poorest man on earth, as could any of us. But I was lucky. My family owns plantations, and my father is a good businessman. Our country grows many things that the western world wants to buy. Sugar cane and cocoa, for instance. Peanuts and coconuts. And palm nuts. That is what my father cultivates. And then he has the palm oil extracted ready to be exported.'

'Palm oil?' Hillie was more than a little surprised. 'That's one of the main ingredients of our candles.'

Patrick's grin widened. 'That was why I was so interested when you said you worked at the candle factory.'

'Only packing candles, I'm afraid.'

'Yes, but you see the end product which must be most interesting.'

'Not when you're doing it day after blooming day,' Gert moaned. 'Here, Jess, your lav out the back? That tea's gone straight through me.'

'Outside?' Jessica frowned. 'No, it's in the semi-basement next to the coalhole. At the bottom of the stairs. But you have to wash your hands in the kitchen just along the passage. I'll show you.'

'Oh, expect I can find it.'

'I'll come with you,' Hillie said, getting to her feet as well. 'And then I'm afraid we'll need to be off.'

'Of course.' Patrick stood up politely. 'I have already detained you too long.'

'No, it's been really interesting, and you've got a few minutes while we're downstairs. Come on, Gert.' And Hillie almost dragged her friend from the room.

'What you doing, leaving them two alone?' Gert hissed as they trotted down the stairs.

'They're not going to get up to anything in five minutes, are they? Look, here we are. This must be it. You go first.'

197

'Cor, this is all right, ain't it, not having to go outside in all weathers? And proper toilet paper rather than torn-up newspaper.'

'Oh, go on, shut the door and get on with it.'

Hillie waited impatiently, taking in her surroundings. There was an outside door, heavily bolted, that she realised must lead to the area steps up to the street – from the days when the house had been built and servants were obliged to use a different door from the owners of the house. She'd noticed that the wooden stairs they'd come down were bare painted wood, unlike those she'd glimpsed going up to the bedrooms that were thickly carpeted, brass stair rods gleaming. The drawing room they'd sat in was twice the size of the front room in her house, with coving around the ceiling and an ornate ceiling rose. It was beautifully furnished, as Hillie expected the rest of the house was, and she couldn't help feeling envious. She could only ever dream of living somewhere like this.

'Your turn, then.'

She used the facilities as quickly as she could, and then joined Gert in the kitchen to wash her hands. Again, the room was large, with a massive dresser on which fine crockery and shining pans were neatly displayed.

'See they still have a bathtub, mind,' Gert grinned, digging her in the ribs and pointing to a smoothly enamelled bath half-hidden behind a badly pulled curtain. 'Can't imagine old Braithwaite or his wife using that, somehow!' she chortled.

Hillie came up beside her. 'I don't know. Look at the quality of it. It's on legs, and it mightn't have taps, but the waste is plumbed in. I'd use it any day rather than the old tin thing we have to lug in from the yard each week. And yours is in a worse state than ours!'

'Well, maybe when I've had this ride in a taxi, I'll be wanting to save up for a spanking new bath and all!' Gert declared in such an airy tone that both girls fell about laughing.

*

Dolly Maguire staggered blindly along the street. Why couldn't the bleeding pavement stay still instead of waving up and down like the bloody sea? Even the blooming houses were dancing round her like a flaming merry-go-round! She'd been having a damned good evening, singing, dancing the can-can and knocking back every drink she was bought by customers grateful for her merry entertainment. It wasn't until she'd tripped over a table – what was the blasted thing doing there? – and thrown up on the floor that the landlord had told her to leave. What? After keeping all his blessed customers happy all evening? And then he'd got two of his lads to drag her outside and dump her on the pavement – and one of them was the boy that Hardwick girl was seeing! Dolly had it in for both of them now!

Was this her street? They all looked the bleeding same. She was so tired now. Just wanted to curl up and go to sleep, but it was cold enough to freeze the balls off a brass monkey and she didn't want to wake up as stiff as a board. She wanted her bed.

Now, wait a minute, this looked familiar. A street, not very long. On one side, a terrace of small houses almost straight onto the pavement. One of them could be hers. On the other side, the houses were a bit more posh. Three with tiny front gardens and bay windows, and then four grander ones with one set of steps leading up to the front door and another, behind railings, going down to the semi-basement. And, yes! At the far end of the street was another pub. This was it. She was home.

*

'That was a great party, best I've ever been to!'

'It's the only party like that we've ever been to!' Hillie chuckled as she corrected Gert from the back seat of the motorcar. 'Do thank your parents again for us, won't you, Rob? We did say thank you, but with everyone leaving at the same time, they might not have heard properly.'

'Of course I will,' Rob answered. 'Down here, you say?'

'Yeah, that's right. Pity Jessica felt she couldn't join us after all. But she was scared she wouldn't be back before her mum and dad.'

'What the—?' Rob had to swerve as a figure staggered out in front of the car.

'Oh, that's old Dolly Maguire,' Gert told him. 'Never mind her. Yeah, this is our house. Thanks ever so for the lift, Rob. I hope we'll see you again.'

'Yes, so do I,' said Rob, getting out of the car to open the doors for them. 'Happy New Year to you both.'

'And you!' they both replied. 'See you soon!'

They stood on the pavement, waiting while Rob drove off and turned out of the street. As soon as he was out of sight, Gert grabbed Hillie's hands and jumped up and down with excitement. 'Oh, I think he really liked me!' she crowed.

'Yes, I think he did,' Hillie smiled, so pleased for her friend. 'Goodnight then, Gert, and a Happy New Year!'

She turned away, waving to Gert, but the smile quickly slid from her face as she took the few yards towards her own house. A bit further down near the corner was the heap in the road that was Dolly

Maguire, and Hillie wrinkled her nose in disgust. But she had more important things on her mind than the slovenly, drunken woman. For if her dad was still up, she'd no doubt have to face the music. Happy New Year? She hoped so. But God knew what it might hold for her.

*

Dolly Maguire fell off the pavement and into the street. What the hell was that noise blaring in her lugholes? Get off the road, bloody motorcar! Just bleeding missed her! She scraped herself off the tarmac as it went on down the street and pulled up outside Stan Parker's house. And would you look at that! Stan's girl – what was her name? Didn't matter. Getting out the front, and some young geezer getting out the driver's side and shaking her hand. And then blooming Hillie Hardwick getting out the back.

Bleeding hell! First her lover boy chucks her out the pub, and now she very nearly runs her over. Dolly wasn't so drunk that she'd forget *that* in a hurry! She'd make the pair of them pay – once her head had stopped spinning and she could figure out how.

But for now, she used the lamp post to drag herself upright and then vomited into the gutter.

Chapter Ten

'Thought you'd get away with it, did you, you sly little slut?'

On the Saturday evening two weeks after the New Year's party, as Hillie let herself in the front door, glowing with the few hours she'd spent with Jimmy, the hand that shot out and grasped her by the collar was so swift that she had no time to dodge it. The next instant, she was being dragged, half choking, into the gloom of the hallway. Her own hands flew to her throat, trying to tear away the strangling grip. Grab the little fingers and bend them backwards. But she was still wearing the woollen mittens her mum had knitted her for Christmas to match the beret, and she couldn't get a hold. She fought to draw breath, air wheezing noisily in her lungs, and even as she struggled, she could feel herself coming over faint.

He slammed her against the wall then, and the pain of it stung through her neck and back, leaving her stunned and winded as she slithered helplessly down onto the linoleum. She was aware of a moment's respite as she heard the front door crash shut. Oh, thank God, it was over…

But in a flash, she was being yanked upright again. Her feet flailed in the air, but she seemed unable to find her footing before a giant fist cracked against her skull. Once, twice, she lost count as black stars wavered across her vision. She felt herself falling into a deep, dark pit. Was she lying on the cold floor again? Consciousness fled, no pain, but aware of the boot that rammed against her ribs again and again. Had she rolled into a ball to try to protect herself? She didn't really know if... or even how.

'For God's sake, get off her!' she heard her mum scream, and when she managed to drag her eyes open a slit, she saw Nell trying to restrain her dad, but he merely threw her off and sprang forward again.

The smell of sweat, of stale beer, of hate, of her own fear in her nostrils. Darkness. Nothingness.

'If I catch you so much as looking at Jimmy Baxter again, I'll kill you. Remember that, you trollop.'

Oh, yes, she'd remember that, all right. And this time, she felt all too well the agony of the vicious kick that split her sides before she passed into oblivion...

Outside, Dolly Maguire had slunk up to the door, her flabby, scarlet-painted lips twisted in a malicious, gloating leer. It had taken her a few days to sober up, get rid of the hangover and thumping head. But when she'd got herself back on her feet, she'd watched and waited for the best opportunity to reveal her secret. It hadn't come for a couple of weeks, until this evening when she'd spied the little tart heading to the cinema, hand-in-hand with her lover boy. Dolly had rubbed her hands in glee, and made her way to Harold's front door. What a welcome committee the floozy would get on her return!

Oh, how she'd enjoyed telling old Hardwick what the girl had been up to behind his back – especially as she'd persuaded him beforehand that he wanted to pay for the knowledge! She was really on her uppers that week. Life had never given her much. Her own father had shown her what men wanted and she'd survived on that since she was little more than a child. But she was getting a bit long in the tooth for it, so now she must live on her cunning and her wits instead.

And what joy to get that Miss Goody Two Shoes into trouble. Teach her to be so bloody righteous when she was just – oh, wouldn't Dolly just love to tell her! Dolly'd been a bit scared for a second, mind, when she'd told the old devil his trollop of a daughter had been deceiving him since way back in the summer. Why hadn't she told him before, he'd hissed, raising his fist. She'd had to think quickly to get out of that one! Well, it might've just been a flash in the pan, nothing for him to worry about, she'd simpered. But now it seemed to have developed into something really serious, and surely he could spare a ten-bob note for the warning?

He'd jerked his fist, but then he'd thrown two half-crowns onto the pavement. Dolly had jumped on them, and then shambled away indoors. She hadn't turned on the light. The meter had run out, so she couldn't anyway, and both her lodgers had left a few days into January, leaving her with no income from there at the minute. She'd stood by the window in the dark, tweaking the curtains and the filthy nets behind, and waited. The little strumpet usually turned up just before eleven, and it wasn't far off.

She didn't have to wait long, and she'd slipped out into the silence of the night, but kept in the shadows of her own doorway to enjoy the spectacle. A grin split her face as she heard Old Man Hardwick's roar, and the bang as he slammed the front door. Dolly couldn't resist creeping up on the outside. Oh, revenge was sweet. She could hear the thumps and crashes from inside. Then Nell's screams as she tried to protect her daughter, but not a peep from the kid herself. That was a pity. Dolly would have liked to hear her squeal.

But never mind. Dolly could feel the two large, silver-coloured coins in her pocket. It was almost closing time, but she wondered if the pub on the corner would still serve her.

*

'Why Hillie not well, Mummy?'

Daisy's worried little voice swam into Hillie's head and she heard herself groan. The grey mist that swirled in her brain was beginning to lift, but her leaden eyelids refused to open. She tried forcing them. Only one eye parted to a hazy slit, the other was stuck fast.

'I told you not to bother her, Daisy. She... fell down the stairs,' her mum lied to the small child, her words frail and faltering. 'Now you know why I always tell you to be careful going up and down.'

'Is she going to die?'

'No, of course not. But she is quite poorly.'

'I'll be all right, Daisy, love.' Hillie tried to smile, but somehow her face didn't want to work properly and even her whispered words were slurred.

'Oh, Hillie dear,' Nell breathed. 'You're coming to. At last. How d'you feel?'

'My head hurts... and... everywhere. I don't know...'

'We should get a doctor.' Luke's suppressed anger vibrated from the doorway.

'There's no money for a doctor.'

'We could get one from the Women's Hospital.'

'Your... dad wouldn't hear of it. He won't accept charity.'

'He's not the one who's hurt. And when it was him who… I'll go and get—'

'No, Luke.' Nell's voice quivered with fear. 'You don't know what you're doing. It'd only make things worse.'

'Worse? What could be worse than this?'

'All right. But we stick to our story. She fell down the stairs. But first go downstairs and fetch her some aspirin. And make sure you put the bottle back where the little ones can't reach it. Can you… manage to swallow a couple, Hillie, love?'

Hillie managed to nod but it made her head explode and she felt her whole body spinning in wild circles. Her one eyelid drooped shut again and she drifted away. The next thing she knew, her mum was lifting her head to get her to sip some water and swallow the vile-tasting pills. She must have lost some minutes, but it was all a bit of a fog.

'You rest now, dear,' her mum was saying from far, far away. Rest? She was incapable of anything else.

*

Footsteps on the stairs. Hillie recoiled from her sleep, terrified it was… But through the slit of her one eye, she saw her brother's tortured face in the doorway.

'Hill?' he murmured, tiptoeing in. 'I was still awake and I heard what happened. I should go to the police.'

'No, Luke,' Hillie managed to mumble. 'He'd only take it out on Mum even worse than this.'

'But they could stop him, and we could get away—'

'They don't like getting involved in domestic stuff. And he hasn't hurt any of you younger ones, and I'm not a child anymore. So promise me, Luke. No police. And then let me sleep.'

It overcame her again, the numbing, welcome nothingness where her head didn't pound and her eye didn't burn. She sank willingly beneath its waves.

*

It had been a week. The kind lady doctor from the hospital had frowned knowingly at the lie, but had prescribed nothing more than painkillers and rest, and now Hillie was anxious to get back to work. Any longer, and she could lose her job. She wouldn't care about it for herself, but her mum needed the money. Without it, she knew Nell would let herself starve while she watched her children eat.

'You fell down the stairs, remember?' Harold hissed in her ear as she poured her bruised body into her coat.

She couldn't even be afraid of him. She still ached too much for that. He couldn't hurt her any worse than he already had. And she was defying him, wasn't she, by returning to work? Showing him she could withstand anything he threw at her. She'd keep to the story, but the way she told it, everyone would realise it wasn't the truth.

'Bleeding hell, Hillie!' Gert gasped as they met on the street corner. 'No wonder they wouldn't let me in to see you.'

Hillie had tried to pull the slack of the beret over the side of her face, but it hadn't worked. Nothing could hide the livid bruise that spread from her forehead down to her jaw, or her swollen, bloodshot eye. And she was walking hunched up and with her arms folded across her sore ribs.

'Fell down the stairs, my eye!' Gert scoffed, her voice sparking with rage. 'It was him, wasn't it? Your dad.'

Hillie succeeded in squinting at her sideways. 'You guessed,' she grated meaningfully. 'I didn't tell you. He found out about me and Jimmy.'

'Well, that don't surprise me. I'll give him bloody what for—'

'No, Gert. Let it rest for now.'

Gert's face looked as if it would blow up with fury and Hillie watched her cheeks puff up like angry balloons. 'All right. But this can't go on. And you sure you should be coming back to work?'

'Oh, yes.' Hillie felt her heart jerk as her resolve strengthened. 'It's a way of standing up to him.'

'Ain't you done enough of that already? And Jimmy'll go mad when he sees you. He was like a cat on hot bricks all last week. I know I wasn't keen on you two getting together, but he's been all right to you, has Jimmy.'

Hillie's hand shot out and grasped Gert's arm. 'You'll have to tell Jimmy the truth. But promise me you'll keep him away from me. For the time being, at least. And keep him away from my dad as well. He'd do the same as this to him, or probably worse. Or he'd take it out on Mum, and that's the last thing I want.'

'Yeah, yeah, I promise,' Gert sighed with bitter reluctance. 'But we're gonna sort this out one way or the other. Things can't go on like this. And you're going in on the tram. You're not walking all that way as well as standing at the bench all day. Here.' She pulled out Hillie's hand and emptied her purse into her friend's palm. 'It's me tea money for the week. I'll just have a glass of water each day instead.'

Hillie stared down at the copper and brass coins. No, she couldn't accept. But it was so tempting. She was armed with a bottle of aspirin, but she didn't know how she was going to get through the day.

Tears of gratitude pooled in her eyes. 'You're one in a million, Gert. I'll pay you back as soon as I can. And… you'll talk to Jimmy for me?'

'Course I will, kiddo. Told you. Mates forever, you and me.'

'Oh, Gert, I'd hug you if I didn't think it'd hurt too much.'

'Well, you just get on the tram. Look, there's one coming,' Gert said, herding her across Battersea Park Road. 'I'll catch up with you later.'

'Ta ever so, Gert.'

Hillie didn't have a chance to say more as she heaved herself up into the crowded tram. She must have looked awful as people glanced furtively at her, their faces either etched with sympathy or frowning in suspicion. At least she was offered a seat straightaway, and she sank into it gratefully.

Her and Jimmy, she thought as the tram rattled along. As if she'd been thinking about anything else the whole week she'd been lying in bed. They'd made up a foursome a couple of times with Gert and Belinda's brother, Rob. But on that last, fateful evening together, it'd just been the two of them, and they'd been oh, so close. Dreaming of their future. Would they continue to live in London, or would they be able to move to a little cottage in the country somewhere? That was what Hillie really wanted, but she realised it could be years before they could do so.

There was no harm in talking about it, though. And Jimmy had shown her his Post Office Savings Book, so she knew he was serious about it all.

But what did it matter now? She was trapped. It didn't really make any difference how much she stood up to her dad, did it? He'd always have the upper hand. His beating had knocked the stuffing out of her, and resignation gnawed at her heart as she began to understand how her mother gave into him all the time.

Was there ever to be a way out? At that moment, she couldn't imagine it.

*

Hillie crumpled into a chair at one of the long tables in the canteen, helped by May and Ethel, two of the older women who'd worked in the candle-packing shed most of their lives. Sitting down wasn't much better for Hillie than standing up, and she reached at once for the little bottle of aspirin in her pocket.

As she did so, she saw Jimmy coming through the doors. His gaze swept along the rows of tables and found her almost instantly. Even at that distance, Hillie saw the horror on his face and he went to bound forward. But Gert had been waiting for him. True to her word, she held him back, though it was clearly a struggle and she was talking to him with obvious urgency. Whatever she said, though, seemed to convince him, and Hillie saw her drag Jimmy to a table on the far side, even though he kept glancing back at her across the room.

'You can't work like this,' Belinda said, appearing from nowhere. 'Several of the packets you did this morning fell apart. Go home. I've spoken to Personnel in the office and you won't lose your job if you don't come in for the rest of the week. And I can help you out with some money.'

Hillie glanced up. Dear Belinda, she was so kind, but she didn't understand. She had to fight this. Show her dad…

'Cor, don't look a gift horse and all that,' May declared almost enviously as she lit a cigarette. 'What I wouldn't give to put me feet up for a week.'

'Come on,' Belinda beckoned, helping Hillie to her feet and ushering her towards the doors. 'And don't look back at Jimmy or anyone else. If there's any more trouble, both you and your dad are likely to be out on your ear.'

'But… I only fell down the stairs,' Hillie protested.

'We all know you didn't. Gert spilt the beans when I pressed her. Not that I've told anyone else. But everyone's guessed it was your dad. We don't know what you did to make him so angry, but his temper's well known. So go home till this all blows over.'

Hillie nodded. Defeated. But only for now. But... until it all blew over? Fat chance of that. Where would it all end? At that moment, she had no idea.

*

She didn't go home. She thought she'd suffocate if she did. She went to Gert's house instead, praying Eva would be in. She was.

Eva's face dropped a mile when she opened the door. Within five minutes, she had Hillie tucked up in Gert's bed with a cup of tea. The good woman must have sworn the little ones to silence as the house soon fell so blissfully quiet that Hillie drifted asleep.

The next thing she knew, Gert was shaking her gently.

'Hillie, wake up. You'd best try and get home before your dad. But first, I've got some news for you.'

Hillie blinked the sleep from her eyes. She still ached but she did feel better for a few hours' rest.

'News?' she mumbled. 'What news? The only news I want to hear is that my dad's walked under a bus.'

'It's better than that. At least, it might be. But first of all, I'll tell you what happened at work this afternoon. After you left, someone knocked their hot tea over your dad's lap in the canteen. Accidentally on purpose, if you know what I mean. And then, as he walked out, someone else stuck out their foot and tripped him up,' Gert crowed, her eyes opening wide with derision. 'And then later on, he got locked in a store room.'

'What?' Hillie might have found it amusing if she hadn't held her dad in such contempt.

'Yeah,' Gert grinned. 'No one knows who did it, but it was ages before he was discovered and he was furious. But…' The laughter slid from her face as she became more serious. 'I've got a message for you from Jimmy. It's a dead funny way to propose, but he wants me to tell you that he wants you to marry him.'

'*Marry* him?' Hillie lifted her head but instantly wished she hadn't and let herself fall back heavily onto the pillow. 'Huh, and how does he think I could do that? My dad's not going to give his consent after *this*, is he?'

'You wouldn't need his consent. Not if you went to Gretna Green.'

'Gretna Green!'

'Yeah. Just over the border in Scotland where you can tie the knot without your dad's consent. And anyone can marry you. Usually it's a local blacksmith.'

'Blacksmith?' Hillie cried in confusion.

'Yup. Over an anvil, apparently. Quite romantic.' Gert took her hands, gazing excitedly into her eyes with such intensity that Hillie found herself sitting up again, but this time more slowly. 'Think about it, Hill. While you're living at home, your dad seems to have some sort of hold over you. But you'd be free of him if you was married to Jimmy.'

'But... what about Mum?'

'You've said yourself, she's a lost cause. Won't leave him. And maybe without you around, goading him all the time – 'cos you do, Hill, you know you do. Not that I blame you. But without you there, things might just settle down. And she's told you to get away before, hasn't she? So now's your chance, girl.'

'But...'

'No ifs or buts. Seems to me the only question is, d'you *want* to marry Jimmy? 'Cos he's keen as mustard to marry *you*.'

Hillie stared at her, chewing her lip and unaware of the aches in her head and body. She was so taken aback that she couldn't think straight right now. 'But... how would we get there, anyway?'

'What, to Scotland? Train, of course. Only problem is, you're supposed to live there for three weeks beforehand. Means you could lose your jobs, but Jimmy says that don't matter. He's got plenty of savings, and he reckons he could work full-time at the pub. Just means when you got back, you'd have to wait a bit longer to move somewhere better than his little bedsit.'

'I could put up with that—'

Gert's eyes narrowed with cunning. 'So you do want to, then? Well, maybe there's an overnight train or something. You know Kit's been working as a clerk in the Station Master's Office since the New Year. He can easily find out for you. The last train of the day, so even if your dad twigged it and tried to follow you, by the time he got there, you and Jimmy could be hiding at a remote farm or something. He wouldn't spend three weeks waiting for you to turn up at one of the places you can get spliced, and I don't suppose he'd spend out the money for the train fare in the first place. And once you got back, if he ever tried to attack you again, it'd be a criminal matter. The police don't like interfering in family affairs. Well, they would if you was a kiddy, but you're grown up now. So if you was Jimmy's wife, you wouldn't be part of the family no more. And I don't think even your dad'd be so stupid. Especially not after everyone's realised what really happened this time.'

Hillie slowly pursed her lips. How much longer could she face her father's temper? She wanted to protect her mum, but she couldn't do so forever. And she did love Jimmy very, very much. The walks in the park, the films that had made them laugh or cry at the flicks, their first proper kiss on the river embankment that balmy summer evening. But did she truly want to become Mrs Baxter? Sacrifice having her dream wedding with all her family and friends there to share it with? At that moment, yes, she did.

She groaned and bowed her head. Though it filled her with shame, deep down, she knew she didn't have the strength to face anything like the beating her dad had given her ever again.

So, she slowly nodded her head.

Chapter Eleven

When Hillie hadn't turned up for the evening meal that Friday night at the end of February, her father had scraped her dinner into the bin.

'Harold, don't do that,' Nell had protested. 'We can't afford to waste good food. She'll be in soon, wanting her dinner.'

'If she can't turn up on time, she'll have to go hungry,' Harold snarled back. 'She knows the rules. Teach her a lesson.'

'She's probably with Gert and just forgot the time. I'm sure she'll be back in a few minutes.'

'Well, she'll be too bloody late. You others, you see what happens when you disobey me?'

Luke glanced up darkly. 'Yes, Dad,' he muttered. But then, driven by his shame at his usual lack of courage, he dared to go on, 'But I'm sure Mum's right, and Hillie'll be back soon.'

'Don't you backchat me, or dinner'll go the same way.'

Luke lowered his eyes and got on with eating. Not that he wanted anything. Every morsel tasted like cardboard.

When Hillie still hadn't appeared by the time the younger children were in bed, Harold was pacing the floor like a caged bear. Finally he slammed his fist on the table, making the ready-laid breakfast cutlery jump in the air.

'She should be bloody back by now,' he barked. 'I'm going to the Parkers' to drag her home by the hair if need be.'

Nell grasped his arm. 'Oh, Harold, dear, don't do that. Don't make a scene. She doesn't deserve it.'

'I'll be the judge of that!'

He stormed out of the front door, slamming it behind him. A brittle silence followed, in which Nell and Luke stared at each other in horror.

'D'you know where she is?' Nell squeaked.

Luke shook his head. But he didn't like lying. Especially not to his mum. 'She's gone,' he admitted, forcing the croak from his throat.

He wished he hadn't as Nell's face drained of any colour it might have had.

'Gone?' she repeated in a whisper.

'Yes, but don't worry. She'll be back. And when she is, she'll be married.'

'*Married!*'

'To a bloke at the factory. The one Dad beat her up for seeing in secret. Gone to that place in Scotland. Be halfway there by now. You have to stay there for three weeks. But when she gets back, as a married woman, there'll be trouble if Dad ever tries anything again.'

'Ooo,' Nell breathed, pursing her lips as the news percolated her stunned mind and thoughts began to chase each other around crazily in her head. It would hardly be the wedding she wanted for her darling girl. She wouldn't even be there to witness it herself. But, oh, the relief that Hillie would be safe at last. Nell might not have met this fellow, but Hillie wasn't daft. She wouldn't marry him if he wasn't a good sort. 'Well, good for her. Oh, watch it. Here he comes.'

The door nearly came off its hinges as Harold crashed back into the room, his puce face almost on fire.

'She's not there!' he bellowed. 'Neither of them are! Gone out and not told me. Well, I won't let her out of my sight from now on.'

'Don't be too hard on her, dear,' Nell ventured.

'D'you know something?' Harold suddenly jumped at her, grasping her wrist across the table.

'Know something?' she replied, wide-eyed with feigned innocence. 'What d'you mean? Why should I know something?'

'Huh!' Harold let go with a jerk. 'Well, I'm off to the pub. And she'd better be here when I get back.'

He turned towards the door, and Nell winked at Luke behind his back. Peace for a few hours – until the fireworks really began. But Nell wouldn't care what happened. Her little girl had done what she'd never had the courage to do. What she'd wanted Hillie to do. And now she had, Nell could be content.

'Why aren't you worried she's not back?' Harold demanded, shaking her awake when he rolled in after closing time. 'You *do* know something, don't you?'

He grasped a hank of Nell's hair, pulling her head from the pillow as she blinked her eyes awake.

'I don't know what you mean,' she managed to gasp. 'She's with Gert, so whatever they're doing, they'll be all right together.'

'I don't believe you!' He gave her a clout that made her teeth rattle. 'Tell me, or you'll get what for.'

'I can't tell you what I don't know, can I?'

'You lying bitch! Always the same, you deceitful little cow! And when I think what I've done for you and that brat of yours, and this is how you repay me!'

He hit her again. She went to curl up into a ball to protect herself, but all of a sudden she felt she'd reached the end of her tether. Had paid enough for her mistake. Hillie had stood up to him, and now it was her turn.

She tried. Fought him off, slapped at his hands. Trying to catch them. It wasn't until she managed to kick the bedcovers clear and bring her knee up where it hurt most that he fell back with an oath that turned the air blue.

'Remember what I've done for you, too!' she grated, and turned her back on him while he nursed his aching manhood. At least he wouldn't want to exercise *that* for a while, she thought triumphantly. And as Harold went quiet and was soon lost to drunken snoring, Nell began to wonder. Her Hillie married. And who was this chap she'd been seeing? But as long as he treated her well, Nell would be happy.

*

Kit couldn't sleep. He'd been tossing and turning for hours, going over the scene in his head. Gert had come to him, explaining everything, and who was he to stand in Hillie's way, especially if it meant she would be rescued from Harold Hardwick's clutches? Kit had worked it all out for them and got Hillie and this Jimmy Baxter on the train. The two hadn't met since the night of Harold's vicious attack on his daughter several weeks past now. Everything had been organised through Gert, and that evening Hillie had rushed into Jimmy's arms, her now mended face aglow.

Kit had remained on the platform, watching her steam out of his life forever. Well, not quite out of his life, or even out of his heart, for she'd stay there until the day he died. And that would make the pain even harder to bear. She loved Jimmy Baxter, not him. This marriage was what she wanted. Kit would have laid down his life to save her from that brute of a father. But Jimmy Baxter had got there first.

Kit got out of bed and padded across the cold, bare floor of his bedsit to the window. Lamp posts cast their circle of grey light on the deserted street below. They'd be turned off before too long as dawn broke. By the time they came on again that evening, Hillie would be hiding out somewhere, hundreds of miles away, and in three weeks' time, she'd be returning as Mrs Hilda Baxter. Lost to him for eternity.

But at least she'd be safe.

He rested his forehead against the cool, comforting glass of the windowpane. And felt his heart tear in two.

*

'Well, how does it feel to be Mrs Baxter?'

They were sitting together on the end of the bed in the little room in the cheapest B and B they could find. But it was clean and the landlady was very pleasant. And so she should be, Jimmy had grimaced, after the wodge of pound notes he'd given her to say they'd been lodging with her for the past few weeks. As far as he was concerned, the quicker they got hitched the better, just in case Hardwick worked things out and came looking for them. And so, after just two days, one of the local blacksmiths had been happy for them to make their vows over his anvil – again in exchange for a sizeable backhander. But it had all been worth it in Jimmy's eyes.

Hillie turned the cheap wedding ring round on her finger. 'Wonderful. Safe,' she murmured. 'Thank you, Jimmy.'

'No need for any thanks,' Jimmy answered thickly. 'I love you.'

He turned to her, his chocolate eyes soft with wonder as his hand caressed her cheek. She tipped her head against his palm, closing her eyes, and he drew her forward until his lips met hers. She kissed him back, loving the feel of her mouth against his. But inside her chest, her heart was thumping. She knew what she had to do, and in a way she wanted to do it. But she was also very scared.

She kept her eyes shut as she felt Jimmy begin to undress her. She dutifully raised her arms for him to pull off her jumper, and then stood up so that he could unzip her skirt. She felt fragile, vulnerable. But Jimmy's own shy smile reassured her.

'I don't think I'm very good with suspenders,' he said playfully. 'And I wouldn't want to ladder your stockings.'

Hillie's mouth curved in an uncertain smile. So Jimmy felt awkward, too. Well, that must be a first for him, she thought fondly as she removed her stockings and suspender belt, and then stood before him in her petticoat. Trembling. Shivering. Her stomach cramped. What next? Should she undress completely, expose herself, her frailty, to him?

'It's freezing in here. Shall we get into bed?' Jimmy gulped.

Weak with relief, Hillie dived in between the sheets. It might be less embarrassing if Jimmy couldn't *see* her. But – oo! The landlady had put hot-water bottles in the bed as she had done in the separate rooms they'd had on the two previous nights. That was thoughtful. At least if Hillie was shaking, it wouldn't be from cold.

She pulled the blankets up to her neck, and now she watched as Jimmy undressed, her curiosity overtaking her nerves. He was slight of build, of course, with a thin chest which he sensibly kept hidden beneath his vest. He kept his pants on, too. Odd, baggy things that nevertheless couldn't conceal his growing excitement.

Oh, help.

He slipped into bed beside her, and they snuggled down together to get warm. Perhaps that would be it. She'd be spared. For now, at least.

But as they warmed up, Jimmy began to stroke her arms and his hands quickly found their way to the steep curve of her breasts. He'd touched her before, through her clothes, and a thrill of desire had slithered down her spine. But now, as he felt beneath her brassière and rolled her nipple between his fingers, she held her breath. It felt, well, not quite right. But she supposed she must grit her teeth. There was more to come. And she did love Jimmy. It must be the same for every young woman the first time, and she'd soon get used to it.

As he kissed her, his lips moving more urgently now, he reached down to the inside of her thighs. He didn't seem to notice her flinch. She almost wanted to push him away, but she mustn't. This was what married couples did. And he'd rescued her from God knew what from her dad.

Jimmy was wriggling down in the bed now, doing something to his own attire. A moment later, he was pulling off her knickers. She stiffened as his fingers briefly probed between her legs and before she knew it, he was drawing her knees apart. She had to stifle her gasp of pain as he pushed himself inside her. He wasn't being rough, she realised that. But it still burned so much as he moved himself in and out, up and down, seemingly oblivious to anything else as he took his own pleasure. He suddenly seemed to judder and then, thank God, he withdrew himself.

The soreness and stinging stayed with her, but it wasn't quite as bad now. Jimmy was smiling so sweetly at her, his dark eyes melting with love. She couldn't tell him how much it hurt. How she felt degraded. And instead she returned his smile. She'd heard women at the factory joking about it. How it got better in time. How you could even come to enjoy it. She couldn't imagine that. But she could tolerate it. Because she loved Jimmy. Really she did. And when she thought of her poor mum being subjected to that by her dad, year in year out, and doubtless more by force and nowhere near as gently as Jimmy had her, she thanked her lucky stars.

'Oh, my love, don't cry,' Jimmy was saying, thumbing away a tear on her cheek.

'Am I?' she asked in genuine surprise. 'I hadn't realised.'

'I know. It's a big thing. We'll take it gently. Come on. Cuddle up. We need to get some sleep. Early start in the morning. We can be back at work on Wednesday. Two days off instead of three weeks. Oh, and Saturday morning, of course. But it was worth the extra money for the bribes.'

'Yes.' Hillie was feeling more relaxed now. 'And maybe when we speak to Personnel, if we're lucky, they'll just dock our pay instead of giving us the sack.'

'Yeah. Price's have always been a good company to work for. Only got to think of their pension scheme for that.'

'Well, I'd rather not have to think that far ahead,' Hillie chuckled now.

'Why not? Grow old together, you and me. Lots of kids and grandchildren. Might've been an unconventional wedding, but the rest of our life together's gonna be great!'

He turned out the bedside lamp, and Hillie was grateful for his comforting arm about her, holding her close. That was more like it. He made her feel safe. Yes, tomorrow they had a train to catch. And then she'd have to face the music. But her dad wouldn't be able to hurt her again now.

Would he?

Chapter Twelve

'Where the hell have you been?' Harold roared as Hillie opened the kitchen door the following evening. And when Jimmy followed her into the room, she saw her father's jaw clench so tightly she thought his teeth might crack. 'Five bloody days! Your mother's been frantic. Been with this bastard, I suppose? Guessed as much, seeing as he'd skived off at the same time. How dare you bring him here when I've forbidden you to see him!'

Hillie braced herself. This was exactly what she'd expected, but she was ready for it. 'You can forbid all you like,' she retorted, eyes glinting like steel. 'Jimmy's my husband now. I've only come to get my things.'

'He's *what?*'

'We was married yesterday,' Jimmy informed him caustically. 'In Scotland. All perfectly legal, so there's nothing you can do about it. Hillie, go upstairs and get your things. We're not staying.'

'My God, I didn't expect even do something as bloody underhand as that!' Harold bellowed. 'And dead right you're not staying,' was the last Hillie heard as she scooted up the stairs, thankful for the few minutes' respite. As she stuffed her few belongings into two string bags, she could hear her father ranting in the room below. It didn't take her long to gather up her clothes, toiletries and the few other bits and pieces she possessed before she hurried back down.

Jimmy was squaring up to her father, his face grim with anger and determination. His slight form was half Harold's size, but he was taller and had both youth and the fire of righteousness on his side. Hillie glanced across at her mother who, despite the shock announcement, appeared to be observing Jimmy with avid curiosity. The younger children gazed on, wide-eyed with bewilderment, while Luke – dear Luke who'd been in on the plan – was successfully feigning total innocence.

'Well, congratulations!' With a sudden rush of defiance, Nell sprang to her feet and hugged Hillie tightly, putting her mouth close to her daughter's ear. 'I knew,' she breathed from between clamped teeth so that no one else could hear. 'Luke told me. Good for you.'

But before Hillie could take in her mum's words, Harold swung round and brutally thrust his wife back down into her chair. 'No!' he yelled at Nell so loudly that Hillie physically cringed. 'You're never, *ever* to see her again! And if I ever catch any of you so much as talking to your sister again,' Harold snarled, eyes stabbing at his terrified children, 'I'll tan your hides so hard, you won't be able to sit down for a week. Now, get out!' he bawled, whipping back round to Hillie and Jimmy. 'Get out, get out!'

'Don't worry, we're going!' Jimmy spat with equal contempt. 'And Hillie won't be coming back. She's my wife now, and if you ever try to hurt her again, you'll have me to answer to. It'll count as assault, and I won't be afraid to call in the police. Remember that. Come on, Hillie, love. We're leaving.'

Hillie hesitated for just one moment. She wanted so much to hug her mum again, but she knew Nell would pay for it afterwards if she did. To forbid her to see her mother or her brother and sisters again was a spear in her very soul. She couldn't even give them one last hug to say goodbye. She met Nell's gaze, their eyes clinging, and Hillie felt her heart clench in agony as Jimmy took her hand and dragged her out of the house.

Oh, dear Lord, what had she done? She'd saved herself, but at what cost?

Just then, she felt like the most gutless coward who'd ever walked the earth.

*

Gert's warm, encompassing welcome a few moments later lifted her from her misery, slipping around her like a soft, cosy blanket on a cold winter's night.

'Oh, you're back! Why so soon? You did actually…? Oh, what am I thinking of? Come on, come inside.'

'Yes, we are married,' Hillie assured her friend as they stepped over the threshold. But somehow the words were coming out of her mouth of their own accord. 'Jimmy managed to charm the landlady into saying we'd already been there three weeks, with a little help from his wallet. And the same with the blacksmith who married us.'

'Golly. Well, congratulations!'

Hillie still felt numb as Gert wrapped her in a bear hug before herding them along the dark passageway to the back room. As she opened the door, the familiar scene suddenly made Hillie want to weep. Why couldn't she just turn the clock back to when they were children? To when, apart from her dad's strict discipline, the world had been a happy place and she'd been too young to comprehend what her mum had been going through.

'Mum, this is Jimmy,' Gert told her mother, and Hillie saw surprise register on Eva's face as she followed her friend into the kitchen. 'You know after Hillie's dad came storming round here, I told you they'd gone to Scotland to get married? Well, they managed to tie the knot within a few days, so now they're back.'

Jimmy held out his hand. 'Mrs Parker,' he said with a smile. 'We met once before, very briefly, in the park.'

'So we did. Charmed, I'm sure.'

Eva shook his hand, but Hillie thought her greeting a trifle tight-lipped. But it had been a long day and she was tired, so perhaps she was mistaken.

'Jimmy,' Stan nodded flatly, dipping his head, 'I hope you're going to take care of this girl of ours now you've taken her away from us.'

Hillie smiled grimly to herself. It was comforting that Stan thought of her as part of his own family. If only she really had been, how differently her life would have turned out.

'Of course,' Jimmy assured him defensively. 'Protect her with me life, I will.'

'Let's hope it don't come to that,' Hillie caught Eva muttering under her breath.

'And… have you see your dad yet?' Gert dared to ask.

Hillie felt as if she'd been doused in icy water yet again. 'Yes,' she murmured, her throat closing up. 'He's… he's forbidden me to see any of my family again,' she blurted out before the strangling tears that welled up inside began to choke her.

'What?' everyone chorused in horror.

'Well!' Eva hitched up her ample bosom. 'We'll see about that!'

'Oh, Mrs P, I know you mean well, but…'

'It's been a long day,' Jimmy interrupted, trying to smooth things over for his new wife, 'and I need to get Hillie home. Expect you're knackered, eh, Hill?'

'Yes, I am,' she murmured, suddenly feeling so tired, she just wanted to hide herself away and curl up into a cocoon, cutting out all else.

'I'll come to the door with you,' Gert announced.

'See you all again soon!'

Gulping down her sadness, Hillie tried to put some brightness into her voice. All her life, she'd been in and out of Number Eight almost every day. She hadn't really considered how much she'd miss that, and regret stuck in her throat. Of course, she could still come round whenever she wanted, but it wouldn't be the same as living almost next-door. For a moment, it made her feel as if she'd lost not just one family, but two.

'Well, I'll see you at work tomorrow,' Gert said, ushering her and Jimmy back along the hall. 'As you've only been away a few days, let's hope you won't lose your jobs. And what about… you know what?' she asked, dropping her voice so that Jimmy couldn't hear.

Hillie felt her heart jump. What could she say? But she knew she had to say something. 'OK,' she whispered, praying Gert wouldn't probe any further. She couldn't tell her that she wasn't sure. That she was dreading getting back to Jimmy's bedsit and having to do 'it' again before they went to sleep. She gave Gert a quick hug and was relieved when Jimmy led her outside before Gert could ask any more probing questions.

When they finally arrived back at Jimmy's digs, Hillie cowered in the damp, dingy hallway while the landlady scrutinised the marriage certificate Jimmy waved under her nose. But it wasn't because of the woman's sour expression, or because of what she'd be expected to do again once they were squeezed into the single bed. No. It was because, with her dad's vicious words still ringing in her ears, Hillie'd had enough of nasty, belligerent people, and this mean-mouthed landlady was too much for her.

Finally, though, the tyrant was convinced and reluctantly allowed them up to Jimmy's room. It was the end of February and so cold. Hillie could feel the dampness exuding from the walls. The smell of it got into her nostrils. At least her old home had been dry, and Hillie felt a twinge of regret. But this was her home now, until they could afford to move on.

'Cor, pretty parky in here, ain't it?' Jimmy was rubbing his hands together. 'Keep your coat on, love, till it warms up.'

Hillie stood, looking about the room she'd only seen briefly before, while Jimmy lit the gas fire and then disappeared with the kettle. There was a single bed with a chest of drawers beside it, an old wardrobe, an armchair with the horsehair stuffing hanging out and a rickety table that evidently served as Jimmy's kitchen. And that was it.

'Bathroom and lav's just along the landing,' Jimmy told her cheerfully as he came back in with the kettle filled with water. He lit the one gas ring and put the kettle on to boil. 'Take a while, that. And then we'll have a nice cuppa and I'll put the hot-water bottles in the bed. Bought an extra one for you, I did,' he grinned, and then, opening the window, brought in a bottle of milk that had evidently been sitting on the sill outside all the time they'd been away, to keep cool, Hillie guessed – even though it was almost cold enough to freeze in the room itself. 'Damn birds've been at it,' Jimmy complained as he pulled off the remains of the pecked silver top and sniffed at the contents. 'Smells a little bit off, but I think it's OK. Course, I wasn't sure we'd be back so quick. You can have Ovaltine if you want. Might as well use up the milk before it goes off completely.'

'That'd be nice, actually,' Hillie replied, feigning a smile.

'Your wish is my command, madam,' Jimmy laughed, measuring milk into two chipped mugs before transferring it into a battered saucepan and swapping it for the kettle on the gas ring. 'Why don't you unpack while you're waiting?'

Hillie nodded, sniffing back the dewdrop that the cold air had caused to form at the end of her nose. She could swear it was even colder in the room than it had been outside as she emptied her possessions onto the bed. Jimmy had as few clothes as she did, so there was plenty of room for her own things in the wardrobe and drawers.

'Here you are, love.' Jimmy handed her the steaming mug and then poured some water from the kettle into the dirty saucepan. 'Have to wash up in the bowl there,' he explained, 'and then empty it down the bathroom sink. You'll soon get used to it. I thought about tarting the place up a bit. But any money I spent'd be money we didn't have for moving on. You OK with that?'

Hillie nodded, trying to hide her true feelings as she wrapped her cold hands round the hot mug. It wasn't as if she was used to the Ritz, but the gas fire was totally inadequate for the room, and the fumes were rasping at her throat. The malty drink was soothing, though, and she drank it down quickly before it cooled down.

'I'll just use the lav and do my teeth,' she said when she'd finished and, gathering what she needed, went along the landing. The toilet and bathroom were like iceboxes, and none too clean. The one thing Hillie vowed she *would* spend some money on was a china wash bowl, the next day if she had the chance.

There was no way she could ever use the green-stained bath with the scum marks ingrained up its sides! A good stripped wash would have to suffice for the foreseeable future.

'You get ready for bed, love,' Jimmy said as she re-entered the grotty bedsit, which was the only way she could describe it. 'I'll be with you in a mo.'

Jimmy left the room, armed with his toothbrush. Hillie took the opportunity to change into her nightdress and slip into bed. She was sure it was damp, and gratefully cuddled one of the hot-water bottles Jimmy had thoughtfully put there, while she put the other one at her feet. At least she should have thawed out by the time Jimmy came back and she had to foray into that frightening world again.

'Bit of a squash, ain't it?' he observed, wriggling in beside her a few minutes later. 'I know this ain't a good start, but I'll make everything all right for you, you'll see. Now let's get to sleep. You must be knackered and it's too cold for any hanky-panky. Anyway, I expect you're a bit sore. They say it takes women a bit to get used to it, and I doesn't want to hurt you. Take things gently we will, just like I said. So nighty-night, love. Sweet dreams. And don't you worry about that bastard of a father of yours. I'm really sorry about what he said just now. But we'll try and find a way to get round it, so don't let him upset you.'

'Mmm, yes. Thanks, Jimmy.'

Hillie turned towards him on her side, her head on his shoulder. Besides, it was the only way they could fit comfortably in the bed. She relished the feel of his warm body alongside hers, even if he was a bit bony. He was going to be a considerate husband. So perhaps the hanky-panky, as Jimmy called it, would come more easily with time, after all.

She lay in the darkness, listening to Jimmy's steady breathing as sleep claimed him. Yes, he *would* make things right for her, she was sure. But would she ever manage to see her family again? The pain of it sliced into her heart. For in solving one problem for her, Jimmy, her husband, had only succeeded in creating another, far worse, one.

*

'Golly, you dark horses!' Belinda chuckled when they went into the office to see to the necessary administration their marriage would create – and whether they'd be able to hang onto their jobs.

They'd been severely reprimanded by the chap in charge of Personnel, but he admitted they were both good at their jobs and it would take time to train up replacements for them.

'And of course, you're Harold Hardwick's daughter, aren't you?' he quizzed Hillie, looking up at her over the rim of his spectacles. 'Hmm. Well, I'll have to dock your pay, both of you, and if anything like this happens again, you'll be out on your ears.'

They'd both thanked him profusely and, filled with relief, had stopped briefly at Belinda's desk as they passed.

'Well, you can understand why we had to keep it all a secret,' Hillie grimaced. 'One hint of it, and my dad would've locked me up for good. So the fewer people knew about it, the better.'

'Of course, I understand,' Belinda grinned. 'Quite cloak and dagger stuff, eh? But… you must have a party to celebrate!' she declared, jumping up and down with excitement.

'Fat chance of that in our little room. And I can't imagine the landlady would agree. You should see her. She'd make the Grim Reaper turn and run.'

'I'll ask my mum and dad, then. They love having parties. And what with our Rob courting your Gert… You could ask whoever you wanted.'

'Oh, no, we couldn't expect—'

'I'll have a word with them tonight. I'm sure they'll be only too pleased.'

Hillie nailed a grateful smile on her face. It'd be so very kind of Belinda's parents, but Hillie's own family, her *real* family, wouldn't be able to go, would they? And she felt the knife twist in the wound.

'Well, I suppose it looks respectable enough,' Charles Braithwaite frowned as the taxi drew up outside the substantial semi-detached Victorian villa in Parsons Green where Belinda's family lived. 'I want to speak with this Belinda's parents before we leave you here, mind.'

'I'm surprised you even considered letting her come at all!' his wife complained. 'Running away to get married, indeed.'

'At least they were doing the honourable thing, Mum,' Jessica protested. 'And it's not as if Hillie was pregnant or anything—'

'Jessica!' her mother cried, aghast.

'Well, she wasn't. And it was the only way to escape her father. He's really violent, you know.'

'Don't we!' Charles put in. 'Despicable brute. Thank goodness we don't need to have anything to do with him. I hate living on the same street, even if we are on opposite sides. As soon as I get my next promotion, we'll be off somewhere better.'

Jessica rolled her eyes. She'd heard that one so many times before. The thing was, there wasn't really anything he could be promoted *to*, unless it was some sort of director, and Jessica could see that would be a long time coming, if ever. It was a case of waiting for dead men's shoes. Besides, her father wasn't as posh as he thought he was, and that's what it seemed to Jessica you needed to be. If only he'd let her go out to work so that she didn't need the generous allowance he gave her. And if her mother would deign to run the house instead of employing Mrs Dawson to do everything, then perhaps there'd be enough in the pot for them to be able to move to a more salubrious neighbourhood. Not that Jessica wanted to. Most of the people living in the area were perfectly respectable even if they were poor, and now that Jessica was friendly with the Parkers, she didn't want to move away.

Not that her parents approved, and they did everything to curtail her relationship with the chaotic family. It was only because Jessica had convinced her father that Belinda's family were a cut above that he'd agreed to consider allowing her to attend the belated wedding celebration. He'd even brought home a box containing what was left of a dinner service that had been dropped at work and half of it smashed, saying that Jessica could give it to Hillie and Jimmy as a present. It was good enough for the likes of them, he'd sneered, but Jessica knew the newly married couple would be grateful.

'Are you coming, dear, or are you going to wait in the taxi?' Charles enquired of his wife now.

'Of course, I'm coming! I want to make sure I approve of these people, too, before we leave Jessica in their care.'

Jessica set her jaw as they marched up the front path. The garden was neatly manicured, the borders colourful with spring flowers, which was a good sign. And when Belinda's parents came to the door, they were so pleasant and, most importantly, well-spoken, that Charles gave his consent for Jessica to go inside. He would send a taxi to collect her at eleven o'clock precisely.

Jessica breathed a sigh of relief as she was shown inside. The party was in full swing, drinks and a finger buffet set out on a side table. Music was playing from a wind-up gramophone, not too loud, but loud enough to be heard above the hubbub of happy voices. People were bobbing around dancing, or spilling out through open French doors into the garden and the mild April evening.

'Jessica!' Hillie called across the room. 'Oh, I'm so glad your dad let you come!'

'Hillie, congratulations!' Jessica called back, shouldering her way through as best she could with the heavy box. 'Where can I put your present?'

'Oh, goodness, that looks exciting! Thank you so much! Jimmy! Jimmy, come here, love. Let me introduce you to Jessica.'

'Pleased to meet you. Hillie's told me so much about you,' Jimmy said, giving his most charming smile.

'Likewise. But could you take this? Your present. It's rather heavy.'

'Of course,' Jimmy replied, obliging at once. 'Blimey, it is, ain't it? Ta ever so.'

'Jess, come this way,' Hillie invited her, leading her across the room. 'I've got a surprise for you.'

'A surprise? For *me*?'

'Yes, look.'

She took Jessica out into the garden, and jabbed her head across the lawn. Standing by an ornamental tree, drink in hand as he chatted to Gert, Eva and Stan, was a tall, broad man immaculately dressed. His skin was as dark as the material of his suit, but when he turned his head and saw Jessica, his face lit up with a huge smile.

'Patrick!' Jessica gasped, and then she turned to Hillie, her eyes bright as stars. 'Oh, Hillie, what a wonderful surprise indeed! Thank you!' And she skipped across the grass.

*

'Oh, Jimmy, wasn't that a fantastic evening!' Hillie breathed as they turned towards the front door of the boarding house. Rob had dropped them home in his car, promising to bring all the presents people had given them the next morning. 'I just wish Mum and the others had been able to come,' she added wistfully.

'Yeah. I wish I could've done something about that,' Jimmy agreed. 'But you know what Mrs P said. She's determined to sort something out. But apart from that, it was as good a party as any proper wedding, and worth the wait. Belinda's mum and dad are the best. To do that for us when we're almost strangers.'

'Yes, well, Gert's no stranger to them,' Hillie chuckled. 'She and Rob are seeing each other during the week as well as at weekends, so things seem to be getting serious between them. So it was a good opportunity for Belinda's parents to get to know Gert's mum and dad better. I'm so glad they could come.'

'And it was good of Kit to turn down his invitation and offer to baby- and granny-sit instead.'

'Yes.' In the dim light from the street lamp, Jimmy saw Hillie's face fall as he put his key in the lock. 'I wish he'd been able to come as well,' she murmured. 'He's been as much part of my life as Gert. And after he sorted everything out for our trip to Gretna Green as well.'

'Yeah, well, perhaps he felt he'd done enough.'

Jimmy stood back for Hillie to go in front of him as they went up the stairs, glad she couldn't see his face. Hillie was his now, but he couldn't help feel a twinge of jealousy. Kit could easily have taken Hillie first, and he'd noticed the way he looked at Hillie sometimes. He was even better looking than Jimmy, and his prospects were far better. As he unlocked the door to their horrible little room, it seemed even more horrible than ever to Jimmy after the evening at Belinda's pleasant house. It broke his heart to bring Hillie back to such dire surroundings. She deserved so much better.

But he *would* provide a better home for her, and soon. There were things... things he could get involved in. Jackson, the bloke at the pub he'd run the odd errand for on occasion. Jimmy wasn't entirely sure what the chap was up to, but he could maybe do more.

In that moment, Jimmy swore he'd make a decent home for Hillie if it was the last thing he ever did!

Chapter Thirteen

Gert glanced around as they sat down at one of the outside tables by the refreshment pavilion in Battersea Park. It was probably safe enough, but you never knew, and she had to make sure. It was a drizzly Saturday afternoon early in May, just over a couple of months since Hillie and Jimmy had got married. Once again, Jimmy was working for Mr Jackson, delivering a package this time. Sensing her friend needed some company, Gert had told Rob she couldn't see him until the evening. Besides, she had something to give to Hillie as soon as possible, and the drizzle should mean less people in the park to notice them.

'Here you are,' she said quietly, drawing a piece of paper from her pocket. 'She gave it to Mum a couple of days ago, but this is the first time I've been sure no one would see.'

She watched as Hillie's face lit like a beacon – or would have done if it hadn't been for the sadness that had haunted her eyes ever since the terrible row with her father.

'A letter from Mum!' she gasped in a whisper, almost snatching the dog-eared paper that had been in Gert's pocket. 'Oh, thanks, Gert. You're an angel!'

'Don't thank me. Thank my mum. She was the one what suggested you kept in contact by letter. I admire your mum, mind, finding the guts to risk it. But she writes them while your dad's at work, and reads yours at our house.'

'Even so, this is only the second one she's dared to write,' Hillie answered, barely dragging her eyes from the letter as she began to read. 'If only I didn't work the same hours as my dad, we could risk meeting up. Oh,' she said in surprise. 'Luke's been working on a paper round this last month. Dad's idea, no doubt, to help make up for my wages,' she scoffed bitterly. 'Oh, yes, that's what Mum's said. And she says Dad's had to give her a bit extra as well. Ha, that'll upset him! But she says things are OK. She's managing. And she says… she loves me.' She looked up, unshed tears spangling in her eyes. 'Oh, Gert, what are we to do? D'you think I'll ever see her or the others again?'

Gert shook her head, totally at a loss. 'I don't know. But what I do know is that something's gotta snap somewhere. But I'm not gonna let it be you.' She grasped Hillie's hand across the table and squeezed it tightly.

Hillie's mouth twisted. 'Thanks, Gert,' she choked. 'You're one in a million.'

'That's why you like me, kiddo,' Gert told her, finally bringing a smile to Hillie's lips. 'So drink up your cuppa before it gets cold, and we'll go for a walk before it starts raining properly. I don't know. Supposed to be May, ain't it?'

*

'Oh, Jimmy, it really is wonderful!' Hillie cried in delight, inspecting the flat up in the eaves of the large terraced house one evening at the beginning of July. 'A separate bedroom, a little kitchenette and our own bathroom! Oh, thank you so much!'

She flung her arms around Jimmy's neck and landed a big, passionate kiss on his mouth, making him grin wickedly.

'And a double bed, which I can't wait to get you in,' he answered, winking playfully.

'Well, you'll have to wait for that until we've moved in,' Hillie told him with teasing haughtiness.

The prospect of making love somewhere comfortable and dry was certainly more appealing than being squashed into the single bed which felt perpetually damp, and staring at the wet patches on the ceiling and the paper hanging off the walls. Her marital duties no longer held any fear for her, but Hillie still couldn't say she exactly enjoyed those most intimate moments. Jimmy was always very gentle with her, and she relished the closeness of the cuddles before and afterwards. But she still didn't feel the physical desire she'd heard others talk about. She wished she did, so perhaps that in itself was a step in the right direction. And she loved Jimmy deeply in every other way, so maybe living in better surroundings would help.

'The sooner we does so, the better, then,' he declared now. 'I only have to give a week's notice, so we can move in next weekend.'

'Oh, I can't wait!' Hillie crowed. But as her eyes swept about her, doubt crept into her mind. 'Are you sure we can afford it, though?'

'Course we can,' Jimmy assured her, taking her hands and looking earnestly into her eyes. 'We've got your wages as well as mine. And with me extra shifts at the pub and the odd errand I run for Mr Jackson, we're doing fine.'

'Well, if you're sure.' Hillie gave a reluctant sigh. 'But with all the extra work you do, I hardly ever see you. You're working seven days a week.'

'We have Saturday and Sunday afternoons together,' Jimmy protested, 'and all the evenings during the week.'

'If you're not doing something for that Mr Jackson.'

Jimmy gave a casual shrug. 'He pays me well, and it's all cash in hand, so I can't say no. Anyway, it won't be forever. When old Matthews retires or pops his clogs, I'll be next in line for his job. And then I won't need to do any extras at all, and we'll have plenty of time together. You'll likely be sick of the sight of me.'

'No,' Hillie chuckled. 'Never that.'

'That's my girl.'

Jimmy pulled her close again, and his mouth came down firmly on hers. Her lips parted in response, and the tingle low down in her stomach as his tongue gently probed between her teeth took her by surprise. Oh, so perhaps it had merely been those long months in the dingy bedsit that had put her off. Summer had arrived, and it felt warm and cosy in this little attic flat with its quirky, sloping ceilings and windows that seemed to let in so much light. Maybe that little flicker inside her would burst into flame in their new home. She certainly hoped it would because she loved Jimmy so much and wanted to make everything right for him, too.

*

Hillie stood back to admire her handiwork with a satisfied sigh. She'd bought some material at the market the previous weekend and spent every spare moment sewing curtains for the sitting room. She'd just put them up and they looked splendid, especially with the July sunshine streaming through the windows. The wooden clock Gert and Rob had given them as a wedding present presided over the shelf above the gas fire, together with the china figurines from Eva and Stan. Belinda had taken a nice photograph of Hillie and Jimmy with her Brownie camera, and had had an enlargement printed from the negative. It hung in pride of place in a shiny new frame from a hook on the wall above the shelf.

Hillie glanced round the room, rocking in contentment. It really felt like home now. The middle-aged woman who acted as landlady for the owners occupied the ground floor and semi-basement. Both she and her husband, who was out at work all day, were nothing like the crotchety tyrant at Jimmy's previous digs, and the elderly couple who rented the flat on the middle floor were very pleasant and as quiet as mice.

It was no wonder Hillie felt so much happier. The door that opened directly into the bedroom was slightly ajar, and Hillie's pulse began to patter as she remembered the previous evening. It being Friday night, they'd treated themselves to fish and chips. Jimmy had brought home a couple of bottles of beer from the pub, and some cider for Hillie. She'd giggled as the sweet, bubbly liquid had seemed to fizz up her nose. The only alcohol she'd ever tasted was the sherry Belinda's dad had given her at their wedding party. She hadn't been keen, and had stuck to Tizer afterwards. But this was a totally different taste, light and refreshing. And relaxing.

A mellow tiredness had seeped through her limbs, and her head was slightly muzzy. Jimmy had kissed her thoroughly as they snuggled on the sofa, and she'd put up little resistance when he persuaded her to finish the bottle.

'Come on, love. I think it's bedtime,' Jimmy said, getting up from the settee and holding out his hand.

Hillie's head swam with pleasant dizziness as she staggered to her feet. 'Oh, dear,' she laughed. 'Am I supposed to feel like this? I'm not drunk, am I?'

'What, on one bottle? Nah, it's not much stronger than lemonade.'

'Well, I feel... Whoops!' she giggled, nearly tripping over the shoes she'd kicked off earlier. 'Oo, where's the bedroom gone?'

The next thing she knew, her head was spinning as Jimmy picked her up and carried her through to the other room where he laid her on the bed. She flopped back, ready to curl up and sleep, not caring that she was still fully dressed. In fact, she didn't care a jot when Jimmy began to peel off her clothes. He'd have to get her ready for bed, since she wasn't capable of doing so herself!

It wasn't until she was down to her brassière and knickers that she began to feel shy, and something twitched deep inside her. She gazed up trustingly into Jimmy's adoring, smiling face as he unhooked her bra, the warm evening air like silk against her naked skin.

'Cor, you're that beautiful, you know,' Jimmy croaked, his eyes almost on stalks.

It darted across Hillie's befuddled mind that on their wedding night, she'd been wearing her petticoat, and that ever since, she'd been changed into her winceyette nightdress because the bedsit had always been so cold, even when the warmer weather arrived. Jimmy had never seen her in the altogether, and though the old awkwardness lingered in the background, Jimmy's feasting, loving gaze made her feel strangely wanted. She felt lost in an unknown world, wanting to resist but somehow not capable of doing so as he pulled her drawers down off her legs and tossed them somewhere across the room. He couldn't wait, and only did the necessary to his own clothes so that he could enter her straightaway.

Hillie smiled wistfully to herself at the recent memory. It didn't hurt any more, and through her wavering stupor, it had even seemed acceptable. She vowed not to get tiddly again, but yes. She'd cracked it. Wouldn't mind it from now on. She could be a proper wife.

It was surprising what surroundings could do to you, she mused. The bedsit had demeaned her entire soul, but now she felt fulfilled with a proper little home to look after. Contented. Or as contented as she could be.

If ever she chanced to come anywhere near her father at the factory, he put his nose in the air and totally ignored her. She didn't mind that. But what she did mind was not seeing her mum or Luke or the girls. The secret letters were all well and good, but she hadn't been able to talk to her family since the day back in February when she and Jimmy had returned from Scotland, and it was breaking her heart.

She had tried, of course she had. At weekends, when Jimmy was off earning extra money, she usually went over to the Parkers' house. Her eyes always scanned the street, eager to catch a glimpse of her younger siblings playing on the pavement, especially when the better weather came. But it seemed Harold had guessed she'd try to make contact that way, as they were rarely outside. On a couple of occasions when she'd spied them there and run towards them, her heart bursting with happiness, Trixie had noticed her first, and quickly shepherded Daisy and Frances inside and shut the door in Hillie's face.

Dear God, had the bastard terrorised them so much that they were afraid to speak to her? Only a devil could be so cruel, and to his own children, too. If he wanted to punish her, then so be it. But if Luke and her little sisters were living in fear, it was outrageous. Or what if he'd told them such vicious lies about her that they didn't *want* to speak to her? And what about her poor mum? He must keep her locked up like a prisoner when he knew Hillie wasn't at work.

Hillie's eyes travelled around the room again, and the comfortable little home she'd created. Cushion covers to match the curtains with the leftover material would be next on her list of jobs, but she wasn't in the mood to start them, now her thoughts had entwined about her family. After leaving the factory at lunchtime, Jimmy had gone straight to the pub where Mr Jackson would be waiting for him with instructions for one of his errands. So Hillie had walked home alone. She'd made her usual detour to the library, but even the prospect of starting a new book couldn't quell the uneasiness that tumbled in her stomach. She'd busied herself hanging the curtains, but now the task was done, she felt restless and oddly agitated.

There was only one thing for it. And on such a glorious summer afternoon, the outdoors beckoned. She knew Rob had taken Gert up to Regent's Park Zoo, so there was little point calling in at the Parkers'. And if she was lucky enough to catch either Joan or Trixie and the little ones playing in the street, she knew what their reaction would be. So she might as well go straight to Battersea Park and enjoy a couple of hours there, taking a leisurely stroll around the lakes, admiring the flower beds and exchanging blinks with the owls in the aviary. She might even indulge in an ice cream to while away the time. Was it over a year since Kit had treated all of his own family and hers to a vanilla cone? She'd scarcely known Jimmy then, and now she was married to him.

But she might never be able to speak to her mother and Luke and the girls ever again.

A wrenching sigh escaped from her lungs as she gathered up her keys and some change from her purse. That's all she'd need. And then it struck her that on her way, she could stop at the telephone box on the corner and see if Belinda wanted to join her. It was quite a long way from Parsons Green, but it was a thought.

Sadly, though, there was no answer, and Hillie pressed Button B to get her money back. She ached with disappointment as she made her way towards the park, her pulse cranking up when she passed the end of Banbury Street. But she must only look forward now, and bury the past somewhere so deep inside her that it couldn't hurt her any more.

In the park, the spring-flowering shrubs had lost their blooms now, but were in full leaf, and summer bedding plants graced the formal flower beds in swathes of blazing colour. The smell of warm earth and grass filled Hillie's nostrils, and the sounds of people enjoying the tree-lined walks and open spaces made her feel more relaxed. The park was a haven of fresh air and leafy shade that tugged at her innermost feelings. She'd never been to the countryside. Her only experience of it was from out of the train window on the way back from Scotland. It had an effect on her she couldn't explain. She and Jimmy had once discussed moving to the country. But she knew it would only ever be a dream.

She found a seat by one of the lakes and sat down to watch some children feeding the ducks. The sight stabbed into her side as she remembered doing the self-same thing with Luke and Joan and the others. Ah… And suddenly the whole scene became false and ugly, especially with the twin towers of Battersea Power Station looming over the end of the park. She'd heard there were plans to double its size in future years, so that there'd eventually be four monster chimneys instead of the present two spewing out smoke. It was due to start generating electricity the following week, feeding all those cables that had been laid beneath the streets, ready to supply almost the entire neighbourhood. All very well, but surely with all the other factories and breweries and everything else belching into the air, they were all going to choke?

Hillie was gazing blindly through the people wandering past her, and then wondered why something in her subconscious clicked her brain back into focus. Walking along the pathway was a tall man with a broad smile that allowed his large teeth to flash in his dark face. In contrast, a beautiful, pale gold dog trotted on a leash at his heels, and on his arm, was a pretty young woman in a floral-printed summer dress. With matching white shoes, handbag and little frilly hat, she looked like a model from a fashion magazine.

'Jessica!'

The fear in the girl's startled, blue eyes was more than evident as she spun round. But then her face relaxed into a smile when she recognised her friend.

'Oh, Hillie,' she said with a relieved sigh as she led Patrick over to the bench. 'I didn't realise it was you. I was worried for a moment it might've been someone I didn't want to see me with Patrick.' Then her eyes filled with alarm again. 'You won't let on, will you?'

'No, of course not. It's good to see you. Hello, Patrick. How are you?'

'Very happy to see you, too, Hillie,' Patrick replied in his lilting voice. 'And also very grateful. Without you, I should not be enjoying such happiness. And how is married life treating you?'

'Very well,' Hillie assured him, swallowing the niggling doubt at the back of her mind. 'We moved into a flat a couple of weeks ago, and it's so much nicer. You must come round.'

'We'd love to, if we can work it out safely.'

'We were just going to take a drink at the pavilion. Will you join us?'

'Yes, I will, Patrick. Thank you.'

'Where is Jimmy, then?' Patrick asked as they set out in the direction of the said pavilion. 'If I had such a lovely wife, I should want to be out with her.'

'Oh, he's running an errand for someone at the pub where he works. A bit of extra money always comes in handy.'

'And what do these errands consist of?'

'I've no idea, to be honest. But I just felt like getting out. With English weather, you can't afford to miss a good day like this.'

'Indeed, one cannot. However, I am obliged to walk Africa every day, even if the rain is coming down in stair rods, as I believe you say,' Patrick grinned, giving his infectious laugh.

'Of course,' Hillie chuckled back. 'But I thought you worked at the dogs' home after your piano lesson on a Saturday, Jess?'

Jessica pulled a wry grimace. 'I gave that up so that I could see Patrick for half an hour instead. I feel a bit guilty about it, but it was the only thing I could think of. Oh, look, there's a table free over there,' she said as they reached the pavilion.

'You sit down, then, and I shall buy the drinks. Lemonade for you both? And then today I shall enjoy the special treat of having two beautiful ladies in my company.'

'Go on with you,' Jessica giggled. 'I'll take Africa for you.'

Patrick nodded, and then went off to join the short queue while the two girls settled themselves at the table.

'He really is so nice, Patrick,' Hillie remarked as she pushed to one side the dirty cups of the previous customers. 'I don't know why you don't feel able to introduce him to your parents. He's kind, polite, educated. A dentist and even a prince, for heaven's sake.'

'I know.' Jessica's lovely face fell. 'My dad has softened up a little, thanks to you. And if it weren't for the colour of Patrick's skin, I might've plucked up the courage. But... I feel ashamed for Patrick's sake. My father calls people of African descent... well... you don't want to know. I just think it's an abominable term, and I'd hate Patrick to be upset. So he's agreed to wait until I'm twenty-one before we tell my parents. And then, if we're still together and want to get married, they can't stop us.' She lowered her eyes almost guiltily. 'I'm afraid I'm not strong like you, Hillie.'

Hillie had to bite her lip. It had been in a moment of weakness, not strength, that she'd agreed to elope with Jimmy. She'd been at her lowest ebb after her dad's assault on her, and it had seemed the only way out. Even Gert, who hadn't been keen on her relationship with Jimmy at first, had agreed. And Kit, who had the most level head of anyone Hillie knew, had helped with the secret plan. And it worked. She *was* happily married to Jimmy and she *was* free of her dad's evil clutches. And yet he still had that cruel hold over her.

She had no chance to reveal her misgivings, though, as Patrick came back with two bottles of lemonade with straws and a cup of tea on a tray.

'Thanks, Patrick,' Jessica said, smiling at him adoringly. 'I mustn't be long, mind. I'm expected home, and there'll be questions asked if I'm late.'

'Aren't you taking a bit of a risk if you're worried about being seen, and word getting back to your parents?'

Jessica's curls danced as she nodded her head. 'A bit. But Dad's at work, of course, and Mum wouldn't come to the park on her own. And she's such a snob, she wouldn't talk to anyone else on the street, and not many other people actually know me.'

'And I have told Jessica not to worry. I should always take care of her no matter what, just as Jimmy takes care of you.'

Hillie had to hide a wry smile as they sat in the sunshine enjoying their refreshments. She managed to change the subject by admiring Jessica's handbag, and before long, her friends stood up to leave. Hillie noticed Patrick place a peck on Jessica's cheek before they parted company.

Hillie sat for a while longer, musing over the dregs of her lemonade. It was only when she recognised a familiar, beloved young voice that she jerked up her head. Trixie! Parading down the path on the opposite side of the grass was her dad, leading all the children in strict crocodile file. Luke was bringing up the rear, hanging his head, but Nell was nowhere to be seen.

Hillie's heart exploded as she leapt to her feet and streaked across to them. She was just in the mood to confront her father, but as she went to speak to her sisters, he swung round and doffed his cap in a low, sarcastic, mocking bow. Hillie was so pole-axed that she stopped in her tracks. Grinning malevolently, her father wagged his finger at his children and then put it to his lips. And then narrowing his eyes at Hillie, he pointed at the children and drew his finger across his throat in a threatening gesture, before moving on, his lips in a vicious leer.

Hillie could do nothing but let them pass, seething with rage. The bastard never came to the park, but he knew that she often did. How many times had he come there, hoping he'd get the chance to taunt her as he just had? She could have screamed, hopping on the spot in a swirling agony of anger and hate.

Luke glanced back over his shoulder, his young brow folded in terrified frustration. And as she watched her family snake away down the path, Hillie's fists balled at her sides, fingernails digging into her palms. For there was nothing she could do.

Chapter Fourteen

'Luke!' Hillie gasped in astonishment, colliding with her brother as she rounded the corner of one of the buildings at the factory one lunchtime in September. She'd been deep in thought, going over in her head the film, *The Private Life of Henry VIII*, starring Charles Laughton, that she and Jimmy had been to see a few weeks before. She'd been so enthralled by it that she still kept thinking about it every now and then. So to bump into Luke so unexpectedly was a bit of a shock. 'What on earth are you doing here?' she asked him.

Luke looked down at his feet, grinding the toe of his shoe into the ground. He stuffed his hands deeper into his trouser pockets, his shoulders hunched. 'It was my birthday a couple of weeks ago,' he said glumly. 'I was fourteen.'

'Yes, I know.' Hillie gave a puzzled frown. 'I sent you a card and a ten-bob note.'

Luke's head shot up in accusation. 'No, you didn't. Just like you've forgotten everyone else's birthday since you got married.'

For several seconds, Hillie felt as if she couldn't breathe. 'You... you what?' She finally forced the words from her throat. 'I sent everyone the same!'

'Well, we didn't get them. And you can't tell me they *all* got lost in the post.'

'No. But I bet I know who made sure he got to the post first on those days.' Hillie's horrified gaze met Luke's as the truth dawned on both of them. 'The bastard,' Hillie mumbled, so enraged she could barely speak. 'He must've opened them and pocketed the money himself.'

'Well, certainly none of us saw any of it.' Luke's face was furious with disgust. 'Not even the cards. Oh, I'm sorry, Hill. I should've known.'

'And I suppose he's running me down to the others all the time as well.'

Luke nodded in response, biting his bottom lip. ''Fraid so.'

'And taking that money from his own children. How could he? I saved hard for it each time. It's a decent sum is ten bob.'

'I know,' Luke snorted wryly. 'Almost a week's wages for me.'

'Wages!' Hillie was appalled.

'Yes. I'm working here now. In the night-light wicking shed. But at least I don't have to do the paper round anymore,' he said wistfully. 'But I wanted to stay at school until I'm sixteen. Go on to college, even. Study engineering, maybe. I'm good with my hands.'

'And your brain. Oh, Luke, I am sorry. I feel as if it's my fault.'

'No. Dad would've made me leave school anyway, so it doesn't matter. I wouldn't have got the chance either way.' Luke gave a mournful shrug. 'He wouldn't even let me stay on till the end of term at Christmas. He said I'd turned fourteen and had to leave straightaway. When the headmistress tried to tell him otherwise, he threatened her. So here I am.'

'Just like he did with me,' Hillie muttered bitterly. 'Oh, Luke, I am sorry. I wish there was something I could do. Look.' She glanced around, fearful their father could be watching them, but she couldn't see him. 'I haven't got any extra on me today. But I'll try to carry the odd spare bob or two and then next time we bump into each other, I can slip you a bit extra for Mum. We'll have to be careful, mind.'

'Can't we make some definite meeting time?'

'That might be difficult, so let me think about it. And if I tell you our new address, can you remember it? Best not write it down in case you know who finds it. We moved into a proper flat in the summer. You must come round when you think it's safe.'

'You and Jimmy doing OK, then?'

'Not bad. You know Jimmy works shifts at a pub at the weekends, and he runs errands for some chap who drinks there. But you'd best go now before a certain person sees us. And give Mum my love. All right, is she?'

'Been a bit peaky lately. But probably 'cos she's missing you.'

'We'll have to see what we can do about that. I wonder if we could possibly arrange something through Mrs P? But it could be tricky and so much the worse for Mum if it went wrong. Anyway, off you go now. And be careful, Luke.'

'I will.' Luke's eyes narrowed. 'Especially now I know what the bastard's up to.'

Hillie nodded as she watched him hurry away. She didn't like to hear such language from her little brother, but she supposed their dad was right in one thing. Luke *was* grown-up now. But he'd never be a match for their bully of a father.

If only there was something she could do. She'd talk to Jimmy about it that evening. He was bound to come up with something, was Jimmy.

*

'Flipping heck, can you hear that? Break the blooming front door down in a minute!'

Hillie paused from the washing-up and raised an eyebrow at Jimmy's words. Certainly someone was hammering on the front door downstairs, making an almighty racket. She hoped either Mr or Mrs Neilson would answer it soon. It was most unnerving that someone was in such a hurry to speak to them.

Ah, thank goodness. The noise had stopped, and Hillie could hear Mr Neilson's deep voice. She liked their new landlord and landlady and hoped nothing was wrong. She could no longer hear Mr Neilson so she supposed everything must be all right. But then there were footsteps thundering up the stairs. And they didn't stop at the flat below.

Hillie's heart clenched. She somehow knew before the first frantic knocking on the door to their flat, and she was already drying her hands as she crossed the room. Her pulse was cracking wildly and she knew instinctively who was at the door.

'Luke! Whatever's the matter?'

The boy's young face was alive with panic, ghostly white, bare cheeks scarlet from running through the cold November night. 'You've got to come, Hill! Quickly! It's Mum.'

Hillie's stomach squeezed even more tightly. 'Mum? What's wrong with her?' she demanded, tearing off her apron.

'I... don't really know,' Luke stammered, still fighting for breath. 'She can't get up and she's gone a funny colour. I got Mrs P. And she said to fetch you, and then to get someone from the Women's Hospital.'

'And where's Dad?' Hillie asked sharply, grabbing her coat. Not that she cared. If her Mum was so ill that Mrs P was sending for a doctor, dealing with her father would be the least of Hillie's problems. And, dear God, if he was responsible…

'Went down the pub a while before,' Luke panted, still struggling to catch his breath. 'After the little ones went to bed.'

'Drinking *your* wages, no doubt. And Mum was all right then?'

'Yes. At least, I thought she was. But then she started groaning and holding her stomach, and then she collapsed.'

Hillie could feel the blood racing about her limbs, making her feel slightly faint, but she must remain in control. Poor Luke was beside himself, looking to her for direction. And she was grateful when Jimmy appeared beside her.

'I'll go to the hospital,' he offered. 'You two go back to the house.'

'OK, Jimmy.' Hillie turned to her husband, and their eyes met in silent understanding. 'And thanks.'

'I'll be as quick as I can,' she heard him say as she and Luke hurried down the flights of stairs. And then as she stepped out into the night air, she heard the familiar click of the flat door as Jimmy followed them down.

The maze of darkened streets Hillie had lived among all her life seemed strange and hostile. Rows of faceless houses, closed up against the night, each one anonymous and yet holding dark secrets of its own. At least, that was how it felt to Hillie as they scuttled from the arc of light from one street lamp to the next. A cold, steady drizzle, misty with the smuts from hundreds of smoking chimneys, made it difficult to see. Grey, murky shadows merged into one, making it impossible to run at speed along the uneven pavements. And Hillie was peering through a fog of anger and guilt. Her dad. He'd been up to his old tricks again, hadn't he? The severity of internal injuries didn't always show itself straightaway. Hillie knew that. She should have stood up to her dad instead of running away like a coward. And now this.

It seemed an age before they reached the house. Hillie could feel herself shaking as they let themselves in the front door. All the old hatred welled up inside. She'd fight her father, and this time she vowed that she'd be stronger than him.

'Up here,' Eva's familiar voice called softly from upstairs.

They tiptoed up. The girls would all be asleep, but more than that, they both felt as if they were in the presence of something enormous and frightening. Hillie thought her heart must have stopped as she gently pushed open the door to her parents' bedroom.

She held her breath. There was only the one bare light bulb hanging from its fabric-covered, twisted cable in the middle of the ceiling. Eva couldn't have wanted to blind her dear friend with such stark brilliance, and with there being no table lamp, she'd lit a row of night-lights along the mantelpiece. In the uncertain, flickering glow, Nell looked a strange grey, her skin pallid and thin. Hillie hadn't seen her mum for nearly nine months, so to find her like this was a spear in her heart. Nell's eyes were shut, and Eva was holding her hand and crooning softly. Eva glanced up when she saw the two young people enter the room.

'Ah, Hillie,' she whispered, her lowered voice quivering. 'And Luke, I thought I told you to get—'

'Jimmy's gone to the hospital,' Hillie told her. 'I hope to God they won't be long.'

Eva nodded, and then turned to stroke Nell's hand as she moaned again. 'I managed to get her up the stairs, but then she passed out. I've put a hot-water bottle in the bed. She seems so cold. Come. You take my place. Talk to her. She might be able to hear you. I don't know.'

In the deathly quiet of the room, they swapped places and Eva stood at the foot of the bed, like a fierce, protective angel. Hillie stared at her mother's jaundiced face, listened to her uneven, shallow breathing. She barely looked alive, and Hillie was choking on her own bitter rage.

'It was him again, wasn't it?' The tortured words tore at her throat. 'It was my fault. I shouldn't have—'

'No. It wasn't your dad.'

Eva's barely spoken words stung into Hillie's heart, and she swung round. 'What d'you mean?'

Eva nodded at Luke. 'Go and put the kettle on, there's a good lad. We could all do with a cuppa.'

Luke blinked at them, and Hillie recognised the gentle indecision on his face. He wanted to be there. With his mum. But he was also scared, and would rather not face the dreadful tension in the bedroom. The kitchen would be an escape, and when he looked at Hillie for approval, she nodded her head.

'I... don't know how to tell you this, luvvie,' Eva croaked once they could hear Luke moving about downstairs. 'She... she... well...'

Every nerve in Hillie's body was ready to snap. If Eva couldn't bring herself to tell her... And then she watched, mesmerised in horror, as Eva lifted the blankets. Her mother was lying in a pool of wet, glistening blood that had soaked her skirt and was oozing down her legs, despite the rolled-up towel that Eva had pressed up between her thighs.

Hillie recoiled in horror, hands over her mouth, as Eva reverently replaced the bedcovers, shaking her head in utter sorrow. Hillie continued to stare in agonised shock, her mind spinning in crazed circles. Surely Jimmy must arrive with the doctor soon!

'A… a miscarriage,' Hillie stuttered.

Then she felt a hand, calm but defeated, on her arm. 'No, not that, ducks. She told me she couldn't face having another one. Another one to protect from your dad. To try and squeeze money out of him for extra food. She said… it'd be better off not living. So she tried to get rid of it. For its own sake. Only she didn't expect this to happen.'

Something like ice streamed through Hillie's veins as the meaning of Eva's hushed words percolated into her brain. 'B-but…' She'd started to shiver, her trembling jaw making it hard to speak. 'I-I don't understand. She… she should've told me. I could've helped.'

But Eva's voice was firm. 'No. I don't think no one could've helped. She'd just had enough. All those years of fighting your dad.'

'And… and did he know?' she spat viciously.

'That she was preggers again? No. She wasn't going to tell no one. It's only you and me what knows.'

'And whoever did this.' Hillie turned a tear-ravaged face to Eva, breaking the woman's heart.

'Did… did she say who it was? I mean… how did she know anyone?'

Eva's face seemed to close up, but then the tight lines about her mouth slackened. 'It's only right that you should know. It was Dolly Maguire,' she barely whispered.

'Dolly Maguire!'

'Sh! Not Dolly herself, but someone she knows. Now don't you blame Dolly,' Eva warned quietly. 'Your mum went to Dolly 'cos she was the only person she thought would know someone.'

'But…' Hillie shook her head in despair. She just couldn't comprehend… The sigh that broke from her lungs was brutal and unforgiving.

Eva stepped noiselessly to the door. 'I'll go and see if Luke's finished making that cuppa yet.'

Hillie hung her head as she was left alone with her mum in the silent room. She couldn't believe what was happening. What her mum had done. It was so unlike her. She was devoted to her children. Couldn't have been a better mother. So it must have been just as Eva had said. She'd had enough. Was at the end of her tether. Desperate.

Hillie choked back her tears and took her mum's limp hand again. Soothed it. Stroked it. But there was no response. Hillie felt so helpless. Useless. If only there was something she could do. But she knew that only a doctor could help Nell now.

She blinked her eyes wide to clear the moisture that was blurring her vision. She let her gaze wander around the familiar room. It was so stark. Nothing personal about it. Because her dad scorned such fripperies. Hillie saw that the cot had gone, so Frances must have moved into the other room when she'd left. Just as well as she was far too big for a cot now.

But it would have made it even easier for their father to force himself on his wife.

Hillie felt as if she would suffocate. Was it her fault for leaving? For abandoning her mum, forcing her to face her dad alone?

'Here you are, dearie.'

Eva, coming in with two cups of tea, rescued Hillie from her feelings of guilt. The quiet clink as she took the cup and saucer and placed them on the bedside cabinet must have been enough to disturb Nell. She groaned weakly and her eyelids flickered half open. Her wandering eyes focused on Hillie's face, and her mouth curved in the shadow of a smile.

'My darling girl,' she rasped in less than a whisper. 'Forgive me.'

Hillie felt a dagger screw into her chest. 'Forgive you?' she choked. 'Of course. But you should've told me. I could've helped.'

'No. Not this.' The words were so low and slurred, barely articulated, so that Hillie had a job to make them out. 'That's... between me... and my Maker. The other thing,' Nell went on, scarcely breathing. 'Eva will tell you. I... did it... for you. But I was wrong. But... you've escaped. I'm... so pleased. So proud of you. Be happy, my darling. And take care of the little ones for me.'

Her eyes closed, and she sank back on the pillows, her face serene. Hillie threw Eva a questioning glance. What had her mum meant? But that could wait. Hillie took Nell's hand again, squeezing it between both of hers. And noticed her own tears dripping onto their joined fingers.

'Drink your tea whilst it's still hot,' Eva instructed. 'It's brass monkeys in here. I daredn't light the fire. I didn't know if the chimney's been swept. Don't want to set it on fire.'

Hillie nodded, and picked up her tea, warming her hands round the cup. No. Her dad didn't believe in fires in the bedrooms, and Eva had guessed correctly that apart from the kitchen, the chimneys hadn't been swept in years. But Hillie really couldn't bring herself to speak. And besides, she was chilled to the marrow, and no fire could hope to penetrate that.

A knock on the front door lifted her from her misery, and her heart rose in reckless hope.

'That'll be your Jimmy with the doctor,' Eva announced, springing to her feet. 'I'll go.'

But Luke had evidently got there first as Eva had scarcely left the room when she came back in again with a middle-aged woman carrying a leather Gladstone bag. Hillie was glad that Jimmy had the integrity to keep Luke company downstairs. This was no place for men.

'Now then, what've we got here?' the doctor smiled with calm confidence.

Hillie exchanged glances with Eva, who quietly shut the door.

'Don't want no one else hearing,' the older woman said in a whisper, turning back into the room. 'She told me before she passed out. She was trying to… well, you know… get rid. She's already had six.'

The doctor scarcely raised an eyebrow, but nodded knowingly. Hillie stood back from the bed, chewing her fingernail, her heart knocking hard against her ribs. She turned her head as the doctor turned down the covers. She didn't want to see again, and was barely aware of the stranger examining her mum's motionless body before pulling the bedclothes back up.

'Can you… say it's a miscarriage?' Hillie just about managed to scrape the plea from her throat. 'Dad mustn't know. He… he's violent. He'll take it out on her when she's better.'

The doctor unhooked the stethoscope from her ears and slung it around her neck. 'I'm so sorry,' she said with genuine compassion. 'He won't get the chance. Her heart's barely beating, and there's virtually no pulse.'

Hillie had to stifle her horror as the doctor's words sank into her brain. 'You mean...? But surely there's something you can do?' she stammered.

But the doctor shook her head. 'Even if we get an ambulance, she wouldn't make it to the hospital. And she certainly wouldn't make it through any surgery to try and stop the bleeding. I really am sorry. It's about the worst case I've ever seen. So... you need to tell me who did this before whoever it was does it to someone else.'

Eva released a heart-wrenching sigh. 'I only wish I could, but she didn't say who it was. Oh, Lordy Love, poor Nell. We've been best mates since we was kids.'

Hillie raised her eyes. But at that moment, she didn't care about Dolly. She only cared about her mum, and accusing Dolly wasn't going to help. Oh, God, her poor mum.

'How... how long?' she managed to gulp.

'I'll stay,' the doctor said. And Hillie knew what she meant.

'Better get Luke,' she whispered, looking at Eva again. 'But don't wake the girls.'

Eva nodded, and did as Hillie asked. The three women and the boy stood around Nell's bed: her eldest child and her best friend holding her hands, her only son and the kindly doctor in the background. A quiet gurgling started at the back of the dying woman's throat, rhythmical, with each slow breath. Hillie sat there, stunned, aching, as the horrendous noise rapidly grew louder. It slashed at Hillie's heart and she wanted to run from the room. But her legs were numbed. This was her mum...

She suddenly realised the rattling noise had stopped. The doctor hurried over with her stethoscope. And then drew in a deep breath.

'I'm sorry. She's gone.'

Hillie stared, blinded by tears. Hearing Luke's young sobs.

'Goodbye, old friend,' she caught Eva's choked whisper.

How long the minutes took to tick by. Or perhaps it was seconds. Hillie didn't know. Or care, really. But then she felt the doctor press something into her hands.

'You'll need this to register the death,' the woman said gently. 'I'm sorry. I can't lie. This sort of haemorrhage from a miscarriage is incredibly rare. It'd raise an inquest, and probably a post-mortem. And you wouldn't want to put your mum through that, would you?'

Hillie wiped the back of her hand across her face, and looked at the piece of paper trembling in her hands. Oh, God. Her dad would have to know the truth. 'No,' she murmured, her voice broken and empty. 'And thank you.'

'I just wish I'd been in time. But... you say your goodbyes. I'll see myself out.'

The doctor tiptoed down the stairs. She'd seen it all before. Many times. Women, girls, in trouble. Married or otherwise. If only this sort of thing could be made legal. So that doctors could perform the procedure safely and with impunity. But she couldn't see that happening in her lifetime. If only the politicians and the religious objectors could see what she had over and over again...

As if to compound her convictions, the front door crashed open just as she reached it and a stocky, lurching drunk in a flat cap staggered inside. He stopped, swaying precariously, and glared at the stranger.

'Who the bleeding hell are you?' he demanded.

'I think... you'd better go upstairs,' she answered levelly, and slipped past him, smelling the beer on his breath as she did so.

She shook her head as she pulled the door shut behind her. And heard the fellow's bellicose roar as he pounded up the stairs. Dear God, she wouldn't fancy being in that poor young girl's shoes just now!

Chapter Fifteen

Jimmy had been waiting down in the kitchen, not wanting to intrude. But recognising Harold's bellowing voice, he ran up the stairs behind him. He might be needed, and he wasn't going to let that monster hurt his Hillie ever again.

He reached the front bedroom just in time to hear Mrs Parker tell Harold in a few words what had happened. It was just as well he was there, Jimmy considered, as Hardwick went berserk, flinging himself about the room in a frenzy so that everyone had to dodge out of his way. Jimmy was about to launch himself on him before someone was hurt, when the devil lurched over the bottom of the bedstead, breaking his stampede. He looked down on his wife, jerking himself into reality, and crawled round the side of the bed to her.

Jimmy sought Hillie's gaze. Her face was white, but she mouthed her thanks at him. 'I'll call if I need you,' she whispered. 'And take Luke with you.'

Jimmy was reluctant to go, but Harold seemed to have calmed down so Jimmy led Hillie's trembling brother down the stairs, followed by an anxious Eva, who mumbled that she'd fetch a bowl of water. They left Harold kneeling by Nell's bedside, holding her hand in his and kissing it repeatedly. 'Oh, my darling, what'll I do without you?' he moaned, his words slurred from a night at the pub.

Hillie watched him, grief, fury, contempt bubbling up inside her. 'Oh, don't play the grieving husband with me,' she growled, burning with disgust as she noticed his eyes were totally dry. 'You never loved her.'

He swivelled round, scarlet rage flushing up from his neck. 'How dare you!' he yelled, letting go of Nell's hand to raise his fist. Then, realising Hillie was towering over him, face set like granite, he appeared to think better of it. 'I did love her. Very much,' he protested – as if butter wouldn't melt, Hillie considered.

'Then you had a dead funny way of showing it,' she retorted.

'Don't you cheek me, you little minx,' Harold grated, his usual ill-temper returning at once. 'This is your fault. If you hadn't run away to marry that scum, you'd've been here to help, and she wouldn't've felt she couldn't cope with another un. And now they're both dead 'cos of you.'

Hillie brushed aside the stab of guilt. Yes, her mother and her baby brother or sister were gone. But she wasn't going to let her father bully her like he had her mum. It was time for some home truths.

'I didn't run away. You *drove* me away. You beat me up for going out and having some fun. And don't think I don't know about you stealing the money I sent for Luke and the others for their birthdays. You're just a damned, bloody bully! And this,' she seethed, gesturing towards Nell, 'had nothing to do with me. And it didn't really have anything to do with the baby, either. She'd have loved it and cared for it just as she did all of us. It was *you* who ground her down. Bullying her, treating her like muck. It was *that* that made her feel she couldn't cope. Well, at least she won't have to put up with you any longer. She's well out of it. Now get your sodding self out of here so Mrs P and I can lay her out.'

Harold's jaw had dropped open several times as he went to interrupt her tirade, but in his drunken stupor, the shock of Hillie's unfettered rage was too much for him. 'And where am I supposed to go?' he whined pathetically, changing tactic as he stood up and yawned, just as if his dead wife wasn't lying there in the bed. 'I'm knackered and I need some kip.'

Hillie boiled over with hatred. He was unbelievable! 'I don't bloody well care where you go!' She rolled her eyes in outrage, her gaze falling on his side of the bed. 'Here,' she snarled, grabbing his pillow and the eiderdown and bundling them into his arms. 'Take those downstairs into your precious parlour. Make a bed for yourself on the floor. It's where you belong. Like the dog that you are, and that's insulting every dog on earth!'

She pushed him so hard as he staggered from the room, that he fell out through the door and only just managed to stop himself from going headlong down the stairs. Hillie watched him, disappointed that he didn't do just that and break his neck. He deserved it, and the world would be a far better place.

Panting as her fury subsided, Hillie stumbled on unsteady legs back into the bedroom, hands over her mouth in horror at her own flaring outburst. She'd argued, shouted at her dad often enough, but she didn't think she'd ever attacked him like that before. Perhaps if she had, things might never have got so bad, and this might never have happened. But there again, Harold hadn't got so drunk in the past as he seemed to now. She was sure the only reason she'd got away with it was because he was semi-paralytic and wasn't capable of retaliating. No doubt she'd pay for it later in one way or another.

'Oh, Mum,' she sighed out loud as she stepped up to the bed and took Harold's place, kneeling on the rag rug over the bare floorboards. She stroked Nell's cheek. It was already turning cold. 'I'm sorry I let it come to this,' she choked miserably, tears streaming unchecked down her cheeks. 'I did try. But I still don't really understand why you wouldn't leave him. And now... now I never will.'

She took Nell's hand, pressing her forehead against it, allowing the grief to pour over her. What had her poor mum suffered since she'd upped and gone away? Was it her fault, or would it have happened anyway?

Hillie gritted her teeth, steeling herself as she heard Eva's heavy footfall on the stairs. She knew the dear woman would be carrying a bowl of warm water to wash Nell's body clean, and that then with Hillie's help, she'd change her clothes, put clean sheets on the bed. Make her friend ready for her journey into the afterlife.

Hillie watched, trembling, as the door handle turned. She'd never expected this. Was it really her fault? Dear Lord, what had she done?

*

Jimmy held her at arm's length, his chocolate eyes deep with earnest. 'I'm so sorry, Hill. I can't come.'

Hillie's face moved into a bewildered, accusing frown. 'What d'you mean, you can't come?' she demanded, pausing as she pulled on her old knitted black gloves to match the coat Belinda had lent her. 'You only went out to get a loaf of bread.'

'Yeah, well, here's the bread. But I bumped into Mr Jackson, and he's got a job for us.'

'A job for you!' Hillie scoffed, halfway between disbelief and outrage. 'The factory've given you a day's compassionate leave to come to my mum's funeral, and you're going to swan off to do some dodgy deal for this Mr Jackson instead!'

'No, Hill, you don't understand. He's giving us a month's wages for just one day's work. I couldn't say no.'

'And you expect me to believe it's all above board?' Hillie was infuriated. 'I've always thought there was something fishy about him.'

'Well, you're wrong. He just moves in very different circles to the sort of thing we're used to. He deals in lots of things, but this is to do with property. Anyway, I've said yes, so I can't let him down now. Besides, your dad might decide he don't want me at the funeral after all. He might turn nasty, and you wouldn't want that, would you?'

Hillie glared at him, her lips twisted. She *needed* Jimmy at the funeral to support her. She was disappointed and deeply hurt. But a month's wages... Besides, she was sure nothing she'd say could change Jimmy's mind.

'But what if it gets back to the factory that you weren't at the funeral?'

'If anyone asks, just tell them I got ill or something,' Jimmy shrugged. 'I am sorry, love. But it was too good to miss. I hope it all goes off... well, as well as a funeral can.' He gave her a quick peck on the cheek before turning back to the door. 'I'll get you something nice to make up for it. And don't wait up tonight. I mightn't be back till late.'

And he was gone, leaving Hillie to stare at the closed door. Her legs felt wobbly, and her hand reached out to feel for the settee. She lowered herself onto it, feeling all topsy-turvy. The funeral wasn't until two o'clock and she was running early, so she had plenty of time to sit quietly for a few moments to put her emotions in order. It was going to be hard enough, and she couldn't waste any of her strength worrying about what Jimmy was up to.

She took a deep breath, putting the lid on her frustrations and sorrow. Time to face the music. And she let herself out of the flat.

It was drizzling and cold, a thoroughly miserable afternoon. When she turned into Banbury Street, already feeling chilled and wretched, a lifetime of memories flooded back. Childhood dreams, playing innocently on the pavement with Kit and Gert, and then Luke when he was old enough, wary of her dad but unaware of the animosity that would eventually develop between them. Above all, her mum, always there to comfort her, bathe a grazed knee, kiss a bumped head. Help her to read her first book, and all those that came after. It was special what they'd had. Was that because she was the firstborn, and the war had meant a four-year gap before Luke came along? Perhaps. And now her mum was dead. Gone. At peace. And somehow Hillie was going to have to make sure her brother and sisters were properly cared for.

The front door to the house was open, and Hillie went inside. The atmosphere was strange. Hushed. The parlour door was ajar, and Hillie peered round it. Her dad was there, staring down at the long, narrow box balanced on two trestles. His expression was unfathomable, hair greased down, his work suit sponged and pressed in an outward show of grief.

Hillie pulled herself up short. On this of all days, she should give him more credit. Surely he must have loved her mum once upon a time. But yet again, there wasn't a tear in his eyes.

His features stiffened when he saw Hillie, but she ignored it and instead stepped forward to look at her mum one last time. Nell looked so peaceful, as if she was asleep. All her cares gone. And Hillie felt sorrow rising in her throat again.

'Have the… the little ones said goodbye?' she managed to croak.

'Yeah. Of course,' Harold snapped back.

Hillie couldn't find it in her to retort, but nodded briefly. Then she gazed down into the open coffin again, imprinting the image on her mind forever.

Kissed her own fingers and placed them on Nell's marble forehead.

'Goodbye, Mum,' she mouthed, unable to voice the words. Grief strangling her.

There were sounds in the hallway, footsteps, muted voices. A couple of men Hillie didn't recognise came into the room and lifted the coffin lid into place. She watched until the last second. The shadow closing over her mum's face. And then she was swallowed up into darkness.

Hillie couldn't bear to watch the lid being nailed down. Gasping for breath, she stumbled out into the kitchen. Luke was there, stone-faced, as he kept an eye on his four younger sisters. The relief as Hillie appeared was palpable, and she scraped herself together for their sakes. They were back to their normal, loving selves again, and Hillie wondered what lies Harold had told about her – or what threats he'd made towards them if they dared to speak to her.

'Get your coats on,' she said gently. She bent to help Daisy into hers and then turned to Frances who was struggling to fasten her buttons.

'Luke says Mummy's gone for a long sleep,' the child told her in a matter-of-fact tone.

'That's right. She was very tired,' Hillie managed to confirm in what she hoped was a normal-sounding voice.

'And we won't see her for a very long time.'

'No. So you all need to be very good for Daddy.'

Hillie straightened up as Luke peered round the door into the hallway. 'Come on. It's time,' he rasped.

They trooped outside just as the plain coffin was being lifted onto the decorated dray-cart from the brewery that owned not just the Duke of Cambridge on the corner but some of the street as well. Some of the people from the brewery still remembered Nell as the sweet little daughter of the grocer who used to be round the corner, and when they heard she was to have the equivalent of a pauper's funeral, they'd stepped in to provide some decent transport for her last journey. The cart had been cleaned, and the massive horses groomed until their coats gleamed, their manes and tails plaited with black ribbons. The sight tightened the constriction in Hillie's throat, and suddenly the street filled with people spilling out of their front doors. Jessica came down the steps of Number Three followed, amazingly, by both her parents dressed immaculately in black, wanting to be seen to be doing the correct thing, Hillie imagined. But it was nevertheless appreciated.

Belinda, although unable to come herself, had also wangled from Personnel a couple of hours' compassionate leave for Stan and Gert, who was holding little Trudy's hand. Eva was trundling

Primrose along in an old pushchair, and then Hillie was happily surprised to see Kit manoeuvring Old Sal's wheelchair over the threshold and onto the pavement.

The clip-clop of horses' hooves drew Hillie's attention back to the cart as it began to move forward. Nobody spoke to Harold as he took up his position immediately behind, shoulders hunched and his face set sourly. Hillie fell into step next, holding Daisy and Frances each by a hand. Luke followed them with Joan and Trixie who, like Daisy, had both been allowed the day off school, and the Parker family and everyone else came on behind.

Hillie's eyes settled on her father's back as the procession moved off. Dampness spangled on his worn coat, dank and depressing. She wondered bitterly what was going on in his head. Was he really sad? Yes, of course he'd be thinking who was going to warm his bed, and who he could bully now his poor, submissive wife was gone. But was he really going to miss her as someone should miss their lifelong soulmate? The other part of their own being that would make them empty and aching for the rest of their life?

Somehow Hillie doubted it very much!

*

'So where was that so-called husband of yours, then?'

Hillie felt a flush of shame warm her cheeks. 'He was going to come, but he's gone down with some sort of tummy bug. Been sick and rushing to the lav all night. I left him in bed.'

She cringed at the deceit, and prayed it didn't show. How could she tell such a lie? But Jimmy had forced her into it, and what else could she do? She hoped to God nobody saw Jimmy out and about. If they did, and accused her of lying, she'd have to say that Jimmy had apparently felt a little better later on and thought a breath of air might help. Oh, crikey, what had he got her into?

'Huh, more likely bottled out,' Harold sneered. 'Too yellow to face me, was he?'

'Who could blame him if he was?' Hillie retorted. Was it nine months of marriage that had given her more confidence than ever to confront her father? Or was she so broken by her mum's death that she'd thrown caution to the wind? But she could see the anger building on her dad's face, and this wasn't the time.

'Look, now everyone's gone, you sit down and I'll make you a nice fresh cuppa,' she pacified him. 'Luke and Joan and I'll clear up,' she grimaced, her eyes roving over the dirty teacups and plates strewn all over the place from the wake. 'And then I'll put Daisy and Frances to bed for you.'

Harold glared at her, lips knotted, but then he nodded, if reluctantly. Easing himself into a chair at the table, he proceeded to cut himself a chunk of what remained of the cake Hillie had baked as her contribution to the wake. He sat, slurping at his tea, and Hillie watched him out of the corner of her eye as she worked. Her two youngest sisters were sitting still as rocks, hardly daring to move. It had been a strange day for them, and they really didn't understand why their mummy wasn't there anymore. Yet their daddy did nothing whatsoever to comfort them, Hillie noted bitterly.

She worked as quickly as she could to have everything washed up and cleared away, leftover sandwiches wrapped in greaseproof paper to keep them fresh, and bits of cake stowed in tins. At least her dad had possessed the grace to offer a wake. Not that many of those who'd come to the funeral had come inside the house. Jessica and her parents certainly hadn't, and one or two others had only popped in for a polite cuppa. Gert and Stan had needed to get back to the factory for another hour or two, and out of the dozen or so people who'd partaken of the tea, it was really only Eva who'd stayed any length of time, as Kit had taken Old Sal, Trudy and Primrose back home.

'Call in for a bit when you've finished here,' Eva had said to Hillie in a muted tone when she finally left.

'Thanks, I will,' Hillie replied with a grateful nod. She couldn't think of anything better after the tensions of the day than an hour with her dear friends, the Parkers. And Jimmy had warned her he'd be late, so the flat would be empty when she got home. Oh, she could throttle him, and just when she needed him for moral support. But she supposed he was right in that the extra money would always come in handy even though they were managing very well, even putting money into their savings every week. Exactly what they were saving for, they weren't quite sure. The cottage in the country seemed but a pipe dream just now. But it would be for a better future life in some shape or form.

'Come on, you two,' Hillie said when all was neat and tidy in the kitchen. 'Use the lav and do your teeth, and if you're good, I'll do you a bedtime story.'

'Oh, ta, Hillie.'

'We haven't had a story since Mummy went to sleep.'

'Daddy said you went away 'cos you don't love us anymore.'

Hillie stifled her gasp. 'No, that's not true,' she answered, casting an angry glare in her dad's direction. 'It's just that I've grown up and got my own home now. Come on, hurry up now.'

'Me don't like Mummy not being here,' Frances complained as they finally climbed the stairs. 'When her come back?'

Hillie bit her lip. Tears were threatening in her eyes at her little sister's distress, but she had to be strong. 'Not for a long time, I'm afraid,' she managed to smile. 'So, what story would you like? The Three Little Pigs?'

'Oh, yes!' Daisy squealed, diving into bed.

'All right, then. Once upon a time, there were three little piggies,' Hillie began and launched into the story.

After much huffing and puffing and blowing, the girls were giggling happily and ready to settle down, clearly far more their old selves.

'Nighty-night, then,' Hillie said, bending to kiss each in turn. 'Sleep well.'

'I wish you'd come back, Hillie.'

The earnest expression on Daisy's little face scythed into Hillie's heart. 'I will if I can,' she promised, although she doubted her dad would allow it.

She went slowly down the familiar staircase, her heart heavy. She wondered if in fact she'd ever come back to the house. She couldn't see her dad changing his mind, and besides, it held such terrible memories for her now. She'd avoided even glancing at the bedroom door behind which her mum had bled to death. And yet she yearned with a burning passion to see her siblings on a regular basis.

Back in the kitchen, Joan was sniffing back tears as she tried valiantly to continue with the jumper Nell had been knitting for Daisy, and Trixie was building a tower with old cotton reels. Luke was gazing motionless into the pathetic fire in the grate, while Harold's palms were placed down squarely on the table in front of him, his head drawn back into his bull neck.

Hillie saw him glance up as she came back into the room, almost as if he'd been waiting for her. Ready to taunt her.

'Well, that's that, then,' he announced, lifting his hands and banging them back down on the table. The force of it made Trixie's tower collapse, and the poor child burst into tears as the tamped-down sadness of the day suddenly erupted. 'Oh, shut up,' Harold snapped. 'It's only a bloody game.'

Hillie's mouth fell open in horrified disbelief. She wrapped her arms round Trixie who sobbed against her, clinging to her in desperation.

'How can you be so horrible?' Hillie grated over her shoulder. 'She's just lost her mother in case you hadn't noticed.' And before Harold had a chance to answer with some scathing reply, she tipped Trixie's chin up to look at her. 'It's been a long day. Why don't you get yourself up to bed?'

Trixie nodded, wiping the back of her hand under her running nose. Her pleading eyes bore into Hillie's. 'I'm glad you've come back,' she mumbled, before shooting out to the closet in the backyard.

Harold glared across at Hillie as if his mere glance would cow her, but she held his gaze in steady, defiant silence. It wasn't until Trixie hurried back through, giving Hillie a final hug and then went upstairs, that Hillie stepped up to her father.

'So what are you going to do?' she demanded fiercely. 'You and Luke are at work all day. Joan's only twelve and won't be leaving school for another eighteen months or so. So you can't expect her to keep house. And Frances won't be starting school for another year nearly, so who's going to take care of her? And then there's after school and the school holidays for all of them. You just going to let them fend for themselves?'

Harold's lip curled into a livid sneer. 'Think I'm stupid, do you? That I ain't got it all worked out? Well, that's where you're bloody wrong.' He leant back in the chair, joining his hands behind his head and looking up at Hillie with malice glinting in his eyes. 'I've taken on Dolly Maguire. She's starting in the morning.'

Hillie almost staggered backwards. 'D-Dolly Maguire!' she stammered, almost choking on the name. 'Y-you can't be serious. You do know…?' She broke off in a turmoil of anger and despair. She was about to say that it was Dolly who'd told her mum who to go to. That without Dolly, Nell might still be alive. But she didn't know how much Luke and Joan understood about their mum's death. Surely to God Harold hadn't told them the truth, that she'd died as a result of a botched abortion!

A sudden surge of fury overtook her shock. Her hand shot out and she shook her father hard by the shoulder. 'No, you can't possibly let Dolly look after the children!' she protested, her eyes snapping dangerously. 'She's little more than a common whore and a drunk into the bargain!'

'Huh!' Harold threw up his head with a sarcastic laugh, but then suddenly he sprang up, poking Hillie in the chest. 'I don't need a little slut like you telling me what I can or can't do! Dolly comes cheap, and since you ran off and abandoned us for that good-for-nothing and took your wages with you, she's all I can afford. So if you want to blame anyone, blame yourself. Now get out of here, and don't you ever come back!'

Stinging tears pricked in Hillie's eyes. For was there some truth in her father's words? But she wasn't going to yield to him ever again, and thrust her nose fearlessly towards his face.

'Yes, I'll go,' she hissed. 'But I *will* be back, I promise you. Bye, Joannie,' she said, turning to give her sister a hug. 'I'll see you soon. And Luke, I'll see you at work tomorrow. And *you*,' she snarled, spinning back to Harold and stabbing her finger at him, 'will not stop me!'

She swivelled on her heel, storming out of the kitchen. Swiftly pulling on her coat in the hallway and slinging her scarf round her neck, she let herself out of the house. She wanted to slam the door, but closed it quietly behind her so as not to wake her sleeping sisters.

Outside, she hesitated in the dark, empty street, clenching her fists at her sides. Dear God, Dolly Maguire! Surely there was something she could do to stop it. Luke was probably mature enough to deal with it, but the idea of that... that *harlot* going anywhere near her sisters was unbearable. Hillie was beside herself, stamping her feet into the pavement in exploding frustration. She really could scream out loud, but instead found herself entwining her fingers in her hair and pulling hard. It didn't help, and she let go, crossing her fists across her chest and bending down over them. She turned in a circle, her face torn in an ugly grimace until the dam burst and tears flooded down her cheeks.

She didn't know how long she stood there, so utterly alone and desperate. Jimmy, her husband, should have been there, but he wasn't. There was only one place she could go. The chaotic place that had been her haven since childhood.

Gulping down her tears, she wiped her eyes dry and found herself running blindly to the house a few doors down the street.

Chapter Sixteen

Hillie waited outside the Parkers' front door, feeling guilty and miserable. She needed to grieve for her mum, and yet overriding all else now was her fear for her younger sisters. To have them cared for by Dolly Maguire was unthinkable, but what could she do about it? She felt so helpless. And was what her dad had said right? Was it all her fault? If it hadn't been so long since she'd seen her mum, maybe things wouldn't have worked out this way. Yet it was her father who'd prevented her from seeing Nell. Oh, whichever way she looked at it, Hillie seemed to be trapped in a deep, dark hole.

When the door was opened by Kit, dear Kit who'd been part of her life since the cradle, it suddenly all became too much. Her mangled emotions rose up inside her and she burst into tears yet again.

The next instant, she felt herself enveloped in Kit's quiet, dependable embrace. She wept against his shoulder, helpless against the sobs that racked her body. She was aware of Kit drawing her inside and closing the door, but he made no attempt to stem the tide of her misery. He knew she needed to cry, and he waited patiently, holding her gently, soothing her, tucking her head beneath his chin. Wishing… wishing…

Slowly, gradually, her soul seemed to be washed clean and she pulled back slightly. She missed his closeness almost at once, but she was regaining control, and she couldn't weep for ever. Sniffing, she began searching in her pocket for a hanky, but Kit was already there, offering a folded, starched white cotton square of his own. She took it gratefully, noticing how clean and pristine it was for a chap who lived alone and did his own laundry. But then, Kit had always been a perfectionist in everything he'd ever turned his hand to.

'Thanks,' she gulped, wiping her nose. 'I'm sorry—'

'Well, don't be. It's been a tough day for you.'

'Yes,' she nodded, giving a watery smile.

Kit smiled back, an expression of such kindness and compassion that Hillie could feel tears welling up again. She forced herself to concentrate on Kit's familiar face instead, his striking blue eyes, the lock of hair that fell over his forehead, his curved, well-shaped mouth. At that moment, his just being there was a comfort.

'Come into the kitchen,' he said in his soft voice. 'Mum said she'd asked you to pop by.'

'I didn't think you'd still be here,' Hillie told him, feeling better as they went down the hallway. 'Not on shift or anything? It was so good of you to come to the funeral.'

'I wanted to come. And for something like this, there's usually someone who's willing to swap shifts. Actually... I don't suppose you want to hear this just now, but I've just been given another promotion.'

'Oh, that's great news, Kit! Congratulations! And on the contrary, that's really something to cheer me up.'

'Thanks,' Kit replied as he opened the kitchen door for her. 'Look who I found on the front step,' he announced as they went in. As Hillie had expected, the four younger children were all abed, leaving the five adults sitting around the table.

'Oh, there you are, you poor lamb.' Eva was on her feet in an instant, squashing Hillie against her homely bosom. 'Stan, you move and let the poor child sit next to the fire, and I'll make her a nice cuppa.'

'That's very kind, Mrs P.' Hillie caught her breath as she was released. 'But I'm awash with tea.'

'You sure? Anything else I can get you instead?'

'No, thanks. It'll just be nice to be with you all for a bit,' Hillie said, sitting down in the chair Stan had vacated for her.

'Your dad been his usual charming self, has he?' Gert asked, pulling an affronted grimace.

Hillie released a torn sigh. 'You won't believe this. He's only getting Dolly Maguire to look after the girls and keep house for him.'

'What!'

'Huh, well, she won't keep the place spick and span like what he made poor Nell do, will she, now?' Eva scoffed bitterly.

'And does he know it was Dolly who... you know...?'

Hillie shook her head in despair. 'I honestly don't know. And I didn't want to bring it up. Not in front of the others, anyway. But I can't bear the idea of her taking Mum's place. But Dad says she's all he can afford.'

'We-ell,' Eva said thoughtfully, rubbing her bottom lip between her forefinger and thumb. 'I suppose I could have Frances during the day. Won't be easy with Primrose and Trudy and me mum—'

'Someone call me?' the elderly woman screeched, suddenly springing to life. 'I think someone died. Sure I went to a funeral today. Who was it died? Wasn't me, was it?'

'Oh, I'm sorry, Hill. The poor old dear—'

'It's all right. I understand.'

'Time you went to bed, eh, Mum?'

'OK, love, I'll take her,' Stan offered. 'Come on, Old Sal.'

'Oh, ta, Stan. What'd I do without you?'

They all had to get up and move round so that Stan could support the old lady as she tottered precariously out of the room. Hillie thought perhaps it should be her cue to leave, but she couldn't bring herself to do so. And she must reply to Eva's generous offer.

'That's very kind of you, Mrs P, but I couldn't expect you to have Frances as well.'

'Well, your Luke and now young Joan've taken my lot to and from school ever since Mum couldn't be left. So I'd only be repaying the favour. Think on it, ducks. But I'm afraid I can't offer to do anything in the house.'

'Oh, Mrs P, you're a gem, really you are. But I don't know if...' Hillie paused, considering what a sincere friend this happy-go-lucky, golden-hearted woman had been to her mum. Memories of the night Nell had died came flooding back. Hillie was sure she couldn't have got through it without dear Eva. 'Mrs P,' she began tentatively, a curious dread taking hold of her. 'That night. Not long before... Mum died, she asked me to forgive her for something. She said you'd tell me. Do you... d'you know what she meant?'

Hillie watched as Eva's ruddy face drained of its usual colour, and the woman's mouth clamped shut. Hillie's stomach started churning as she realised Gert and Kit were both looking at their mother with searching curiosity. It was several moments before Eva spoke, and when she did, her voice was almost inaudible.

'Yeah. I do. And she obviously wanted you to know. But… maybe not…'

She gestured towards her son and daughter, but Hillie shook her head. 'Whatever it is, I don't want there to be any secrets between us,' she whispered.

'Well, if you're sure. But this goes no further than this room,' Eva said sharply, gathering her wits again as she jabbed her head towards Gert and Kit. 'Your dad's always known, of course. But we was always sworn to secrecy.'

Hillie exchanged confused glances with her two friends. Whatever was this all about? Her heart raced as she waited for Eva to begin, the very air seeming to quiver with tension.

'Your mum, my dearest Nell, was in love,' the older woman spoke at last in a low, steady tone. 'Stan and me was already married, living in this very house, and we already had you, Kit. Anyway, Nell was a pretty young thing. And she fell in love. Really nice young fella he was. And they got engaged. And everything was hunky-dory.'

A frown puckered Hillie's forehead, and she shook her head in bewilderment. 'And it wasn't my dad?' she questioned. 'So… if everything was going so well, why didn't Mum marry this chap? I don't understand.'

She watched as Eva pursed her lips, and in the ensuing silence, listened to the clock ticking on the mantelpiece, the fire crackling in the grate. She was willing Eva to continue, and yet she was suddenly afraid of what the good woman was going to reveal. Hillie realised she was holding her breath, and Gert and Kit were waiting without a word, too.

'It... it was the war,' Eva finally continued, the words clearly coming with difficulty. 'The chance to see another country. It'll be over by Christmas. You've heard how it was. Nobody thought of getting killed. Leastways, the lads didn't. Nell's young man – Will Norton his name was – he joined up straightaway. Said it was his patriotic duty. Poor Nell was all overcome, and I suppose with her feelings all over the place, she... well, they... they did you know what before he left.'

Eva paused, her cheeks flushing, and she lowered her eyes for a moment before she looked up again and fixed her gaze, intense with compassion, on Hillie's face. 'I don't think I need to tell you, dearie, do I? Ain't you ever wondered where you got your height from? And them eyes? The colour of your hair?'

Hillie was staring blindly at her, Eva's words becoming a fading jumble in her head. Her stomach turned somersaults as the fog began to clear and the truth clawed its way into her brain.

'You… you mean…?' she barely articulated. And something seemed to land heavily in her chest as Eva nodded slowly.

'You was Will's child. And he was killed right at the start of the war. Never even left British soil. Training accident it was. Terrible.'

The words tore at Hillie's heart and she felt slightly faint as the strength seemed to drain out of her, leaving her lost and fragile. She glanced at Gert and Kit. Saw the same shock on both their faces. Her head swam and she could feel herself going limp.

The next second, Kit's strong arm was about her, holding her up. 'Get her some water, would you, Gert?' she heard him say. And then, as he helped her to sip some of the cool, refreshing liquid, the room wavered back into focus.

'And… and Mum?' she managed to mumble, turning back to Eva. She knew there was more and was grateful when Kit still kept his arm about her shoulder.

'Realised she had a bun in the oven same time she got the news,' Eva went on slowly. 'I think knowing I was preggers again made her realise. It was my second, of course, so I recognised it early on. And when I told her how I felt, she realised she felt the same. She was broke with the news over Will. And she panicked, I suppose. Didn't think she had the strength to face the, what shall I say, stigma of having a baby out of wedlock. And she reckoned it'd bring shame on her parents. That customers'd boycott the shop.'

'But... surely that sort of thing happened a lot during the war?' Kit put in, his frown deepening.

'It did. But people can be cruel. Too bloody righteous to put themselves in someone else's shoes. And this was right at the start of the war, remember. Before people'd got used to things like that. I mean, I told Nell to take no bleeding notice of anyone else. Me and Stan said we'd take her in if it helped. And I'd've given what for to anyone what was nasty to her. But poor Nell was so grief-stricken over Will, she couldn't think straight. And she was frightened, but more for her parents and the baby than for herself.' Eva turned to Hillie, moisture glistening in her eyes. 'She didn't want you growing up being called a bastard. She could've gone away and had you in secret and then given you up. But she wasn't having none of that. You was all she had left of Will. So she did what she thought was best for you. Something what I think took a hell of a lot more guts than facing vicious gossip. She married another man. A man what she didn't love 'cos she was still in love with a ghost.'

312

Eva paused, her face twitching. Hillie watched her, a magnitude of sorrow and jumbled emotions heaving inside her.

'My... my dad,' she finally croaked.

Eva nodded with slow, disgusted reluctance. 'Except he wasn't your dad, of course. Harold had been after your mum for a while. Nell'd turned him down several times in favour of Will, even though he was blooming persistent. But, being Nell, she'd turned him down gently. Just as well, 'cos it made it more believable when she accepted his advances soon after Will was killed. They was married within a couple of months. As luck would have it, you was a small baby, and Nell wasn't showing.'

Hillie blinked hard, her senses dropping away as realisation dawned. 'You mean... he didn't know?'

Eva met her gaze. 'No. He was cock-a-hoop at getting Nell. Till he found out. And then he went mad. Called her all the names under the sun. The whole bloody street heard. And then he buttoned his lip. His pride was hurt that he'd let hisself be tricked, and he didn't want no one to know. So, to the outside world, he behaved as if you was his.'

'But in private, all he did was punish Mum and me,' Hillie murmured as the truth sank in.

'Oh, things wasn't quite so bad at first. Your mum respected Harold for bringing you up as his own. I think she even did love him for it once, in a funny sort of way. And he always loved her. He was just eaten up with jealousy. He just couldn't ever *forgive* her, if that makes sense.'

'No. No, it doesn't. If you truly love someone, you do so unconditionally. Even if they love someone else and not you, their happiness is all you want.'

Hillie's eyes flashed at Kit at his words. Eva's revelation had been swirling about her numbed brain in a mist, the words sinking in like drizzle, falling softly here and there, the full impact only slowly gathering strength. She was glad of Eva's stream of speech, almost like a dream she had no need to interrupt. But Kit's murmured comment broke the spell. She came back to reality, forcing herself to start making sense of Eva's tale.

'So… she stayed with him for my sake? Put up with all the abuse because of me?'

'Well, as I say, it wasn't like that at first. Once Harold got over the shock, they both seemed to come to terms with what they had. Made the best of it. And maybe things might've been OK if Harold hadn't had to go off to war himself. Being made sergeant brought out the bully in him, and it never left him. And then Luke and the others came along, and Nell was trapped.'

'But… she could've left him as we got older. God knows, I tried to persuade her, but she wouldn't hear of it. She said it wasn't possible to divorce him, and I think she was too frightened of him to try to escape. But I reckon there was something else, too.'

'Oh, well, the lines between love and duty and familiarity can all cross over when you're in a rut. And poor Nell felt she *deserved* all the punishment he meted out to her. But *you* didn't. She married him 'cos she thought it was the best thing for you. But it wasn't. *That's* what she wanted you to forgive her for.'

'Oh.' Hillie's brow compressed into deep folds as she slowly broke free from her shock. 'Poor Mum. All those years. The man she really loved dead, and having to put up with Dad's cruelty instead. And to keep it all secret.'

'*Not* your bleeding dad, remember,' Gert put in fiercely, emerging from her own shock. 'You need to forget he ever pretended to be, and double quick. He's nothing but bloody Harold Hardwick to you now. To any of us.'

'Ah.' Stan came in just then, carrying Old Sal's chamber pot. 'You... told them, then? I'll just empty this and I'll be back.' And he went through to the yard, leaving them all in pensive silence.

'So, Mum,' Kit said a few moments later, focusing all their thoughts, 'Hillie's real father, this Will Norton, what of him? What about his family? Maybe Hillie has grandparents, aunts and uncles, cousins, somewhere?'

But Eva shook her head sadly. 'No. His parents was already dead. He had a sister what he never got on with, but she'd gone to Canada with her husband and they'd lost touch. That's why Nell was down as Will's next of kin. Why she got the telegram.'

Hillie hadn't realised, but she'd clasped her hands in front of her. Now she rested her chin on them, her eyes lowered sightlessly. Her poor, poor Mum.

'Could I... have that cuppa now, d'you think?' a voice that sounded like hers asked as Stan came back in, washing his hands in the scullery sink.

'Course, love,' he answered amiably.

'And then I'll walk you home,' Kit put in firmly. 'You shouldn't be alone tonight.'

'Yeah. It's a lot to take in. Oh, come here,' Gert said, coming round to give Hillie such a tight hug, it almost squeezed the breath out of her.

It was half an hour later when Hillie and Kit set out together. Winter was coming on hard, and there was frost in the air, the pavements slippery with ice in places. Kit offered Hillie his arm and she took it gratefully, huddling close to him for warmth. It felt comforting and natural, for wasn't Kit just like a brother to her?

'You know, I could give your dad, I mean Harold, some money each week so that he could get in a proper housekeeper,' Kit offered as they hurried through the bitter night air. 'I'm getting a good salary, and I've only got myself to keep.'

Such a tide of gratitude surged through Hillie that the horrors of the day seemed to melt away. 'Oh, Kit, you're so kind,' she answered. 'I really appreciate it, but *Harold*,' she enunciated with distaste, 'would never accept. And he'd probably thump you one into the bargain. Besides, I'm not so sure the money's not just an excuse. He probably could afford more, especially if he didn't go down the pub every night. He's just using it as another way to go on punishing me.'

'Then he really is a bastard.' They'd reached the front door to the house now, and Kit turned her round to face him. 'But if you think of any way, any way at all, I can help, you just let me know, eh?'

Hillie smiled up at him, his face so familiar in the lamplight, and nodded. 'Bless you, Kit, I will,' she replied, and reached up to plant a kiss on his cheek.

He hugged her tightly, making her feel secure and safe. It was with reluctance that she pulled away, waving to him as he walked back down the pavement. He turned to glance at her over his shoulder and raised his hand as he rounded the corner of the street and disappeared.

Hillie let herself quietly in the front door, then padded up the two flights of stairs to the flat.

'Jimmy?' she called softly. For how she yearned for him to hold her, to drive away all the demons, soothe her stretched nerves. But to her dismay – and a little annoyance – he wasn't there. So when she climbed into bed ten minutes later, she felt alone in the world and abandoned.

Chapter Seventeen

'Sorry I was so late back last night, love,' Jimmy apologised, coming up behind her the next morning as she prepared their sandwiches, and putting his arms round her waist. 'So how did it go yesterday?'

Hillie glanced over her shoulder, then got on with spreading fish paste on the bread. 'The funeral was all right. As you'd expect. Lots of people turned out. Even Jessica's parents.' She snapped the lid back on the little pot, her need to talk quelling her irritation with Jimmy as she swivelled round to face him. 'It was what happened afterwards that was so awful. My dad says that the only person he can afford to pay to keep house for him and look after the children is Dolly Maguire. You don't know her, but she's the last house in the street, and she's the one who... well, she's basically a drunk and a prostitute, and I can't bear the thought of her going anywhere near the girls. And then Mrs P told me my dad's not my dad at all. My real dad was killed at the beginning of the war, and Mum tricked Dad – or should I say Harold – into marrying her. He made her pay for it for the rest of her life, and that's why he treats me like he does.'

Jimmy's face had visibly lengthened as he listened to her outpouring of emotion, and he blinked his eyes wide. 'Blimey,' he breathed incredulously. 'And you never knew? And there was me not there for you. Oh, love, come here. I'm that sorry.'

He opened his arms and Hillie fell into them, her pent-up anguish bursting open as she sobbed against him. He held her tightly, hushing her and stroking her hair.

'We'll think of something, love,' Jimmy assured her. 'And look at it this way. It means you're totally free of him now. And this'll cheer you up. Look how much Mr Jackson gave me,' he said, taking a wad of pound notes from his pocket and waving them under her nose. 'Going to put this lot in our savings account at lunchtime, I am. And he says there's more where this came from. Now I know that's some pretty tough news you've had to take in, but we ought to get off to work. We'll talk about it tonight. It'll give me some thinking time and maybe I can come up with an idea for your kid sisters. Leave it with Jimmy, eh?'

He cupped Hillie's face in his hands, tipping it upwards so that she was looking at him. Her trusting eyes met his, and his smile seemed to instil faith in her. She nodded, sniffing back the remnants of her tears.

'Thanks, Jimmy,' she mumbled with a watery smile.

'You ain't married to Jimmy Baxter for nothing, you know,' he winked.

Hillie felt calmer. For now, at least. But what Jimmy could do, she had no idea. And the thought of Dolly Maguire taking care of Frances all day while the others were at school filled her with horror.

*

'Right, you. Get out. Now.'

Hillie's eyes flashed around the room. She'd let herself into her old home using the key that hung through the letter box on a length of string. Considering her sisters would be home from school, the house seemed much too quiet.

When Hillie opened the door to the back room, the sight that met her eyes made her seethe. Little Frances was on her hands and knees sweeping the floor with a dustpan and brush. Daisy, who wasn't yet six, was sat at the table cutting up carrots with what Hillie knew was a razor-sharp knife. Out in the scullery, she could see Trixie standing on an old orange-box in order to stir something in a large saucepan on the gas stove, and Joan was dunking sheets up and down in the copper full of steaming water. Meanwhile, Dolly was sitting in Nell's chair by the fire, feet up on the fender, sipping tea and eating cake while the girls slaved away at chores she should have done during the day.

Dolly slipped her feet from the fender and sat up with an affronted expression on her face. 'Who the hell d'you think you are, barging in here like you own the place? This ain't even your home no more.'

'But these are still my sisters,' Hillie retorted coldly. 'Sisters *you're* supposed to be looking after, not the other way round. Girls, stop doing all that at once,' she commanded, and then turning back to Dolly, she spat accusingly, 'How dare you get them doing all that when it's *your* job! Boiling saucepans and sharp knives at *their* ages? Are you out of your mind, you drunken old sow?'

'Don't you go accusing me, young madam!' Dolly rose to her feet with a malicious curl of her lip. 'Or should I say, you little bastard? 'Cos that's what you are!'

'You can say whatever you like as long as you get out and don't come back. Your so-called services are no longer required.'

But Dolly stood her ground, crossing her arms over her chest and wrinkling her mouth. 'I don't know what you think your dad's gonna say about this,' she gloated.

'It doesn't matter what he says, 'cos you're leaving of your own accord.' Hillie came up to her now. She cringed at the unwashed smell coming from Dolly, but forced herself to put her mouth close to her ear in order to whisper, 'I know the part you played in my mum's death. If you don't leave, I'm going to the police.'

She saw fear flash across Dolly's face for a split second before the woman sneered, 'But didn't stick the needles up her. And your beloved mother conceived you the wrong side of the blanket. If you make me leave, I'll make sure it's common knowledge.'

'Huh, go ahead,' Hillie scoffed. 'I know all about it, so you can't hurt *me*. And you certainly can't hurt Mum, so I wouldn't waste your breath. Whereas if I go to the police, you could be charged as an accessory to my mum's manslaughter.'

Dolly's jaw fell open. 'A... a what?' she murmured before she could stop herself.

'Means you were part of it, you ignorant old cow. So if I spill the beans, you could be facing a prison sentence. So I suggest you leave right now.'

'B-but... this is the first proper job I've had in ages—'

'And it's going to be the last.'

'But I ain't been paid fer this week.'

'How much was Harold paying you?'

'Twelve and six. Precious little fer all what he expected us ter do.'

'Well, it's Wednesday today, so by my reckoning, that's seven and six for this week,' Hillie grated, taking two half-crowns from her purse and pushing them into Dolly's greedy hands. 'But I'm going to make that five bob. Not that you deserve a penny of it. Now get out before I throw you out. And remember what I said. It wasn't a threat; it was a promise.'

She gave Dolly a shove towards the door and then followed her down the hallway. She grabbed the woman's filthy coat from the stand and thrust it into her arms before she bundled her outside. Dolly tried to turn back in protest, but Hillie shut the door in her face and yanked the key from its string in case she tried to let herself back in.

Hillie stood there for a moment, breathing heavily. Then she slapped her hands together. One down and one – the worse one – to go. She set her chin determinedly as she went back into the kitchen.

'Oh, Hill, you came back!'

'I knew you wouldn't let us down!'

The four young girls crowded around Hillie, hugging her, the little ones clinging onto her legs. She had to bite back the tears that pricked her eyes, and peeled her sisters' arms from about her.

'Come on. We've a lot to do. Daisy, Frances, you clear away the things that witch was using, then go and get a clean tablecloth from the drawer and lay the table,' Hillie instructed, since she felt she owed it to her mum's memory to keep up standards. 'Joan, leave the washing and take over the pan,' she went on, tying on one of Nell's old aprons and getting stuck in. 'I'll finish chopping the vegetables, and, Trixie, you just take them over to Joan as I do it. Helping out is one thing, but doing *everything* is another. Why didn't you tell Dad what was going on?'

'We tried, but he wouldn't listen. Said we were lying that Mrs Maguire wasn't doing anything.'

'I'd've thought that was obvious,' Hillie observed, glancing at the thick dust on the side-dresser and the accumulated ash in the hearth.

'We haven't had a cloth on the table since Mummy died,' Joan told her ruefully as Daisy and Frances spread the pristine damask out between them.

'Really? And what did your father have to say about that?'

'He didn't seem to care.'

Hillie raised an eyebrow. Didn't care? So bullying her mum all those years into having the table set as if for royalty all the time was simply part of his punishment, was it? Grrrh! She could cheerfully throttle him!

'Right, let's get the rest of the veg in the stew, and then, Joan, if you can peel some spuds ready to boil, I'll finish off the washing.'

In no time at all, the dinner was simmering on the stove, Hillie had given the room a lick and a promise, and the younger girls were playing on the hearth rug, just as they should have been, Hillie observed with satisfaction. She and Joan between them had finished the laundry which consisted mainly of Frances's sheets, since – no surprise to Hillie – the poor child had gone back to wetting the bed since her mummy had gone away and Dolly had been ordering her about and terrifying her all day long while the others were at school. By six o'clock, everything was in order, and the atmosphere was utterly changed from when Hillie had walked in the door two hours previously.

'Your dad'll be home soon,' she warned. 'There's likely to be a huge row, so the minute he gets in, I want you lot upstairs and making yourselves scarce until I call you back down. OK?'

dad, father. So far, that had sounded all right, and she didn't think even Joan had latched onto what Dolly had said. Hillie would have to explain at some point, but not just now. They'd been through enough. The two little ones would be too young to understand anyway, but when the moment was right, she'd tell Luke, Joan and Trixie. After all, they'd want to know why she'd be calling their dad Harold from now on, while Daisy and Frances should be young enough just to accept it. She'd reveal the truth to them when they were older.

Her younger sisters all nodded, Joan casting her a knowing, wary look that said she was glad she wasn't in Hillie's shoes. So when they heard Harold's key in the front door, Joan swiftly herded them all upstairs.

'What's going on?' Hillie heard him bellow from the hallway as the girls retreated upstairs. 'Where's that Dolly Maguire…?'

He stopped dead as he flung open the kitchen door. The delicious aroma of something cooking on the stove – far more tantalising than anything Dolly'd ever thrown together – filled his hungry nostrils. The table was set with an immaculately laundered cloth and perfectly arranged cutlery. The whole room was generally cleaner and more orderly, and for a second Harold was confused. It was as if Nell had come back from the dead. This certainly wasn't Dolly's handiwork.

And then he realised it was Hillie standing at the far end of the table, arms folded fiercely across her chest and her face set with challenging ferocity.

'What the hell are doing here?' he bawled, striding forward. 'And what the blazes have you done with Dolly?'

'Stop… right… there!' Hillie commanded icily. 'Dolly's gone. Said she couldn't cope with everything you wanted her to do, so she left.'

'You mean you threw her out, you bloody liar!'

He raised his arm as if to cuff her across the face. But Hillie was too quick for him and dodged the blow so that he banged his wrist against the chimney breast instead. He gave out a yelp of pain, and bent over to nurse his injury.

'No. She left of her own accord,' Hillie hissed in his ear. 'Ask her if you don't believe me. And I warned you not to try hitting me again. So you just listen to me. Dolly's gone, but you've got me instead. You can pay me the same as you were paying her. You won't get anyone else to do it for that money.'

'You're my daughter and you'll do it for nothing!' Harold spat, straightening up menacingly as the pain wore off.

'Well, that's just it, isn't it? I'm not your daughter. I know the truth now. You have no hold over me at all any more. Yes, that's right, Luke,' she said more gently, gazing across at her brother who'd just come in the door and was standing on the threshold, aghast at what he'd just heard. 'I'm sorry you found out like this. I wanted to tell you in a quiet moment, but forced my hand. We're all half-brother and sisters. That's why this monster always treated Mum and me so badly.'

'I suppose it was that bitch, Eva Parker, what told you!' Harold fumed. 'Well, I'll bloody teach her a less—'

'No,' Hillie interjected, her brain racing. 'Mum told me herself as she lay dying,' she lied, since she didn't want Harold doing anything to dear Eva. 'She wanted me to know the truth before she went. So from now on, you listen to me. I've given up my job at Price's. So I'll be here every morning before the girls go to school so I can look after Frances and keep house for you. And I'll stay until either you or Luke get home from work. We'll hardly see each other, which will suit me fine, too. I'll do everything Mum did, and you'll pay me twelve and six a week, same as Dolly.'

'Twelve and six, she said, did she?' Harold chortled. 'That what she told you? Well, it was only ten bob, so how you going to manage on that if you're not working at Price's no more?'

Hillie was fuming, but she had to think quickly. Dolly could well have been lying in order to get more money out of her, but Harold seemed to be coming round. If Hillie held out for twelve and six a week, he might change his mind. So instead she went on calmly, 'Jimmy's doing perfectly well, if you must know. And he does shifts at the Falcon at the weekends, so don't you worry your ugly head over our finances.' She wasn't going to tell him about

Jimmy's work for Mr Jackson. It was all cash in hand, and she wasn't sure it was all above board, despite Jimmy's assurances. But it had been Jimmy's idea, bless him, that she gave up her job at the factory to look after her half-sisters instead of Dolly. 'So, enjoy your meal,' she went on. 'It's all ready on the stove. All you've got to do is serve yourselves, and leave the washing up. I'll do it when I come back in the morning. Oh, and leave me some housekeeping money. Dolly helped herself to almost everything in the larder and I'll need to do some shopping. And no arguing, 'cos you know I'm right.'

Without giving Harold a chance to come back at her, she slipped out of the door past Luke. 'I'll tell you everything later,' she whispered to him as she passed, and then retrieving her coat from the hall stand, called the girls downstairs. 'I'll see you all bright and early in the morning!' she sang out, and went out through the front door.

She paused for a moment, glancing up and down the familiar street. Phew! She wouldn't want to live through all that again! But it was done now, and hopefully she'd sorted everything out. Harold might try and stop her, but she doubted it. The arrangement would suit his mean pockets too much!

So she set off through the dark, freezing streets feeling more than pleased with herself. Dear Jimmy would be home by now, and they could have a lovely evening together, the first time she'd felt happy since her mum had passed away. And she hummed to herself as she made her way home.

*

Hillie walked briskly along the street, Frances skipping along beside her and both of them wrapped up against the December cold. They'd been shopping, as with a little more money in her pocket this year, Hillie had planned a slightly better Christmas for her family, and she wanted to make up for their mum not being there. Harold had even agreed to let her cook the Christmas dinner, so she'd see her brother and sisters for a little while. Jimmy, however, was excluded, but he would wait for her at the Parkers' house.

What she cooked would depend on what money she could wangle from Harold, of course, but she planned on making Christmas Day as enjoyable as possible. Among other little treats, they'd just now called into Jon Jax Corner, where she'd bought some little toys for the younger children to exchange, including some plastic farm animals for Trixie who was always so enthralled by the deer in the enclosure in the park. She'd also noticed a tiny doll in a little bed that she knew Frances would like, but she'd have to get that when she was on her own on Saturday afternoon.

'Can we wrap them up when we get home?' Frances asked happily.

'Yes, of course,' Hillie grinned down at her youngest half-sister. 'And we'll make some little decorations to hang on the tree when the others get in from school,' she added, since she was determined they'd have a tree this year. 'That's what the glue and the glitter are for.'

'Oh, goody,' Frances cried, hopping about Hillie in excitement.

Hillie smiled down at her, feeling her heart warm. It was good to see the little ones happier than they had been since Nell had died. Frances and Daisy had seemed quite content with the explanation that their mummy hadn't been well and had gone away for a long time to get better. Hopefully their memories would gradually fade. Luke was grieving in an adult way, so it was mainly Trixie and Joan that Hillie was most concerned about. But there was definitely relief that Dolly Maguire had gone, even if she did still live a few doors away. And Hillie was making a great effort to be cheerful for her sisters and make life as much fun for them as she could, even if her own heart was heavy with grief.

In some ways, though, she was really enjoying her new role as surrogate mother to her siblings. Her mum had been a good cook and taught her well how to make a tasty meal out of cheaper ingredients. But Hillie's main satisfaction was seeing Luke and her sisters sitting down eagerly to their meal as she left each night, their appetites returning. She had kept her promise to her mum, and that was the most important thing to her.

She unlocked the front door to Number Twelve and ushered Frances inside, not noticing the man in the long raincoat and trilby hat who'd been trailing her ever since she'd left home that morning. Earlier, he'd loitered on the corner of the street. If she hadn't emerged from the house with Frances not long after Harold and Luke had left for work, and the girls for school half an hour later, he might not have hung around – and come back again another day. But as it was, he slowed his step as they went back inside, and then went to wait at the end of the street. Just to see what happened next.

It wasn't long before an older woman came out from the house on the end. She looked a bit down at heel, a grumpy expression on her face and a battered shopping bag dangling from her arm. But she might be useful to him.

'Excuse me, madam,' he addressed her, bounding up and doffing his hat. 'I'm looking for a Mrs Hilda Baxter. I believe she lives on this street.'

'That bitch!' Dolly Maguire sneered down her nose, still seething from having been thrown out so recently from what she'd considered a cushy job. 'No, she don't live here no more.'

'Oh, I must be mistaken—'

'Yeah, but after her tart of a mother died, she's here every day, keeping house and looking after the little brats.'

'Oh, yes?'

'Yeah. Number Twelve.' Dolly jabbed her head at the Hardwick front door. 'Probably there now.'

'Ah. So she has younger brothers and sisters, does she?'

'Yeah. A boy just started work, three girls at school and a little one. Why d'yer wanna know?'

'Oh, just finding out for a friend.'

Dolly's eyes suddenly gleamed. ''Ere, that sounds a bit dodgy. Guess yer want me ter keep me gob shut about yer snooping? Well, it'll cost yer. Ten bob.'

The man raised his eyebrows in surprise. 'Five.'

'Eight.'

'OK. Seven and six,' Jackson laughed, putting his hand in his trouser pocket. 'You sound like a woman after my own heart. Wouldn't be interested in making a bob or two on the side, would you? I might need someone like you occasionally. Someone who knows how to keep things to themselves, if you know what I mean?'

'Depends. I might be,' Dolly answered shiftily.

'Then you and I should get to know each other better. Pubs'll be open soon. Fancy a drink?'

'Yeah. As long as it's a double. And not 'ere at the Cambridge. Make it the Falcon.'

'Exactly where I was going to suggest. Ah, didn't I see you there last New Year's Eve? Singing and dancing, the life and soul of the party?' Until she was so drunk that she fell over, he added to himself.

'Yeah, that was me,' Dolly nodded, preening herself that someone remembered her. Not that she remembered him. In fact, all she really remembered about that evening was nearly being run over on her own street and Miss Hoity-Toity Hardwick sneering down at her. So if this chap was going to give her a chance to get back at her, so much the better. 'Lead on, mister,' she grinned, lacing her arm through his. 'The shopping can wait.'

Chapter Eighteen

Hillie glanced up from the ironing. 'Oh, sounds like we have a visitor, Frances,' she told her little half-sister in surprise. 'Shall we go and see who it is?'

Frances had been sitting up at the table, concentrating on filling in the colouring book Hillie had given her as a second present at Christmas. Now she slipped down from the chair and skipped out into the hallway with Hillie on her tail. When the door was opened, they found a familiar figure dressed against the January cold in a smart winter coat.

'Oo, it's Auntie Jessie,' Frances beamed in delight.

Hillie, too, was delighted to see her friend. It seemed that since the tragedy that had befallen the Hardwick family, Jessica's parents had softened in their attitude a little, and they had allowed their daughter more freedom to see Hillie and the children, even if they didn't entirely approve. But it meant the girls had seen quite a lot of each other lately, and their friendship had deepened.

'Jess, hello!' Hillie exclaimed happily. 'Come on in. It's freezing out here.'

'Mmm, yes, I will. Thanks,' Jessica said, huddling her arms across her chest. 'Not disturbing you, am I?'

'Give me an excuse to have five minutes' break,' Hillie grinned back. 'Cuppa?'

'Yes, please,' Jessica answered as Frances proudly took her hand and led her down the hallway.

'Come and look at my colouring,' the child invited her.

It was cosy and warm in the kitchen, the air scented with the smell of fresh ironing. The second Jessica took off her coat and sat down, Frances climbed up onto her lap.

'What d'you think?' she demanded, showing Jessica the book.

'That's very good. You've really kept the crayoning inside the lines.'

'And look, I can write my name. Hill taught me. And I can count to a hundred.'

'Well, you'll be top of the class when you start school.'

Hillie rolled her eyes heavenwards. 'That won't be soon enough for me. She's got such an enquiring mind, she could do with school now. I'm constantly trying to think of ways to keep her occupied, but it's difficult when I've got so much to do.'

'You've certainly got a pile of ironing there! I'm glad to see you've got an electric iron, though. So much easier. I imagined you might be stuck in the dark ages with a flat iron.'

'I would've been if Jimmy hadn't got this for me,' Hillie told her, reaching up to disconnect the wire from the ceiling light. 'He got me one for myself at home, too.'

'Spoils you, then?'

'He does when he can. Oh, there's the kettle singing its head off. I'll just make the tea.'

A couple of minutes later, they were sitting at the table together, with Frances absorbed in her colouring.

'So, how are you coping with all this?' Jessica asked, gesturing about the room. 'And how's it working out with your... I mean with Harold?' she corrected herself, since Hillie had told her about Harold not being her real father, although she'd sworn her to secrecy.

'Fine, actually,' Hillie shrugged. 'I mean, I hardly ever see him. Joan's OK to hold the fort until it's time for school, so I don't need to get here till then, and Luke and his lordship leave for the factory long before that. Then at night, I have the dinner ready and waiting on the table for when they get in, so I only see him for a few minutes. And it's much the same Saturday lunchtime. I get a meal while they're at work in the morning, and push off as soon as they're back. Although a couple of times I've stayed on to take the girls to the park in the afternoon, and it's the only time I get to see Luke.'

'And… Harold's all right with that? Even though he banned you from the house when you married Jimmy?'

Hillie gave a wry grimace. 'I reckon he thinks it's a small price to pay for having a housekeeper for the princely sum of ten bob a week.'

'Is that all he pays you?' Jessica looked utterly shocked.

'Dolly said he paid *her* twelve and six, but she might've been lying. Anyway, that's what we agreed, and I'm just happy to know my family's being properly cared for.'

'But that must be far less than you earned at the factory. Are you managing all right moneywise? I mean, Dad gives me a generous allowance, and I could—'

'Goodness, you're a true friend, Jess, but we're managing fine. Jimmy's not badly paid at Price's, and you know he does shifts at the pub on Saturday *and* Sunday now, and sometimes during the week as well. And he does a bit of work on the side for some chap called Jackson, too. So, all in all,' she assured her friend, 'we're doing quite well. And I certainly don't miss standing at the factory workbench all day, I can tell you!' she grinned mischievously.

'No, I bet you don't,' Jessica chuckled. 'Oh, yes, that's very good, Frances,' she said, turning her attention back to the little girl on her lap. 'What colour are you going to do the butterfly?'

'I miss being with Gert all day, mind,' Hillie went on, smiling across at little Frances whose tongue was stuck out of the side of her mouth in concentration. 'But we still see a lot of each other. I'm often at a loose end when Jimmy's doing his extras, so I see her then. Unless she's out with Rob, of course. I play gooseberry sometimes, but I can't do that *all* the time. And sometimes Belinda and I go to the flicks or whatever together. But that's enough of me,' she said decisively. 'Does your mum know you're here? I'm surprised she lets you come so often.'

'Yes, she does know. And she's not that happy about it. But Dad says you're not *that* bad and we should show some compassion. So as long as your dad's not here, I can come. Well, of course, *they* still think he's your dad, anyway. But they draw the line at Gert's house, which I think's rotten.'

'Huh, well, so do I. Salt of the earth the Parkers are, all of them. But if your dad's being a bit more lenient, d'you think he might be OK about Patrick? You are still seeing each other?'

'Oh, yes!' Hillie saw the other girl's face light up like the sun. 'The more we see of each other, the more we grow to love each other. We seem to think the same about everything. And he's so interesting. He shows me all the letters he gets from home, and sometimes there are photos as well. I feel I know all his family already. And they're quite happy about his English rose, as he calls me. He's asked me to go with him next time he goes home, whenever that might be. Don't you think that's exciting? Imagine, *me* in Africa!'

Her eyes were shining with excitement, and Hillie's heart bled for her. She clearly adored Patrick, but realistically, could there ever be any future for them?

'And… what about your own parents?' she hardly dared to ask. 'I assume you haven't told them yet?'

Jessica lowered her eyes, her face saddened. 'No. Not yet. You know I told you we decided to wait until I'm twenty-one? And that's not till the end of this year. We want to get married, but I'm so scared of what Mum and Dad'll say. They're still my parents, after all, and I do love them whatever happens.'

'Yes, I understand that,' Hillie murmured, thinking how much she'd loved her own mother and had felt so guilty about marrying Jimmy in secret. If only her mum was still there instead of lying deep in the grave that Hillie visited once a week, taking a little bunch of flowers when she could afford it. 'But you've got to do what's right for you,' she went on. 'If I'd been stronger and stood up to Harold a bit more in the past, none of this might've happened. So learn by my mistake, and don't leave it too late.'

She almost wished she hadn't spoken as Jessica twisted her head in a silent groan of anguish. But Jessica had become a good friend and Hillie didn't want to see her trapped in a situation like she was herself. Joan wasn't yet thirteen, and even if she left school at the earliest opportunity, Hillie couldn't see her being able to cope with running the house straightaway, and she'd feel guilty at saddling Joan with everything, anyway. It wasn't that she wanted to abandon her siblings, but it would be nice to have a life of her own one day. But for now, she was probably just as stuck as she'd been before Jimmy had rescued her.

But at least he'd be home that evening to comfort her, and they could cuddle up on the settee together and listen to the radio, and let their cares drift away.

'I know it's cold, but if we wrap up warm, d'you fancy a quick walk in the park when we've finished this?' she asked Jessica brightly.

*

Hillie closed the door to the flat behind her and put her shopping bag on the floor while she hung up her coat. Damn. Jimmy's old work jacket wasn't there. He usually beat her home by about five minutes –

unless he called in for a swift half at the Falcon. Only it wasn't always so swift if Mr Jackson was there or had sent a messenger to look for Jimmy. It was all very well the extra cash Jimmy got for the errands he ran, but sometimes Hillie wished the suspicious Mr Jackson would disappear off the face of the earth. But there again, these regular windfalls made more bearable the drastic drop in Hillie's wages so that she could take care of her family, so she supposed she should be grateful.

With a deep sigh, she went to the kitchenette and put the cheap, tasteless sausages in the little lead-lined cupboard with its marble base that served as their cold larder. Jessica had told her that in the semi-basement kitchen at Number Three, they had one of those new-fangled electric fridges that kept meat fresh for several days and vegetables for nearly a week. How wonderful it'd be to have one of those! But since Hillie had to shop every day for her family and did her own shopping at the same time, it didn't really matter. But it didn't hurt to dream.

But what was that? An extra package already in there. Hillie knew it hadn't been there this morning. She carefully unwrapped it. A thick, beautifully lean lamb chop, the expensive sort Hillie would never contemplate buying. So where had it come from?

It was only then that she spied a note in Jimmy's untidy scrawl on the table. *Don't wait up. Working*

for Mr Jackson. Little present for you in the larder.
Love you, Jimmy xx

Hillie drew in a disappointed breath. Jimmy must have popped in just before she'd got home. So she could only have missed him by a few minutes. Oh, she'd been so looking forward to a nice cosy evening together, and bitterness filled her as she put a match to the fire she'd laid that morning. It was March, and the winter was seeming so long. There was little sign of spring, except in the park where daffodil buds were bravely beginning to unfurl, but everywhere else was so grey. Grey streets, grey houses, the very air seemed grey, especially when all the factories and now the first two chimneys of the new giant power station were spewing out smoke. A relaxing evening in with Jimmy might have brought a little brightness into her life, and now she had been denied even that.

Hillie stayed on her knees in front of the fire as she coaxed it into life. The scrunched-up newspaper and kindling caught instantly, and she expertly added some coal, a little at a time. She waited while the growing flames licked about the black lumps until they were burning, too, and then she added a little more fuel to build up a good heart so that there was no danger of the fire going out.

Just to be sure, Hillie remained by the hearth, and anyway, she didn't have the heart to start cooking straightaway, even if the thought of the juicy chop was enticing. She just wished Jimmy was there to enjoy the evening with her. She hadn't expected married life to be like this. Lonely. She'd expected to *share* her life with Jimmy. She appreciated how hard he worked and that it was meant to be for their future. But, quite honestly, the dream of leaving London behind and moving to a pretty cottage in the country with chickens at the bottom of the garden and fresh, clean air to breathe was fading into the ether.

She finally dragged herself away from the fire and went to cook the chop. They didn't have a grill or a proper oven. Just two gas rings. So she fried the meat to perfection over a moderate heat while a couple of potatoes boiled on the other ring, and finally she lightly cooked some cabbage while she prepared the mash. Placing the meal on a tray, she sat down in a chair by the fire to eat it. The meat was delicious and succulent, but Hillie didn't enjoy it as much as she knew she should. It would have tasted so much better if Jimmy had been there to share it.

She washed up and then prepared Jimmy's sandwiches for the next day. She turned the radio on for a bit of company, but she wasn't really listening to it. She sat down for a while, darning a pair of Jimmy's socks. There was other mending to be done, but she couldn't settle to it. Instead she made herself a cup of tea and lost herself in a book.

Ten o'clock. Well, it was an early start in the morning, and time for bed. Jimmy had put in his note that she shouldn't wait up, so she wouldn't. Still feeling disgruntled, she made herself a hot-water bottle, got herself ready for bed and climbed in between the sheets.

Heaven knew what time it was when Jimmy fell into bed beside her, and within a few minutes, he was breathing heavily in a deep sleep. His arrival woke Hillie up and she turned over huffily, cursing him as she waited for sleep to overcome her again. The extra money was all very well, but they both had a proper job to get to in the morning!

Hillie woke again at the normal time and went to get the day started. She'd leave Jimmy asleep as long as she dared, and only wake him at the last minute. It wouldn't do for him to be falling asleep at Price's! It was, after all, their main source of income.

It was then that she noticed something draped over the back of the settee. A beautiful Fair Isle cardigan in the softest wool, a silk petticoat trimmed with lace and a couple of pairs of silk stockings. Everything appeared brand new, and then Hillie spied another note in Jimmy's hand. *A present for my darling Hillie.*

Hillie stared at the items of clothing. Were they really for her? They certainly were lovely, but surely they should be spending their money on more important things or saving it for their future? She didn't know whether to be cross with Jimmy or delighted.

She got herself ready and had breakfast on the table before she shook Jimmy awake. He came to, bleary-eyed, but grinned at her almost at once.

'Did you find the things I got for my girl?' he demanded, leaping out of bed. 'You'll look a proper treat—'

'Jimmy, we can't afford things like that,' Hillie interrupted him. 'It's a waste of money when—'

'Course we can,' Jimmy insisted, pulling on his trousers and disappearing into the bathroom. 'I told you, Mr Jackson pays us well.' His voice came to her through the partly open door and she could hear water sloshing about in the basin. 'And I wanted to get you something to make up for being out so late.'

'So, what were you doing, then? And are you sure this is all above board?'

'Well, more or less. Last night it was a card game. Gambling. Serious stuff.' Jimmy emerged from the bathroom, naked to the waist after his wash. 'I'm not exactly sure how legal it was. But everyone there obviously wanted to be. No bad blood or anything. A lot of money changed hands, though. Mr Jackson won loads and gave us another wodge of notes.'

'So what were *you* doing there?'

'Serving drinks,' Jimmy shrugged, pulling on his vest and shirt. 'Just as well, 'cos I don't know nothing about card games.'

'Don't you?' Hillie eyed him suspiciously. 'I'd've thought—'

'Nah, never interested us. So don't you worry,' Jimmy said, stuffing toast and cheap streaky bacon into his mouth and slurping down a mug of tea. 'Now, you enjoy being spoilt once in a while. Pretty as a picture you'll look in those, my princess. Well, time I was off. See you tonight, angel, and I *promise* I'll be in all evening.'

He dropped a kiss on her hair, collected his packet of sandwiches and then scuttled out of the flat door, plonking his cap on his head and shrugging into his jacket as he went. Hillie watched him leave, holding her breath in exasperation.

She hoped to goodness he knew what he was doing!

Chapter Nineteen

'Right, girls, stand back. I'm bringing the big saucepan across.'

Daisy and Frances at once stopped leaping about in anticipation of the fun they were going to have, and obediently stepped back. And just to make sure, Trixie put a restraining hand on each of their bare little shoulders.

It was June, and Friday evening, so time for the weekly ritual of the bath. Joan had helped Hillie lift the galvanised tin tub from its hook on the wall out in the yard, but today there was no need to drag it inside and place it in front of the fire. It was so warm that even though the yard was mainly in shadow, there was still one sunny patch where the girls could enjoy their bath outside and splash around to their hearts' content. But they would still want warm water, which needed to be heated on the gas stove in the kettle and every available saucepan.

'There. That feels about right,' Hillie announced, testing the temperature of the water. 'In you get.'

The two little ones had already stripped off and clambered over the sides, although Frances had to be helped. Hillie gave them both a good wash with some nice soap Jimmy had brought home from Price's.

Rejects that had been handed out to the staff, he'd said. At first, Hillie had been inclined not to believe him and suspected him of pilfering. But Gert had confirmed there'd been a batch where the colour hadn't mixed in properly, and it had been a bit of a bun fight among the women to grab one of the handouts. As Jimmy had been the one to distribute them around the factory, it was no surprise he'd nicked an entire box for himself and Hillie first.

But why did Hillie feel the need to distrust him, she asked herself with a distressed sigh?

She left the girls playing with a rubber duck that had seen better days, and went indoors to prepare the family supper and heat up another consignment of water for when it was Joan and Trixie's turn. Hoots of laughter reached her from the yard as she cut slices of bread. It was only going to be a simple meal that night – baked beans on toast with a poached egg on top – as Hillie needed all the bathing to be over by the time Harold and Luke got home from work, and tea on the table as they came in the door, enabling her to make her exit immediately. She still felt that the least time she spent in Harold's company the better.

'Come on, you two, out now,' she ordered with a chuckle as she went back outside. 'We'll get you dry and into clean clothes, so you make sure they stay that way until bedtime.'

'Oh, just five more minutes,' Daisy begged.

'No, sorry, love. Your sisters've got to have theirs before your dad and Luke get in. Come on. Let's see which one of you can get dry and dressed first,' she said, turning it into a game.

She wrapped them in towels and topped up the hot water so that the two older girls could have their baths, each holding up a large towel for the other in order to provide privacy from any prying eyes from the other houses!

By the time their father and brother got in from work, all four sisters were clean and respectable, the bathtub was hanging back on its hook in the yard, and tea was on the table.

'That's everything done, then,' Hillie told Harold curtly as he sat down in front of his meal. 'I'll be back in the morning, so you'll have your dinner waiting on the table as usual when you get in from work. And don't forget to have my wages ready.'

Harold looked up at her darkly, his mouth in a disgruntled bunch. But he said nothing as he stabbed his knife and fork into the beans.

'I'll see you out,' Luke said, leaping to his feet.

Hillie saw Harold glare at his son, but then he couldn't really protest. Luke could easily walk out, taking his pay packet with him, and Harold wouldn't want that, would he, Hillie grimaced to herself?

'Everything OK, Luke?' she asked as her half-brother came down the hallway with her.

'Yeah. As good as it can be without Mum,' Luke answered. 'In fact, in some ways, Dad's not as bad-tempered as he used to be. I mean, he rants and raves about *you* sometimes. But he knows which side his bread's buttered, I reckon, so he's not going to stop you coming to do all the housework and everything.'

'No, I don't suppose he is,' Hillie agreed, and then she frowned. They were standing now on the front step Hillie had donkey-stoned that morning, and Luke appeared to be hovering as if he wanted to say something but didn't have the courage. 'Is there anything else?' she asked. 'Only Gert and me are going out this evening, 'cos Jimmy's working at the pub and Gert's not seeing Rob tonight.'

'Oh. Well,' Luke faltered. 'Actually, there was something. I… I thought you ought to know. I heard Jimmy being told off at work today. Sounded like he'd nodded off on the job.'

'What!' Hillie's heart crashed to her feet, her earlier semi-contentment fled. 'Oh, Lordy. I keep telling him he's working too hard with his shifts at the pub,' she told Luke, covering up. For, somehow, she didn't want anyone knowing the truth about Jimmy's activities with the mysterious Mr Jackson! 'Oh, I'll have to tell him to cut down.'

'I... I did right to tell you, then? I didn't want to worry you, but—'

'No, thanks for letting me know.' Hillie squeezed Luke's hand. 'Now, you get back and eat while it's still hot. And I'll see you tomorrow lunchtime.'

'Yes. Thanks, Hill,' Luke said, and went back inside.

The smile faded from Hillie's face as she stepped along the pavement to Gert's house. That side of the street was still bathed in evening sunshine, the smell of heat and dust coming off the tarmac. Summer was the best time of year, no matter what one was doing, and Hillie had felt light of heart as she was about to leave the house. She couldn't bring her mum back, but she'd managed somehow to create a happy atmosphere in the home for her sisters, at least. And she'd been looking forward to her evening with Gert. A stroll in the park, or maybe going to the flicks.

But now, because of what Luke had just told her, all was in ruins.

She'd have to have it out with Jimmy. The shifts at the pub were all right, but she'd have to insist he gave up his work for Mr Jackson. So often it was two or three in the morning before he got in, and with his work at Price's the next day, it just wasn't worth taking the risk. And to be honest, Hillie would be relieved. Jimmy insisted it was all legitimate, but often he couldn't – or wouldn't – tell her exactly what it was he'd been doing. And when he did, she sometimes felt he was fobbing her off with some cock-and-bull story.

She'd thought marrying Jimmy would be the end of her problems, hadn't she? She couldn't have predicted what happened to her mum, of course, but in between the happy moments, her life sometimes seemed just as fraught, if not more so, than it had been before. Especially after what Luke had just told her. They simply couldn't afford for Jimmy to lose his job at Price's for the sake of the extra money he earned from this Jackson fellow!

She knocked on the front door to the Parkers' house, hoping the happy welcome she knew she'd find there would make her feel better. And when Gert opened the door, beaming from ear to ear, she felt, as ever, as if she'd truly come home.

'Come on in and have a cuppa,' Gert invited her. 'Only just got in from work, so I haven't had time to change yet. And, Hillie, I'm ever so sorry, but I can't come out with you tonight, after all. Rob sent us a message through Belinda. He's got tickets for a West End show. Coming to pick us up in half an hour.'

'Oh, how exciting!' Hillie declared, trying to hide the fact that her heart had sunk. She'd wanted to talk to Gert in confidence about her misgivings over Jimmy's outside activities, and now she wouldn't get the chance. 'What you going to see?' she asked instead.

'Dunno. It's a surprise, he said. But I don't care. Never been to a proper live show before.'

'Me neither. But you make sure you remember every little detail to tell me tomorrow, Miss Parker!'

Gert's glowing face had made Hillie get over her disappointment almost at once, and she was grinning as they went into the back room. The entire horde was there, the younger children racing in and out of the back door to the yard. Even Old Sal was sitting up quite alert for once.

'Hello, everyone!'

'Hello, Hillie, love,' Eva beamed. 'Tea in the pot if you want to help yourself.'

'Thanks, I will. Oh, hello, Kit. How are you?' she said as Kit came in from the backyard. 'Haven't seen you for ages.'

'I'm very well, thanks. You look nice. New cardi?'

'Yes, Jimmy got it for me,' Hillie answered, blushing slightly, although not so much at Kit's compliment as at the memory of the frustrating evening when Jimmy had produced the said item of clothing. 'I wore it 'cos Gert and I were supposed to be going out, but now she's going out with Rob. To a West End theatre, no less!'

'So I've heard.'

'Oh, I really am sorry to let you down, Hill—'

'Now don't you worry. Go upstairs and get yourself ready to paint the town red!'

'I take it your Jimmy's working?' Kit put in. 'Well, I'm at a loose end tonight. Fancy doing something?'

'Oh.' Hillie was taken by surprise. But as she thought about it, the idea of spending the evening with her old friend was really quite appealing. 'What did you have in mind?'

'Oh, I don't know really. Anything on at the pictures you wanted to see?'

'Not particularly. And it's such a lovely evening, it seems a shame to spend it indoors, even if some of us are!' Hillie teased, raising her eyebrows in Gert's direction.

'Oh, get away,' Gert laughed back. 'But I must go and titivate meself for me special night out!' she went on with a mock expression of superiority as she disappeared out of the door and an instant later was heard clomping up the stairs.

'Tell you what, then.' Kit drew back Hillie's attention. 'We'll have a walk in the park before it closes. I know you like that. Then we'll cross over the bridge and head up the King's Road. There's bound to be a café or something open and we can get something to eat. If you're sure Jimmy won't mind, of course.'

The little catch in his voice didn't register with Hillie and she smiled back. She almost wanted to say she wouldn't care if Jimmy *did* mind, but instead she answered, 'No, of course he wouldn't.'

'OK, then. You wait here and I'll pop home to change out of my uniform. See you all later, then! Night-night, you little toe rags,' he chuckled, scooping up Primrose and Trudy, one in each arm, to give them both a kiss. 'I expect you two to be nicely tucked up in bed when I get back.'

He blew a raspberry onto each of their tummies before he set them on their feet again, making them giggle furiously and jump up for more.

'Just one each, and then you get ready for bed,' he laughed, readily obliging, his wide mouth spread in a handsome grin before he slipped out of the door.

'How you getting on then, without poor Nell?' Eva asked as she wiped the two little ones' faces with a grubby-looking flannel.

'Oh, OK, thanks, Mrs P,' Hillie replied, her spirits a little dampened again at Eva's question. 'We all miss her terribly, of course. Frances and Daisy don't ask about her quite so much, though. They don't really understand, but I think they're getting used to her not being there.'

'Poor little mites,' Eva tutted. 'Stan, put these toads to bed, would you? And Jake and Mildred, you wash your faces and do your teeth ready for when it's your bedtime, and all.' And then, when Stan had taken the two youngest girls into the front room where they slept with Old Sal and Jake, Eva turned to Hillie, her face creased with compassion. 'And how are *you* coping, Hillie, dear?'

Hillie blinked at her as her own emotions clambered over each other. But before she had a chance to reply, there was a brisk knock on the front door, followed by the thump of Gert flying down the stairs.

A proud smile spread across Eva's lined face. 'Never expected our Gert to find someone posh like this Rob. Lovely lad, he is. And right smitten.'

'Gert's got such a warm personality, Mrs P. That's what he loves about her. It's what love about her. What I love about you all.'

Unusually for Eva, the woman seemed to blush to the roots of her hair. 'Oh, get away with you,' she flustered.

'No, it's true,' Hillie insisted, suddenly wanting to open up all her suppressed emotions. 'You're all so wonderful and kind. You. Stan. Gert, Kit. Even the little ones. I don't know how I'd have got through all this without you all.'

'It's what friends are for,' Eva nodded modestly.

But Hillie knew the whole family was more than that to her. She loved each and every one of them as if they were her own. And there were times like this when she almost wished she'd been born one of them, and not Hilda Hardwick. Either that, or that her real father hadn't been killed and she'd been brought up as Hilda Norton instead. How different things might have been then! She sometimes wondered about Will Norton, what sort of man he was. Eva had told her he was good and kind, but sadly, she had no photograph of him. And if Nell ever had, Hillie knew what would have happened to it!

But there was no good thinking of what might have been. You couldn't turn back the clock, could you?

*

'Oh, Kit, it's been a lovely evening. Thank you so much.'

They were sauntering back across the bridge, arm in arm, Hillie leaning slightly against Kit's shoulder. She felt totally at ease, as if all her cares had melted away in his company. They'd come back, of course. But it had been glorious to lose herself in Kit's warmth and kindness for a few hours.

'I'm glad you enjoyed it,' Kit's voice murmured from somewhere just above her head. 'I only wish…'

His words trailed off, almost as if he regretted speaking them. Hillie's eyebrows lifted. She shouldn't press him. But curiosity got the better of her. And he *was* like an elder brother to her, so they shouldn't have any secrets.

'You only wish what?' she asked lazily.

It was a few seconds before Kit replied. And his answer was preceded by a rueful sigh. 'I only wish I'd been able to protect you,' he said at last. 'From your father. Or Harold, should I say. From everything that's happened. I should've done more than help you catch a train to Scotland.'

'Bless you, Kit.' Hillie's heart swelled with affection for this man who'd been part of her life since the day she'd been born. 'Harold's a hard man to fight against. You've always been such a good friend to me. And that counts for so much.'

She stopped for an instant, reaching up to give him a peck on the cheek before linking her arm through his again before they wandered on. It was such a natural, spontaneous gesture that she scarcely thought about it as they continued over the bridge.

It was a balmy summer's evening, reminding Hillie of the time two years previously when she and Jimmy had admired the sunset from that very spot. He'd made her laugh so much with his antics. He rarely did that now. Things had changed between them. The magic had gone and life seemed to be so much more serious.

Hillie glanced up now at Kit's strong, familiar face. Thank goodness all was still the same with him.

The way he'd always looked out for her and Gert since they were children. And Hillie shuddered as she realised she felt more at home, more protected, with Kit than she did with her own husband. There was always a tension with Jimmy nowadays, and it was all to do with Jackson. But after what Luke had told her, she was going to insist that Jimmy stopped working for him. And then all would be well again.

'And you, Kit,' she asked as they sauntered along. 'Still no young lady in your sights?' He was, after all, a good-looking fellow, she considered, kind and thoughtful, and would make some lucky girl a super catch. In fact, she wondered if it had been Kit she'd been seeing and not Jimmy, Harold wouldn't have objected. After all, he'd always allowed her to go out with Gert.

At her question, Kit's handsome face seemed to come over serious. 'No,' he answered in a matter of fact tone. 'I'm concentrating on my career. I'm still determined to be a stationmaster one day.'

'But wouldn't you like to settle down ever? Marry and have a family?' Hillie persisted.

But Kit replied with a shrug. 'I thought I did. Once. But not now. My work's more important to me.'

'But what if the right girl came along and you fell desperately in love?'

Kit gave a wry smile. 'She won't.'

'You don't know that.'

'Yes, I do. And you, young lady, are asking too many questions,' Kit admonished with a chuckle. 'Just because I take you out for an evening as a friend, doesn't mean you can give me the tenth degree. Now, I think I'd better get you home. We've both got work in the morning. In fact, I'm on an early shift.'

Hillie pulled a face. 'At least I don't have to worry about arriving on the dot. It's Saturday, so no school and Joan can hold the fort till I get there.'

'So, d'you think she'll take over from you when she leaves school?'

'I don't know.' Hillie shook her head. 'I'd feel guilty about lumbering her with it. She'd be trapped for years.'

'And you're not?'

They'd reached the house where Hillie and Jimmy had their flat. It was relatively early, dusk only just beginning to fall, and as Hillie turned to Kit, she could still see his face quite clearly. But somehow she couldn't quite read the expression in his eyes. Concern, yes. But there was something else she couldn't quite fathom. It unnerved her, setting butterflies fluttering in her stomach.

She answered his question with an arch of her eyebrows, as her mouth curved into a half-smile.

'Well, goodnight, Kit. And thanks again for a lovely evening.'

He returned her smile, his eyes soft and melting. He bent his head and she felt his cheek brush against hers.

'My pleasure. Glad you enjoyed it,' he said, pulling back. 'Give Jimmy my regards.' Then he was walking away down the street.

Hillie stood on the pavement, a multitude of emotions strangling her as she searched in her handbag for her keys. She was still grieving for her mum, her lost baby brother or sister, and the father she'd never known. She had found contentment looking after her siblings, but Harold was still a thorn in her side and ever would be. And Jimmy, well, he was exasperating, and she was also worried about what he might be mixed up in. Thank goodness she had people like Gert and Kit and Mr and Mrs P, or she'd probably lose her sanity!

*

'Promise me!' she grated at Jimmy through clenched teeth when he finally rolled in at half past eleven and came into the bedroom where she was already in bed, waiting for him. If she hadn't been worried about waking the other people in the house, she might have yelled at him. She cringed at the thought that this was the first time she'd ever raised her voice to Jimmy. But this was so important and he was wriggling his mouth in reluctance.

'I know what happened at the factory today,' she went on, determined to convince him. 'You can't keep pushing yourself like this. If you fall asleep at the factory again 'cos you're out till all hours with this Jackson chap, you'll get the sack, and then where will we be?' she demanded, her chest heaving breathlessly.

Jimmy glared at her, pursing his lips. And then he lowered his eyes like a naughty schoolboy who'd been caught in the act of some prank. 'All right. I promise,' he finally agreed. 'But Mr Jackson ain't gonna like it. And I've already promised to do some work for him over the next couple of weeks. But I'll tell him I can't do any more after that.'

Hillie drew in an exasperated breath. 'All right. If he can't find anyone else. But no more after that!' she told him in no uncertain terms.

'Anything to make my girl happy,' Jimmy chirped, changing tack. 'But what about me shifts at the pub? We really need the extra money.'

'Well, yes, I suppose so.' Hillie nodded reluctantly. 'At least that doesn't keep you out so late.'

'Yeah. So let's get to sleep, eh? And look, I got this for you. Nipped out at lunchtime, I did, and bought it in Arding and Hobbs. Right under old Braithwaite's nose. You should've seen the look on his face!'

'Oh, Jimmy, he's not quite as bad as we thought, you know.'

'Maybe not. But I don't think he ever expected to see me buying something like this. Go on. Open it!' he instructed, beaming gleefully as he thrust a fancy box into her hands.

Hillie frowned. But she couldn't quell her excitement as she opened the box. Inside was the most exquisite glass vase she'd ever seen, heavy and deeply cut in a symmetrical pattern so that it refracted the light coming from the bulb in the ceiling into all the colours of the rainbow.

'Oh, Jimmy,' Hillie breathed in wonderment.

'It's what they call lead crystal,' Jimmy told her knowledgeably, pulling his pyjama jacket on over his head. 'Sorry it's only small, but it was all I could afford.'

'But we *can't* afford anything like this.'

'Oh, yes, we can. Mr Jackson gave us some extra cash last night. And I thought I wanted to treat my girl,' Jimmy grinned as he got into bed beside her. 'But I won't be able to afford anything like this again. Not if I have to stop working for him—'

'Jimmy,' Hillie warned. 'You promised.'

'Yeah. I know. And I will. Keep me promise. Now,' he said, turning off the light and groping his way over to the bed, 'let's get some shut-eye.'

'Yes. All right, Jimmy. And Jimmy,' she said as her eyes adjusted to the near darkness and she was able to replace the vase in its box, which she then carefully stowed under the bed, 'thank you for the vase. It really is beautiful. I'll treasure it always.'

She snuggled down under the blankets. She was sorry she'd been so cross with Jimmy. But they really couldn't risk him losing his job at Price's. And she did love the vase.

Jimmy's breathing was soon deep and heavy, so Hillie knew he was asleep. But it took her some time to settle. He hadn't asked how her evening had been with Gert, and she hoped he didn't in the morning! She didn't want to lie to him, but for some reason, neither did she fancy telling him she'd been out with Kit instead. Especially after his gift of the wonderful vase. Not that there'd been anything in the evening she'd spent with Kit. But there was some unnerving sensation niggling at the back of her mind that she couldn't quite identify.

Chapter Twenty

'Can we go to the park yet, Hill?'

'Yes, I do believe we can!' Hillie beamed down at Daisy. 'Thanks to Joan's help, I've got everything done nice and early. So go and spend a penny and tidy yourselves up. Can't have you going to the park looking like ragamuffins, can we?'

The girls didn't need telling twice. It was near the end of the school summer holidays. Hillie had tried to keep her younger siblings occupied with drawing and painting and suchlike as much as possible. On a nice day, they'd walked the three miles to Buckingham Palace, Hillie and Joan piggybacking the little ones much of the way, and cajoling them with promises of seeing the king. They didn't, of course, but they did go on to feed the pigeons in Trafalgar Square which had made them squeal with laughter, before marching on to stand below Big Ben as it chimed. Utterly exhausted, they'd caught the bus home from there. Hillie felt satisfied that she'd given the girls a good day out, the nearest they'd ever come to a holiday! Nevertheless, the little ones decided that they'd rather have just gone to the park.

Not so the day that Hillie had actually managed to wheedle some money out of Harold to take them to

Regents' Park Zoo where they'd marvelled over the animals. Trixie was so taken that she announced that evening that she was going to work there when she left school.

'Won't catch me going to work at boring old Price's,' she'd declared.

Hillie had been picking up her handbag ready to leave, and snatched in her breath. Oh, crikey. What was Harold going to say to that? Nell had been sure he'd never go for the younger children – presumably because they were his own flesh and blood, as Hillie knew now she wasn't. Was Trixie's affirmation going to test how right their mum had been? Hillie soon had the answer.

'You'll go to Price's and lump it,' Harold had snapped. 'And it's got a good pension scheme.'

'I hardly think I'm going to be worrying about a pension scheme when I'm only fourteen,' Trixie answered back. 'If I want to work with animals at the zoo, then I will.'

Hillie's eyes had flicked from Trixie's mutinously set mouth to Harold's menacing glower. Oh, dear. In the nine months since their dear mother had died, Hillie had managed, more or less, to keep the peace. Trixie was apt to be quiet and brooding, so to hear her speak out so adamantly was a bit of a shock. Was she going to be the one to defy her father?

Hillie was, in a way, pleased that someone was likely to stand up to Harold. And Nell might have been right in that Hillie would have received a clip round the ear if it had been her speaking to Harold like that and not Trixie. But Trixie was only ten, and Hillie didn't want her being on the receiving end of Harold's wrath just yet!

'I didn't notice if they had any female keepers. Did you?' she'd intervened, trying to pour oil on troubled waters.

'No, I didn't,' Trixie admitted. 'But there's always a first time for everything. I'll go and ask nearer the time. Anyway, who knows if Price's will still be going by then? Who's going to want candles when we're all getting the electric?'

Hillie blinked in surprise. She was stunned that her younger sister should have thought of such a thing. But by the look on his face, it'd been enough to take the wind out of Harold's sails.

'People will always want candles,' he'd said gruffly.

'But not in the same way as they used to. We did it in history at school last term. You know, when they only had candles and not even gas lights.'

'So that's where you got that nonsense from—'

'But anyway, working at the zoo'd still be a paid job. Maybe even better paid than at Price's. And people will always want to go and see all those animals.'

'Well, you're probably right there,' Hillie put in. 'But you've got another four years at school where you've got to work *very* hard to get any sort of job afterwards, don't forget. Right, I'm off, then. See you in the morning.'

She'd left the house that evening feeling that she'd smoothed things over, but now the tense scene came back to her as they got ready to go to the park. Trixie had always been the one who wanted to stop at the aviaries and deer enclosure and who observed the tiny differences between the ducks they fed. So perhaps it was no surprise that she wanted to turn her interest in animals into paid work when the time came.

Just like Kit and his passion for trains.

The thought flashed across Hillie's mind with a pang of guilt as she herded her little tribe out of the front door. The memory of that evening when she'd felt so close to Kit made her feel disloyal to Jimmy, even though there'd been nothing really in it. And Jimmy had kept to his word. He'd given up his work for Jackson, which was such a relief to Hillie as she was never quite sure what it entailed. Jimmy would never give her a direct answer, and given his past, with things *falling off the back of a lorry*, she wasn't convinced Mr Jackson and his doings were strictly legal. But nowadays, Jimmy was always home from his shifts at the pub by midnight at the very latest, and Hillie felt she could relax on that score, at least.

'Hello, you lot. Off somewhere nice?'

Hillie turned round from locking the front door. Jessica was standing there, almost loitering on the pavement. She didn't look her usual self, and Hillie thought her eyes were a touch swollen and red.

'Just to the park for an hour or so. Want to come with us?'

'Would you mind? I'm at a bit of a loose end.'

Hillie instinctively felt it was more than that, but was more than happy for her friend to come along. She had thought of calling in to see if Eva would like her to take her little tykes off her hands for a while. But now Hillie had the sensation that something was up with Jessica and that she maybe wanted to talk. But with the Parker children in tow as well, there'd be fat chance of being able to.

'Can we go on the boating lake, Hill?' Joan pleaded as they set out along South Carriage Drive.

'Oh, Hillie, plea-ease,' the others chorused.

'No, I'm sorry. I've no money to spare. You've had enough outings this summer. You'll just have to go and play,' she said, crossing them over towards the grass. 'Jess and I will sit here and watch you.'

As the children raced off, she and Jessica found an empty bench overlooking the vast area of grass. Hillie sat down with a heartfelt oomph, and Jessica settled herself beside her as the four girls chased each other around in a game of 'It'.

'What it is to be young,' Hillie sighed dramatically.

'You make it sound like you're really old.'

'Oh, I feel like it sometimes. I can understand how my poor mum felt with so much work to do. And I don't have a cruel, abusive husband to cope with.'

'You must… miss her so much,' Jessica suggested delicately. 'I'd miss mine, even if she can be so… so horrible to me sometimes. She and Dad both.'

Hillie glanced at her askew. 'I thought you looked as if you'd been crying. Something up?'

Jessica nodded, downcast eyes riveted on her joined hands. 'Yes.' She gulped, seeming on the brink of tears. 'Mum's got toothache. Only she's scared of going to the dentist because our usual one hurt her so much last time. Anyway, you can imagine I saw it as an ideal way to introduce her to Patrick. I know he uses local anaesthetic, you see. But I didn't want her to know I already knew him, so I pretended I'd asked at the library and said they recommended him as having a good reputation. She seemed quite keen and then she asked me his name. Well, I had to tell her, didn't I? I couldn't very well pretend they hadn't told me at the library. So when I told her, she said what sort of a name was Akpobio? I didn't know what to say, so like a fool, I said I thought he was from Nigeria. And both she and Dad said they'd never let a… well, I won't tell you what they called him, look in their mouths, and they'd sooner suffer the pain.'

Oh, dear. Hillie could see moisture collecting in Jessica's eyes, and the girl thumbed them away.

'Well, more fool them—' Hillie started to say, but Jessica couldn't contain herself.

'And just when… Oh, Hillie, I'll be twenty-one at the end of the year. And we really were going to break it to them then. But now I'm not sure we ever can.'

'Oh, now you listen to me.' Hillie turned to her friend with a sudden passion that astounded even herself. 'Patrick's a good catch. Your parents'd be idiots not to see that. And more importantly, you really love each other. Waiting so long is proof of that. And once you're twenty-one, you can marry who you like, and your mum and dad can't stop you.'

She saw Jessica wring her hands, her pretty mouth twitching. 'But I don't want to hurt them,' she moaned. 'Or… or lose them.'

'But what's more important to you? They've made their lives, now it's time for you to make yours. If you give Patrick up now, you'll always feel resentful towards your parents. But one day, they'll be dead and gone, and you'll still have your life to live. Don't make a mistake you'll regret forever.'

Jessica met her gaze, wide-eyed, and Hillie watched the minute changes in the older girl's expression as her impassioned words sank in. But where had they come from? Somewhere so deep inside that she hadn't known they were there herself. It was almost as if she was talking about herself.

And... was she?

Ever since that evening out with Kit, she'd been wondering. No. If she were truthful with herself, it went back way before that. When she'd begun to wonder if she hadn't made a mistake in marrying Jimmy. She'd thought she loved him. And she still did. But not with the intensity she knew lay somewhere inside her. Jimmy had been fun when she needed cheering up. He was exciting, and had proved himself hard-working. And in her time of need, he'd been her knight in shining armour. But was he really right for her?

Whereas that evening she'd spent with Kit, she'd felt so at home. They were on the same wavelength. Had more of the same tastes. It'd been a long time since she'd had a serious discussion with him. Years. But they found they'd read some of the same books – when Jimmy confessed to never having read an entire book in his life, even when he was supposed to have done at school.

As she sat on the bench with Jessica, she remembered Kit's animated face as they'd discussed *Cold Comfort Farm*, which they'd both recently read. And then they'd talked about more serious matters, Oswald Mosley's British Union of Fascists rally and then another hunger march at the beginning of the year, and the politician Winston Churchill's speeches about what was going on in Germany.

And then Kit had finished on a lighter note. 'Of course, all Dad's going to be interested in is the cricket and the British Empire Games coming up in August!' he'd laughed, making Hillie feel so relaxed and happy that, for a second or two, she couldn't help herself considering his strong jawline, his even teeth when he gave that engaging smile. The way a rogue lock of hair always flopped over his brow, giving him such a boyish expression. Could it be that she was finding the lad she'd always looked upon as an older brother increasingly attractive?

The thought that invaded her mind made her break out in a cold sweat and she hurled it aside. But what did it matter, anyway? She was married to Jimmy now, for better or for worse. And what an ungrateful cow she was, after all Jimmy had done for her!

But if she'd made a terrible mistake, she wasn't going to sit back and let her friend do the same!

She was relieved when Jessica stopped staring at her and then blinked. It was almost as if realisation or maybe acceptance was dawning on her face. A slight frown settled on her brow, but at the same time, her lips were curving upwards at the corners.

'D'you know, you're right,' Jessica finally spoke. 'I've been too worried about upsetting Mum and Dad all along. Look how they let me make friends with you and Gert in the end, even if they don't really approve, if you don't mind my saying so. Oh, Hillie, thank you! We'll still wait until after my birthday, but then we'll announce our engagement.'

'They'll come round,' Hillie assured her. 'They won't want to lose you, either.'

'Well, thanks again, Hillie. You've convinced me. Given me hope. So, shall we join in this game of tag?' she asked, her eyes glistening now with joy rather than tears as she gestured towards where the four sisters were racing around like lunatics.

'Yes, I think we'd better before war breaks out,' Hillie laughed, grateful for the diversion as she noticed the frustration on Frances's face at being 'caught' yet again. 'I think we've been far too solemn this afternoon, don't you?' And she charged across the grass, burying her thoughts in the deepest recesses of her mind.

*

Now what?

Hillie was lounging on the settee in the flat, twiddling her thumbs. It had been a long, busy day as usual at the little house in Banbury Street. But today had been different, and that's why she couldn't settle. For Frances, her baby sister, had started school.

Hillie had been looking forward to it. Frances was a bright little thing and needed the stimulus of the classroom. Much as Hillie had tried to keep her youngest sibling's mind occupied, there was so much to do that she didn't have sufficient time to devote to her sister's needs.

Frances had been so excited and there'd been no tears at the school gate as she'd skipped into the playground surrounded by her sisters and the Parker children. Hillie had felt she ought to go with her for the first few days, but there clearly wasn't going to be any need after that.

Hillie had done the day's shopping on her way back and then let herself into the house. Time to catch up on some of the jobs she'd neglected during the summer holidays. Not that there was anything dire, but she wanted to keep the place as pristine as her mum would have done.

But the house was just so quiet. She'd never known it like that. In the past, even if she'd been alone there, it was only ever for a short while, never the whole day. The silence pressed down on her in a way she hadn't expected. This was it now. Her life. She felt Nell's spirit brush past her shoulder. Could she understand what her mum had done – and given her life in the process? She'd asked herself that question a million times. How could such a devoted mother do what she had, and keep it a secret – as it would have been if things hadn't gone so horrifically wrong? But yes, Hillie was beginning to see how it could happen if you were worn down to nothingness.

She'd literally shaken herself and forced her attentions onto the housework, the washing and cooking that she needed to do. There wasn't even a radio to listen to. Harold didn't believe in such things, and wouldn't entertain the inconvenience – or the expense, no doubt – of having to take the batteries in to be recharged regularly. So Hillie had to put up with the deafening silence that somehow made her stomach trundle.

It had been a joy when it came to three o'clock and it was time to set out for the school. Frances was full of her first day, chattering all the way home. When Luke and Harold eventually got in from work, Hillie was only just beginning to feel her normal self. Part of her would have liked to stay on for a while to hear Frances's account of the day all over again, but the other part wanted to get away from Harold as swiftly as possible!

As she opened the front door, she'd almost collided with Gert who was walking along the street on her way home from work. Hillie spilled over with relief to see her old friend.

'Hello, Gert! Good day at the factory?' she asked, trying to sound cheerful.

'Blooming same as ever.' Gert rolled her eyes. 'How did Frances get on? You wanna come in for a cuppa?'

'Thought you'd never ask!' Hillie had laughed, forcing a grin onto her face.

But Gert pulled in her chin with a frown. 'What's up then, Hill? Can't fool me. I can see something's wrong.'

Hillie glanced at her, chewing on her lip. But she knew there was no getting away with it with Gert. 'Oh, I don't know,' she gave in at last. 'I just feel a bit down in the dumps. Life's running away with me before I've had a chance to achieve anything.'

'That's what comes of being such a clever clogs,' Gert chirped back. 'Anyway, you don't know what the future holds. You won't be tied to your family forever.'

'I feel as if I will.'

'Nah. Anyway, you'll probably have a family of your own soon with Jimmy. I'm surprised you ain't started one already.'

'We've been trying to have a family,' Hillie confessed. You couldn't keep anything from Gert! 'And to be honest, I'm not sure…' She'd found herself on the brink of saying it. That she was beginning to feel it had been a huge mistake, and that she shouldn't have married Jimmy in the first place. But how could she when Gert had supported her? Done so much to help them elope? So instead she went on, 'I'm not sure I could cope with a baby as well at the moment. And it wouldn't feel right, not so soon after Mum—'

'Not that soon. Nearly a year, you know. But at least you've got your own little home with Jimmy. I can't wait till Rob and me have a place of our own. Only he wants to save up so we can buy somewhere and have a mortgage thingy before we tie the knot. But then I guess he would, working in a bank and all.'

Hillie cocked an envious eyebrow as they went into Gert's house. 'You deserve to be happy,' she said wistfully.

'You make it sound as if you're not,' Gert frowned at her.

'Well, it's just that Jimmy's out so much, I guess. He's working at the pub almost every evening this week.'

'Oh? I thought he only worked there weekends?'

'He does normally, but he's filling in for someone.'

'Oh, well, you can have a bit of company with us, then, instead. Kit should be here, too. Said he'd call in on his way to work. He's on nights for a bit. Hello, everyone!' Gert called, pushing open the door to the back room.

'Hello, love.' Eva had welcomed them with her usual beaming smile. 'And Hillie, too.'

'Hello, Mrs P, everyone,' Hillie nodded, her heart skipping as she saw Kit looking alarmingly handsome as he raised his mug of tea to her in greeting.

'Haven't seen you in a while,' he said amiably.

'I hear you're on nights,' she answered, wondering why she felt a little unnerved.

'For my sins, yes,' he joked. 'But I rather enjoy it. The station's so different at night. Has an atmosphere all of its own. And how are you? Jake tells me Frances started school today. How did she get on?'

'Loved it,' Hillie chuckled. 'Still talking about it just now,' she informed him, thumbing back over her shoulder in the direction of her old family home.

'Good for her. Well, I must be off. Thanks for the tea, Mum. See you in a few days. Bye, Gran,' he said, placing a kiss on the old lady's gnarled cheek before heading towards the hallway.

'I'd better be going, too,' Hillie announced. 'Jimmy's out tonight but I've got a few things to do.'

'Oh. Oh, all right, then,' Gert looked vaguely put out.

'Cheerio, then. See you anon!'

Hillie hurried out of the room, suddenly driven by some force she could neither comprehend nor resist. She caught Kit up as he crossed the street.

'You leaving, too?'

'Yes. Things to do. But...' The words cascaded out of her mouth as if they had a life of their own. 'We should do what we did before. When you're back on days. Go out somewhere. I get so fed up with Jimmy not being there half the time. We could go out with Gert and Rob,' she added as a safety measure. 'And ask Luke along as well.'

Kit blinked at her in mild surprise. 'Yes. That'd be nice. Could be fun. But I must be off. Can't be late.'

He walked briskly away, and Hillie watched him for a second or two before turning for home in the opposite direction. She couldn't believe she'd just done that! But it had seemed perfectly natural, hadn't it? And after all, if Jimmy insisted on being out so regularly, what could he expect? And it'd only be going out with friends.

But now, as she sat in the empty flat, Hillie wasn't so sure and guilt flooded over her. Jimmy was working all hours God sent to provide for her and so that they could afford for her to look after her sisters for the pittance Harold paid her. On the other hand, she just felt so… empty was the only way she could describe it. And even more lonely without Frances to keep her company, hard work though she was. And then there was Kit. Hillie loved him like a brother, nothing more. Didn't she? So what harm could there be in seeing him once in a while?

But try as she might, Hillie couldn't reason herself out of her present mood. She picked up the newspaper she'd bought and flicked through it. Nothing much there. The unemployment situation. A bit about Germany and this chap, Adolf Hitler, who'd recently proclaimed himself Fuhrer and Chancellor. Some more warnings about the Nazi Party by the politician, Winston Churchill. And then there was an article about a spate of raids on jewellery shops in the area. Armed gangs or something.

Well, nothing that could be of any concern to her. Except the business with Germany, which Kit had said was a bit unsettling when they'd discussed it. So, what was on the radio? She turned it on. Nothing. Oh, blast. Jimmy was supposed to have taken in the discharged batteries and swapped them back for the recharged ones. But he'd either forgotten or not had time. And he didn't like Hillie doing it because they were quite heavy and sometimes leaked acid. At least he was being gallant, Hillie supposed.

So, what could she do now? She stepped over to the window and gazed down on the street below. The day was beginning to fade, but it was too early for the street lamps to come on. The early September evening was still mild and inviting. Oh, she should have stayed at Gert's house for a while, just as she'd been asked, rather than rushing out after Kit. What on earth had possessed her to chase after him like that?

Ah, Jimmy. If only he were there to cuddle her. Make her laugh. Reassure her that he was the only one for her and that their marriage was rock solid.

But – why on earth hadn't she thought of it before? If Jimmy couldn't be at home with her, there was nothing to stop her from going to him! OK, pubs were really a man's domain. It was frowned upon for women to go in alone. She remembered how awkward she and Gert had felt that New Year's Eve when they'd sidled in together. But maybe she could sit up at the bar near where Jimmy was working. He could explain to the customers who she was, and that'd make her feel more comfortable. She might even enjoy herself and meet some interesting people. Not everyone went to a pub just to get drunk!

She went to the mirror and took the pins out of her hair, letting it tumble down her back in a riot of curls. Should she have it cut? Not too short, but maybe shoulder length? It'd be more manageable and she wouldn't need to scrape it back into a bun for the business of the day. It could make her more attractive. To Jimmy. To anyone. To… to Kit?

Angrily, she grasped her handbag and careered down the stairs, gasping at the dusty evening air and the smell of warm tarmac outside. She must get to Jimmy, to her husband, to make herself see sense. She raced along breathlessly, eventually turning down Falcon Road and passing the back entrance to the station with the row of sealed railway arches that acted as warehouses. They could be creepy at night, dark, dirty and faceless, but during the day were often a hive of activity. Under the succession of railway lines crossing above the road, then, the throaty rumble as a goods train clattered overhead, making the ground shake. By the time Hillie reached the corner of the street and entered the Falcon, she wondered quite what she'd been thinking of, letting her frustrations turn her towards dear, trusting Kit.

There weren't so many customers, it being a weekday. A few eyes turned on her, looking her up and down, and she felt like fleeing back the way she'd come.

'Hello, darling. Fancy a drink? Or maybe somefing else?' some chap leered at her, and then chortled as he dug his mate in the ribs.

Well, Hillie wasn't going to be cowed by them. 'Not with the likes of you, chum!' she retorted, and strode confidently up to the long, snaking, continuous bar with its polished wood and gleaming pump handles. She couldn't see Jimmy, but it was a vast pub and he could easily be round the other side of the circular bar and hidden by its huge central service area.

'Don't mind them, miss,' an older man in an apron greeted her from the opposite side of the bar. 'All mouth and no trousers. Now, what can I get you?'

'Oh, nothing at the moment, thank you. I'm looking for Jimmy. Is he around?' Hillie enquired with relief. This fellow, the landlord she guessed, had put her at her ease.

'Jimmy? What, Jimmy Baxter, d'you mean?' The man's face darkened. 'Hasn't worked here for months. I sent him packing. Caught him with his fingers in the till. Lucky I didn't call in the coppers, he was. Not seen hide nor hair of him since, not that I ever want to. So what's a nice girl like you want with him? If you'll take my advice, don't have anything to do with him. Oh, my, you've gone as white as a sheet. Not gone and left you up the duff, has he?'

The man, the bar, the sparkling mirrors swayed in front of Hillie's eyes. She rocked on her feet, waiting for the grey veil of shock to lift, for her heart to sink back into its proper place. She swallowed hard, nearly choking, as her brain swam back and forth and finally started to function again.

'No. No, nothing like that,' she mumbled. 'Thanks for your time.'

'Not at all, miss. And you two can stop sniggering,' he chastised as Hillie turned, blundering into the two customers before hurrying back outside, the ground waving up and down beneath her feet.

*

'You've been lying to me, Jimmy!' she challenged him, fury blazing in her eyes. 'All these months, you've been lying! So if you haven't been working at the pub, where have you been, eh? Working for that blackguard Jackson, I suppose, when you promised me—'

Jimmy wriggled his head on his neck, scarlet flushing up through his face in a rash. 'We-ell, I was going to tell you. I was waiting for the right moment, that's all. I knew you'd be upset—'

'Upset? Upset!' she yelled. 'I'm not upset, I'm bloody livid! You betrayed me, lied and lied—'

'Oh, come on, Hill. It's not that bad. I've only been doing small things for him. Running errands, nothing more. I've been home by eleven thirty every night, just like you asked.' He reached out a placatory hand to take her by the arm, but she angrily threw him off.

'Yes! Deceiving me even further! How can I ever trust you again? *And* you were caught stealing!'

'Oh, yeah?' Jimmy half sneered. 'He didn't have any proof of that. Did he tell you that's why he didn't call in the old bill? No, he wouldn't, would he? He couldn't prove it was me 'cos it wasn't.'

'But how can I believe you, Jimmy? How can I ever believe a word you say to me anymore?'

'Look!' Jimmy spread his hands in exasperation. 'So I didn't tell you I was working for Mr Jackson and not at the pub. It's not such a big deal. I'm bringing in money we need if we're to go on living here and you're looking after your sisters for next to nothing. You should be bloody grateful. And it's only 'cos of Jackson that I can put money in our savings account for the future. I'll get you that cottage in the country one day if it's the last thing I ever do,' he cajoled with a half-pleading, half-cheeky smile.

'Blow the cottage in the country! Fat lot of good it'll be if you're behind bars!'

'I keep telling you, I'm not doing anything illegal.' Jimmy was becoming angry now. 'Why won't you believe me?'

'I'd've thought that was obvious. I really don't feel I can trust you ever again. Now here's a blanket and a pillow,' Hillie hissed, stepping into the adjacent bedroom, pulling the said items from the bed and thrusting them at him. 'From now on, you sleep on the settee until you stop lying to me!'

And she went back into the bedroom, slamming the door behind her before she burst into tears.

Chapter Twenty-One

He was laughing, that soft, light, familiar laugh that sent delight tingling down Hillie's spine. His head thrown back, mouth stretched wide, revealing his even, white teeth. Chortling herself, Hillie stole a secret glance at Kit, her heart missing a beat. She couldn't even remember what outrageous remark Gert had made a few moments earlier that had made them all roar in merriment. Nor did she care. All she knew was that for just a short while, she could be herself. Be happy.

It wasn't fair on Jimmy, the way she was feeling – she had to admit it to herself now – so attracted to another man. And it certainly wasn't fair on Kit. He appeared quite content, though, to come out in a group when his shifts allowed, not realising how Hillie felt. Sometimes it was just the four of them; other times, they were joined by either Belinda or Luke. The more the merrier, as far as Hillie was concerned. It was easier to hide her feelings when they were a bigger group. Made her feel safer.

Kit always joined whole-heartedly in the fun or more serious discussion if the conversation went that way, and then took himself off home with a cheery wave. He might give Hillie the occasional special smile or squeeze her hand, but she was sure she was just reading something into it that wasn't there and that he was oblivious to how his very presence lifted her soul, giving her the strength to carry on with her doubly trapped life. Trapped into working for Harold whom she despised, and trapped into her life with Jimmy whom she couldn't trust anymore.

And yet she wanted to take care of her younger sisters, and she wanted her marriage to repair itself. She wanted Jimmy to come back to her. Or rather she wanted to feel she could *let* him, since she was the one who'd put the distance between them. She still *wanted* to love him, but she felt betrayed. She wasn't ready to forgive.

What Jimmy was up to half the time, she didn't know. She wasn't even sure that she cared anymore. She'd had enough of worrying about him. Since the night of their terrible row, she'd let him get on with his dubious activities without interfering. She felt that whatever she said, however she pleaded, he wouldn't listen anyway, so there wasn't much point. She'd even allowed him back into the marital bed to sleep, although nothing more. She simply couldn't give herself to someone she couldn't believe in, even if he was her husband.

'I'm gonna be in every night this week,' he'd told her shortly afterwards. 'See if I'm not. And all over the weekend. Don't want my girl getting all upset again.'

He'd said it as if it were some sort of triumphant sacrifice, Hillie considered, silently pouring scorn on his words. She was about to retort that she'd believe it when it happened, when he pulled her into his arms and covered her mouth with his in a passionate kiss. She didn't resist, hoping it would stir something inside her. But it didn't. The magic had gone and she felt herself stiffen. When she didn't respond, Jimmy simply released her.

'Are you gonna punish us forever?' he grumbled.

'That depends on whether or not you can go back to keeping your promise,' Hillie answered almost under her breath.

'Oh, Hill.' Jimmy shook his head. 'You know I still need to do *some* work for Mr Jackson. That is, unless you go back to work at Price's. Then maybe we could manage this flat and still be able to save a bit. And even then, earning a bit on the side wouldn't come amiss.'

'So now it's my fault, is it, for wanting to look after my sisters?'

'Hill, I didn't say that—'

'It's what you meant. And if you hadn't got yourself sacked from the pub, we'd have been all right anyway. Well, I'm not going to let the likes of Dolly Maguire near the girls again! We'll just have to muddle through until they're a bit older. Use some of our savings.'

'But we've gone without to save that money,' Jimmy protested. 'I love you, Hill, and I want to make that dream of yours of a cottage in the country come true.'

Hillie had softened then, and placed a peck on his cheek. 'Well, we'll just have to be more patient, then, won't we? I know you're doing it for the sake of our future, but I just don't want you getting into trouble.'

'I won't, I promise. So, if I only do things like serve drinks at Mr Jackson's gambling parties, can we be friends again?'

Jimmy had tipped his head, half cajoling, half teasing, and Hillie had relented. Almost.

'Well, let's see how it goes,' she'd said.

That had been a few days after she'd discovered he'd been lying to her. Could they be reconciled? She'd hoped so. But although Jimmy wasn't absent quite so much as before, he was gradually slipping backwards. And Hillie began to give up hope again. She'd heard it all before.

The start of October had produced some pleasant days, and here they were, Gert, Rob, Hillie and Kit, whose shifts had allowed him to join them on a Sunday afternoon. When Jimmy had disappeared God knew where, Hillie had gone where she always did in times of crisis – to Gert's. Rob had been there and so had Kit, and the four of them had decided to go out together. They'd gone to the park, of course, taking with them a picnic to enjoy in the autumn sunshine, possibly their last chance before the colder weather arrived.

They found an empty bench in the sunshine and sat down to munch the hastily made sandwiches Eva had insisted they take with them, and a bottle of ginger beer she'd unearthed from the larder.

'We could take the little ones—' Kit had offered.

'No, you young people enjoy yourselves on your own for once,' Eva had insisted. 'It's not often you get the chance.'

'If you're sure—'

'Go on. You're a good lad, Kit.'

And so they'd arrived in the park unencumbered by any of their junior siblings, laughing and joking in a relaxed mood. Hillie had felt her depressed spirits slowly rising, pushing her cares aside for a couple of hours. The sun was warm enough to penetrate her clothes, and she unbuttoned the Fair Isle cardigan she kept for better occasions, despite its associations. It certainly made her feel more uplifted to wear something less drab than normal, and she was secretly grateful to Jimmy – not that she'd ever admit it to him. She wondered vaguely what he was up to just now…

'Here you are, Hill,' Gert said, passing her a half of one of Eva's doorstep sandwiches. 'Just a bit of tongue inside, but it's better than nothing.'

'Thanks. Very kind of your mum.'

'Well, you know our dear mum.' Kit jerked his head as he opened the bottle of ginger beer that resounded with an explosive pop. 'Always likes to put food inside us, whatever it tastes like.'

'Mmm,' Hillie chuckled by way of reply as she took the sandwich from Gert. Tongue was one thing she couldn't stand. She'd rather have bread and dripping, but she couldn't very well refuse. And she hadn't eaten since breakfast. She hadn't felt like it after Jimmy had announced he was *just popping out*, and still hadn't returned a few hours later.

Now, suddenly, with the good company and the sunshine, Hillie felt ravenous, and bit into the sandwich with gusto. To her delight, she found that the half-piece Gert had handed her had missed the slither of tongue but was tastily laced with mustard instead.

'Funny how food tastes so much nicer when you're outside,' she observed through a mouthful of bread.

'Yeah. Pity all we've got is a piddling backyard,' Gert complained. 'It's so nice at Rob's house to have a cuppa or something out in the garden. His mum keeps it so lovely. Been teaching me about plants and things for when Rob and me have a place of our own.'

Hillie noticed the way Gert smiled adoringly at the young man sitting on the bench beside her. 'D'you think you'll have somewhere with a proper garden, then?'

'I certainly hope so.'

'Well, don't get too impatient, love,' Rob warned, lifting an eyebrow. 'It'll be a while before we've got enough for a deposit. But if we move out a bit, maybe we can get a nice little semi in one of those new suburb estates they're building, and I can commute in every day on one of Kit's trains.'

It was a serious observation, but in the light-heartedness that seemed to have invaded them all, it was met with a chuckle. Hillie, though, had to move her face into a smile as envy pricked her heart at the evident love between Gert and Rob. How good and solid their plans were, whereas she hadn't had the courage to tell even Gert about how Jimmy had lied to her and the rockiness of their circumstances. She felt almost ashamed, as if it were partly her fault. And… well, maybe it was. If only this, and if only that…

But the sun shone down, enticing the fragrance of warm earth and grass. Overhead, a light breeze made the autumn-kissed leaves dance in the trees. And Kit was there, silently and unknowingly bringing her some peace. Their fingers had touched as he'd handed her the bottle of ginger beer they were all sharing, and their eyes had met in a mutual smile. Did it mean anything? Did Hillie *want* it to mean anything? But it made her feel relaxed and happy.

And yet there was a sting in the tail of that brief contentment. When Hillie was with Kit, her heart secretly soared recklessly, as if everything was magically going to turn out all right. But how could it? And it made the inevitable fall when they parted so much worse. She always felt as if she was plummeting down through the air, a wingless bird with nothing to stop her crashing to the earth and smashing into a million pieces.

For how was it all to end?

*

'I told you that ne'er-do-well you married was good for nothing!' Harold crowed triumphantly as he burst into the back room after work one evening a few weeks later. 'Should've listened to me in the first place. Well, you're in a right old pickle now, my girl.'

Hillie jerked up her head as she placed the sizzling rabbit casserole on the table next to a tray of baked potatoes, and she felt a spike of dread as she saw the delight gleaming in Harold's eyes. 'W-what d'you mean?' she stammered.

'Got the sack, ain't he? For falling asleep when he'd been warned about it before.'

'What?'

'You heard me,' Harold almost grinned back. 'Lover boy's let you down good and proper, just like I said he would.'

Panic gripped Hillie by the throat. 'No. I don't believe you. You're lying. Luke?' she questioned, seeking reassurance from her brother as he slunk awkwardly into the room behind his father.

But even as she spoke the words, Hillie knew that Harold wasn't lying at all. The scene that morning sprang back so vividly into her mind. Jimmy had indeed been out the previous evening, and she'd had no idea what time it was when he'd stumbled into bed. Twice that morning she'd had to wake him and he'd fallen back asleep. She'd needed to push him out of the flat with neither a wash nor breakfast so that he wouldn't be late for work. And now this.

Daisy and Frances were clambering up to the table, oblivious to the conversation, but Joan and Trixie understood what it meant. Hillie shivered as she saw them exchange glances, and then she met Luke's anxious gaze. Oh, good Lord. It must be true.

'Bye, girls,' a hoarse voice that must be hers, but that she hardly recognised, scraped automatically over the top of Daisy and Frances's heads. Her limbs moved as if in a dream, or more likely a nightmare, as if she had no control over them, but fortunately they knew what to do. She picked up her handbag and moved towards the door, her heart hammering. 'See you tomorrow,' she mumbled, and then staggered down the hallway. She swiped her coat from the stand, but was too poleaxed to put it on. She just wanted to rush home, speak to Jimmy, find out it was all a mistake. Although she knew it wasn't.

'Oh, Hill, I'm so sorry—'

Luke had followed her out into the hallway and she caught his voice over her shoulder. But she ignored him and stepped outside, sharply pulling the door to behind her. She couldn't face his sympathy. She just needed to get out. Gulp at the November evening air. Let the murky drizzle calm the tortured energy that surged through her veins.

Her legs broke into a run.

*

'Hello, love.' Jimmy threw her a cheeky smile as he looked up from laying the little table. 'Thought I'd surprise you and have supper ready. You been running? You look all puffed.'

Hillie stared at him in disbelief. He was acting as if nothing had happened, and her brain swirled in confusion. *Had* it all been a dream? Had Harold set her up? Bullied Luke into playing along with him? It was the sort of mental cruelty he was capable of. And when Luke had said he was sorry, was that what he'd meant? That he was sorry for falling in with Harold's nasty game because he was scared to do otherwise? Not that he was sorry Jimmy had lost his job because, in fact, he hadn't?

Hillie had been close to tears as she'd raced headlong through the darkened streets, almost pushing people out of her way in blind panic. What would happen to them without Jimmy's wages? It was hard enough for anyone to get a job. Not so hard, so she believed, as in the north of the country where unemployment was rife, but hard, nonetheless. And Jimmy wasn't exactly going to get a glowing reference from Price's, was he? They'd have to leave the flat. Go back to some godawful little room with a shared bathroom and toilet, probably with damp paper peeling off the walls, mould on the ceiling and windows that were cracked and loose in their frames, and rattled in the wind.

She could maybe face that. But even if she was lucky enough to get her old job back at the factory with her own reputation of being such a good worker, could she face leaving her sisters to fend for themselves? Or worse, have Dolly Maguire come back to lord it over them? For that was probably what Harold would do, bring the old hag back, deliberately to spite Hillie. It wouldn't be *quite* so bad as before, now that Frances was at school all day, but it would still be bad enough. Dolly taking the place of their dear mum. It was unthinkable.

But here was Jimmy, as calm as a cucumber, setting the table, with something sizzling tantalisingly in the pan and steam wafting gently from a saucepan on the other ring. It was all so normal. Had Hillie imagined it, after all? Or fallen for another despicable trick of Harold's?

She hung up her coat, aware of her hands shaking as she did so. She ignored Jimmy's last remark and instead consciously rearranged her face into a smile. 'And a lovely surprise it is, too. Did you… get home early for some reason?' she found herself probing.

'No, not especially.' Jimmy shrugged slightly. 'I caught the tram 'cos of the rain. And I thought I'd spoil my girl for once.'

Hillie bit the inside of her lip. Rain? It had been drizzling, not proper rain at all. Although it could have been raining harder a little earlier. She might not have known with the curtains drawn, and the pavements had been quite wet.

'Mmm, that smells lovely,' she said, forcing herself to receive Jimmy's peck on the cheek. 'Be with you in a mo.'

She went into the bathroom, used the toilet and then stared at herself in the mottled mirror over the sink as she washed her hands. Was it her imagination, or did she look pale, her eyes sunken with shock? Had Jimmy noticed?

She took a deep breath and walked calmly back into the living area, sitting down at the table. In the kitchenette, Jimmy was serving up the meal. He carried her plate over in one hand, tea cloth folded over his other arm, and bowed as he placed her dinner in front of her.

'Here you are, madam,' he announced with mock servility.

Hillie's heart squeezed. When Jimmy dropped into his play-acting, it was often for a reason. *Was* there a reason this time? She watched as Jimmy sat down and began to devour his own meal, but Hillie scarcely noticed what was on her plate. It stuck in her throat as she tried to eat, and she had to take a large gulp of water to swallow down each morsel.

She was only halfway through when she simply couldn't stomach any more. She felt too sick. She lay down her knife and fork, waiting for Jimmy to notice. He finally looked up, chewing vigorously.

'What's up, love? Not hungry?' he asked casually, then immediately went back to preparing the next forkful to launch into his mouth.

Hillie lowered her eyes. 'When were you going to tell me?' she murmured.

She heard the little rush of air as Jimmy snatched in his breath. 'Tell you? Tell you what?' he asked lightly, but she could hear the change in his voice as he spoke.

'I think you know.'

A split second's silence before Jimmy found his tongue. 'Oh, what, you mean about Price's deciding they no longer need me services?'

'So... it's true, then? I thought as much. It must be all over the factory. So how long were you going to keep it from me?'

'We-ell, I was waiting for the right moment to tell you. But now you know, I won't have to, will I?' Jimmy went on glibly once more. 'Anyway, I'm better off without them. They didn't even give me notice, so I walked out straightaway. I've been to see Mr Jackson, and he says he's happy to take me on full-time, so Price's've done us a favour. I'll be much better off working for him.'

Hillie felt a flush of icy water pass through her. 'Oh, Jimmy, a bit of cash in hand is one thing. But... well, I don't trust this chap. I mean, who exactly is he? All this work and money he's offering you? What exactly is his set-up? And what about tax and National Insurance?'

'Oh, don't worry about all that,' Jimmy assured her with his usual grin. 'I'll make sure it's all done proper, and I'll buy me own stamp at the Post Office.'

But Hillie shook her head. 'Oh, I don't know, Jimmy. It just doesn't seem right.'

'Now don't you worry your pretty little head about it, and eat up before it gets completely cold. Everything'll be perfectly OK, just you wait and see. Better than before. We'll be able to get out of London so much sooner and then I promise you I'll settle down to a nice little job. Tell you what, would you fancy running a little shop of some sort and we could live over the top? In a village or a small country town? I know it wouldn't quite be what you wanted, a cottage with roses round the door. But it'd be a good, solid income, and I've got loads of contacts for stock.'

Oh, yes. More likely stolen goods, Hillie thought to herself. She didn't answer. Because she truly didn't know what to say.

Chapter Twenty-Two

Now, how was she going to make Christmas special for her family, Hillie was asking herself as she scrubbed the butler sink with Vim? The previous year's Christmas had been somewhat subdued with Nell not yet cold in her grave, and Frances and Daisy still asking for their mummy. But Hillie had tried so hard to keep their minds so full and busy, and given them so much love, that as the months had passed, their memories of the woman who'd held their lives together seemed to have faded. But for herself and the older children, she felt Christmas would always be a bit sad, coming as it did not so long after the anniversary of Nell's death.

At least money wasn't so tight that Hillie couldn't afford to buy some decent presents to put around a decorated tree that she herself would also need to purchase. She'd given up worrying about Jimmy. Her mind was so saturated in anxiety that it really couldn't absorb any more. True to his word, Jimmy was producing a proper payslip each week. Their savings were growing, hopefully bringing the yearned for move to the country a little closer. It wouldn't be for years yet, but by then, the girls would be old enough for Hillie to feel she could pass her housekeeping duties on to someone else. And Hillie would insist Jimmy left his connections with Mr Jackson behind, even if it meant he had to work as a farm labourer or some such, and they had to struggle as a result. And yet despite all their logical plans, it still seemed like a pipe dream to Hillie.

She was so lost in thought that the knock on the front door made her jump. Now, who could that be? She wasn't expecting anyone. She dried her hands on the rough towel as she went down the hallway, her forehead in a slight frown. When she opened the door, she expected to see an adult, Jessica perhaps. But she looked down on a small child who obviously hadn't thought to put on her coat and was shivering on the doorstep.

'Trudy! What are you doing here? Oh, come in out of the cold,' Hillie instructed.

The child stepped inside, unusually for her, a little warily. Worried that Harold might be around, Hillie considered grimly.

'Now, what can I do for you, love?' she asked to distract Trudy's saucer-eyed stare.

'Mummy said can you come? Straightaway.'

'Oh.' Hillie's frown deepened and alarm bells started ringing in her head. It was a highly unusual request from dear Eva. Trudy was only a few months younger than Frances, but her birthday was just after the cut-off date, so she couldn't start school until the following year. But she was old enough to take a message from her mum to Hillie. Usually it was an invite to call in for a cuppa, but never anything like this. And Eva would normally have wrapped Trudy up warmly, even if it was only a few doors down.

'Yes, of course. I've got something simmering on the stove. Let me just turn the gas off, and I'll be with you.'

Hillie nipped back to the kitchen to make sure all was safe and then moved her face into a smile as she let herself and Trudy out of the house. She locked the door behind them, taking the key with her. Ever since she'd thrown Dolly out, she never left the key hanging on its string through the letter box!

'What've you been up to today?' she asked as brightly as she could as they covered the few yards to the Parkers' house. After all, if something was up, there was no need to upset Trudy. It was probably just that Eva needed a hand with something, or that she couldn't tune in the radio, a modern technology she'd never entirely managed to get the hang of!

'Making paper chains for Christmas,' Trudy answered with excitement. 'Mummy cut the newspaper into strips and I've been painting them. Only Primrose keeps trying to take them before they're dry.'

'Hmm.' Hillie gave a false chuckle. 'Little brothers and sisters can be a nuisance, can't they? Still, I expect you're looking forward to starting school next year, aren't you?'

'Yeah,' the little girl replied, pushing open her front door that was only ever locked at night. 'Wish I could've started with Frances.'

'Oh, well, never mind,' Hillie pacified her, following her into the back room where Trudy at once climbed back up to the table and resumed her painting of the newspaper strips.

Hillie paused for a moment, observing the scene. Primrose was happily playing on the floor with a couple of crude miniature horses Stan had carved for her out of some leftover wood at the factory's sawmill. Eva, though, was standing motionless, one hand at her throat and the other resting on the table next to her. Her normally ruddy face was grey, her gaze fixed on Old Sal sat in her chair next to the fire.

Hillie knew at once and her heart dropped.

'I-I can't wake her up,' Eva gulped without turning her head.

Hillie stepped forward, her pulse rattling. Her mum had been the only experience of death she'd ever had, and then, the kind lady doctor had been there. But now she had to take a hold of herself. Be practical as well as strong. Especially for dear Eva whose own generosity knew no bounds.

Old Sal's head was slumped forward, eyes closed for all the world as if she was asleep. Hillie, though, couldn't see her chest moving. She placed her fingers under the old lady's wrinkled jaw, just as she'd seen in films at the cinema. Nothing. And when she felt Old Sal's brow, it was already cold and hard, like marble, despite being by the fire.

'Oh, Eva,' Hillie said so quietly. 'I'm so sorry. She's gone. A little while ago, I think.'

Eva's face crumpled as she nodded slowly. 'I know,' she croaked. 'I just hoped... I didn't notice. I-I thought she'd been asleep a long time, even for her. I should've... been holding her hand.'

Hillie came over and, pulling out a chair, gently pushed Eva down onto it. 'You couldn't have known,' she whispered. 'She went peacefully. In such a happy home. You couldn't have done more for her, Mrs P.'

'Eva. Please.' The older woman turned glistening eyes on her. 'You and me, we've been through quite a bit together, ain't we? Even before you was born, really. I'm sure Nell would've approved.' She attempted a wry smile as she fought off her tears, and sadness pierced Hillie's heart.

'Yes. Eva,' she agreed, nodding her head. 'Can I make you a cuppa?'

'No, it's all right, love. I'll get one meself in a minute. I need to stay here with the little uns. But I'd be grateful if you could do the necessary. Go to the undertakers'. And we need a doctor for the certificate, don't we? And… and Stan. Perhaps they'd let him come home early.'

'Yes. Yes, of course,' Hillie replied, her brain whirring into action. 'I'll leave my key with you in case Joan gets back from school with everyone before I do. I'll just pop home to get my coat and then I'll bring the key back here.'

'Yeah, of course, ducks. I just wish…'

She broke off, choking on her words, and Hillie patted her hand.

'Yes, I know.'

But the girl didn't know, Eva thought to herself, cross that in her grief she'd nearly let it slip. What she'd secretly wanted all along. Hillie was like another daughter to her, and she'd longed to welcome her into the family officially. But it was too late. Had been for a while. And it could never be.

And Eva must keep that secret longing hidden safely in her heart for always.

*

When Hillie turned the corner back into Banbury Street with Gert and Stan, the light was already fading from the cold, damp, miserable day. Outside Number Eight, a horse stood patiently between the shafts of a black-painted cart with white lettering on the sides. Hillie hadn't known how much money the

Parkers might have to spend, so had chosen the cart, which was cheaper than the motor-driven hearse. With no spare room to hold Old Sal for the few days until the funeral, her body had to be taken away. It was the same firm who'd provided Nell's coffin and other services, so Hillie knew the old lady would be treated with respect, be it cart or limousine.

The gentleman in the office had offered to telephone for a doctor to certify the death before they removed Old Sal's body. At no extra cost, he'd said when Hillie'd explained that she didn't think the family had much money to spare. He'd remembered Hillie from her own mother's funeral just over a year previously. How could you forget a beauty like that? he'd thought privately. Such dignity, too. And the way the brewery had stepped in with the decorated dray-cart had been remarkable. He wondered if they'd do the same for this old lady who'd lived on the street even longer.

Hillie had been met with equal understanding when she'd gone into the offices at Price's. It seemed so strange, walking into the factory again. She went straight to find Belinda, who'd been promoted to working in Personnel.

Her friend's face folded into compassionate lines when Hillie told her the sad news. 'Oh, no, not dear Old Sal? She was such a character.'

'I know. Poor Mrs P's going to miss her terribly. And after losing her best friend last year,' Hillie added almost under her breath as she lowered her eyes. And then she felt Belinda's hand on her arm.

'Yes. Your mum,' the other girl said with feeling. 'You go and find Mr Parker, and Gert, too. I'll square it with the powers that be here.'

'Thanks, Belinda.'

'Can you remember the way?'

'Yes, I should think so,' Hillie grimaced, and set off through the eleven-acre site she knew like the back of her hand.

God, what a place it was, she thought grimly as she set off towards the sawmill to find Stan first. The original founders and subsequent management had always been benevolent, but the factory itself seemed even more depressing than ever. Hillie thanked her lucky stars she wasn't working there anymore, so perhaps there was a silver lining to Jimmy's *change of employment*, after all.

'What the hell are you doing here?'

A hand dug cruelly into Hillie's shoulder and she was spun round to meet Harold's menacingly glinting eyes. And then his expression altered to a gloating sneer. 'Or have you changed your mind and want your old job back now that useless husband of yours has lost his?'

Hillie had to knot her lips fiercely to stop her fury bursting out, and her own eyes flashed like cold steel. 'As it happens, no,' she all but spat back, 'though it's doubtless what you'd like to see. Old Sal died this afternoon, so I've come to fetch Mr Parker.'

'Oh.' Harold's face fell as the cause for his glee was whisked from beneath his feet. But not to be defeated, he went on with a malevolent curl of his lip. 'And there's me thinking you was maybe hankering after the old place. But...' He leant forward, grasping her arm this time, and poking his nose so close to her face, she could see the saliva oozing from the corners of his mouth. 'You'll be back here, mark my words.'

Hillie angrily pulled away. 'It's being so nasty that keeps you going, isn't it?' she grated, turning her back and storming off.

But somehow Harold's words kept echoing in her brain.

*

The hearse had gleamed crisply in the clear, frosty morning. So much less depressing than the wretched drizzle on the day Nell had been buried, Hillie thought. It was sad, of course, that Old Sal had passed on. And poor Eva was quite devastated, even if it was going to make life so much easier for her. But Sal had recently turned eighty-nine and had been senile for so many years. She'd had a good life, so you couldn't complain.

But the old lady's funeral had reopened the wound of Nell's death just as it was beginning to heal. The agony of grief came swirling back into Hillie's soul. Oh, how different life might have been for them all if their mum had still been alive. Hillie would still have been working at Price's, and with her wages coming in, Jimmy might not have felt the need to work for Jackson and lost his job at the factory as a result. Above all, Luke and the girls would still have had their loving mother at home.

And when it came down to it, all their troubles had been Harold's fault. He hadn't even bothered to get a couple of hours off work to go to Sal's funeral, Hillie scoffed bitterly. But at least her resentment towards him helped take the edge off the sadness that swelled in her throat.

'You did Old Sal proud, Eva,' she said to the poor woman whose eyes were still bloodshot from crying at the funeral. 'You sit down and let me help with the drinks and things.'

'Thanks, Hillie,' Eva said, gratefully easing her well-padded figure onto a chair. 'It wasn't us. We could only've afforded the cart. It was Kit forked out for it. Thought the world of his gran, he did.'

Hillie lifted her chin slightly. Now why didn't that surprise her? Kit had always been so fond of Old Sal.

She squeezed through all the people squashed into the back room of Number Eight, helping Stan, Gert and Kit serve tea and biscuits to everyone. Unlike when Nell had died and the many who'd gone to the service had found excuses not to enter Harold Hardwick's house, almost the whole street seemed to want to cram into the Parker home. They were like sardines in a tin. Hillie noticed Jessica talking to Eva, evidently having defied her parents' ban on her visiting Gert's house. She'd be celebrating her twenty-first birthday in a few days' time. Hillie wondered if she'd found the courage yet to tell them about Patrick. But now wasn't the time to ask.

'I gather it was you who paid for the hearse,' she said to Kit as she joined him in the scullery waiting for the kettle to boil on the gas stove to make yet another pot of tea. 'That was good of you.'

Kit gave a wistful shrug. 'I was very close to Gran. I suppose it was being the eldest, I spent more time with her while Mum was looking after the little ones. She had a wicked sense of humour before her mind started going.'

The way he looked at Hillie made her stomach melt, the memories creating a closeness between them. 'Yes, I can remember that. But it was good of you anyway.'

'It was the least I could do for her. Mum and Dad couldn't afford it, and well, I've got a good job now.

Oh, hello, Jimmy,' he said flatly, nodding briefly as Jimmy came up beside them.

Hillie's body stilled as a spark of electricity seemed to sizzle through her. Her husband, and the man she was finding increasingly attractive and certainly respected more, standing one on either side of her. Was it her imagination, or was there a tension between them?

'It's going well, then? As a senior clerk?' she asked, the only thing she could think of to steer the conversation in a sensible direction – as much for her own sake as anything else, for she'd successfully hidden her feelings from both of them as far as she was aware.

'Yes, I love it,' Kit told her, as if her question had lifted him from his sorrow. 'The whole operation's so complex with all the goods trains that come through the station. It's utterly fascinating. And we're being extra vigilant at the moment. There've been a lot of armed raids throughout London over the past year. Mainly on jewellers' shops, but other things as well. Delivery lorries and so forth. Really organised stuff, so we don't want any of our trains to be held up.'

'Gosh, d'you really think that's likely?'

'Well, I'd love to stay and chat,' Jimmy broke in a little hastily. 'But I came over to say I need to go.'

'It was good of you to come.'

'Just wanted to show me respects, even though I scarcely knew the old dear. See you later, Hillie, love,' Jimmy concluded, kissing her on the cheek.

Hillie nodded, but didn't even turn her head to watch Jimmy leave. She didn't want him to see the contempt on her face. *Old dear*, indeed! Old Sal *had* been a dear, but not in the sense Jimmy meant, she was sure.

'Ah, kettle's boiled,' she announced, smiling up at Kit instead.

*

'Is this what you're looking for? I found them quite by chance. They must've fallen out of your pocket.'

Hillie had been sitting quietly on the sofa pretending to read, but out of the corner of her eye, she'd been watching Jimmy searching high and low for something. He'd been looking in the pockets of his coat and jacket hanging on the pegs by the door, and riffling as surreptitiously as he could through every drawer in the bedroom and then in the kitchenette. When Hillie saw the panic growing on his face, she finally held up the little package she'd found that had obviously slipped down between the cushions of the settee.

Relief broke out in Jimmy's eyes and he reached out for the brown paper packet, but Hillie snatched it away.

'No,' she said defiantly, her heart racing. 'Not till you tell me what's going on. I've looked inside. They look like pieces of glass or clear stone or something. But they're not, are they? I'd hazard a guess they're uncut diamonds.'

She watched as Jimmy's face twisted, and then turned thunderous.

'You shouldn't have been looking, Hill—'

But anger, exasperation, fear steamed inside her and she interrupted him with, 'Tell me the truth for once, Jimmy! You said you weren't doing anything illegal, but explain to me how this isn't. These are stolen, aren't they?'

Her eyes narrowed and she gave him a dangerous, implacable glare. She could almost see the cogs of his brain turning as he tried to concoct some lie. But when he finally spoke, she felt he was telling something near the truth.

'All right,' he said. 'But these ain't stolen. They belong to Mr Jackson, honest they do. But they ain't as good as they look. They're flawed. Only... Let's sit down and I'll explain.'

'I think you better had!'

Jimmy spread his hands as he perched on the sofa next to her. 'Mr Jackson takes in perfect – or near perfect – diamonds from dealers. He has them cut and mounted by the cutters and gold- and silversmiths he employs in his factory. Then he returns them to the dealers, and charges for his services. All completely above board.'

'So... why all the secrecy?' Hillie demanded, still suspicious. 'And what are you doing with these flawed ones, then? You say they belong to Jackson himself? I don't understand.'

'Ah, now, here's the clever bit.' Jimmy puffed up his chest almost proudly. 'But you mustn't breathe a word of this to no one, or I'll be sunk. Mr Jackson buys a certain amount of uncut diamonds, but flawed, not good ones, on the open market, so all totally legit. Then I take them to a secret location – often in the night so no one'll see – where we have a couple of master cutters. They're both so brilliant, they can virtually disguise any flaw by the way they cut them. Not many cutters are that skilled. They're so good that once the stones are mounted, you wouldn't know. Not even the dealers.'

'And... they're swapped. So Jackson gives back the mounted flawed ones to the dealers, who think they're getting the original ones back, that would obviously be worth more?'

'Exactly. The master cutters match them in size, clarity and colour – I think I've got that right – so without unmounting them which they're never gonna do, it's almost impossible to tell the difference. And even then, it'd be virtually impossible to prove it wasn't the same original stone. And then Mr Jackson sells *them ones* to some other dealer he knows in Amsterdam for a fat profit, and nobody's any the wiser. Even the setters in the factory don't realise where the stones come from. They just work with what they're given. So the whole business appears legit. All I do is act as courier. I didn't find out for ages what it was all about, and only then, quite by chance. It's not the only thing Mr Jackson deals in, of course. But you see how fool proof it is, so you ain't got nothing to worry about.'

'But how can you possibly claim it's all legal?' Hillie fumed, shaking at the thought of what Jimmy was involved in. 'It's stealing!'

'No, it ain't. The dealers don't lose no money over it. Nobody does.'

'So why doesn't Jackson just use these master cutters to get the best out of the flawed ones, and never mind the swapping and cheating? Then it all be legal.'

Jimmy shrugged. 'Easy. 'Cos he wouldn't make nearly as much money. And nobody gets hurt.'

Hillie ran her hand frantically through her hair. 'And are you sure that's all this Jackson fellow has his fingers in?'

'Well, there's the bit of illegal gambling, but it don't seem like nobody's forced into that. And he owns property and makes sure people pay their rents, but that's all.'

But by the evasive look on his face, Hillie wasn't convinced he was telling her the entire truth. But she wouldn't know how – and was a bit too scared – to try and find out anything about Jackson herself. So she cried in desperation, 'Oh, Jimmy, you've got to find a way out of this. What if it all gets discovered, and you're implicated? No. Find yourself a proper job before it's too late. Does Jackson know you know?'

Jimmy wagged his head awkwardly. 'He didn't at first, but he does now.'

'Well, you just keep quiet about it all. And after Christmas, find another job, no matter what it is. Sweeping roads if you have to. And I'll try and think of a way I can go back to work as well. How does that sound?'

Jimmy worked his lips, but to Hillie's relief, he nodded slowly. 'Mr Jackson ain't gonna like it, but I want to make my girl happy. I promise I'll go down the Labour first thing in the New Year. But you've got to keep your side of the bargain, too.'

'Yes. Yes, I will. Somehow. And then, Jimmy, maybe we can start building up the trust between us again. Be a proper husband and wife again.'

'Cor, I'd like that more than anything, Hill. But now, I need to go. Mr Jackson'd murder us if he thought I'd lost them stones. So, will you give them to us?'

Reluctantly, Hillie held the package out to him. She didn't like this one little bit. But now she knew the truth, maybe – just maybe – they could put things to rights again.

But a dreadful doubt persisted at the back of her mind. She liked the sound of this Jackson chap even less than before. And as for her sisters and how she was going to care for them as well as going back to work at Price's, at that precise moment, she had no idea!

Chapter Twenty-Three

Hillie wasn't, however, going to let worrying about Jimmy spoil her Christmas plans for her family, and managed to put it all to the back of her mind. As the previous year, she wanted to make the most of it for Luke and the girls. While Jimmy was still putting money in her pocket, she'd buy little presents and a tree, though she felt ripped by guilt that it was his work for the criminal Mr Jackson that was paying for it. For criminal she was convinced he was. But Jimmy had promised her it would all be over in just a few days, but whether or not he meant it this time, she couldn't be sure.

'Glad to see you haven't got that wastrel of a husband with you,' Harold sneered as she arrived on Christmas morning. 'Not that I'd've let him in.'

'And you think he'd have wanted to come?' Hillie snapped back.

But just then, Frances and Daisy rushed into her arms. 'Look what Father Christmas put in our stockings!' they cried, both showing her the tiny bracelets made of plastic beads on elastic they wore.

'Oh, yes, aren't they grown-up?' Hillie smiled, feigning surprise as she came into the kitchen. 'Hello, Happy Christmas!' she called to everyone else, and there were hugs all round. 'Oh, Joan, you've prepared all the vegetables. Thank you!'

'Trixie helped,' Joan beamed. 'Our Christmas present to you. Seeing as we don't get pocket money to buy you anything,' she added under her breath.

'Well, let's get the joint in the oven, and then we can open our other presents,' Hillie beamed. 'Oh, and doesn't the tree look pretty?' she declared as the light coming through the window caught on the shiny tinsel she'd splashed out on this year as well as the tree itself.

A little while later, they were all sitting round the table. The little ones' eyes were shining with expectation, while Joan and Luke were more subdued. But Hillie had either bought or made them all reasonable gifts, and they exchanged those she'd got for them to give to each other – even for their father. Harold produced packages for each of his five children, too, although noticeably there was nothing for Hillie. Not that she'd got him anything either. But having worked at Price's for a few months, for the first time in his life, Luke had been able to purchase small items of his own to give to his family, and Hillie saw the pride in his face as he handed them out. Not that Harold let him keep much of his wages, she knew!

The time passed reasonably amicably, and to Hillie's relief, Harold was in a good mood, actually playing with his children. It made Hillie think back to what her mum had said, that he'd never harm any of his own. At least Nell had been right in that, and when Hillie eventually left – among protests from her younger siblings – after she had washed up and cleared away after the dinner, she felt all would be well for the remainder of the day.

'Thanks, Hill,' Luke said, coming to the door with her. 'I think Christmas has been OK 'cos of you.'

'Yes, I hope so,' she smiled back a little wistfully. 'Thank you for the present, and enjoy the rest of the day.'

'Yeah, think we will. Thanks for your present, too. And enjoy the rest of your day, as well.'

'Thanks, Luke. Take care of yourself.'

She covered the few yards to the Parkers' house, knowing she'd be in time to hear the king's speech on their radio, only the third royal Christmas broadcast ever. She wasn't sure, however, if she felt relieved to be going to Number Eight or not. Jimmy was going to be waiting for her there, too, and she hoped, prayed, he would keep his promise. And then her heart lifted because she knew Kit would be there, too.

*

'No.'

Jimmy could feel his guts twisting as he screwed up enough courage to continue, 'No, I'm sorry, Mr Jackson. Cheating on dealers, illegal gambling, a bit of theft and even squeezing exorbitant rents out of tenants is one thing, but armed robbery's another. That guard what got shot last time could've died. No, I'm sorry,' he repeated. 'But I'm not gonna be involved no more.'

Sweat was oozing through Jimmy's palms as his eyes warily followed Jackson who was walking up and down. The silence was palpable, the air quivering with tension. Jimmy gulped as Jackson finally turned to him.

'You're only the lookout, for God's sake,' the fellow grated, his eyes steely.

Jimmy thought that at any second, he was going to see his own heart break out of his chest, it was crashing so hard against his ribs. 'Even so,' he managed to answer. 'Someone could get killed, and I ain't gonna be part of that.'

Jackson suddenly stopped his pacing and put his mouth right up to Jimmy's ear. 'You already are a part of it. It's taken months to plan this. I didn't give you that money to get your wife a vase for nothing. It was so you could suss out the lie of the land for your part in this. I know we've got someone on the inside, but we need you as well.'

But Jimmy stood his ground. 'No. No, you don't. You've got enough other people working for you. Get someone else to do it. And you can have your blooming vase back if you want.'

Jackson gave a bitter laugh. 'You think I care about that?' Then he motioned to the 'heavy' standing behind him. An instant later, Jimmy gasped in agony as his arm was being wrenched up his back.

'But not many of my *employees* realise what's really going on like you do. And I want to keep it that way. No. You're already involved, whether you like it or not.'

Jackson jerked his head, and Jimmy sagged with relief as his arm was released. But Hillie's words were ringing in his head, and he wanted more than anything to do what she'd asked of him. She was right. And he loved her and wanted her back, to be a proper husband and wife again. If only he hadn't got mixed up with Jackson in the first place! But the easy money had been so tempting, and to be honest, the thrill of something not quite legal had been enticing. But now...

He glowered at Jackson to show his displeasure, and thrust his lips forward as if coolly considering the situation when in fact he felt sick, his stomach was clamped so tightly. 'All right. But this is the last time. And only 'cos I know your plans. And then I don't want to know nothing more about what you're up to. I've been grateful for all you've done for us, and I'll never grass on you. But it's time for us to part company.'

He waited, holding his breath, for Jackson's reaction. The other man's expression was inscrutable for a few seconds, and then Jimmy relaxed as a smile edged onto the fellow's lips.

'Hmm, we'll see.' Jackson flashed his eyes towards his heavy again. 'Bruno hasn't used his blade for a bit, have you, Bruno?' he said in such a meaningful way that the thug grinned as he pulled a flick-knife from his pocket and clicked it open.

'Pretty wife you've got, Jimmy,' Jackson went on. 'Pity if her face got rearranged. And then there's those little girls she looks after. Her sisters, so our informant told me. Wouldn't want any of them to get hurt, now, would we?'

Jimmy's eyes widened and he stepped forward with hatred blazing in his heart. 'You bastard!' he snarled, but Jackson merely smiled.

'You can call me all you like,' he chuckled. 'But I know all about your wife's family. And her friends. Oh, yes. I make it my business to have eyes and ears everywhere. Be a tragedy if one or other of their houses burnt down in the night, and they perished in the flames, wouldn't it? Oh, dear, oh, dear. So, I think you could be working for us for some time, don't you agree? So, you come along as planned, or there could be consequences. Run along now, and we'll see you then. Bruno?'

Bruno had been fondling the knife in his hands and now, snapping the blade back into the handle, he returned it to his pocket and went to hold open the door. Jimmy was rooted to the spot with sickened, maddened fury. But what could he do? He felt such a bloody coward, but he couldn't risk Hillie…

He did the only thing he could. Leave. But with his head held high and his gaze burning into Jackson's face.

Outside, he scurried down the darkened alley. But when he turned the corner, he sank onto his knees and vomited up his terror.

*

'So, what did your parents say when you told them about Patrick? Have you introduced them yet?'

Hillie and Jessica were sitting at the table in the back room enjoying a cup of tea and the remnants of the Christmas cake Hillie had baked. Daisy and Frances were flitting about playing at being fairies, each with a pair of gauzy wings Hillie had made for them strapped to their backs, and waving wands fashioned out of cardboard and glitter. Trixie was devouring the illustrated version of *The Jungle Book* that Hillie had bought her for Christmas, and Joan had begun working on the little tapestry set.

Christmas seemed an age ago now, even though it was but a few days. And at that moment, Hillie was all ears to hear what had happened with Jessica over the Yuletide period. But to her dismay, her friend sucked in her cheeks and cast down her gaze.

Hillie's expectations sank. 'Don't say you still haven't told them?'

Jessica flashed up her eyes. 'Well, I know I said I would after my birthday,' she answered defensively. 'But that *was* only a few days before Christmas and the atmosphere could've been *awful* if it went badly, and I didn't want to spoil Christmas. They might even have thrown me out, and just think how dreadful that would've been! I'd have gone to Patrick's, of course. But if we never made it up, there'd always be that memory at Christmas, and it'd never be the same. So, I'm going to try and break it to them *gently* in the New Year. At least they're letting me go to the party at Belinda's rather than the stuffy affair I usually have to go to with them. And Patrick'll be there, so at least we'll have a lovely evening before facing the music.'

'Oh, Jessie—'

'But I swear I'll do it next week,' Jessica went on earnestly. 'I mightn't tell them we're actually engaged straightaway. I might work up to that in time. But it really will be a case of a new year and a new start.'

Yes, Hillie thought, suppressing her disappointment. A new year and a new start. It was going to be the same for her and Jimmy. He'd promised her. And once he had a proper job again, her love for him would be rekindled, or so she hoped. But how she was going to bury forever her growing passion for the man who was good and kind and honest and lit a beacon inside her, she really didn't know.

Chapter Twenty-Four

Hillie gazed at her reflection in the old mottled mirror Jimmy had bought second-hand, considering the dress she'd sewn for herself for the New Year's Eve party at Belinda's. It was only cheap taffeta from a street stall, but the powder-blue suited her colouring and the little pearl buttons down the front gave the dress some class. Beneath the white knitted bolero she'd also made herself, the bodice of the dress clung to her small waist, and the full skirt swung attractively below her knees. She'd also had her hair trimmed, not fashionably short, but so that it brushed against her shoulders rather than tumbling down her back as before. Overall she was quite pleased with how she looked. New dress, new hairstyle, new year.

But who was it really for? It was uplifting to feel good about oneself, of course. But was it for Jimmy? To make him appreciate her more and want to make the effort so that they could be a proper couple again? Or deep down, did she want Kit to notice her, since she knew he'd be coming along to the party later on? But that would be cruel to both him and Jimmy. And it was a torment to herself.

She heard Jimmy come up behind her, and she turned to him with a smile painted on her lips. But the muscles around her mouth slackened as she took in what he was wearing. Instead of his best flannels and the shirt she'd washed and ironed especially, he'd put on some old black trousers and a dark, frayed jumper.

Her brow compressed into a frown. 'Jimmy?' she began in a quiet, uneasy voice. He'd seemed on tenterhooks the last couple of days. Was she about to find out why?

'I'm sorry, love.' Jimmy gave her a furtive, sideways glance as if he didn't have the courage to look her straight in the eye. 'I can't come to the party.'

Hillie's heart groaned. 'W-what d'you mean you can't come?' she demanded.

'I've… Mr Jackson's got a job for me,' Jimmy mumbled back.

Hillie stared at him in disbelief. And then all the pent-up frustration and feelings of betrayal erupted in a shower of fury. 'Oh, but Jimmy, you *promised*!' she squealed as angry tears welled in her eyes. 'You said in the New Year—'

'But it ain't New Year till tomorrow.'

'B-but you've known about the party for ages! So why didn't you tell him no? Or did you know about it all along?'

Jimmy's silence as he wriggled his lips awkwardly gave her the answer.

'You did, didn't you?' she fumed. 'Well, you can jolly well go and tell Jackson that you had a prior engagement and can't do whatever underhand job it is he's got for you!'

But Jimmy's eyes flicked nervously at her, and she caught the glint of fear in them. 'No, Hill, you don't understand. Mr Jackson's not the sort of man you say no to. I'm really sorry, love. But… I've got to go. I-I ain't got no choice.'

Hillie's face stilled as Jimmy met her gaze and the terror she saw there stung her to the core. She watched, stunned, as he put on his new jacket and his old overcoat on top, checking something black and knitted – was it a balaclava? – in the pocket. A moment later, he was gone, and Hillie lowered herself onto the settee. She could feel herself shaking with each pounding beat of her heart. Dear Lord, what was Jimmy mixed up in?

Her brain was still whirling when she heard the knock on the front door. She dragged herself across to the attic window and looked down onto the street. Rob's car, and she could see the top of Gert's head as she waited by the door. Rob would have picked Gert and Jessica up, and now had come to collect Hillie and Jimmy as arranged.

Good, strong, dependable Gert. Hillie shook herself free from her shock, grabbed her coat and catapulted down the two flights of stairs to the front door.

When she opened it, she met Gert's frowning face on the other side. 'Hello, Hill. Was that Jimmy I saw disappearing round the corner? Ain't he coming?'

'Gert, listen to me.' All of a sudden, Hillie's brain seemed crystal clear. 'Jimmy's got himself mixed up in something. I don't know exactly what. There's been dodgy diamond dealing—'

'What—?'

'Yes, but I think this is something much bigger. Something Jimmy can't get himself out of. I saw the fear in his eyes. You've got to believe me, Gert. I want you to go to the police and convince them something's going to happen tonight. Tell them there's a man called Jackson at the heart of it. It might mean something to them, I don't know. Meanwhile, I'm going to follow Jimmy.'

'Follow him?' Gert's eyes stretched wide. 'But it could be dangerous. We can't let you—'

'Just do as I say,' Hillie called, already running down the street. 'If I see anything, I'll find a phone box and get the operator to put me through to the police.'

'Hillie, you be careful—'

But Gert's voice was lost as she turned the corner and broke into a run. She couldn't see Jimmy, but he couldn't have gone far…

*

It wasn't easy, following Jimmy through the darkened streets without losing him or being seen. Hillie kept telling herself it was utterly ridiculous, tracking her own husband. But she was terrified. Not of Jimmy, of course, but of what she might discover. And yet that was exactly what she wanted. Alert the police, put a stop to whatever it was. Save Jimmy from himself, even if it meant a spell in prison to rid himself of this Jackson blackguard.

Nearly ten o'clock on New Year's Eve, so there were more people out and about than normal on such a cold, dank and drizzly night. And yet, with work the following morning, the number of revellers was limited. The pubs would doubtless be busy, with more women accompanying their menfolk than usual, it being more acceptable on a special occasion. Others would be going to family or friends, if only for a short while and not necessarily to see in midnight and listen to Big Ben chiming twelve o'clock on the radio.

So, although Hillie couldn't lose herself in crowds, she came across couples and small groups on every street, making her feel less conspicuous and yet more alone. Here were people going off to enjoy themselves, while she... Well, she wasn't quite sure what she was doing. All she knew was that she had to do it for Jimmy's sake. For the sake of their future. If she really believed they would have one.

Her nerves were taut and ready to snap as Jimmy wove his way through the warren of back streets they both knew so well. Hillie had several times to dodge back round a corner as Jimmy checked around him, and then run to catch him up. After a while, though, he left the area she knew intimately, and Hillie had to look up and memorise the names of the streets.

At long last, they came to a wide back alley. Hillie retreated, hiding behind the corner, crouched down and peering round the wall of a house. The alley was in darkness but for the square of light from a couple of windows in the long terrace of houses that backed onto it. They had small backyards, just like the poorer side of Banbury Street, but most of them had ramshackle sheds or outhouses opening onto the alley. Jimmy stopped in front of one of them, looked furtively about him, and then slipped inside.

Hillie's heart bucked painfully. Now what? Surely the police would need more than this? As her eyes adjusted to the increased darkness, she spotted some dustbins in a pitch-black corner by a shed. She'd have the perfect view and yet would be hidden from sight.

She checked the alley and then scurried across to settle down behind the bins and wait. Her wildly beating pulse thrummed in her ears, every nerve alert to the slightest movement or sound. A dog barked in the distance, happy laughter wafted along the adjacent street, then all went quiet again.

Hillie shivered, realising that her nervous sweat as she'd hurried through the streets was now turning ice-cold as she squatted down, not daring to move. She needed something to happen, and yet she was petrified that it would.

The flimsy dress beneath her coat was no match for the damp that seemed to penetrate her bones, and her cramped limbs were aching. She felt as if she'd been folded into her hiding place for hours, but if nothing happened soon, she'd go to the police anyway.

She was just about to give up when the purr of an engine tightened every muscle. A car turned into the alleyway, dimming its lights and crawling to a stop. Three men got out and, without a word, went inside the outhouse Jimmy had gone into earlier. Was one of them Jackson? Hillie wondered with contempt.

It was too dark to read the number plate, but then a van rumbled past her, illuminating the first vehicle. But all too briefly, its lights and engine were turned off, and more figures disappeared into the outbuilding.

Hillie watched, her heartbeat echoing in the silence. It was time to act. Would anyone else be arriving? She waited for what she hoped was sufficient time before checking the alleyway. All was clear. Her limbs protested as she made them move, and she had to force her muscles into action. Cautiously she extricated herself from behind the bins, being careful not to knock them or make a sound.

She turned to hurry back down the alley.

'What 'ave we 'ere, then?'

Suddenly, three silhouettes appeared from out of the darkness, virtually blocking her path – two tall, broad shadows and a smaller one in the middle. Hillie's brain froze, and yet somewhere in the depths of her mind, the voice sounded familiar.

But there was no time to think of that now. One of the black forms went to grab her. Instinct, years of dodging Harold's blows, made Hillie duck sideways, avoiding the swiping arm. But the gap was narrow and as Hillie plunged through it, the other larger figure launched itself at her, closing firmly about her waist. She struggled, kicking out backwards. A male voice cursed as she felt her shoe crack against his shin. An instant later, other arms locked about her shoulders. She tried to sink her teeth into whatever she could, but her mouth found only the thick material of a winter coat. Panic streamed through her, but she fought like a wild cat, lashing out as best she could. But she was helpless against the two men, and felt herself being dragged along the alley and into the meeting place.

Inside, the glimmer from a single bare light bulb diffused through a fug of cigarette smoke. Hillie stopped struggling. Her instinct for survival told her it'd be better to use her wits if she was going to stand any chance of escaping.

'Look who I found spying on us outside.'

The familiar woman's voice again. Hillie felt her heart skip a beat as Dolly Maguire stepped forward, and a tall, thin man in an immaculate dark overcoat spun round, looking Hillie up and down.

'You're Jimmy Baxter's wife, aren't you?' he growled, scowling with annoyance.

'What!'

Hillie heard an intake of breath that could only be Jimmy's, and the crowd of men parted as Jimmy gazed across at her, white-faced. Hillie's eyes swivelled about her, trying to take everything in. Spot a means of escape. And what the heck was Dolly Maguire doing there?

'Hill, what the hell are you—?'

'Was she alone?' the man Hillie imagined must be Jackson barked again.

'Yeah. We clocked 'er a few streets away, and when she turned into the alley and 'id, we thought we oughta stop and watch 'er. We was there for bleeding ages to make sure. I'm bloody frozen.'

Jackson nodded, and two men took hold of Jimmy and marched him forward. 'Betrayed us, have you?' he snarled.

'No,' Jimmy protested in desperation. 'I ain't told her nothing. She's supposed to be at a party.'

'Well, we can't have grasses. Take them to the lock-up and we'll deal with them later. Bruno, I need you on the job, but you know what to do afterwards,' he said, dropping his voice so that Hillie couldn't hear him clearly. 'Lose the bodies downriver just as the tide's turning, and they'll get washed out to sea.'

'Yeah, boss.'

'No. She don't know nothing—'

Hillie's knees had turned weak with terror. As Jimmy tried to break free from the hands that held him, a giant of a man sprang forward and landed him such a blow in the belly that he doubled up in agony. Hillie barely had the chance to gasp before something – was it a sack? – was pulled over her head, plunging her into darkness. There was no point in struggling as she was bodily picked up.

Dear God, what had she done?

Chapter Twenty-Five

'Hmm.' The police sergeant pinched his bottom lip between his forefinger and thumb. 'That isn't a lot to go on, miss. And if there is something going on, it mightn't be on our patch. Could be anywhere in the entire metropolis. And our men are going to be busy keeping drunks and overenthusiastic revellers at bay, it being New Year's Eve.'

'Forgive me, sergeant,' Rob put in, 'but wouldn't that be exactly why a criminal would choose tonight for a major crime?'

The sergeant lifted a considering eyebrow. 'Perhaps. But I can't call a major alert for something that's just hearsay, especially when my officers are busy keeping the peace. You sure this friend of yours is reliable?'

'Course she is,' Gert bristled. 'It's her husband what's got caught up in this. She'd hardly inform on him if she wasn't worried sick, would she?'

The sergeant pulled his lip harder. 'And you can't tell me anything more?'

'Oh, wait a jiffy,' Gert frowned. 'She did say she thought there was a man called – oh, what was it? That's right. Jackson, I think. He seems to be the ringleader.'

'Jackson?' The officer straightened up abruptly. 'We've had someone called Jackson under suspicion for some time. If it's the same fellow, he's a slippery customer. Never seem to be able to get enough evidence to charge him. But a nasty piece of work. Wait here a minute. I'll go and get my superior.'

'Could I possibly use a phone?' Rob asked, getting to his feet. 'Just to ring my parents. They're having a party we're all supposed to be at, and they'll be worried we haven't turned up.'

'Of course. Come this way.'

The two men left the room, and Gert began chewing her nails. 'I'm really worried, Jess,' she muttered, turning to her friend. 'I shouldn't have let Hill go off on her own. You heard what the officer said about this Jackson fellow.'

'Hillie's not stupid,' Jessica tried to reassure her. 'You just tell them everything you know.'

'But as he said, that ain't a lot.'

'But if the police already know of this Jackson chap—'

The door opened again, and another man came back in with Rob.

'I'm Inspector Chamings,' he introduced himself, sitting down at the table. 'Now, Miss Parker, I want you to tell me absolutely everything. Every detail, however trivial it might seem.'

'Can't tell you much. Only what Hillie told me. I mean, we all knew her Jimmy's been running errands on the side – I guess for this Jackson fella – for ages. None of us thought nothing of it till now.'

'All right. Start at the beginning. Take your time.'

Gert did her best, trawling her memory for any small clues. There didn't seem much. Just Jimmy's frequent absences that eventually cost him his job at Price's.

'But then he went to work full-time for this chap,' Gert concluded. 'Hillie never mentioned his name before. Or that there was anything dodgy about it. But I don't think she really knew much about it until now. But he seemed to be paying Jimmy OK. Even before that, Jimmy'd turn up with a nice present for Hillie. Clothes. Stockings. Oh, and she was thrilled with a little cut-glass vase he bought her in Arding and Hobbs back in the summer. Not the sort of thing you'd ever think they could afford.'

'And now… you think it could've been stolen?' the inspector suggested.

'No, I know the vase wasn't,' Jessica told him. 'My father's manager of the jewellery and expensive gifts department. It was a while ago, but I remember him being put out when Jimmy bought the vase. He's sort of accepted Hillie, but Jimmy, well… He couldn't understand how he had the money to buy something like that.'

The inspector lifted his chin. 'Could've been a ruse of some sort. Casing the joint, but making it look innocent. Now, I need to talk to the Chief Inspector. In the meantime, I'll have some tea sent in for you.'

Gert nodded, but her pulse was trundling. Fine New Year's Eve this was turning into. And she had work in the morning. The tea tasted bitter in her mouth. Hillie was out there somewhere, alone and in danger. If anything happened to her, Gert would never forgive herself.

The tea dregs had gone cold by the time Inspector Chamings returned.

'Right. Everyone's on the alert. All over London. Sent messages to our bobbies on the beat to keep their eyes peeled.'

A knock on the door interrupted him, and the sergeant poked his head into the room. 'Sir, we've just had a phone call from a night-watchman at Arding and Hobbs. Something's going on. Then the line went dead.'

Gert felt her heart bounce and she sprang up. But the inspector put out his hand. 'No. You lot must stay here. We'll do all we can to protect your friend. But you, miss,' he said, addressing Jessica, 'we need to contact your father at once.'

'That's easy. He's at the Arding and Hobbs party. At his boss's house. They'll all be there. All the directors, everyone. I'll give you the address.'

Gert gazed about her, dumbstruck with fear. Now she knew there was definitely something happening, she was terrified that Hillie might get hurt. Horror tumbled in her belly and she burst into tears in Rob's arms.

*

Kit nodded at the night porter who was locking up the gates at the back entrance to Clapham Junction Station, and the two men wished each other a Happy New Year. Kit's shift had finished a little while ago, but he'd been reluctant to leave and had supped a welcome cuppa with a colleague before setting off home.

Except he wasn't going home, at least only to change. He was expected at the party at Rob and Belinda's parents' house. Brother and sister had become good friends to him, and he really liked Belinda. He wished he could feel attracted to her, but he couldn't. The fact was that he wasn't over Hillie yet. He still loved her. Always would.

His heart bled whenever he was with her. The times they all spent together as a group were exquisite torture for him. He felt awash with a warm gladness in her presence, and yet his soul was in torment. For she would never be his.

Oh, what a damned fool he'd been! He'd wanted to do everything right, be able to offer her a good home, a secure future, before he told her how he loved her. Beg for her hand. Why, oh why hadn't he said something sooner? Before Jimmy Baxter had rescued her from that brute they now knew wasn't her father at all? His own stupid pride, his need to prove himself worthy of her, had got in the way. And maybe he'd have been too dull and boring for her anyway. Unlike Jimmy who was fun and exciting.

The pain was bearable – just – when Jimmy wasn't there. When she was happy and laughing. So beautiful. The scent of her so enticing. But Jimmy would be at the party, and Kit was dreading it. To see Jimmy kissing her at midnight would be agony. He couldn't get the image of it out of his head. So much so that he'd tried to get out of the party by offering to babysit so that his mum and dad could go instead. But to his dismay, Eva had insisted he went. It wasn't so long since Old Sal had died, and Eva just wanted a quiet night in after all the jollifications over Christmas.

Kit dragged himself along beneath the lines of raised railway track that would cross Falcon Road at the far end. The long way was dimly lit, the iron pillars silhouetted like eerie sentinels in the gloom.

All was dark and empty with the station locked up and only the night staff on their shifts for the goods trains. The long row of arches beneath the multiple tracks, each closed off by heavy doors and iron grilles, were silent and creepy. Banana arches some people called them. Some nights the scene was a hive of activity, but tonight all was deserted.

Or was it? Kit saw a van turn in from Falcon Road and stop by the third arch in, the last of three smaller ones sealed off with just one door. Nothing unusual in someone turning up at their lock-up late at night. But what happened next was.

The back door of the van was opened and after looking furtively about them, the driver and his mate dragged two figures from the vehicle and manhandled them across to the arch. Kit instinctively pulled back behind one of the pillars to observe. One of the victims was a man, a bit skinny, but a man nonetheless. The other – Good Lord – was wearing a skirt. Tall-ish for a girl, but definitely a girl, kicking and struggling like a wild thing, until she managed to shake off the sack or whatever it was over her head.

Jesus Christ, she looked like Hillie. It *was* Hillie! And… and the man had exactly the same physique as Jimmy.

Kit's heart reared up, and he shrank back behind the pillar, leaning against it as his spinning brain tried to make sense of what he'd seen. What the hell…? His Hillie was in trouble. Deep trouble by the looks of things. His heart was galloping. He'd never trusted that Jimmy, and now he'd obviously got Hillie into danger. Kit had to rescue her, but what in God's name could he do? Think. *Think!*

He peered round the corner of the pillar again. Hillie and Jimmy were bundled inside, and their abductors went with them. Kit waited, straining to stay put. He was no coward, but there were two of them and only one of him. And there could be others inside. If Kit went blundering in, he could be overpowered as well, and then none of them would have a chance of escape.

He waited in an agony of frustration until the men came out again and drove off, and then he ran up to the arch. The heavy door was locked, but with a mortice rather than a padlock. That could possibly mean that there was someone else already there who could operate the lock from the inside. Maybe even more than one person. In which case if Kit called out to let Hillie know that help was on its way, they'd be alerted as well and all could be lost. Kit simply couldn't take that chance.

Kit closed his eyes, forcing his brain to function rationally.

Get the police. Though it ripped him apart, it was the best thing he could do.

Kit ran as if he had wings on his heels.

'What the bleeding hell was you doing, Hill?' Jimmy demanded when all fell silent. 'I warned you Jackson ain't the sort of man to mess with.'

'In that case, you shouldn't have got mixed up with him in the first place,' Hillie retorted into the darkness.

'Yeah, well, I didn't know what he was like then, did I?'

His voice was sharp and Hillie drew in an exasperated breath. 'Well, I was only trying to get you out of it. I sent Gert off to warn the police.'

'Oh, yeah? And now no one knows we're here. A proper mess you've got us into. You should've left things alone, like what I said.'

'Maybe I should, and I'm sorry for that, Jimmy. But that's not going to help. We need to think. And what the blazes was Dolly Maguire doing there?'

'What, that woman? Is that her? I had no idea. Jackson said he was bringing in another lookout, so must've been her. I didn't know, Hill, honest.'

Hillie let out a weighty sigh. Thank God they were arguing. It gave her mind something to focus on other than the terror that drummed in her chest. It would be so easy just to sit, quaking, on the floor where they'd been pushed, and await their fate. But Hillie had faced fear so many times before. The answer to Harold's violence had always been to fight back. And she wasn't going to change now.

Her eyes were adjusting to the faint strip of light coming in under the door. In that split second before the thug had replaced the sack over her head, she'd recognised where they were. And, as if to confirm it, what was obviously a long freight train rumbled past overhead. The railway arches.

'So, this is Jackson's lock-up, is it?'

'One of several,' Jimmy murmured in reply.

'And what was going on tonight? A robbery?'

'Yeah. Oh, Hill, we know too much. Jackson… he won't let us go. You realise that.'

A tiny strangled sound gurgled in Hillie's throat as abject terror shot through her. But though her nerves were stretched to breaking point, she wasn't giving in. 'Yes, that's what he meant, wasn't it?' she gulped. 'So we've got to find a way out of here.'

'Oh, yeah? With our hands tied behind our backs?'

'Hmm. Let me think. Come over to the door. There's a bit of light underneath. I'll kneel down and try and get my hands in it, and you see if there's any way you could get me free.'

'Huh,' Jimmy scoffed. But he did as Hillie instructed anyway. 'Move a bit further back into the light,' he directed her. 'That's it. Hmm, no. Them knots look really tight. But you have a look at mine.'

They both twisted round so that Hillie could peer at the rope that bound Jimmy's wrists. The knots were pulled tight, but maybe…

'Keep still,' she ordered, bending so that her mouth was on a level with his hands.

'Why? What you gonna do?'

'Work at it. With my teeth.'

'What?'

'Shut up and let me get on,' she snapped.

The rope was horrible in her mouth, dry and hairy, and she kept stopping to spit out the tiny fibres. Nothing seemed to be happening, but she had to keep trying to distract her mind from its terror. Her knees hurt from kneeling on the bare concrete, and her neck and shoulders screamed in protest at bending and twisting to get at Jimmy's wrists. Every now and then, she changed position, lying down on her side, but the floor was so hard and cold, and it made her neck ache even worse.

'This is bloody hopeless,' Jimmy moaned after what seemed hours.

'You got any better ideas?'

'No. But they could be back soon. It wasn't gonna be a long job. But whatever happens, Hill, you must understand I did it all for you. I love you so much, and just wanted to make you happy.'

Hillie was about to accuse him of going about it in the wrong way, but she managed to restrain herself. It hardly mattered now. If what Jimmy had implied was... Dear God, she must redouble her efforts. Take the rope between her teeth. Ease it. Little. By little. Now the other loop of the knot.

'Jesus, Hill—'

'I'm not giving up. You look around. See if you can make out anything useful.'

'Huh, it's so bleeding dark. Oh, Hill—'

She turned rigid. 'Wait. Wait a minute...' She went back, got a purchase on the rope. Pulled. Less resistance. It... Glory, it was coming. Back to the other loop. Back again. Looser every time. Until... One final long pull. And it came.

'Jimmy, I think I've done it,' she whispered, hardly daring to believe it. 'Try wriggling your hands. Gently. That's it. OK. No, hang on. Let me give it one more tug. There, now pull!'

He did. And miraculously, he was able to squeeze his hands through the loosened rope. Their eyes had adjusted to the gloom, and they stared at each other in reckless hope.

'Right, now you,' Jimmy breathed, turning her round.

But then the sound of an engine. A closing van door. Heavy footsteps.

Jimmy's brain finally snapped into action. 'You sit back down where they left us,' he hissed. 'I can see a crowbar over there. I'll hide behind here with it and clonk them one from behind.'

Hillie didn't answer but scurried to the back of the lock-up where they'd been pushed. She crouched down, her stomach in an iron vice, praying the men wouldn't realise in the dark that Jimmy wasn't behind her. What if there were too many of them? Could Jimmy possibly fell them all? Would all her efforts be in vain?

She kept still, not daring to move. Hardly daring to *breathe* even, as the door was unlocked. In came just one man, pushing the door to behind him but not locking it. Could they escape through it, or would they be... be... Just one man, but the mountain of a man who'd punched Jimmy in the stomach earlier. The one Jackson had ordered to... to... And he was angry. Dear God, he was angry, hurling boxes and cartons aside as he aimed towards his captives.

Hillie gulped, staring up at him. But she must hold her nerve. She wanted to escape her hiding place. Run, even though she'd have no chance of getting past the raging giant. She must stay put until he was close enough for Jimmy to spring out behind him and axe him with the crowbar. And then they could run...

Flash of movement. Hillie snatched in her breath. The thug spun round, caught the crowbar in hands of steel as Jimmy swung it with all his might. But it was wrenched from Jimmy's grip. Horror on Jimmy's face. Stepped back as the monster flicked something from his pocket. Glint of metal. Thrust.

Jimmy was lifted from his feet, bent over. Eyes huge. Choking. A gurgling, sucking sound, as he was thrown in the air again and then crashed to the floor. Wheezing. Squelching.

Oh, dear God, Jimmy!

The heavy turned to Hillie.

She froze.

Couldn't move.

Shut her eyes. Didn't want to see it coming. Hoped it'd be quick. Held her breath and waited.

Through her closed eyelids, she was aware of the lock-up flooding with flashing lights. Men's shouts, footfall.

Her eyes instinctively opened. Saw the ogre lurch, crumple, topple on the floor in front of her. Behind him, Kit tossed the crowbar aside. At once, he was on his knees beside her, holding her fragile, trembling body. Pouring his strength into her.

'Jimmy!' she heard a voice scream. Someone else, in a crazed nightmare, pulled away from Kit, crawled to the body on the floor. There was something warm and wet and sticky. Everywhere.

'Hill.' A tiny, grating rasp scraped from Jimmy's throat. 'Love… you.'

She felt someone – was it Kit, one of the other men? Were they policemen? – do something with the ties about her wrists. Her hands came free. She wasn't sure how.

'Jimmy, my love, I'm so sorry,' she somehow croaked. 'This is all my fault.'

'Nah. N-not, my girl.' Dark liquid running from his mouth now. Hissing, bubbling in his lungs. 'M-my… jacket. J-jacket.'

His hand limply grasped Hillie's coat lapel. She forced a smile. Through tear-blurred vision. *It would be all right*, she wanted to tell him. Took his bloodied hand. Kissed it.

Saw him shut his eyes. Smile. His face slackened. Body went limp.

Something took a stranglehold on Hillie's throat, and the shadows closed in.

*

'I told you nothing good would ever come of your association with this riff-raff,' Charles Braithwaite growled as they all sat round in the interview room at the police station.

'For heaven's sake, man, have some pity,' Kit retorted, glancing anxiously over at Hillie who was shaking like a leaf in Gert's arms.

'That's right, Mr Braithwaite,' Inspector Chamings agreed as he came into the room. 'This poor young woman has just lost her—'

'And she got my daughter mixed up in it as well!'

'No, Mr Braithwaite.' The inspector's voice was firm. 'I was just coming to tell you all what's happened so that you can go home. I can assure you it was the phone call from your night-watchman that alerted us to the robbery itself, no one else. We'd barely had the chance to talk to Miss Parker properly. She hadn't even made a statement before we received the phone call, so there's no official record that either she or your daughter were ever here. It might've prompted the general alert, but we often get anonymous tip-offs. Sergeant Hoskins and I are agreed that was what we had, if you understand my meaning. So there's nothing at all to connect Miss Parker or your daughter with the case. Jackson and his gang were caught red-handed at the store. And now we'll have evidence, maybe confessions, that'll lead to other crimes, including an earlier robbery where a guard was shot and wounded. They'll all be put away for years. Jackson's heavy, let's call him, will hang. And I reckon there's a good chance Jackson will, too. But all any of them will ever know is that we got the call from your night-watchman. Who's come round from the blow to his head, thank you for asking. As for Mrs Baxter, she was merely concerned for her husband and followed him. She had nothing to do with the gang being caught either. It was just lucky coincidence that Mr Parker saw something suspicious on his way home from work. Otherwise things might've been even worse. So you see, Mr Braithwaite, your daughter wasn't involved in any way, and nobody has anything to worry about. I will need to interview you again, Mrs Baxter, but not until you feel up to it. Can she possibly go home with you tonight, Miss Parker?'

'Yeah, course.' Gert rubbed her hand up and down Hillie's back. 'Some New Year's Eve, eh, kid?'

Hillie peered out from Gert's protective embrace. She felt as if someone was cranking a handle to pump the blood around her body, since she was so numbed, she was sure it couldn't manage of its own accord. The beautiful dress she'd made for the party was ruined. Stained with blood. It had dried down her legs. Her hands were painted deep crimson, caked in her fingernails. She'd have to wash before she went to bed…

'Ah, our police surgeon.' Inspector Chamings stood up as the door opened. 'He'll take a look at you, Mrs Baxter, before you leave. And… oh. Who have we here?'

As Sergeant Hoskins showed the doctor into the room, he stood back to allow someone else to enter as well. A tall, young black man dressed in a long, colourful robe with beads hanging round his neck. Despite the tense, tragic atmosphere, surprise and a general sense of something uplifting permeated everyone's spirits.

'Patrick! What are you doing here?' Jessica gasped.

'I arrived late at the party because I had an emergency at the practice. So when they told me what had happened, I came straight here. I am so sorry, Hillie. This is terrible news.'

'Sergeant Hoskins, why have you let this man—?'

'Yes, who the devil is this… this darkie?' Charles Braithwaite demanded. 'Get him out—'

'As it happens, I do know this gentleman,' the sergeant began to explain.

'That is right.' Patrick drew himself up to his considerable height. 'My name is Patrick Akpobio. Back in Nigeria, I am a tribal prince. Here, I am a dentist and your sergeant is one of my patients. I qualified here in London and I have a thriving practice in Chelsea. And I know these people. They are my good friends, and I have come here to support them.'

With his lilting accent and calm voice, Patrick appeared to have mesmerised everyone, including Inspector Chamings whose eyebrows seemed stuck to his hairline. Charles Braithwaite's face, though, was set like thunder.

'Well, you've got no place here—'

'Yes, he has.' Hillie suddenly emerged from the mist of shock that had closed down her brain. 'He's a friend, and I want him here.'

Somewhere at the back of her mind fluttered the injustice of Mr Braithwaite's words. Jessica's face was white, and Hillie prayed she'd said the right thing. How she'd thought that, she had no idea. Not when… when Jimmy… Jimmy was dead. He was, wasn't he? Or had she dreamt the whole thing? Had it really happened? That dreadful nightmare in the shadows? But why else were they all here in a police station? Or was she dreaming that, too? 'Well, I shall take my daughter home, now,' Charles Braithwaite announced.

'Of course, sir. But we'd be obliged if you'd come back in the morning.'

'Indeed. They'll be a lot to sort out at the store, as well.'

'Naturally. My men are there now, taking fingerprints and so forth. Not that there's any doubt. The wretches were caught red-handed and, as I said, I'm hopeful we can match evidence to link them to other robberies. And some of the other goings-on we believe Jackson ran, as well. Right then, sir,' the inspector continued, addressing Rob, 'are you OK to drive people home when the doctor's had a word with Mrs Baxter, or shall I get a police car?'

Twenty minutes later, Gert and Kit were helping Hillie to totter across the pavement from Rob's car to the Parkers' house. It all felt so unreal to her, as if she was inside a glass ball that was totally unconnected from all that was going on about her. The look of horror that came over Stan and Eva's faces. Their words muffled and disjointed. Gert gently bathing her hands and legs while Kit explained in a low, seemingly incomprehensible whisper what had happened. Gert and Eva helping her as she stumbled upstairs. Helped out of her soiled clothes into Gert's spare nightdress. Taking the sleeping draught the police surgeon had prescribed. Getting into Gert's bed. She'd slept there once before, hadn't she? But this was far, far worse. The relentless juddering until Gert squeezed in beside her. Held her tightly. And slowly, Gert and Jessica and Jimmy and Kit and the huge angry man and Charles Braithwaite and Patrick merged and danced, the colours gleaming and fading and swirling, until finally the drug claimed her into a deadened sleep.

Chapter Twenty-Six

Somehow, time had passed, though it was all somewhat of a blur to Hillie. It was now the end of March, and she was just beginning to piece her life back together. 'Oh, Eva, I really hate to ask you,' she began awkwardly, sitting in Eva's kitchen and stirring the tea the good woman had set before her. 'But it's the only thing I could think of. The thing is… Could you possibly keep a lookout on the girls for me when they come home from school? Make sure Joan doesn't need any help or anything? It's just that I want to stay on at the flat if I can, rather than moving to some grotty bedsit. And the only way I can afford it is if I go back to work.'

'Course I can, ducks.' Eva's double chin wobbled up and down. 'Your girls are welcome to call in or ask me to help any time. And anyway, since me mum died, things are a lot easier for us, even if I do miss the old dear. Oh, Lordy Love.' She clapped her hand over her mouth. 'I shouldn't have said—'

'It's all right, Eva.' Hillie gave a wistful smile. 'You're just as entitled to miss Old Sal as I am to miss my mum. And… and Jimmy. I do miss him, no matter what he got himself mixed up in.'

She felt the familiar scratch in her throat and was grateful when Eva nodded, her lips drawn in knowingly. 'So who's gonna do all the housework and cooking and everything? And all the washing with all them lot?'

'Joan and I'll just have to muddle through between us. I hate having to put so much on her shoulders, but I don't know what else to do. And the others are that much older now and can do a bit to help. I'll go in for a few hours every evening after work, and then over the weekends, so we should get everything done. Harold might not be too happy, but he'll just have to lump it.'

'Well, all I can say is that your mum'd be proud of you and what you've done for those kids. But you'll be worn to a frazzle, girl.' Eva frowned with concern. 'Working every hour God sends. You'll have no time to yourself at all. Well, at least let me do a bit of ironing or something for you. Nell was me best mate, and it'd be a sorry thing if I couldn't help her family out now she's gone.'

'You never know, I might take you up on that. And… thank you.'

'Well, we can't let that Harold find another Maguire woman to look after the girls, can we, the old cow?'

'Absolutely not!' Hillie felt the bile rising inside her. 'I just can't believe what she did to get back at me for throwing her out. Telling a total stranger all about me and my family when Jackson came to snoop on me so that he could get some sort of hold over Jimmy. And then for her to join Jackson's mob.'

'Just the sort of scum she is,' Eva scoffed.

'Yes. And then when I bumped into her at the police station when I went in to make my statement and she was being moved to prison, she spat at me and said she was the one who told Harold about me and Jimmy, well... I think she wanted to goad me into going for her, and get me into trouble, as well.'

'Well, at least she'll be banged up now until her trial. Didn't they say she's likely to get some years? Even if she did testify that Jackson ordered his heavy to, well, you know, that'll probably help send him to the gallows?'

'Yes. Might've been her first provable offence with the gang, but it was an armed robbery. At least I'll have nothing to do with the trials on that side of things. But I'm absolutely dreading Jackson's trial. It was just so horrible with the robbery itself being in the papers, and the way it was foiled. But having to face him in court and... and Jimmy's murderer. I just can't bear...'

The agony scorched in her throat again, and she joined her hands over her mouth to swallow it down. At once, Eva came to put her arms round her for the umpteenth time since Jimmy's death.

'Now don't you upset yourself, Hillie, love,' she crooned, rubbing Hillie's arm. 'We'll all help you through it. And there's that nice new family what's moved into Dolly's house, so she'll never be coming back here to bother us again. But...' Eva hesitated, tipping her head enquiringly to one side as she pulled back to look into Hillie's eyes. 'You sure you wanna be on your own? You'd be welcome to come and live here. With me mum gone, we could easily fit you in.'

Hillie could feel tears beginning to swim in her eyes. 'Oh, Eva, you really are the kindest person who ever walked this earth. And I love you and all the family to bits. But... I feel I need to have my own place. Somewhere that's properly mine. And it was Jimmy's and my home. He was... so proud and excited when he got it for us.' She paused, chin quivering as she remembered Jimmy's face when he'd first taken her to the flat. 'I feel near to him there. I know he was far from perfect, but I did love him. And I don't feel ready to move on with my life just yet.'

Eva gave a short nod as she sat back down. 'Yeah, I understand, love. But you know where we are if you change your mind.'

'Yes, I do. And thank you. But you might regret the offer if I take you up on it,' Hillie joked, forcing some levity into her voice.

'Nah, never,' Eva smiled back. 'So, when you gonna start job hunting?'

'Oh, no need. Got my old job back at the factory. Ethel's had to give up 'cos of her knees, but she was coming up to retirement anyway. But with Price's pension scheme, she'll be OK, and her husband—'

'You're never going back to Price's?' Eva cried, aghast. 'Clever kid like you? Ain't they got no jobs in the office, at least?'

'Not at the moment. And to be honest, a bit of familiarity is what I need. For the time being, at least. And I'll be with Gert all day again.'

'But she won't be working there forever, you know,' Eva frowned, pausing as Primrose came over and climbed up onto her lap. 'I know they've kept their engagement low-key. Rob had planned on proposing at the New Year's party, but because of what happened... Well, you know they're planning on getting married summer after this, and moving out to Surrey. Building some nice new suburbs, they are. Three-bed semi-detached with black and white fronts like what they had in the old days. And not only blooming long back gardens, but front ones as well. Place called Stoneleigh, Rob's got his eye on, 'cos it's got a station on a line straight up to London for his work.'

'Yes, I know,' Hillie smiled wistfully. 'I'm sure Gert'd like to talk about it all the time. But bless her, she doesn't. She thinks it might upset me, talking about her future married life, when I've just... But it won't. Just the opposite. It's lovely to see her so happy. She's even trying to talk posher. Have you noticed?'

'Yeah, but I'm not sure she'll master it. Gert'll always be Gert.'

'Yes, I know!' Hillie grinned now. 'And I'm so looking forward to working with her again.'

'When d'you start?' Eva asked, shoving a Rich Tea biscuit into Primrose's grubby hands to stop her whining.

'In a week. When Ethel leaves, I'll start straight after. Gives me time to sort some things out. Jimmy and I had some reasonable savings. But I don't want to spend too much of them. I want to keep them for something in the future. I'm not quite sure what yet, but I'm not going to spend the rest of my life packing candles. It just suits me for now.'

'Good girl. I'm pleased to hear it,' Eva beamed. 'Now, is there anything else I can do for you?'

'No, thanks. Although... come to think of it,' Hillie faltered as the lump swelled in her gullet again at Eva's kindness, 'a hug'd be nice.'

Eva at once dumped Primrose back on the rug and came round to Hillie's side of the table again. Hillie felt the warm softness of Eva's voluminous bosom against her own pert young breasts as the older woman's arms enclosed her slender frame. In Eva's compassionate embrace, it was easy to believe that everything would turn out all right in the end.

But Hillie had a feeling in her gut that she had a long way to go before she could find any lasting peace.

*

'Right, you lot,' Hillie addressed her three youngest sisters after she'd cooked a Saturday lunch of mashed potato with cheese melted into it. She'd been working at the factory bench all morning, of course, and Luke – to Harold's derision – had insisted on washing up, even though he'd been at his work in the night-light wicking room as well.

'My sissy son doing girl's work,' Harold had sneered, making Hillie suck the breath through her teeth to stop herself from retaliating. But as she'd been working all morning, she didn't see why her little sisters couldn't pull their weight as well.

'I want you three to help Joan tidy up the bedroom while Luke and I heat up the water for the washing. And Trixie, it's your week to have clean sheets, so if you can strip your bed, I'll help you remake it later. Go on, up you go!' she shooed, playfully clapping her hands behind the last of her siblings. 'And, Luke, could you get the clothes horse out, please? It's bucketing down outside, so I'll have to dry everything inside, and there won't be room for it all on the ceiling rack.'

'Shouldn't be doing washing on a Saturday,' Harold grumbled. 'Monday's washday.'

'And I happen to be at work on Mondays in case you hadn't noticed,' Hillie retorted. 'You just don't like it 'cos it disturbs your afternoon. And it reminds you of all the hard work Mum did that you never appreciated.'

'How dare—'

'And if you want clean sheets this week, you'll have to go and change them yourself. I haven't got time.'

'That's not my fault, now, is it? You're the one what decided to go back to work.'

'I wouldn't have to if you paid me a proper housekeeper's wage.'

'You know bloody well I can't afford to.'

'You could pay me a *bit* more if you didn't go to the pub so often.'

'Just drowning me sorrows over your mother,' Harold attempted to whimper.

'Don't give me that. You're just sorry you have to pay someone to do all the work for you Mum did for free all those years.'

Hillie stood, hands on hips, glowering at Harold while she waited for the water in the kettle and the three largest saucepans to boil on the gas stove. It had been her choice, of course, to go back to work and yet still squeeze in everything she had to do for her family. But the main problem was that it meant she saw a lot more of Harold, which she could well do without!

He was glaring back at her now, ready for the challenge. 'Well, if you can't fit everything in and I have to do half your work for you, I'll have to halve your wages.'

'What! Changing your sheets is only a fraction of what I do!'

'Then I'll reduce your wages by a fraction,' Harold smiled with triumphant satisfaction. 'And the girls are all helping you, not forgetting your dear nancy brother. So from now on, I'll be paying you eight bob instead of ten.'

'Oh, no, you won't—'

'And if you argue with me, I'll make it seven and six.'

Hillie's eyes blazed with anger. Harold knew he had her over a barrel, didn't he? He hadn't shown her an ounce of compassion over Jimmy's death, and seemed to treat her even worse than before. How she'd have loved to storm out and leave him in the lurch. But she needed every penny to keep on the flat, and Luke and the girls would suffer. And at least this way, she saw plenty of them. Whereas if she left,

Harold might try to sever her contact with them again. So, though it galled her beyond imagining, she'd have to put up with it.

She turned back to the stove, struggling to hold her frustration in check. Lifting off the heaviest saucepan and pouring the boiling water into the washtub, she refilled it and returned it to the gas. She was doing the same with the middle-sized pan when she sensed Harold standing behind her. When she spun round to face him, pan still in her hands, he was leering cajolingly at her.

'Well, are you going to change your sheets, or what?' she demanded.

'In a minute, yeah, all right. But I just wanted to say there's a perfectly good answer to all this.'

'Oh, yes, and what might that be?' Hillie snapped.

'If you come back to live here, of course. Then you wouldn't need to find no rent, and you wouldn't need to go out to work. You could even have the parlour as a bedroom all to yourself. You could make it all pretty, however you wanted it. So,' he said, looking at her expectantly, 'what d'you say?'

Hillie stared at him open-mouthed. She really couldn't think of anything to say, she was so flabbergasted. The effrontery of the man! And after all she'd been through…

'What, and let you go back to bullying me like you did all those years?' She finally found her tongue, ignoring his last remark, it was so repulsive. 'Punishing me just for being who I am? Oh, no!'

'Oh, come on, Hilda, don't be like that.' Harold put his hand on her arm, and she gazed down on it with vitriolic contempt. 'We could be one happy family again.'

'We were never that,' she spat back, pulling her arm free. 'And don't you try threatening me, either. You *need* me. Dolly Maguire's not going to be around for some time, and you won't find anyone mug enough to do all that needs doing for the pittance you pay *me*!'

She slammed the saucepan back on the stove so hard that the water slopped over the brim, making the gas below flutter and hiss. She saw Harold shrug and, muttering something under his breath that sounded like *Suit yourself,* take himself out of the kitchen. A moment later, she heard him go upstairs to his bedroom. The parlour, indeed! Did he honestly think she'd fall for that one? That he'd give up his precious room to entice her back? He must think she'd fallen off a Christmas tree!

Hillie added some cold to the boiling water in the washtub, tipped in some Persil and swished it round so furiously, the bubbles frothed up to the rim. She threw in everybody's nightwear first, the least dirty items, thumping them up and down and round and round. Who needed one of those new-fangled electric washing machines when you could vent your anger like this? And when Harold's pyjamas came up on top, she plunged the wooden dolly into them even harder.

As he helped her, Luke watched silently. You knew when Hillie was in a bad mood, but you could hardly blame her after what his dad had just said. Personally, he'd have loved his big half-sister to come back and live with them, but he understood why she refused. If only his dad would let *him* have the front room instead of sleeping on the foldaway bed in the kitchen. But he daren't suggest it. He was too scared of what his dad might to do him if he did!

With rain pouring down outside, they could only open the scullery windows partway to let out all the steam. The panes ran with condensation, and Hillie was sweating from punishing the laundry, running it through the mangle, rinsing it in fresh water and putting it through the mangle once again. The ceiling rack was hoisted up, laden with sheets and towels, while everything else steamed on the rails of the clothes horse.

Later, when everything else was done, Hillie cut generous doorsteps of bread, ladling on dripping from the fat cup, for Luke and the girls. But she took great pleasure in scraping a meagre smear onto Harold's portion.

She glanced around with grim satisfaction. Everything was finished, the others all sitting at the table before their plates, waiting for their father to come in. Woe betide anyone who started before him! There was a pot of fresh tea with milk for the youngest, and three apples to share between them all for afterwards.

'Right, kids. I'll be in early in the morning. I've got scrag end of lamb as a treat, but the longer it stews the better. My plan is to do some of the ironing while it cooks, and then if you help me with everything else and it's not raining, I'll take you to the park in the afternoon.'

Hillie picked up her handbag and made for the door. But as she did so, Harold opened it from the other side.

'Off home to a night all by our lonesome, are we?' he sneered. 'That little bugger left you all on your own 'cos of his shenanigans, didn't he? Always told you he was a good-for-nothing bastard, but, oh, no. You wouldn't listen to me and now look where it's got you.'

Looking back, Hillie thought that if she'd had the kitchen knife in her hand at that moment, she might have stuck it in him. As it was, she lashed out at him with her tongue instead.

'That's my dead husband you're talking about!' she yelled. 'He might not've been perfect, and yes, he got himself mixed up in something that was far too big for him. But he was good and kind, and twice the man you'll ever be. I loved him, whereas *you*, I despise. So get out of my way before I do something I regret!'

Using both hands, she shoved him aside, then shrugging into her coat in the hallway, she flung open the front door so that it crashed against the wall. But as she hurled herself out into the darkening street, all she heard was Harold's mocking laughter as he came to close the door after her.

Hillie paused on the pavement. She hadn't stopped to fasten her coat and it flapped about in the driving rain. But it was hardly worth doing it up, even though water was already dripping down the back of her neck. There was only one place she wanted to go now, and it was only a few steps away. Tears of anger and grief trickled from her eyes, mingling with the rain. She brushed them away as she lifted her hand to knock on the door. It was rarely locked, but she always liked to announce her arrival before she went in.

Just as she was about to do so, however, the door opened from the other side. Kit jerked back in surprise.

'Hillie! I was just leaving, but come on in. You're getting soaked. I'm afraid no one else is here. They've all gone over to Rob and Belinda's parents' place for tea.'

'Oh, stupid me, I'd forgotten,' Hillie muttered, stepping inside. 'Of course, Gert told me—'

'What's up, Hill? You're crying. What's that bastard done to upset you now?'

Kit's voice was so soft, so caring, a voice she knew she could trust. Her defences collapsed and she put her hands over her face as her tears flowed unchecked. She heard Kit quietly shut the door behind them. And then his arms came around her, strong, gentle, silent, as she wept against his chest. It was such a good feeling to let everything out, and she didn't feel the least embarrassed. This was Kit, who'd been part of her life, looked out for her, since she was a babe in arms.

At last, her shoulders stopped shaking and she hiccupped away the last of her sobs. She felt Kit's finger lightly under her chin, tilting her head up to look at him, and he thumbed away her tears. She sniffed, and his eyes smiled tenderly at her.

'I'm almost as wet as you now,' he teased, brushing the front of his coat and making her return his smile. 'I'd only called in to leave some bananas we'd been given at work. Got too bruised in transit to sell, but I know Mum won't mind that. But let's put the kettle on and have a brew. And you can tell me all about it. Or not, just as you wish.'

Hillie nodded, and followed him into the back room. It seemed strange with nobody else there and without the usual chaos. But Hillie had to smile to herself at the half-loaf abandoned on the table, with crumbs scattered all about. No doubt Eva had been running late and they'd gone out in a rush. But the mess was comforting and Hillie was grateful for it. She took off her coat and hanging it over the back of a chair, sat down at the table.

'Here.' Kit pushed a mug of tea in front of her and sat down opposite her. 'Now, d'you want to talk, or shall I mind my own business?'

Hillie cupped her hands around the hot mug and gave what she hoped appeared as a casual shrug. 'Oh, it was just Harold being his usual horrible self. You won't believe it, but he suggested I went back to live there. He said then I wouldn't need to go to work to pay the rent on the flat. Can you imagine? He wants me to take Mum's place so he can treat me like a slave just like he did with her.'

'Huh, the fellow must be mad if he thinks you'd agree to that! But I can see how that would've upset you.'

'But not as much as the nasty things he said about Jimmy as I was leaving.'

'What!' Kit's face screwed up with rage. 'The bastard! I'll give him a piece—'

'Oh, no, Kit. It's sweet of you to take my side, but it'd do more harm than good. And the thing is…' Hillie hesitated, chewing her lip. She hadn't said this to anyone else. Not even to Gert. Her dear friend was so open and honest that she might spill the beans elsewhere. But Hillie knew she could trust Kit to keep it to himself. 'Well,' she went on, gazing down at the mug of tea. 'I've had a lot of time to think. Three whole months on my own. And now Jackson and that… that brute are behind bars and awaiting trial, I can stop blaming them for everything and get down to the truth.'

'Which is…?' Kit asked softly after a moment's silence.

'That a lot of what Harold has said is true,' she answered, her voice low and trembling. 'Jimmy was fun, and he was kind. And he loved me. But he did enjoy the excitement of being involved with something that wasn't above board. But, when he said he was doing it for me, that was true as well. He knew I've always wanted to get away from here. From the noise and the dirt and the overcrowding.' She lifted her head and met Kit's gaze, giving him a tearful smile. 'We had a dream, you know. At least, *I* did, and Jimmy went along with it. Wanted to make it come true. A cottage in the country with roses round the door. Can you imagine the stupidity of that? Two lowly factory workers wanting the impossible. But Jimmy wanted to give it to me. And that was part of the reason he got mixed up with Jackson. I know it turned out to be something much bigger than he realised. Something he couldn't get out of. But he *was* a fool to have got involved in the first place, so Harold was right in that respect. But I did still love Jimmy, for all his faults. And he died because of me. I shouldn't have interfered. He'd still have been alive if I hadn't.'

'No. It really wasn't your fault, Hill.' Kit reached across the table and touched her hand reassuringly. 'And Jackson would still have been swindling and bullying innocent people, and carrying out armed robberies in which others could be maimed or killed. A whole load of other rackets were uncovered because of you, Hillie. Fraud, demanding money with menaces, illegal gambling and firearms. The list was as long as my arm. A dozen or more criminals are being brought to justice. The last thing you must do is blame yourself. You weren't the one who got involved, and God knows, you've been through a terrible ordeal. It'll take more than three months to get over that, and Harold saying nasty things about Jimmy isn't going to help.'

Hillie nodded her head jerkily, and then looked Kit steadily in the eye. 'And I would've died, too, if it hadn't been for you. You saved my life, Kit. And I haven't said it properly before. But… thank you.'

She noticed an odd expression come over Kit's face, and he lowered his eyes. 'If only I'd been a few seconds earlier, I'd have saved Jimmy, too. Or if I'd broken the door down in the first place instead of going for help.'

'You wouldn't have been able to on your own. No. You did the right thing. So *you* shouldn't blame yourself, either.'

Kit raised his head, and gave a wry smile. 'Then I guess we're quits. And you know that whatever happens, I'll always be here for you. Talking of which, when you're ready, I'll walk you home.'

'But it's out of your way—'

'That doesn't matter. You should have company to your front door, at least. And what else have I got to do with my evening?'

He lifted one eyebrow in that quizzical way he had, and Hillie suddenly felt warm and comforted inside, her sorrows and anger melting away.

'D'you know, I should like that very much,' she smiled back.

Chapter Twenty-Seven

'Patrick's late,' Jessica grumbled, stirring her tea as they sat at an outside table by the park's refreshment rooms. 'Still,' she brightened, turning her dazzling smile on Hillie, 'it gives you and me time to catch up. I'm so pleased Dad relented and let me see you again.'

Hillie gave a half-smile. 'And I'm pleased I had some time to spare. I'm usually up to my eyes in housework or ironing or something on a Sunday. But with it being Easter, I got ahead of myself on Friday. And as it's the school holidays, Joan's been helping a lot.'

'But you must be exhausted, doing two jobs at once,' Jessica sympathised.

'Well, I've only been doing it three weeks, but it's not so bad. The others all help, and Joan's going to take over most of it when she leaves school at the end of next term. Besides, being so busy keeps my mind off... off things.'

'Jimmy, you mean?' Jessica suggested gently. 'That night... it must've been dreadful for you.'

Hillie sucked in her cheeks and nodded. 'I keep having nightmares about it. And I'm going to have to relive it when the trial comes to court. Give evidence.

And, oh, I miss Jimmy so much. I feel... I don't know, so empty. And torn. Sometimes I feel I just want to go away and start a completely new life. Forget the past. But the other part of me needs to stay. To be among my friends. You and Gert. And my family, of course. But I can't leave anyway,' she shrugged wryly. 'Not until Joan's able to cope on her own. And by then, who knows? I might feel totally different. But *you*, my dear,' she said, jabbing her head towards her friend, 'when *are* you going to stand up to your dad? Patrick's been incredibly patient. But you can't expect him to wait forever.'

It was Jessica's turn to grimace. 'I know. But you saw how Dad was about Patrick on that night. He'd have a blue fit if he knew about us. Not just friends, but more than that.'

'Then let him. And if he refuses to accept it, then just pack your bags and leave.'

'It's all right for you to say that... Oh, there's Patrick coming now! See you in a minute.'

Jessica shot up out of the chair and ran across to where Patrick was coming along the path, an impressive figure in his smart coat, and with Africa padding along obediently on the lead beside him. Even at a distance, Hillie saw the white slash of his teeth in his dark face as he grinned at his approaching English rose. Hillie watched as Jessica ran into his arms. They kissed unashamedly and at length. Then, as always, Patrick withdrew the little box from his pocket, and slid the engagement ring onto her finger. Jessica glanced down at it, then reached on tiptoe to kiss Patrick again. She only wore the ring when they were together.

Hillie released an exasperated, envious sigh. If only she still had Jimmy to embrace. If only there hadn't been that distance between them when… when he'd died. She could feel her eyes filling up with tears again, and she turned her gaze away, concentrating on the nearby flower beds instead. Red and yellow primroses lifted their faces to the weak sunshine, and daffodils nodded their heads in the breeze. It was near the end of April, Easter being late that year, and spring was well on its way. Hillie prayed her heart would feel lifted with the better weather, but just now, the future seemed to stretch ahead of her in a dark, empty tunnel.

A man's raised, angry voice made her turn her head. She peered round a group of customers who'd paused in front of the table and drew in a gasp. Oh, Lord. Charles Braithwaite had appeared from out of nowhere and was standing in front of Jessica and Patrick, wildly gesticulating with his arms. Hillie could see that her friend was cowering, but as Charles went to grab her, Patrick swiftly stepped forward to protect his fianceé from her own father.

Hillie hesitated but an instant before she leapt to her feet. She was near enough to see Patrick trying to argue back, but Mr Braithwaite was so enraged, it seemed he couldn't get a word in edgeways. Hillie could imagine sweet, quiet, calm Patrick being incapable of raising his voice sufficiently to make himself heard, let alone listened to. But Hillie – well, she'd had enough experience of slanging matches with Harold to beat the best of them.

She only slowed her headlong sprint as she neared them.

'Your piano teacher rang to ask when you were going back to your lessons!' she could hear Charles shouting. 'That's why I let you go back to seeing your little friend so that I could follow you and find out what's been going on. You haven't been to your lessons in months, have you? And all the while, you've been seeing this... this native instead! Deceiving us, week in, week out. This is going to kill your mother! Have you no respect for the Christian values we—?'

'But I *am* a Christian—' Patrick tried to intervene.

'And a better one than you!' Hillie couldn't contain her fury any longer. It broke out of her like water breaching a dam, all the horror and agony of the past few months bursting out in a torrent. She saw Jessica's eyes open wide with fear, but what did it matter? Things could hardly get any worse.

'As for you,' Braithwaite snarled, spinning round to face Hillie, 'you've done enough damage, so you can damned well keep out of it!'

'No, I won't! Patrick's a fine man! He's kind and clever, and he can give Jessica a good, secure future. If it weren't for the colour of his skin, you'd be falling over backwards to have him as your son-in-law.'

'My *what?*'

'You heard. They've been secretly engaged for ages, but poor Jessie's been too frightened to tell you. Because despite the fact that you're a bigoted bully, she still loves you. But if you don't come to your senses and realise that she's a grown woman with a life of her own to live, you're going to lose her.'

Hillie stopped, panting, sweat running down her back. Braithwaite was glaring at her, face purple with rage.

'How dare you!' he finally grated. 'You have no idea—'

'What it's like to be bullied and tormented? Oh, yes, I have. A whole lifetime of it. You're no better than… than my own father.'

'Oh, you've no idea what you're talking about. It's not like that at all.'

'Then what *is* it all about? Explain yourself, Mr Braithwaite,' Hillie growled, breathing hard as she realised he seemed to be calming down, thank God.

'Oh, you wouldn't understand, you little minx.'

'Of course, I won't. And nor will Jess unless you tell her your side of things. Why you've kept her wrapped up in cotton wool and not let her have a life of her own.'

Braithwaite's mouth tightened further as he glowered at her, but then his expression appeared to soften slightly. 'All right,' he said crisply. 'If you must know, my wife had two stillbirths before Jessica came along, so she's very precious to us. I vowed to protect her in every possible way. And that included keeping her at home.' There was a catch in his voice, and no one else spoke for a moment as his words sank in.

'Oh, Daddy, why did you never tell me?' Jessica said gently, placing her hand on her father's arm.

'And I'm sorry for what I said, Mr Braithwaite,' Hillie apologised. 'I understand how that must make you feel. But you've got to let go of Jessie some time. She's an adult, and needs an adult's life.'

'And I promise that I will protect her to the very last breath of my body.' Patrick was finally able to enter the conversation, and his reserved, liquid voice seemed to pour oil on the troubled waters around them. 'I appreciate that I come from a totally different culture, but that is no reason why we cannot integrate with one another. I love your daughter, sir, and I would lay down my life for her.'

Hillie saw Charles stare up at Patrick, and the anger on his face began to dissolve.

'Mr Braithwaite, why don't we all go back to the café and discuss this over a cup of tea?' Hillie suggested, leaping in while the going appeared good. 'I know this is all quite momentous and a big shock for you. But if only you'd get to know Patrick, you'd see for yourself what a good man he is.'

'W-w-well—'

'Oh, thank you, Daddy!' Jessica danced around him as he took a reluctant step in the direction of the tables.

'God knows what your mother is going to say about this—'

'Then you're going to have to persuade her, aren't you, Daddy?'

'I haven't given you permission to... to... see this... this gentleman yet—'

'But you will, though, Daddy, won't you?' Jessica begged, eyebrows knitted with expectancy.

'Oh, dear, what have I let myself in for?'

Hillie stopped, and watched as the three figures made their way over to where her own cup of tea was going cold on the little table. They didn't need her. She'd probably only put her foot in it. Had her argument with Charles Braithwaite made any difference? She wasn't sure. Best to let them get on with it without her.

She turned, and began to wend her way towards the Sun Gate entrance to the park. Back to the empty flat and the rest of her lonely life.

*

'Right, come on, my girl, you're not spending the day working!' Gert declared, grabbing Hillie's arm as she walked down the street. 'It's supposed to be a bleeding, I mean, flipping public holiday. And you're gonna spend it with us! The king's gonna be out on the balcony at Buck Palace later on, and we're all gonna be there to wave back!'

'Oh, but—' Hillie protested, trying to break away.

'Oh, but nothing,' Gert insisted. 'It ain't every day the king has a silver jubilee. Me and Rob and Belinda are going, and Kit's not on shift so he's coming, too.'

'But what about—?

'Luke and Joan and Trixie can come if they want, but Harold'll just have to be a dad for once, and look after the younger ones himself. Not having your day being spoilt by having to trail them along.'

'But what about your mum and dad?'

'There's a street party round the corner. They said they'd rather go to that than get squashed in the crowds. So, what you waiting for, kiddo?'

'Oh, well.' Hillie's heart began to dance as the idea took root. 'I'll just go and tell Harold, and see if Luke or the others want to come.'

'Just the older ones, mind,' Gert called after her. 'And tell old Harold to jump in the lake if he tries to stop you!'

A few moments later, she all but did just that. She'd only agreed to come in after her work at Price's, she'd told him firmly. Just because it was an extra public holiday, it made no difference. He couldn't expect her to work all day, and she'd be back in time to cook the evening meal as usual. So saying, she stormed out of the door, Luke and Joan seizing the moment and leaping after her, while Harold stood in the kitchen, mouth opening and closing like a goldfish.

'You did it, then?' Gert chortled, beaming from ear to ear.

'Yup!' Hillie cried, feeling inspired by her fight with Harold. 'Trixie didn't want to come, though. She actually made him promise to take them all to the park instead.'

'So, you're coming, too!' Kit grinned, as he and Rob and Belinda emerged from Number Eight. 'I'm so pleased. It'll do you good. And it's such a lovely day for the beginning of May.'

His smiling eyes gazed down on her, and as he held out his hand, something warm, like liquid honey, seemed to slither through her veins. She hesitated just a moment, the sensation taking her by surprise. And as she took his hand, it just felt like the good and right and natural thing to do.

Chapter Twenty-Eight

'Oh, damn, it's starting to drizzle. Don't want me new hairdo getting wet.'

Hillie watched as Gert patted her frizzy halo that she'd just had cut into a shorter, more sophisticated style. Hillie considered that it rather suited her, and that it would be more apt for the new, middle-class housewife role her dear friend would be taking up in a year's time. Life without Gert. Hillie could scarcely imagine it, and it lay heavily on her heart.

It was lunchtime at Price's, and many of the workers had flocked to the canteen. Others who lived within a few minutes' walk, had popped home to eat. Unlike the gloriously sunny day they'd spent in London for the king's jubilee the previous month, the air was chilly on this late June day and the sky overcast, so not many had ventured out to the narrow strip of the company's wharfs alongside the river.

'You'd better go in, then,' Hillie forced herself to chuckle. 'Can't have it getting ruined.'

'You not coming, then?'

'Think I'll stay out here a bit longer. Get a few more minutes' fresh air. See you back at the grindstone,' Hillie finished with a mock grimace.

'OK. But don't get soaked.'

'I won't.'

Some of the wharf men were still lingering outside in small groups, mainly puffing at their cigarettes and breathing out little clouds of smoke. They were going to get wet anyway if the rain came down more heavily, so Hillie supposed the drizzle meant nothing to them. But almost everyone else had retreated inside, and Hillie found herself virtually alone.

She stared out over the vast, grey width of the Thames as it flowed down towards the series of bridges on its way to the City of London and the docklands beyond, before reaching the estuary and the open sea. Wild and free. Hillie envied the majestically moving water, but life wasn't like that, was it? Everyone had ties. Unless you were someone like Jimmy. Was that why she'd taken to him once she'd seen past his cocky exterior? Because of his devil-may-care attitude that had made her feel unshackled?

But it had been her desire to tie him down, her dream of a home, a cottage in the country, that had killed him. Justice had been done. Both Jackson and his henchman had been tried during the previous fortnight, and both sentenced to the gallows, Jackson for giving the orders, and his heavy for carrying them out. The trials had been horrendous, but Kit had been there, buoying Hillie up, comforting her.

Giving evidence himself, although it hardly seemed necessary, as the policemen had arrived with him at the lock-up, just in time to witness the murder as well. It was over. But none of it would bring Jimmy back.

Ah, Jimmy. She remembered that summer lunchtime, three years ago now, when he'd started chatting her up. At this very spot. What a lot of water had passed by in the river since then. And now he was dead.

Hillie could feel the constriction in her throat. Best not dwell on it. Better to rejoin her friends in the canteen. Gert, Belinda. Other of her workmates.

The site of the factory was split into two by Battersea Creek. On this side, where Hillie and Gert worked in the candle-packing shed near to the site's border with York Road, the land was so densely developed that each building abutted the next. So the only way to return to the front, where the canteen also stood, was to weave one's way through the various worksheds. It felt odd and vaguely unnerving with just a few workers keeping an eye on things here and there while everyone else was at lunch. But Hillie was so familiar with the place, not to mention lost in her own morose thoughts, that she scarcely noticed it.

'You thought any more about my proposal, then?'

Harold's voice at her shoulder made her jump sky-high. Her swift glance took in the vast interior of one of the boiling houses where molten candlewax bubbled gently in ranks of heated vats. The place appeared deserted. Hillie felt a shiver of fear pass through her, but her contempt for her stepfather overrode it.

'And what proposal might that be?' she demanded frostily.

'You know very well. I've asked you enough times. To come back and live with us.'

'And I've told you enough times that you need your brains testing. That's if you've got any,' Hillie snapped, trying to ignore him and walk on.

But Harold caught her arm and wrenched her round to face him. 'No need to be like that,' he snarled. But then he seemed to change his attitude. 'Come home,' he cajoled. 'Where you belong. So I can look after you.'

Hillie was stunned. '*You*? Look after *me*?'

'Course. I'm not so bad really, you know. Your mother loved me, and—'

'*Loved* you? She was terrified of you. It was *you* who drove her to what she did. And when it comes down to it, *you're* the one to blame for everything. Mum, Jimmy—'

'Don't give me that. Your mother only had herself to blame. And as for that little runt, I didn't tell him to get mixed up with some gang, did I?' Harold spat, his eyes blazing. But then his expression hardened from rage to something disturbing Hillie couldn't identify. 'Oh, please come back, Hillie. I need you, really I do. I miss your mum so much, and you're so much like her.'

He came up so close, his fingers digging painfully into her arms, he was holding her so tightly. His nose was almost touching hers, and her eyes narrowed in disgust. For what the hell was he hinting at?

'Well, I'm not coming back, so get used to it,' she grated. 'So kindly let go of me!'

'Oh, come on, Hilda.' He began to pant now, and she could see globules of sweat forming on his upper lip. 'I want you to come home.'

'Well, I'm not. All I'm doing is for my family, not you. I hate you, so get off me!'

She watched the pleading lines on his face move into a mask of fury. For a split second, he was off guard, and she used that moment to try to break free, managing to rake the fingernails of one hand down his face as her only means of defence. Harold winced, letting go of one of her arms to feel his cheek. But he held onto her tight with the other and flung her back against the wall with such force that her head was thrown back and cracked against the bricks. Black stars danced across her vision and the silence in the workshed rang in her ears. Dear God, where was everybody? Surely someone must come soon? She wasn't going to be beaten up by him again!

She forced her eyes open. Harold had her pinned up against the wall with the weight of his body pressing against hers. She could feel his heavy breath hot on her neck as he began to slobber his lips over her skin. Outrage stung through her and, somehow, she found the strength to free one of her hands and yank on his hair. His head went back, distracting him enough so that she was able to bring her knee up hard where it hurt most.

He gave a yelp of pain and half stepped backwards, bent over as he nursed his crotch. Hillie was too transfixed to move, but an instant later, her feet were running as she blundered down the workshed. Her pulse was pounding, pounding, in her skull, blinding her with panic. She stumbled, went down painfully on her knees. Dear God, the man must be deranged! She dragged herself up again, staggered on. Where the hell was everyone?

Nearly there. The doors.

Lungs snatching at the air.

Harold must have gone round the other way and now he sprang out in front of her from behind one of the vats.

'You bitch!' he yelled. And slammed a backhander across her face that sent her reeling.

She saw him standing there, hands on hips, gloating, drooling, his eyes glazed in demented fury. Hillie turned and fled back the way she'd come, dodging in and out of the maze of hot vats as she tried to outwit him, hiding here, his leering face again there, slip past, run, skid around another vat.

Someone help me, please!

His hand shot out from between two vats and grabbed her shoulder. Was that a scream that lodged in her throat? But the momentum as she was swung round pulled Harold off balance, and she was away again. Scooting down between the rows of steaming vats, leaping over buckets and jugs and avoiding protruding taps. So hot. How did the workers in their overalls stand it in here?

'What the hell's going on, mate?'

'It's that odd bloke from moulding, ain't it? Gone bleeding beserk. Chasing some kid.'

'Not any kid. It's his daughter. Come on!'

Shouting. Footfall. Too late, too late. Which way now? This way? That way? Breath burning.

'You won't bloody get away from me!'

He was behind her. She spun round. In her mindless panic, she'd run into a corner. No escape as he stood there. Leering, grinning. Get away, away. Only one way, up the ladder hooked over the rim of the giant vat. Feet sliding on the rungs, slippery with candle grease.

Gasp as she reached the top. The lid was partly open. She couldn't get across! Below her simmered the sea of molten wax.

Slowly, she turned to gaze with petrified eyes over her shoulder. Harold was climbing the ladder behind her. Rung after rung. She saw him put one foot on the same rung as hers. Reach out to grab her as he heaved himself upwards.

This was it. She shut her eyes just as she had once before. She was back in the shadows of the lock-up beneath the railway arches. Didn't want to see it coming. Kit, oh, Kit. Where was Kit?

Harold would drag her down. Throw her to the floor. Mad with anger and lust and revenge for not being his.

No, she wouldn't let it happen!

She flung herself sideways off the ladder onto the concrete just as he launched himself at her.

Pain in her chest as she landed. No breath to call for help. But someone was shouting, yelling. Man in white overalls and rubber boots shinning up the ladder. Grabbed the pair of legs flailing in the air at the top.

'Help me get him out!'

Another man in overalls standing at the bottom of the ladder, reaching up. And then they pulled out the grotesque figure, head, arms, torso dripping thick, pale wax. Bubbling, wheezing from its mouth as it gasped for breath.

'Get an ambulance!'

Hillie peeled herself from the floor. She could barely breathe from the agony in her ribcage. How was she supposed to get to the office to call an ambulance? She couldn't move.

But as she strained to lift her head, there were other white-clad forms returning from their lunch break.

'I'll go!' one of them called, and he ran off.

The writhing monster was laid on the floor at the far side of the ladder. It looked like something from a horror film, Hillie's shocked brain mused. It was horrible. Inhuman. Gurgling. Sucking sound as it struggled to breathe.

Oh, Jimmy. Not again.

'Hillie!' a high voice squealed.

And there was Gert, face white with horror. Dear, good Gert. Everything would be all right now.

Hillie looked up. Went to draw in a deep breath. But her head swam, the room spun and darkness closed in.

Chapter Twenty-Nine

'D'you think you'll be OK to go back to work when they said?'

Hillie was following Luke down the hallway to see him off to the factory. 'I'm sure I will,' she said to his back. 'My ribs are starting to feel better already. I might even go back earlier.'

'What?' Luke turned round to face her. ''Cos we need the money? Oh, Hill, you shouldn't do that. Why don't you call in the Means Test man?'

'You must be joking,' Hillie scoffed. 'You have to have sold almost every stick of furniture and the clothes off your back before they'll give you anything. Don't worry. We can manage. And we've got the compensation from Price's.'

'That won't go far, though.'

'But we were lucky to get what we did. They didn't have to give us anything. It wasn't their fault Harold lost his temper like that. Or that the chap supposed to be keeping an eye on things over lunch happened to pop to the lav just then.'

'Sod's law that was.'

Hillie raised her eyebrows in disapproval at his language. But she supposed Luke was growing up fast, so she chose to ignore his remark. 'Anyway, it all happened so quickly, who knows if it would've made any difference. Now you get off to work, and don't worry about things. I mightn't earn as much as he did, but I won't be spending half of it down the pub.'

'Better not!' Luke grinned now, going out into the street. 'Ta-ta, then. See you tonight. But...' He hesitated after only a few steps and turned back to her. 'D'you think it was wrong of me not to have gone to the hospital with Dad?'

Hillie closed her lips in a moment's reflection. She'd been taken to the hospital in the same ambulance as Harold, and had watched him struggling for breath, his airways severely damaged, confused and semiconscious with shock, his face raw and peeling. It had come as no surprise that they told her his heart had stopped and he'd died soon after he got there. Watching him had been a horrible experience, one that she wouldn't have wished on Luke, and now she put her hands firmly on his shoulders.

'No. And I don't want you ever feeling guilty about it. He probably wouldn't have known you were there, anyway. So let's hear no more about it and get on with our own lives now we're free of him.'

Luke nodded thoughtfully, then his young face spread into a smile. 'Thanks, Hill. You're the best big sister anyone could have.'

He set off down the street, and then turned with a cheery wave before disappearing round the corner.

Hillie went back inside to where the girls were finishing their breakfast, the atmosphere so much brighter since Harold had gone. 'Hurry up, you lot,' she chivvied her sisters. 'Toilet and teeth, and then off to school.'

'Only two more weeks for me,' Joan boasted, shoving the last piece of her bread and margarine into her mouth. 'And then I can join you at Price's.'

'Oh, no, you won't!' Hillie was adamant. 'You'll take whatever time it needs to find a job you like. And you can go to evening classes so you can get an even better job later on. And Luke can do the same.'

'But... can we afford to do that? And what about you, Hill? You're cleverer than all of us.'

Hillie gave a rueful smile. 'I'm not sure about that. And I've got you lot to take care of for now. But who knows what'll happen in the future? I might get my chance later. But in the meantime, Jimmy... Jimmy and I had some reasonable savings,' she went on, chasing away the catch in her throat. 'I can dip into those if need be.'

'OK, Hill. But that money's rightfully yours.' Joan squeezed her sister's shoulder as she got up from the table. 'You sit down and have a cuppa. I'll see to the others.'

Hillie nodded her thanks, mouth curving upwards at the corners. Yes, she could do with a sit-down. Not because her ribs were aching from the fall off the ladder – or more accurately, the landing on the concrete below – since what she'd said to Luke was true. Physically, she was feeling much better. But it was making sense of everything that had happened that was troubling her. Just over six months ago, she and Jimmy had been living at the flat in relative harmony as they rebuilt their trust, unaware of how things were going to explode with Jackson. But now both Jimmy and Harold were dead and Hillie was happily living back in Banbury Street – ironically, just as her stepfather had wished.

But at least not under his terms. She'd well and truly rung the changes. Luke was sleeping in a proper bed for the first time in years, up in the smaller room at the back of the house that the four girls had once shared. Trixie, Daisy and Frances now occupied the larger bedroom at the front, and Hillie and Joan slept in Harold and Nell's double bed that Kit had helped Luke move downstairs into the parlour.

Yet again, Kit had been a tower of strength. Now, as she pondered her feelings for him, Hillie questioned her loyalties to Jimmy. In her grief and with all the upset of the trials from the Jackson case, and having to go back to work and endure Harold's taunting proximity even more than ever, there hadn't been room in her strung-out emotions to think about Kit. She'd just accepted his support with grateful thanks.

But now, with Harold gone and the horrors of the past beginning to fade a little, she was starting to put some order back into her life. Into *her* life, and Luke's and her sisters'. It had started with the practicalities in the house, and now things were settling down, with nobody seeming to be missing Harold in the slightest, Hillie could think about what was going on in her heart.

She'd been wrong to let her affections err away from Jimmy while she was married to him. So had everything that had happened been her fault, some sort of divine retribution? She'd been through hell, but it was Jimmy who'd lost his life. And if she hadn't interfered, he'd still have been alive.

But would it be wrong now for her to give in to her feelings for Kit? To seek some happiness for herself? Did she deserve it? Or was she destined to be a widow for the rest of her life? To accept that her role in the scheme of things was to care for her siblings and make sure they enjoyed a good future? Hardly a penance, but it'd mean saying goodbye to any life of her own.

The tea she swallowed tasted bitter as a tumult of tortured thoughts tumbled about in her head. Kind and supportive though he'd always been, Kit would doubtless be horrified to learn of her feelings anyway, especially so soon after Jimmy's demise. Perhaps it would be best if she drove them out of her head and knuckled down to devoting herself to her family instead. Her own future would have to take care of itself.

She breathed out a tormented sigh. There was no point dwelling on what might or might not be. She had plenty to do. No heavy work, the doctors had said. But easy, day-to-day tasks were fine. Clear the table, wash up… and then steel herself to sort out Jimmy's clothes. Though Harold's she'd disposed of already, her mouth curling up in contempt as she touched them, as yet she hadn't found the courage to sort out Jimmy's. But now she'd moved back into her old family home, she felt it was time to put the past behind her as best she could. And this would be another step in the right direction.

Gert, Rob and Kit had helped her pack all her possessions from the flat and load them into Rob's car. There hadn't been much, and one trip had sufficed. Back in Banbury Street, Hillie had unpacked the household items they'd accumulated, and the cut-glass vase had been given pride of place on the mantelpiece in the front room. But Jimmy's clothes… She hadn't touched them until now.

Gert, bless her, had folded them with the utmost care. Hillie sat on the double bed now and, gritting her teeth, began to lay the items out beside her. Underclothes were too personal to use even as rags, although Jimmy's vests still had some wear in them and might be useful for Luke. Likewise some shirts and trousers, as Jimmy had been the same height and slight build – if Hillie could bear to see her brother sporting Jimmy's attire. That just left his best Sunday coat and his jacket – the very same he'd been wearing when he'd been stabbed.

Hillie gazed down at the bloodstained garment in her hands and felt hot tears scorching the back of her eyes. And as she held the jacket to her face, breathing in Jimmy's smell, fat, salty pearls dripped down and spangled the thick, dark material.

She lost track of how long she sat there, motionless and drenched in sorrow. Her marriage to Jimmy hadn't been made in heaven, and he hadn't been her ideal partner in life. But she'd loved him, and he hadn't deserved to die.

She didn't know what to do with the jacket. The extensive crimson stains would be impossible to remove, so it couldn't be worn again. It was only fit for the dustbin, but could she bear to part with it? And such a pity as it was almost new.

Hillie hadn't realised that her tears had dried as she arranged the garment on the bed, and then opened it up to inspect the lining. It was in perfect condition, and a rich, deep blue. Jimmy had bought the jacket from his ill-gotten gains from Jackson, and had been as proud as a peacock of it. No wonder he'd mentioned it in his dying breath. Almost as if he was trying to tell her something. Remind her that it was good quality and worth a bob or two? But he wouldn't have realised about the stains…

The lining was a lovely colour, though, and she could probably salvage enough material to make a skirt for Frances. It seemed a shame to cut it, but it was the best use Hillie could make of the jacket, and she might then feel justified in keeping the rest of it for sentimental reasons.

Wait a minute, though. Hillie frowned. It looked as if a couple of inches of the lining hem had been badly sewn. So perhaps it had been a second, and therefore cheaper, which was why Jimmy had bought it. But why just in that one place?

Hillie's curiosity was aroused, and she went to investigate further. It felt, well, as if something had been caught up in it. How odd.

A few moments later, she'd armed herself with some scissors and began to snip the stitches. The scissor blades scraped on something small and hard. Hillie put down the scissors and smoothed out the hem that appeared to have been carefully rolled up, concealing something inside.

Out fell a dozen or more tiny, multi-faceted, twinkling stones.

Hillie stared at them as they gleamed on the bedspread. Stunned. Amazed. Shocked. And yet somehow, utterly calm. She didn't need telling. Diamonds.

So Jimmy *had* been trying to tell her something. Somehow, in his dealings with Jackson, he'd managed to steal from the blackguard himself. Trick him. Getting his own back, perhaps. A secret satisfaction. But, more than that, a way of securing their own future.

But how was Jimmy intending to turn them into cash? Some were only tiny. You could scarcely pick them up between finger and thumb. But others were relatively large, and from what Jimmy had explained to her, these all appeared to be ready cut and polished. The colours differed slightly, some being whiter or yellower than others. But overall, they must be worth a small fortune, or would at least have boosted their savings enormously. Making enough for a deposit on a house, perhaps?

Oh, bless you, Jimmy.

But what could Hillie do with them? She had no idea where to sell them. And were they hers to sell? She knew they weren't, of course, but she jolly well felt they should be! Recompense for her widowhood.

A gentle knock on the front door shattered the silence and made her jump. Quickly, she scooped up the diamonds and slipped them into a drawer before stepping out into the hallway.

'Kit!' she greeted her visitor, disguising the disquiet in her voice. 'Oh, come in. Day off?'

'Yes,' he confirmed, coming inside. 'How my shifts worked out, at least. I've just been into Mum's. But I thought I'd pop in and see how you're doing.'

'Oh, that's kind of you,' Hillie smiled, even though she felt all upside-down inside, what with the discovery of the diamonds, and then Kit's arrival making her feel so happy and yet almost afraid of her feelings for him. 'Cuppa?' she asked, grasping at the answer to all ills.

'No, thanks,' Kit replied, following her into the kitchen. 'I had one with Mum. You know, Hill, you mustn't go back to work before you're ready,' he went on with concern. 'You mustn't worry about money. I can help you out.'

Hillie caught her breath. Oh, Kit. He was such a good man. Strong and dependable. Had been her rock. And glancing at him over her shoulder, her heart skipped for the umpteenth time.

'That's so kind of you, but we'll be fine,' she smiled back. 'Joan will be job hunting when school finishes in two weeks, so her wages will help when she starts. And Trixie's always been good at looking after the little ones, so it'll all work out OK.'

'As long as you're sure.' Kit still looked anxious. 'And Hill, you'll always come to me if you need anything, won't you? I mean, anything at all. Not just money.'

Hillie blinked at him. There was something in his eyes that made her heartbeat accelerate. The words flowed out of her mouth almost before she'd thought of them. If she could trust anyone in the world, it was Kit.

'I want to show you something,' she told him, and instead of sitting down, led the way into the front room. 'Look,' she said, opening the drawer. 'I found these. Just two minutes ago. Sewn into the lining of Jimmy's jacket. I think that's what he was trying to tell me.'

She watched Kit's eyes widen, and then his lips pursed together as he whistled.

'Blimey.'

'Exactly,' Hillie murmured. 'What... what d'you think I should do with them?'

She mentally crossed her fingers. Kit dealt with all sorts of merchandise coming through on freight trains. Surely he had connections with the companies involved. But... diamonds? And stolen diamonds, at that?

'You'll have to hand them in to the police,' Kit said levelly. 'They might be able to trace who they belong to through all the shenanigans of the trials. They're stolen, after all.'

Hillie sighed with reluctant relief. Yes, of course. What had she been thinking of? Trying to sell the diamonds was out of the question. Even if she knew how, the guilt would have dogged her for the rest of her life. It would have been wonderful not to have to worry about money again, mind. But as always, Kit was right.

'Yes, of course,' she muttered. 'It was just such a shock, I couldn't think straight. I'll find something to put them in, and take them along to the police station.'

'I'll come with you. Maybe we should take the jacket along, too. But first,' Kit said with a certain urgency, 'I actually came to tell you something. I haven't told anyone else yet. Not even Mum and Dad.'

'Oh, yes?' Hillie dragged her eyes from the diamonds, and saw that Kit's face had moved into solemn lines. Dread took hold of her even before he spoke.

'I'm leaving,' he announced in a low, steady tone. 'There was a job as senior clerk at a station called Edenbridge Town. It's a small town – well, obviously it's a town – in Kent. But it has a busy goods yard and employs several people. The senior clerk's retiring and nobody else there is experienced enough to take over. My boss put in a good word for me, and the job's mine. I start at the beginning of September.'

Hillie stared at him. And her world splintered. Life… without Kit. It was inconceivable.

'B-but I thought you always wanted to be station master here?' she stammered in appalled desperation.

But Kit shook his head. 'That's never going to happen. Clapham Junction's enormous. And it'll get bigger. I'd never be able to be my own boss, even if I did get to the top. Always answerable to the bigwigs. But at Edenbridge Town, who knows, I could be SM one day, and really happy.'

'Oh, Kit.' Hillie was too numbed to say anything more. Everything was falling apart. Her mum, Jimmy, and now Kit. Who she… she knew with certainty now… she loved. Oh, no, she couldn't bear it.

He was looking at her oddly, his mouth twisting. 'The thing is,' he hesitated, 'you and Luke and the girls could come with me. Give you all a fresh start.'

Hillie frowned in confusion, and then the meaning of his words came like sunlight breaking through a mist. 'Yes,' she articulated in a tiny whisper. There was no need even to think about it.

'It's a nice little town surrounded by countryside,' Kit was continuing. 'But the station's right on the edge. The job comes with a house. There are three pairs of semis, painted white and quite attractive, but hardly a cottage with roses round the door. And they overlook the goods yard at the front and only have small backyards, but they back onto open fields.'

'Yes.' Her voice was stronger this time.

'Three bedrooms, I think, but we could work that one out, I'm sure. People might assume that you and me... but they could think what they wanted. The thing is, Hill,' Kit faltered, and she noticed colour flooding into his cheeks, 'I've never said it before. And then Jimmy got there first. But... I guess I can tell you now. All I've ever wanted is to be with you. To look after you. And everything that's happened to you has broken my heart.'

He took her hands in his, and she could feel him shaking. Her own heart was soaring, spinning circles, and yet somehow she felt perfectly calm. Could it possibly be that Kit had felt the same way about her all along? The same way that she knew had been deep inside her, too, but she'd been too blind to see until it had been too late?

She watched, joy spiralling up inside her, as he raised his eyes slowly to hers.

'Hillie, this might not be the right time, but... I love you. I think I always have done. I'd understand if you didn't want to, but I'd like you to come to Edenbridge with me, and then I can help you start a new life, get back on your feet. All I want is to see you happy. Settle down, maybe find some nice lucky chap and get married again. Have a family.'

Hillie stared at him, losing her gaze in his. 'Oh, Kit, that's so typical of you,' she whispered. 'So unselfish. Wanting to do everything correct and proper. That's why... why I love you, too.' She reached up and tenderly brushed his cheek, watching the astonished expression on his face. 'I think I always have, too, but it's taken all this to make me realise.'

But then Kit's eyebrows met in a frown. 'Are you... sure? But... Jimmy?'

'I did love Jimmy, yes. But I know he wouldn't have wanted me to be a grieving widow for the rest of my life. He thought life was for living.'

'Well, in that case ... If you really are sure.' Kit dropped down on one knee. 'Hilda Baxter – no, let's say Hillie Hardwick who I've loved for so long – will you do me the honour of becoming my wife?'

'Nothing would give me greater pleasure,' Hillie agreed, quietly and calmly. And never having felt more sure of anything in her life before. 'Except this.'

She took his hand, pulling him gently to his feet and tilting her head upwards. She saw the love in his eyes, and wondered how he'd managed to keep his feelings hidden. But all that could wait as his lips brushed against hers, sending shivers down her spine. His breath softly fanned her cheek before he kissed her again, gently and caressing.

For just a second, another face swam before her, echo of another time. Another life. It smiled, giving its blessing, and then it was gone.

A new and joyous future was waiting…

*

'You know, I think I'm going to miss this place in a strange sort of way.'

Hillie's gaze swept over the short street with its grander houses on one side, and humble terrace on the other. It had been her lifelong home, and now she was moving on. They'd gone to see the parish vicar straightaway, and had the banns published so that they could be married on the twenty-fourth of August, a week before Kit was due to start his new post. This would also give them plenty of time to settle into their new home with Luke and the girls who were all delighted at the idea of moving to the country as well as seeing their big sister so happy. She and Kit weren't having a honeymoon, for surely starting their new life would be like a perpetual honeymoon, stretching before them in endless delight?

Unlike at her previous wedding, Hillie had been surrounded by all the people she loved. If only her mum and her real dad had been there to share this most wonderful day, but somehow Hillie had the fancy that they were looking down and giving their blessing. Perhaps they'd even been reunited in some other realm.

They'd had a small reception at the Duke of Cambridge on the corner, and now it was over, they'd called into the house for the final time to collect the last of their luggage. They stood on the pavement with Luke and the girls, waiting to say their goodbyes. The entire Parker family littered the pavement, of course, Eva dabbing at her eyes, and Rob and Belinda and their parents were there, too, and some colleagues from Price's and from the railway station.

Charles and Hester Braithwaite had even accepted their invitation to the wedding, accompanied by Jessica and Patrick, who'd dressed in his colourful tribal robes for the occasion. They were courting openly now, and Jessica's parents were slowly coming to accept that their daughter had found her own happiness in an unconventional way. The couple hoped to marry the following spring, and then take a boat to Nigeria for a second ceremony with Patrick's family and tribe, but it was going to take some organising.

'Not as much as I'm going to miss you, kiddo!' Gert answered Hillie, enveloping her in a bear hug, and then pulled away, sniffing back a tear as she held her lifelong friend at arms' length. 'You look absolutely gorgeous. Can I borrow your dress for my wedding next year?' she asked, dipping her head at the cream hem that frothed below Hillie's knees. 'Must've cost a pretty penny.'

'Kit insisted I used some of the reward money I got for returning the diamonds. Said I deserved it after everything.'

'And so you do. You've got a good man in my brother. You deserve him, too. Took you two long enough to get together, mind. And now you're going to be the best sister-in-law ever! You know,' Gert added, lowering her voice, 'I think Belinda held a torch to Kit, but she looks to be getting on well with that friend of Kit's from work,' she smirked, using her eyes to indicate where Belinda was engaged in conversation with Kit's now to be ex-colleague.

'Sorry to break up the party,' Kit interrupted the hubbub of chatter, 'but my wife and I,' he said, grinning down proudly at Hillie, 'and the kids have a train to catch.'

'Oh, come on, last hugs, then!' Eva cried, bustling forward and crushing Hillie against her. 'Nell would've been so proud of you today, girl,' she whispered in Hillie's ear as she released her.

Hillie felt a tiny twinge in her heart and was grateful when her darling Kit came up beside her.

'Time to go, sweetheart,' he said quietly, and her love for him spilled over.

'I'm going to miss you all!' she called out to everyone.

'Well, you're not going to have far to walk from your front door to get on a train!' Gert called out in return.

Kit picked up their small suitcase. Everything had already been moved into the house next to Edenbridge Town Station, so it just contained a few personal items. The children grouped about Hillie and Kit, eager to be off on this new adventure themselves. Luke and Joan also carried a case each, and Trixie fell into line behind them, holding Daisy and Frances each by the hand.

Kit took Hillie's hand in his free one and they walked to the corner of the street among a chorus of shouted good wishes. Hillie paused to give one last wave, choking back tears of mingled joy and sadness. Goodbye, Banbury Street.

Then she looked up at Kit. His handsome smile filled her with confidence, and they rounded the corner, Luke and the girls chatting excitedly as they followed, leaving their old life behind.

Their new, happy future stretched before them. This was just the beginning…

We hope you enjoyed this book.

Tania Crosse's next book is coming in winter 2018

More addictive fiction from Aria:

Find out more
http://headofzeus.com/books/isbn/9781786692573
Find out more
http://headofzeus.com/books/isbn/9781788541473
Find out more
http://headofzeus.com/books/isbn/9781786692986

Acknowledgements

Once again, I must thank my wonderful agent, Broo Doherty, and the lovely team at Aria for bringing this, my third novel with them, to life. There is nothing more wonderful for an author than seeing published a story that has been so much a part of their life for so long.

In this case, it couldn't be truer as I was actually brought up in Banbury Street for the first five years of my life. Amazingly, I have some very vivid memories of living there, particularly the general area, Clapham Junction Station and visits to Battersea Park, although in later years, even though we had moved out to the country, my mother used to bring us back to visit the park on occasion. It is my brother, thriller writer Terence Strong, however, that I must thank for the idea of basing my story around Price's Candle Factory. I had no memory of it, but being that much older, he remembered it well.

There are many other people who have contributed to this novel and to whom I must extend my sincere gratitude. Firstly, to dear, long-standing friend, Colin Skeen, barrister and magistrate, who once again delved into the laws of the past so that I could give an accurate picture of the legal matters in the book. If I have made any errors, they are my mistakes. Huge thanks also go to the Wandsworth Heritage Service at Battersea Library for digging out all kinds of obscure documents for me, including historic tram and bus route maps and detailed fire plans of the factory. The London Transport Museum also contributed details of public transport of the time. Railway historian, John Billard, suggested Kit's career path, and my dear friend, Michael Willats, shared his experiences of having been a diamond sorter in his youth. Again, if I have misinterpreted any of their ideas, it is entirely my own fault. The Friends of Battersea Park provided a detailed history of the park from its beginnings to more recent years, which not only proved so useful for this book, but will also do so in the future. Because, yes, there will be a sequel set in Banbury Street in the years immediately after the Second World War!

The person I must thank most of all, though, is my fantastic husband, for all his love and support throughout the years. Without his encouragement, I would never have been able to pursue my dream of becoming a historical novelist.

Last but not least, I should like to thank you, my faithful readers, for sharing my imaginary worlds. I do so hope that you are enjoying this, my new series with Aria, as well as my earlier titles based on the history of my beloved Dartmoor. A little different from Battersea, but variety is the spice of life, as they say. Many thanks again and happy reading!

About Tania Crosse

Delaying her childhood dream of writing historical novels until her family had grown up, TANIA CROSSE eventually completed a series of published stories based on her beloved Dartmoor. She is now setting her future sagas in London and the southeast.

Find me on Twitter

https://twitter.com/TaniaCrosse

Find me on Facebook
https://www.facebook.com/TaniaCrosseAuthor

Visit my website
http://www.tania-crosse.co.uk/

A Letter from the Author

Dear Reader,

Thank you so much for sharing my characters' journey. I do so hope you enjoyed it.

I get so emotionally involved with my stories that to me they are real, and I hope you felt that way, too. If you would like to share that emotion with others, then please do write a review or spread the word on your preferred social media. I'd be most grateful and so would my characters!

I write gritty tales about women facing terrible challenges in real-life historical situations. Sometimes they already have a problem, or sometimes it's historical fact that brings the problem to their door. Sometimes both! But in every case, they have to find the strength to survive whatever life throws at them.

For further details of all my novels, please drop by my website, where you can also sign up to my newsletter which will keep you up to date with publications and other matters of interest. I'll look forward to meeting you there, just follow the links below.

Happy reading!
With love
Tania

Find me on Twitter
https://twitter.c.om/TaniaCrosse

Find me on Facebook
https://www.facebook.com/TaniaCrosseAuthor

Visit my website
http://www.tania-crosse.co.uk/

Also by Tania Crosse

Find out more
http://headofzeus.com/books/isbn/9781786694928

Find out more
http://headofzeus.com/books/isbn/9781786694966

Find out more
http://headofzeus.com/books/isbn/9781786694973

Visit Aria now
http://www.ariafiction.com

Become an Aria Addict

Aria is the new digital-first fiction imprint from Head of Zeus.

It's Aria's ambition to discover and publish tomorrow's superstars, targeting fiction addicts and readers keen to discover new and exciting authors.

Aria will publish a variety of genres under the commercial fiction umbrella such as women's fiction, crime, thrillers, historical fiction, saga and erotica.

So, whether you're a budding writer looking for a publisher or an avid reader looking for something to escape with – Aria will have something for you.

Get in touch: aria@headofzeus.com

Become an Aria Addict
http://ariafiction.com/newsletter/subscribe

Find us on Twitter
https://twitter.com/Aria_Fiction

Find us on Facebook
http://www.facebook.com/ariafiction

Find us on BookGrail
http://www.bookgrail.com/store/aria/

Addictive Fiction

First published in the United Kingdom in 2018 by
Aria, an imprint of Head of Zeus Ltd

9 7 5 3 1 2 4 6 8

A CIP catalogue record for this book is available
from the British Library.

ISBN (E) 9781786694973

Aria
c/o Head of Zeus
First Floor East

5–8 Hardwick Street
London EC1R 4RG

www.ariafiction.com

17660516R00287

Printed in Great Britain
by Amazon